To Tracie,
Well here's the book
Best wishes! x
Brian Short 2016.

WHEN GOD CAME

BACK

by

BRIAN SHORT

CHAPTER ONE: RETURN JOURNEY

Although mankind didn't know it, many millions of miles away a part of Space was in the process of being changed, and in doing so would never be quite the same. What Earth's scientists proudly proclaimed as universal laws did not apply there in those brief Nano seconds. What man called dark matter was torn, manipulated and rearranged to suit another's needs. The matter was torn down to it atomic parts, with protons and electrons simply moved by will alone to facilitate movement. Having altered the atomic structure, minute parts were exchanged with the outer layer of the entity that was tearing through it. The entity itself was by all meaningful but unimaginable criteria, the oldest and most intelligent being in the universe that was known to mankind, even if mankind did not yet know it. Even if it had known of the man-made scientific laws it was breaking, it would not and could not have been constrained by them. Long before the Earth had coalesced into a planet it had evolved into an entity that had no need of a physical body. It was an immense life force made up of pure energy and pure intelligence. It could, if needed, manifest a physical form at the merest thought of doing so, but this would only seek to slow its progress through the material of space that is thought of as home. It moved merely by wanting to move and moved as fast or as slow as it thought necessary to be where it wanted to be. It knew more of what mankind called dark matter than scientists would ever know and the although it did not know of Einstein's work, it knew instinctively and by long held experience how to manipulate space, time or spacetime when it needed to. It moved inexorably towards its destination, passing through light years of space and whole Galaxies in moments of Earth time. It knew exactly where it was, where it was going and when it would arrive. A small part of its vast intelligence that it reserved for universal roaming registered a million thoughts and projections on its progress towards its destination. Imperceptibly it started to slow down, as it was aware it could destroy stars, planets or any heavenly bodies with the sheer speed and force at which it travelled. It thought itself slower, thereby becoming slower, moving down through several phases of motion before eventually arriving at a relatively sedate number, a number that perhaps some men on earth might just be able to understand. At this speed space was now changed again as the transference was made differently, the entity made use of what men called Axiom dark matter to move itself. At this relatively lower speed the outer edges of the being created heat and light where it now contacted its surroundings. The many tens of millions of small flashes it created became as one, physically showing the path of the being through Space as a long effervescent tube like structure. Whilst it slowed even more, other dormant parts of its intelligence began to awaken, integrating back into the one whole superbeing in preparation for arrival on Earth. It was nearly there, God was returning.

CHAPTER TWO: THE HANGOVER

Gary slowly used his fingers to push his greasy hair back from his face before covering his eyes with his hand. He felt like crap and it was all his own work. Still shielding his eyes from the strong sun light that was streaming through the curtains and hurting him, he took a deep breath and tried to understand which part of him hurt the most. Yes, he'd had hangovers before but this was one was way off the Richter scale. Not only did he have the usual hangover dizziness, dehydration and a deep sickening in his stomach, parts of his body that he wasn't familiar with were bruised and complaining of being recently abused. Slowly some basic and deeper brain functions kicked in and he worked out that somehow in last night's drunken stupor he had fallen over, or down, or out of something. Steeling himself for the inevitable pain he slowly removed his hands and squinted first at the window then quickly away from it as his iris adjusted to the light pouring into the room. He moved his head from side to side and experienced a sharp stabbing sensation across the back of his neck, which he rubbed in a vain attempt to alleviate the pain, but the movement only succeeded in increasing the dizzy feeling. Forcing back down an acidic regurgitation from his stomach, he raised himself onto his two unsteady feet, gained some semblance of balance and stumbled clumsily towards the kitchen. Coffee is what he thought his body needed, so in the forlorn hope that it would cure most of his ills he began foraging around the kitchen. At the third clumsy attempt he managed to turn on the coffee machine, which given his current condition he regarded as a major coup. He found the nearest mug, which although was dirty was soon rinsed of yesterday's remains and put in place under the coffee maker. There was still one basic ingredient missing, namely coffee, so he commanded his hand to reach into the container for a fresh coffee pod. With his fingers grasping fresh air, it slowly dawned on him the container was empty and the challenge for coffee went up a notch. He rested both hands on the kitchen worktop, closed his eyes and thought about the problem. Deep in some minute recess of his brain a small electrical charge passed across a neuron and a memory stirred of a recent shopping trip, so somewhere he reasoned he must have coffee. Still supporting himself with one hand on the worktop, his other reached up and opened the kitchen cabinet above the coffee machine. Much to his surprise there sat a fresh box of coffee pods, which he grabbed and held it in front of his eyes whilst he checked the blend. Not that it really mattered what blend was in the box as today he would have drunk the cheapest instant coffee slop that any greasy spoon café would have served. He tore at the 'easy opening' strip along the stop of the box, which despite its name put up something of a fight. Not yet having the delicate muscle control needed for such a task, he applied a lot more force to the strip than was needed and felt it start to tear. What he couldn't do in time was stop the applied pressure, resulting in the box disintegrating before his eyes and distributing the twenty coffee pods around the kitchen. "Fuck it" he said quietly under his breath as he sought the nearest available pod, which had landed on top of his bare left foot. Without thinking about the possible repercussions he commanded his battered body to bend at the waist to pick up the much needed pod. As he moved in deliberate slow motion he felt twinges and complaints from other parts of his body, but with a grimace he gallantly pressed on towards his goal. Despite the slow speed of movement, the various pain messages to his brain distracted him to the point he was unable to stop his forehead impacting the sharp corner of the kitchen worktop. His second word of the day was also "Fuck it" as he rubbed away at the quickly reddening welt on his forehead. Having learnt his lesson the hard and painful way, his second attempt at retrieving the pod was successful and he managed to put it into the machine without further injury. The machine took thirty seconds to heat the water and for twenty eight of those Gary just stood holding onto the worktop. Eventually the machine completed its part of the bargain and noisily filled the mug with coffee. With a mug of steaming java in one hand and two paracetomol in the other, he carefully walked into the area that estate agents would refer to as the living room, although he silently conceded the word living was stretching the meaning a bit far. Having cleared the end of the sofa from newspapers, some crumpled trousers and unmatched scatter cushions, he managed to slowly sit himself down with only a minor spillage of his coffee, which joined the many other stains on the cushion. His body was still sending him hurt messages when he moved but by sitting still and drinking slowly he could minimize the pain. Hoping to avoid the gag reflex he popped the two pain killers into his mouth and brought the mug of hot coffee to his lips. However, in his caution he was too slow in sipping the coffee, allowing time for one of the pills to stick unkindly to the roof of his mouth and the other to slip between his cheek and gum. After much facial gurning and teeth versus tongue action, he managed to wrangle the pills back into position, washing them down with coffee and a deep sigh. "Fuck it" he said for the third time that morning before silently complimenting himself on getting that far in just twenty minutes. With this kind of heady progress he might make the shower in little over an hour. He risked moving his eyes to glance at the wall clock, which mockingly confirmed to Gary that he was already nearly two hours late for work. He knew that wouldn't be going down well in the office and that prick of an editor would already be either preparing a bollocking or writing out Gary's P45 dismissal notice. In truth Gary would have gladly taken the later, in fact it would have been a welcome release from that miserable job had he not needed the money so badly. He knew that he had better have a fire proof excuse when he did eventually get there later that day, or tomorrow, or whenever he made it in to the office. The coffee and painkillers just started to work and he went from feeling just fucking terrible to just fucking awful. Although this was something of an improvement, he was still not well enough to consider venturing outside in general or to work in particular. With the television remote control within arm's reach, he decided to cheer himself up by watching the news to see what had occurred in the world during his eighteen hour drinking bender and ten hours of snoring unconsciousness. Nothing puts a hangover into perspective better than other people's misery, so he headed for the news. Flicking through the channels he found the dozen or so back to back news channels, each trumpeting their channel idents in the corner of the screen. Although there was no sound as yet, each of the news programmes seemed to be running with a major weather. They each had selected experts, computer graphics and anchor-men, all apparently trying to outdo each other in a sincere look frenzy about whatever it was that was happening. Gary's cheap satellite TV box eventually settled down and grudgingly allowed him sound to go with the images. He choose the Global American NCN channel, for no other reason than he liked the pretty female anchor onscreen.

In between admiring her carefully coiffured hair and the vast expanse of thigh on show, he took in the gist of the big story. It seemed something strange was happening to the world's weather. Cold countries were suddenly getting hotter and hot places were also getting hotter but wetter. A strange phenomenon was indeed taking place and from the news report it looked like people, governments and more importantly news anchors were stating to panic. This did three things for Gary. Firstly, he realised as a reporter, albeit for a small regional newspaper, that he really ought to be interested in the top story in the world. Secondly, as a resident of planet earth he thought that this could have a big impact on where he takes his holidays. Lastly however, he brain grasped at the notion that perhaps this could actually be the excuse he needed for being late for work. How could any editor be cross when he could claim he was working on the biggest story sweeping around the world? He carried on channel hopping across the various news programs until one image in particular caught his eye. As with most things in Gary's life the satellite box also had an inherent fault, doing everything with a playful two second delay. No sooner had he spotted something he wanted to see then a few seconds later the box would catch up and switch channels or offer up some random channel or radio station. From years of bitter experience Gary knew that stabbing wildly at buttons only produced a slowly but ever changing image, but that didn't stop him stabbing wildly at the buttons. Eventually, getting a grip of his anger and frustration, he took a deep breath and patiently brought the box back under control. Allowing for the delay, he eventually found the channel he was looking for and in particular the female reporter who had caught his eye. The attractive and shapely brunette certainly had that fake American news look but there was also something familiar about her. He turned the TV volume up and leant forward on the sofa, not quite ignoring the pain it brought to his head but also not acknowledging it either. As the now obviously British voice of the woman came through the speakers it pulled at some distant memory, but one that he just could not bring into focus. There was something familiar about her voice and mannerism he thought as he strained his brain to put all the elements together. Gary closed his eyes and tried to put this woman in context, as he was sure he knew her from somewhere but just couldn't complete the thought loop. Having no success and temporarily beaten by the hangover, he reached again for his coffee mug and took a swig, but in doing so caught his mouth on the chipped rim of the mug. He ran his tongue around his lips to check it they were not cut and in doing so put all of his available brain into the process. Once he established there was no damage, what available brain function he possessed was released back to the memory task. This momentary distraction followed by the subsequent influx of memory resources instantly found the connection with the woman he had been seeking. "Joanne fucking Grayond!" he said out loud once the realization had set in. Yes, she was all made up like Hilary Clinton's dog, but there on his screen was Joanne fucking Graymond. He felt justified inserting fucking as a middle name for her because that is exactly what he had done to her at university all those years ago, well eight years ago actually to be precise. Gary was amazed that someone who once swam in the same shallow intellectual gene pool as him, had now made it to the realms of television, and satellite television at that! He took a moment to ignore the main story she was reporting, and the fact she seemed to have 'made it big' to reflect back on their student sexual fumbling. He couldn't actually remember any of the fine detail of their love making because none of was fine, just a distant memory of a moist premature something, followed by a look of little or no fulfilment from her. What he could remember was not very flattering towards him and he knew it would have been of little satisfaction to her, so he shook his head and tried to erase that uncomfortable memory. With nothing good or sexually pleasing left to focus on, he returned to the story Joanne fucking Graymond was reporting, but this time he used the word fucking in an ironic kind of way to alleviate his fucking poor performance. She it seemed had a pretty good handle on how this story about the eccentric world weather was panning out. The more he listened the more he understood, which was not always the case in Gary's world. It seemed from her report that she access to details and information that none of the other channels seem to have. Even though he worked in the lowly world of regional newspapers, Gary had been a reporter long enough to spot when someone else had an inside edge on a story, because that is what mostly happened in his world. This particular edge he reasoned must be some scientific source that Joanne no longer fucking Graymond had found. Despite the crap start to the morning, Gary now thought he had a good chance of getting on board this story and out of the shit with his boss, in one easy to imagine coup. All he had to do was get the lovely Joanne to share her source with him, and why not, they did have some history together he wrongly reasoned. He applied his self-delusional filter and simply left out the memory of their unsatisfactory sweaty coupling, thereby he figured making everything just fine. He was wrong.

CHAPTER THREE: PURSUING THE UNEATABLE

He stood still in the shower, letting the hot water run down his slightly overweight body, whilst his brain was shut up inside his head doing what he called 'thinking'. He liked to think that some of his best ideas had come to him whilst soaking in a bath, shower or hot tub, but so far not one of these ideas had ever come to fruition or made him any money. After many minutes of trying to think it through, the simple thought process was complete. A plan, or rather 'The Plan' as it was now called, slowly appeared to him out of the steam of the shower and made pretty pictures in his head. It was like when he single finger typed onto a computer keyboard, heavily bashing out each letter, making mistakes every other word and spending a lot of time correcting, but eventually getting a full sentence. Slowly conceived or otherwise, he figured his idea could not fail as like him it was simple but believable in the right light. He was going to spruce himself up, get his ass down to the London NCN news channel offices and woo that Joanne fucking Graymond into giving up her secret source to this story. By the end of the day he would a hero in the office and given half a chance a hero in the bedroom. Surely Joanna would not turn down the chance of a repeat shagging, especially since Gary was now also a fellow journalist and something of a stud, at least in his own mind. Now the overall plan was formulated, he looked into some of the detail but carefully to glossed over some of the more negative points. His mind fast forwarded to the point where he bedded Ms Graymond as he now called her, so he could put right his student days shagging fiasco. He also allowed himself the luxury of imagining how their future love making would be, and whilst doing so soaped his nether regions in the hope he could encourage his penis to get involved. However, despite being controlled centrally, most of Gary's body parts held their own views on his sexual prowess. His penis wasn't going to be fooled by a few cheap thoughts and two rubs with a bar of soap, so decided it was not going to play today. Ever so slightly disappointed he put a positive spin on it. "Still" thought Gary, "at least it's clean now" Invigorated by the coffee, shower and a mind full of fresh ideas, Gary quickly dressed himself in his least creased suit and the less stained shirt from the washing pile. A quick look in the mirror convinced Gary if no one else, that he was a sharp reporter out on the hunt for a particular story and sex of any kind. Such was his buoyant mood, the aches, pains and hangover from earlier were pushed to the back of his mind. He never even broke step or swore when he saw the parking ticket stuck on his car windscreen, merely pausing to snatch it up and screw it into a ball. Once in the car he simply threw it into the passenger foot well with all the others. A quick goggle search on his phone revealed the London offices of NCN were in North London, as luck had it not far from the county court where he sometimes sat reporting on public misdemeanours and paying his own parking fines. That's as far as his luck held because the next hour saw him swearing and cursing his way through the then seemingly endless London traffic. Although it did not dampen his enthusiasm for the task in hand, the fraught journey did provide him with some thinking and quality swearing time. When he arrived at the spacious corporate TV studio complex he saw that the few parking spaces near the entrance were all filled with TV executive's Porches' and BMW's. He followed the visitor parking sign but was met by an endless sea of Fords Aztecs & Renault Clio's, obviously belonging to the lesser paid worker drones at the station. He quickly became frustrated with driving laps around the car park looking for a space and so returned to the front of the building and just stopped his car on the public road alongside double yellow lines. Scrabbling in the foot well he recovered the screwed up parking ticket from earlier, and spreading it flat he once again stuck it back on the outside of the car window. He hoped this well used subterfuge would save him the cost of a ticket or yet another court appearance, just as it had not done many times before, but he was nothing if not optimistic this morning. Looking every inch the proverbial sack o' shit but feeling just like the sack, Gary stood up tall and marched confidently towards the security man stood outside the main entrance revolving door. Either his confident manner, or the scrappy Bromley Herald press ID card he flashed was enough to fool the less than minimum wage Polish security guard so he passed through unchallenged, albeit with a suspicious look from the poorly paid eastern European. Gary's eyes took in the cavernous reception area that in itself was much bigger than the whole of the offices where worked. He walked briskly up to the modern reception island

and picked the least threatening of the three immaculately dressed receptionists sat within it. The pretty black girl he chose had obviously excelled on the customer greeting part of her receptionist training. With her face showing none of the inner disgust she felt for the shabbily dressed man standing before her, she robotically intoned `Good morning, sir, how can I help you today?` Gary coughed slightly before replying `Yes, I am here to see Joanne fuc…em Graymond please`. The girl's professional façade slipped as her body language revealed the hint of a raised eyebrow. Given that Joanne Graymond was one of the rising stars of the TV Station the receptionist was used to visitors, some who had genuine appointments but others who were barely able to talk. Some were even potential stalkers who wanted to meet her or worse ask for an autograph. She saw herself and her profession as the first and last line of defence. She would one day be fierce enough to be a doctor's receptionist. `Do you have an appointment, sir? ` She asked, but the way she asked the question made it clear she thought he did not. Gary thought for a second before replying with a resounding `No but Yes`, trying to sound both positive and yet somehow mysterious. The receptionist was now convinced she had a stalker or worse, but she needed a little more confirmation before dismissing Gary completely. `I am sorry sir but Ms Graymond is very busy and does not see anyone without an appointment. `Well I think she'll see me, as I am her... her um boyfriend` he lied, using a sweep of his hand for dramatic emphasis. Now completely convinced that Gary was not the full ticket she became bolder in her challenge, `Sir, I happen to know Ms Graymond's fiancé and you are most certainly not him!` Realising that the first round of his little game was up, Gary looked at her nametag and quickly changed tack. `Look miss...Babette, I must see Joanne today, not only is it a matter of life or death, but also my job is on the line, and besides I do really do know her` Babette took a deep breath, whilst under the counter she pushed the silent alarm button that would summon security. `That may be so sir, but I still cannot allow you into the building` Gary was suddenly aware of a presence both behind and beside him, as he was flanked by several burly cheap suited security personnel. `Is there a problem here sir? Asked the security guard in yet another heavy eastern European accent. `No problem` replied Gary, `I was just explaining to Babet..` but he was cut off in mid-sentence by Babette `This gentlemen wants to see a senior reporter but does not have an appointment or understand what the word no means` Before Gary could offer further meaningless excuses, he felt two firm hands cup his elbows and he rose up onto his tip toes. Gary started to struggle but the grip became firmer and his toes rose even higher. He raised his voice and proceeded to berate the two guards who were now starting to turn him away from the reception desk towards the main doors. One of the guards failed to notice the yellow warning cone `CAUTION, SLIPPERY SURFACE` as he moved backwards and skidded a little on a coffee spillage. It wasn't much but it gave Gary just enough time to very nearly escape the clutches of the two guards. The incident was just being raised to the official British level of a commotion, which brought matters to the attention of other visitors and staff. Having recovered his footing, the security man reaffirmed his grip on Gary and protesting loudly he was firmly ushered towards the entrance. Just as the trio passed by the row of lift doors, the executive lift door opened and a group of three people exited into the lobby. They were surprised to see the guards almost carrying a scruffy loud man and stood back to allow them to pass. One of the three, Joanne Graymond herself, did a double take. `Gary? ` She said out loud, immediately wishing she had kept quiet.

`Joanne` shouted Gary, `tell these people to let me go. you remember me right?` The taller of the two guards nodded towards Gary and asked her `Ah Miss, do you know this uh this …um gentleman?` before she could formulate the much needed lie she needed in her head, Joanne's mouth mistakenly jumped in `Yes, I do know him, you can let him go` Suddenly Gary was dropped back onto his own two feet, shook his shoulders and walked away from the pair. `Thank you guys, you may carry on` he said. The guards ignored Gary's comment and spoke to Joanne `Well miss, if you are quite sure. We will be just over there if you need us` `Thank you` replied Joanne. `Well Gary Barnet, what the hell are you doing here and what was all that about? `Well nice to see you too `Gary replied sarcastically. `And its Barnes by the way, my surname is Barnes, using the annoying Australian upward cadence which makes everything into a question. `I thought you would have remembered me, after all we meant to each other back in Uni` Joanne snorted something like a laugh but with much more derisory undertones `Gary, those teenage fumbles at university parties were I recall few and entirely unsatisfactory for all concerned` Gary instantly regretted bringing it up `well I enjoyed it!', he said defensively, but quickly realised that put him in a minority of one. After the longest embarrassment of any short moment ever, Joanne broke the crushing silence `Well as nice as it is to see you again Gary, unless there is something specific you want then I really have to get back. I have an appointment in a few minutes. ` Gary went to speak but gagged on the question as the full realization of what he was going to ask dawned on him. `Well I do need a favour` he offered slowly as a starting point. She looked quizzically at him and said equally slowly `What kind of favour?` Encouraged Gary said `I work for a local newspaper and I need some help with a story` Joanne looked relieved `Phew, thank god for that, I thought you were going to ask me to sleep with you again. By the way you do know I am engaged right?` `Yes` he replied, `the receptionist told me` Joanne took a deep breath `What story' she started to say before the realisation set in. 'not the crazy weather we are having, you can't expect me to help you with that!` she spat the words at him. `Well that is exactly what I was hoping for` he replied. `In truth Joanne my neck is on the line and you are the only one with an inside track on this story. Besides, how often does an ex-girlfriend have a chance to help out an old flame? ` He asked in what he hoped was a cheeky but lovable fashion. One again horrified at the reminder of their earlier coupling, Joanne was shocked back into the now moment.` I am sorry Gary, you must know as well as anyone that reporters do not share their sources, especially when they have a good one. This story is the biggest thing happening right now and I have the best possible source` Gary raised an eyebrow `Well if yours is so good then why do they not appear on your reports as an expert, instead of you just quoting them onscreen` he said in the hope this would unnerve Joanne into given up information. `Gary, it's none of your business, but basically she is a boffin, the quiet studious type who wouldn't go down well on camera. Plus, my director always has an eye on the instant viewing figures and …` Gary jumped in `and the public prefer to have their news read by a pretty girl instead of someone who actually knows what they are talking about?` Now irritated by Gary's cheap remark Joanne replied `I am a bloody good reporter Gary, but if how I look makes people take a second look at the news, then so be it!` Gary realized he had overstepped the mark and had set himself up as opposition. He started to apologise `I am sorry Joanne…I am a bit` but he was cut off by Joanne who was now looking over his shoulder. `Sorry Gary, my appointment is here. Sort of lovely to see you again and sort of good luck but I just cannot help you, understand? `No' replied Gary 'But I'll get over it`. He lent forward to kiss her goodbye in what he hoped would be a poignant and touching farewell moment, but Joanne recoiled and replaced his kiss with a patronizing and awkward rub of his arm. This was made all the less meaningful by the way she then looked at her hand before wiping it on her skirt. `Goodbye Gary` she said quickly as she side stepped him and moved to meet her guest at the reception desk. Gary intently watched her go, aware that the two security guards were also intently watching him. He was savouring those last few seconds when yet another commotion broke out at the reception desk as the visitor accidentally opened her brief case and then dropped the contents onto the polished floor. The situation was made worse when Joanne bent down to help recover the paperwork, only to crack heads with the patently clumsy and nervous visitor, sending them both backwards onto their behinds. The two security guards rushed forward, each helping one the two floundering women to their feet. Gary watched as Joanne started to bend forward again to assist her guest but thought better of it, and so just stood and regained her composure. The other woman quickly gathered most of her papers back into her briefcase, but in her haste left several pieces of paper protruding from the edges. Just as she seemed ready to proceed, her dark rimmed spectacles also slipped from her face onto the floor, cracking one of the lenses. As both women made to pick them up they were stopped by one of the guards who held up his hand to avoid a further collision of heads. He then slowly and deliberately bent down to recover the spectacles and handed them back to her. The whole thing had taken perhaps no more than twenty seconds but the fiasco had made an impression on Gary. Here was a clumsy, yet obviously important female visitor that required Joanne to meet her personally in reception. When added to what Joanne had already let slip, namely that her weather expert was a 'she' and now here was an awkward but welcomed guest at the NCN station, Gary put two and two together and for the first time in his life was correct. `Voila` he said out loud, this was the expert he needed. Formalities completed, Joanne now shepherded her guest towards the lifts, but seeing that Gary was still stood there she moved towards the furthest door so as to deliberately avoid Gary. This only confirmed in Gary's mind that the visitor was someone that Joanne did not want him to meet. Seeing the two guards now walking towards him Gary held up his hands in silent submission and moved towards the front doors of the building. Once outside he stood in a pretend admiring the day fashion before speaking to the door security man. 'I have to wait for the doctor that just came in. Did you see where she parked her car?' The guard was only too happy that someone actually wanted to talk to him and offered in his eastern European accent 'You mean Professor Rowlinson, who just went in?' 'Yes, sorry professor Rowlinson, what was I thinking? 'Replied Gary. The guard pointed towards a row of cars in the reserved parking bays. 'As she is an important visitor they have given her special parking place with bosses cars' Gary was pleased with himself and decided to push his luck a little further. 'Do you know which is her car? ` The guard laughed out loud 'Yes, but go see for yourself if you can spot car for crazy professor lady, it should not be difficult'. Gary, for the first time in his life winked at another man in what he hoped would be a conspiratorial way. For the guard, in his culture this was something of a major insult and his demeanour suddenly changed whilst he spat out the word 'Dupek!' Having no idea what the word meant but understanding he had committed some international faux pas, Gary just nodded apologetically and quickly went down the steps towards the car park. He thought about the guards comment as he walked amongst the gleaming Mercedes, Porsche's and BMW's of the executive parking area. Amidst the rich money motors he suddenly came upon a shabby little blue car, which he would later find out was a Hillman Imp. Not only did it stand out because it came from a different era, it was also noticeable because the owner seemed to have parked across the parking bay line at a jaunty angle, giving the impression it had more been abandoned than parked. Given the fracas he had seen the visitor create just by turning up for a meeting with Joanne, he was in no doubt this would be the clumsy professor's car. He chanced a look at the security guard, who whilst offering him a middle finger salute also grudgingly confirmed he was in the right place. Gary settled down to wait.

CHAPTER FOUR: COME TO DADDY

Gary was feeling rather smug. Not only was he now working on an international story, but he was also minutes away from meeting and interviewing the world's leading expert. If Joanne fucking Graymond wouldn't share, then *'fuck it'* he thought *'he would just take!'*, now using the fucking word with a definite negative connotation. After the initial flush of success had begun to fade Gary started to get bored and tired of just standing around. He had only been waiting fifteen minutes but his unfit body and hangover began to complain, plus he was also starting to feel a little conspicuous just hanging around the car park in full view of the office windows. He moved to the back of a gleaming silver Porsche that had the private number plate 1AND. He sat down gently on the rear wheel arch and felt the car move slightly under his weight. He then immediately jumped up in fright as the car alarm suddenly blared out a series of loud high frequency beeps, along with flashing of all the lights on the car. Gary looked around as nonchalantly as he could, as if to see who had caused the commotion other than himself. The alarm suddenly ceased and was replaced with a knocking sound. Looking around Gary eventually found the knocking to be coming from an office window on the second floor. A tall male with red braces was holding a key fob and had obviously reset the alarm whilst also give Gary an internationally recognised signal whilst mouthing the words 'FUCK OFF!' Gary shrugged his shoulders in fake innocence but moved away from the car anyway. Still not happy with standing, he decided the professor's car was too old to have anything like a car alarm so he thought he would alight there for a while. Settling as gently as he could onto the rear boot of the little car, he slowly transferred the rest of his weight and enjoyed the relief it bought to his aching back. Seeking further comfort he lifted the heel of his left foot up and hooked it over the silver rear bumper. Settling in for another wait, Gary was once again caught unawares when a hidden rusted bolt snapped causing half the bumper to fall onto the ground with a loud bang. He bent down to see if he could quickly mend the bumper before the owner returned and saw the damage. He was busily engaged holding it up and willing it to stay in place when he became aware of a shadow of someone standing over him. 'What have you done to my car!' said a stern female voice. Gary looked up but the woman standing over him was silhouetted against the sun, and although he could not see her face he knew who it must the professor. 'I was just trying to fix it' Gary quickly lied. Gesturing over his shoulder towards the Porsche he hoped to continue the lies. 'One of those posh jobs reversed into it before driving off without stopping' Gary stood up and looked into the face of Professor Emma Rowlinson. 'Hello, I'm Gary' he said, holding out his hand 'You must be Professor Rowlinson? She looked confused but slowly shook his hand 'Yes, but how do you know my name?' Gary had used the waiting time wisely, if a little immorally to work out a covering tissue of lies and deceit to use on the professor. 'I am a friend of Joanne's…. Joanne Graymond, who you have just been meeting with?' Relaxing a little she replied 'Oh that Joanne. She didn't mention a Gary during the meeting?' 'Well no, she wouldn't would she' said Gary 'I asked Joanne to introduce us but she thought it a bit difficult to do in her offices, so she suggested I wait here to introduce myself' She was struggling to see the relevance in all this and impatiently asked him 'well what do you want? I am very busy at the moment and now I have to get my car fixed! ` Gary did not always recognise an opportunity when it presented itself, but he saw this one. 'Well firstly I know somewhere that can quickly fix your car, so that's one less thing to worry about ' Her expression softened a little 'Go on' Gary looked around in what he hoped would seem a mysterious way 'And Prof, I need to talk to you about the weather' he said, using the bunny ears for "The weather". Emma was not impressed by the scruffy man or his talk of the weather, but she did need her car fixing so decided to go along with him for the moment. 'Well firstly 'she said 'drop the professor thing, and call me Emma. Secondly, everyone knows the weather is all messed up, so why would you want to talk to me?' Gary quickly considered his options. He could either be completely straight with the woman and hope for the best, or be creative and help manage the situation along a bit. The sneaky part of his brain won the argument in the briefest of moments. 'Yes, the weather is strange but it is going to get worse isn't it' he ventured. 'And, you are the expert who knows more about it than anyone else, that is why Joanne values you. Am I right…Emma?' He obviously knew more than she had first thought but held back a little 'So Gary, what's your interest in all this?' He struck what he thought was a thoughtful gaze across the car park 'I just want to help to keep people informed of what is going on in the world' he offered. She took a deep breath 'I don't think the world is quite ready to hear what I think is going on. Even Joanne is shying away from some of my detailed analysis of the situation' Seizing the moment Gary jumped in 'Well, I am ready to hear what you have to say and give the public the right to know!' Suddenly a light came on in Emma's head 'Give the public the right to know? Are you…are you yet another reporter?' Realising he had jumped too soon Gary tried a recovery 'No, well yes, but not like them in there, I work for a newspaper' If he thought this would help matters the change in her expression told him otherwise. 'A newspaper! Yes, I see now. You are just another greasy reporter type, who just wants to sensationalise this whole thing to sell newspapers. I should have known' Emma sighed and walked towards driver's door of her little blue car. Gary tried to cut her off whilst he protested his innocence, all the while insisting he was in it for the public good. He was helped in his endeavours when Emma for the third time that day dropped he briefcase, spilling papers and charts around and under her car. Gary helpfully joined in the scramble to gather up the papers before they blew away and between them the stack was soon recovered back into the briefcase. 'Thank you' said Emma in a slightly embarrassed way. Seeing his chance to make a full regain, Gary spoke. 'Look, I can see why you would be suspicious of yet another reporter, but I am not out for the sensational story and quick buck' he lied convincingly 'So, why not let me strap your bumper back into place, take you to a garage I know where it can be fixed and whilst they do it I can buy you a coffee. Now, if by the end of the coffee I haven't convinced you I am a fit and proper person to talk to then I will just walk away and leave you alone for ever… deal?' Emma weighed up her options; broken car, less than useful meeting with Joanne and the urgent need for some coffee, and now here was someone offering to put all three things right! 'Okay' she said 'much against my better judgment and everything my father taught me, I will accept your offer'. Gary went to speak but she held up her finger 'But, once the car is fixed and your real motive oozes out, then it is goodbye Gary, got it? He nodded 'Got it'. He smiled, rubbed his hands together and proceeded to look around for something to strap up the bumper for the drive to the garage. Next to a nearby waste bin he spotted a cardboard box that had been flat packed for dumping complete with the plastic banding still wrapped around it. It was a simple task that Gary made look difficult by first cutting his finger on the sharp edge of the banding and then proceeding to bleed over everything. Between sucking his bleeding finger and rolling around under the car, he eventually secured the loose bumper temporarily back on the car. 'What sort of car is this?' he asked as he wrestled with the ancient and non-retracting seat belt. Emma clunked the car into reverse 'It is a Hillman Imp and before you say anything else you ought to know it used to be my father's, so I don't need a critique of its faults and failings thank you. I love daddy's car' Gary sat amidst the loose tentacles of the ineffective seat belt strap 'Oh I wouldn't dream of being critical, especially since it has so much character and charm' which although he said in an ironic way, he hoped it would ingratiate him a little more with the prof. After a couple of minutes of trying to figure what part of the belt went where, he gave up and just laid it across his shoulder and lap like a thin grey scarf. The garage was nearby and he figured he could risk it. This somewhat casual attitude to risk taking was soon challenged when Emma started the car, crunched it into several gears, before speeding off around the car park like she was driving a go kart at a race track. Gary was flung around the interior of the small car and looked around for a hanging strap or anything to hold onto. Finding nothing of substance to grab he renewed his efforts with the seatbelt and with the sense of urgency provided by self-preservation managed to plug one of the many buckles into something silver between the seats. It wouldn't save him he thought but it certainly made him feel better. 'Wow, where's the fire lady!' he exclaimed in a faux American accent that he hoped would hide his real British fear. Emma gave him a sideways glance, 'Daddy always said life is too short to waste sat in a car, so he taught me to drive as if I actually want to get somewhere to do something' Gary looked across at the crazed face of the prof and then back to the front just in time to see them exit the car park and momentarily take flight as they hit the speed bump. Hoping that perhaps her style of driving was reserved for car parks and not the public roads, Gary was sorely disappointed and even more frightened when the journey became a blur of near misses, shouted threats and blaring horns from other road users. His voice went up an octave as he shouted directions to the garage, with each word getting emphasis as yet another road disaster was barely avoided. He felt like the co-driver in a manic rally car, shouting instruction from pace notes to the driver. He looked over appealingly at the prof. and noticed that she was now wearing glasses and that both lenses had large cracks across the lenses. 'What happened to your glasses?' he shouted in an attempt to take her mind off the imaginary race they were now seemingly engaged in. 'Oh these old things? I only wear them for driving, they used to be my dad's but I dropped them back there is the foyer and the security guard stood on them' He shook his head and tried to bite his lip to help contain the fear he was feeling before asking 'So you have the same lens prescription as your father, that is lucky'. She shot him a glance through broken the specs and replied 'No, not the same, just a similar stigmatism in one eye' Gary was further horrified and hoped that his inevitable death would be both swift, painless and reported on favourably. Following Gary's instruction as if she really was the driver of a rally car, Emma squealed around the last corner and onto the winning straight that was the railway viaduct garages. Hitting the brakes, the car skidded to a halt just outside the large archway doors, making the two mechanics working inside look up. With the engine off the car was silent except for the pounding of Gary's own heart in his own ears. He sighed out loud 'Houston, the eagle has landed'. Emma said nothing and expertly unbuckling her seatbelt climbed out of the car. Gary attempted to follow but the tentacle like seatbelt now held him tight. The buckle that earlier he could not do up, would now not undo and refused to release him back into the wild. He could see the crazy prof stood at the front of the car impatiently waiting for him and gesticulating that he should hurry up and get out of the car. With great difficulty and by stepping through the lap belt, he somehow managed to be free himself from the restraint device and extricate himself from the vehicle. He looked loathingly down at the quietly hissing and ticking car as it sat benignly cooling down after the race. They walked into the garage where the podgier of the two mechanics spoke first 'Hello Gary, been a while since we've seen you down here'. Gary nodded in moot acknowledgment. Everyone present, except for Emma, knew the reason Gary had not been to the garage recently was because he lost his driving licence in a drink drive related incident earlier in the year. 'Hello Dave, how's things?' said Gary, who then hoped to jump straight to the reason he had brought the prof to garage before his little secret came out. 'Good Gary thanks' replied Dave 'isn't that right Steve?' to the skinny mechanic still tinkering under the bonnet of the red Ford Escort. He looked up 'Well last year was much better when we had your business Gary, but of course without a licence we don't get to see you much these days, do we Dave?' Both of them laughed out loud. Emma looked across at Gary 'No licence! Then how come you dare to criticize my driving?' 'It's a long story' said Gary wearily 'I'll tell you about it later'. He turned to Dave and in a sarcastic way said 'Thanks Dave! Look, the Prof here just has a loose bumper and we were hoping you could have a look and quickly fix it? The dust in the garage visibly moved as both mechanics in unison gave a sharp intake of breath. 'Oh Gary, we would really like to help wouldn't we Steve' said Dave. 'Oh yes' replied Steve 'But we gotta get this knocked out urgent like and then bodge those two through an MOT by the end of the day. Dave jumped in 'Look, Gary, as you're a regular' 'or at least wuz a regular when you had a licence' chimed in Steve, allowing both of them a little further chuckle at Gary's expense, 'How about we say we can have it ready by tomorrow lunchtime?' Having played this game before Gary looked at each of them in turn. 'What if we said ten o'clock tomorrow morning and there will an extra drink in it for you?' They two exchanged glances and Dave looked like he was about to speak when Emma burst forth 'That is simply not good enough gentlemen. I am far too busy to not have a car for 24 hours, especially with everything else going on.' Both the mechanics looked ruffled by the outburst and were rolling their shoulders ready to respond. Gary put his hand over his eyes as Emma continued 'I need it done today, within the hour. It is a simple bolt that is broken, so, I will pay fifty pounds for the job and another fifty if it done within the hour... agreed?' Without even checking with Steve, Dave bit the proverbial hand off 'Yes miss, be done wivin the hour, right Steve' 'Right Dave!' he replied. Gary, not for the first time that day was both amazed and horrified. Firstly that the prof had managed to get Dave & Steve to change their minds about something, but also that she was paying way too much for such a simple job. He took her by the arm and turned her away from the Dave and Steve. 'That's is way over the odds just to replace a bolt, any fool could do it, especially at that that price! She removed her broken glasses 'Do you want the job Gary? If you can do it within the hour I will pay you the hundred pounds!' He knew she was teasing him and he breathed in to keep from saying something even stupider than what he was actually thinking

'Fine!' he replied. Trying to recover some of his lost masculinity he turned back to the mechanics 'Right then Dave, I will take the good professor for a coffee and we will back in about an hour for the motor. 'Yeah, you do that Gary' he heard Dave reply, along with some less than discreet sniggering from Steve under the car bonnet. Gary and Emma turned and walked down the road to where Gary hoped to find a coffee shop instead of a greasy spoon. Emma spoke first 'Gary, you called me prof again, so for the last time please refer to me as Emma.' 'Why?' he asked 'It must have been hard getting a degree and a professorship, aren't you proud of the title?' She stopped and looked at him 'Gary, I have three degrees and two doctorates in various scientific fields. I have been nominated for two Nobel prizes for my work and I am on the United Nations Panel for Science and technology. But, none of that will matter unless I can complete my studies into this weather phenomenon and try and find a way out of it', you see? What Gary did see was that there was a lot more to this weather thing than he first understood, but he let that slide for the moment. 'But Prof...' he began. She cut him off 'There you go again. Every time you say Prof you and everyone else expects me to perform like some deranged boffin, talking like Stephen Hawking and solving the world's problem. Then I get a plethora of stupid questions, none of which helps me to actually solve the world's problems. Do you get that!?' Gary could see she was getting wound up and since he knew he was soon to asking her those stupid questions himself decided to try and calm her down a bit. 'Whoa, calm down pro... Emma. Look, let's take this one step at a time. First coffee, then the car sorted and then I will buy you dinner'. Where Gary came from dinner was a lunchtime meal, but he had read enough about posh women to know dinner for her would be in the evening. Emma took a deep breath 'Yes, you are right I do need to calm down, have a strong cup of tea and get the car fixed' Gary noted there was no mention of his dinner invitation, which in his world meant a rebuff, so he didn't mention it again. They walked in silence for a bit, which although they had only met a short while earlier that day was still awkward. Gary was smarting over the moot dinner refusal and Emma was considering everything that was flying around her head, along with the dinner invitation. She had heard his offer but it had caught her unawares and with everything else going on it was something she could not even contemplate at the moment. Besides which, she was starting to formulate a plan that might include Gary in the bigger picture. They reach the road junction and there in the distance there was the corporate beacon of an international non UK taxpaying coffee chain. He gripped her elbow as they waited to cross the road, which prompted her to look down at his hand on her. Gary noticed 'Just in case someone comes along who drives like you!' he said. The humour was duly noted and she smiled but not because of the attempt at a joke, but because it reminded her of something her dad would have done. Gary, unknowingly, had chipped a small piece away from the ice maiden.

CHAPTER FIVE: TEA FOR TWO

Having successfully crossed the road, Gary released his hand from Emma's arm and led the way to the coffee shop door. Out of character for him, he pushed the heavy door open and then held it open so the she could go through ahead of him. She smiled and was grateful, he smiled back but he was also curious as to which part of his brain was responsible for that. Was that, as he suspected, the devious Gary, just playing the game part of his brain, or was there something else going on? As Emma was leading she chose a plastic table and bench combination seat in the main window and they sat down opposite each other. 'What will you have then?' started Gary, continuing the gentleman of concern routine. Looking at the menu he began reading from the long list of coffee options and variations on a theme 'Americano, Latte, Skinny, Cappuccino, Mocc...' She held up her and hand and cut him off 'Tea please' Gary was somewhat perplexed. He couldn't imagine starting any day without at least two cups of coffee, and you can make that three on days when he had a hangover, which was most days. He tried once more 'Are you sure, there's a whole world of coffee to be had right here?' he said in a fake Italian accent. She smiled politely but in a way to confirm her decision not to change it. 'Coffee mid mornings, but today just some ordinary English tea would nice, thank you' Gary made as if to get up and order the drinks but she stopped him. 'I will treat you. What do you want?' Gary started to make some modest protest but she quickly added. 'It's the least I can do since you found a place to get the car mended' Gary nodded, 'Okay I will have a black Americano with some milk on the side please' With that she slid out of the plastic seat and went to the counter to order. Gary, as all men would do, watched her walk away and for the first time realized the prof was a real woman with a real woman shape hidden under her less than flattering professor clothes that she had hung on her body. Her shoulder length hair had some shape to it but she was obviously not a woman who spent a lot of time on her appearance before leaving her house in the morning. Since he was in full critique mode and with little else to do, he waited until she turned sideways on to see if she was equipped with breasts of the female kind. However, before he could tell what was happening under her blouse or smock or whatever it was, he was forced to look quickly away as she turned and looked back towards him. He returned to reading the menu to occupy his mind whilst he waited and learned in the small print that VAT was indeed included in the price, and that any nut allergies should be notified to the staff. In his peripheral vision he was aware of her approaching the table so he sat back and cleared room for her to put the cups down. She seemed to take this simple thing the wrong way 'I am really not that clumsy!' she said in a mocking tone. Gary responded 'You forget, I saw your grand entrance to the television station' in an attempt to lighten the mood again. His words did not exactly lighten the mood, but they were a good precursor for what was to happen next. With the cups and saucers now safely on the table, both of them looked down at the saucers which were swimming in spilt liquid from her clumsy carriage of them from the bar. Gary made an exaggerated sideways look at the saucer and raised an eyebrow in what he hoped would be a quizzical, yet humorous look. The tension broke and she gave a small laugh, allowing Gary to join in. 'See, you don't always have to be such a little miss iron pants' She picked up her spoon and slowly stirred her tea before adding some milk from the jug. Still stirring she looked down into her drink and said thoughtfully 'I don't want to be a little miss iron pants anytime, it's just with so much happening right now I am finding it difficult to know what to do' Gary knew from experience as a reporter that this was a chink he could capitalize on, but strangely enough found himself regarding this statement as a friend sharing a concern. 'So what is bothering so much that even a cup of tea with Gary Barnes won't fix?' he asked. She continued looking down, stirring her tea and biting her bottom lip as if considering something. 'Well Gary Barnes, the company is fine thank you and the tea is good, but the world is fucked' Gary gagged at hearing her swear and spat his coffee back into his cup rather than splatter Emma with it. It made her smile 'Surprise you did it that little miss iron pants can swear?' 'Yes, well there's no denying that it did rather catch me on the hop' he replied, as he used the napkin to wipe the coffee from his lips and fingers. 'Well Gary, be warned I can swear in five languages!' 'Okay I got that' he smiled 'Perhaps I've misjudged you' It was her turn to raise an eyebrow. 'How so?' she asked. He took a breath, like so much of Gary's life it was going to be all or nothing. 'I thought you were a brainbox, a boffin, a clumsy but clever tight assed professor, who is full of academic qualifications but without any common sense or humour' he stopped and thought shit I have done it again. He waited for the deluge to begin, the shouting, the anger the throwing of the tea cup at him but nothing happened. She sat silently, still stirring her tea for another ten seconds before looking up. 'You are right, or at least part right. I am all those things Gary and a hundred more besides, all of which are on the dull side. I've kidded myself for years that once I had completed all my research projects I would be able to kick back a little and start to enjoy life, maybe have a holiday, a relationship, maybe even a family' Gary spoke 'So why can't you? You are not too old for those things'. She looked at his face 'I am currently 32 years old Gary, and if I am right about this weather situation' she paused 'I will never be 33'. Confusion was etched onto Gary's face as he struggled with what she had just said but before he could ask the question she continued. 'If I am right Gary, it means that me, you and ALL of those out there are going to die sometime in the next six months.' Gary's brain tried to compute the information it had been given but there was no rational or emotional thoughts that could adequately deal with them. His mouth opened and shut a few times as he tried to speak but no words came out. 'Gary I am sorry to burden you with this but everyone has to know sooner or later, it just happens that you are the first, or technically the second if you include me'. Since he couldn't deal with it directly Gary's brain was trying to swerve around it and provide alternative scenarios. After all, as bright as she was Emma could also just be a nutter, a bit cuckoo or just a religious nut job, just like so many of the 'end of the world' purveyors. 'Let's face it' he thought, 'not one of them has ever been right yet, why should she be the one.' With a little tension in his voice he tried a rational question 'What makes you so sure that you are right and this is going to happen?' She looked around the coffee shop to make sure no one else could hear what she was saying.' The weather Gary, like it or not it is one of the fields I specialise in. I am also one of very few scientists who also have a doctorate in astrophysics and degree's in Physics and Chemistry. In fact Gary I am the only person in the world with that combination of qualifications, and published research in all four sciences. Does that make any sense to you?' Although all the long words and titles meant very little to Gary, the overall evidence was impressive so he pushed on, waiting and hoping for the flaw or religious argument that would undermine her whole theory. 'Go on, I'm listening' He said. 'Using all the resources at my disposal, checking individually with the finest scientists in their fields and crunching all he available the data over and over leads me to the same conclusion.' Gary jumped in impatiently 'which is what?' She continued 'That something is gently pulling the whole of Earths weather systems in one direction. Our clouds and associated weather patterns are slowly being slowly dragged across the planet and unless something can be done, in six months they will be drawn off completely into space' Gary sighed, there was nothing obvious he could challenge there but asked the question anyway. 'Assuming you are right, and I am not totally convinced as yet, so what if all the clouds and rain piss off into space, won't we just be left with a sunny planet all over. Everywhere will be a holiday destination? He added the last bit in the hope that some humour may just help the situation. It did not. She did not smile 'Well for those that live through the raging storms that will happen in the next few months, yes they will get some sunshine. That might seem like an ideal until you realise with no cloud cover the earth's water will slowly evaporate and everyone will be exposed to huge amounts of solar radiation. In short it is not a question of how life will die out, just the small matter of when. Gary swallowed hard and spoke 'This all sounds very farfetched, the whole world's weather being screwed and sucked around?' Emma tilted her head 'Have you ever been to the seaside Gary and watched the tide go in and out?' 'Of course' he replied, 'we all have' 'And do you know what causes the tide to go in and out? She asked in a very patronizing tone.' Gary switched to his sarcastic voice 'Of course, everyone knows that the moon influences the sea with gravity. Whilst I don't understand gravity at least I know it is a proper thing'. 'So there Gary, you accept that something outside of the Earth can influence and pull something as dense as water around the planet using gravity. Now I am telling you something else is also pulling our weather towards it, and I am doing my best to find out what it is before it is too late'. Somewhere in the deep recesses of Gary's mind a wooden wheel and a cog meshed together, giving Gary the first inkling that this may actually be happening and she was not the fruit loop he first thought and hoped she was. 'Well assuming I believe or just accept the possibility this might be happening, just what can you do about it?' 'Nothing' she quickly replied 'At least nothing unless I can discover what is causing the phenomenon'. In a more panicky voice than he would have liked Gary said 'Well shouldn't you be in your lab and white coat, testing and sorting this shit out!' 'And that is where I have been these last four months, in between answering stupid questions from reporters and TV stations' she replied. The irony was not lost on Gary and he gave a sheepish kind of grin. 'Present company accepted' she added, which made Gary feel a little better. 'So what about your meeting with Joanne Graymond this morning, what was all that about?' It was Emma's turn to look sheepish. 'I have been their science source for the last few months, giving them updates on the deteriorating weather situation. It was only a few days ago that I was in a position to put all the pieces together and see the terrible end result.' 'So did you tell Joanne all this?' Gary asked. 'No, it wouldn't be right to give this information to just one TV station. There would be panic, looting and chaos everywhere' I just gave Joanne the immediate weather update and then told her I would not be available for a few weeks as I am off to Hawaii' 'And just why did you tell her that? Asked Gary 'Because that is exactly where I am going. There I can have the use of one of the largest telescopes on the planet, access to data from radio telescopes and be able to complete my studies away from them. Once I have crossed referenced the information from all the different sciences then I can ask other scientists to check my results and then confirm them.' 'But how long will all that take?' he asked 'If it all goes really well and confirms my earlier work then about one or two weeks' she replied. Gary looked intently at her 'and if it doesn't go well? She paused but not for effect 'possibly six months to a year'. Gary's coffee cup fell from his hands and clattered around the table as he sought to catch it 'But if you are right six months is too late' 'Correct Gary. Shall we get going?' She quickly drank the remaining tea in her cup whilst Gary dabbed at yet more spilt coffee from his jacket front. As soon as they were outside the coffee house Gary's brain began started to process what it knew. In the space of four hours he had gone from being the hangover king to ace reporter, then boffin navigator to a doomed member of planet earth, and all before he had stopped for lunch. He started to gabble out questions, but as varied and many as they were, they also lacked thought or substance. He did not even notice that Emma had now taken hold of his arm and was escorting him safely back across that same road. Once back on the pavement she stopped him. 'Gary, can I suggest you stop babbling like an idiot and take stock of your own situation first, otherwise you are going to be no use to me in Hawaii' She stepped off again leaving Gary stunned and rooted to the spot 'Hawaii…. HAWAII! What the fuck would I be doing in HAWAII?' She came back to him. 'You are going to help me Gary' He looked dazed 'Me, how can I help you… I can't even spell astro turf, or whatever it is' She took his hand ' At some point Gary this story will break or will have to be broken, and I will need an ace reporter. That's you right? Isn't that what your whole career has been about so far, the big scoop? Isn't that what your whole day has been about, getting the crazy professor to spill the beans? Well I am offering it to you Gary, there on a plate. Not only the biggest scoop of the day but in the whole history of mankind!' Gary was stunned for the third time that day 'But why me?' he mumbled. 'Because as you have pointed out time is an issue and I don't have time to find another reporter who can drop everything and fly off to Hawaii to save the planet. And besides Gary, you are the only person yet who has driven with me and not jumped out at the first set of traffic lights'

Her crude use of humour worked and woke Gary from his stupefying wonderment. 'Okay, if I can get the editor to let me run off to Hawaii with you AND cover the expenses then I will do it!' Emma shook her head, there isn't time for all that. Ring him if you feel the need but I will cover the immediate costs out of my research grant and money daddy left me. It matters little if I am right, as money will soon be obsolete anyways!' She took Gary's arm and ushered him back along the road towards the archways garage. Her little blue Hillman Imp was just being pushed back out of the garage by the two mechanics as they arrived back. 'All sorted miss, good as new' said Dave, as Steve wiped his oily hand on an oily rag and said 'She'll take you to the moon and back' which caused both of them to chuckle. Gary stepped forward 'well as long as it get us to Hawaii, eh Emma' She smiled and 'yes Gary, Hawaii!' Somehow feeling they were now out of the humour loop caused Dave & Steve to exchange awkward confused glances. Emma took advantage of the moment and taking some cash from her shoulder bag she pushed it into Dave's overall top pocket. 'Now gents, we are in a bit of a rush, so if you will excuse us' said Emma before she jumped into the driving seat. Gary winked at the two bewildered mechanics before getting into the passenger side and started the process of strapping in. Before Gary had found any of the many silver buckles belonging to the seat belt, Emma had selected reverse gear and roared backwards onto the road. She then crunched the gearbox into an unnamed forward gear before releasing the clutch and tearing up the road and back into the manic London traffic that suited her style of driving. Whilst still fighting with the grey nylon seat strap contraption Gary suggested 'would it be best if I drove?' which only produced a wry smile from Emma and further acceleration of the demon Hillman Imp. Gary remained quiet and gripped the edge of

the seat for comfort, if not for safety.

CHAPTER SIX: WELCOME TO AMERICA SIR, BEND OVER.

After a life and underpants changing drive across London, Gary had collected his passport, thrown some items of unwashed clothing into a suitcase and put on some new clothes. They literally were brand new clothes he had mail ordered the previous year but have never tried on, opened or even paid for. Whilst he looked somewhat smarter, all the clothes has the tell-tale crease from where they had been originally folded and wrapped in some Indian sweatshop some time ago. He had insisted Emma stay in the car, telling her the area was probably not safe to leave a classic car like hers parked, but they both knew the real reason. Batchelor pads in the daylight are seldom the natural habitat of single women. 'Well' she said, 'you do look…em different, better…very smart' as she tried to convey the right compliment whilst hiding her horror at the creased cheap polyester suit and shirt Gary was wearing. This was completely lost on Gary, as having at last opened his new clothes for this special occasion he imagined he must look the proverbial million dollars, so he took the compliment at its two faced value. The time was just after three o'clock in the afternoon as they tore through the traffic to where Emma lived. Although the drive was just as frightening as before, Gary distracted himself by calling his offices where he worked. 'Good morning, Bromley Mercury office' the cheery female voice intoned. 'Hi Sarah, its Gary here' the cheery female voice instantly changed to a much less cheery one and hissed, 'Gary, where the hell have you been? Nick is doing his nut. You had better have a good excuse or he will have your balls' 'I'm fine, thanks for asking' Gary replied sarcastically. He had an idea that Sarah had a soft spot for him but that her own particular soft spot was being filled by the editor Nick. 'Look, I need you to pass a message to Nick for me. Tell him I am on to something really big. This is the biggest story in the world today and I have got the inside edge, the skinny, the scoop!' He paused to let the information sink in with the reliable but none too bright Sarah. She spoke 'That's all very well Gary, but you are scheduled to cover the council's planning application meeting this afternoon and the new supermarket opening tonight. Peggy from Enders is cutting the ribbon you know!' Either she had not heard him or she was less than impressed with world events, especially when set against 'EastEnders' the long running TV soap. Gary tried a different tack and spoke slowly 'Listen Sarah, I am not coming in to the office for a few days, so someone else will have to cover for me. I am following the weather story and flying out to Hawaii today' A strangled voice of apoplexy came back to him down the mobile 'Hawaii! Hawaii!' she shouted twice, briefly reminding Gary of that old song 'Goodbyeee, Goodbyeee' 'What the hell are doing heading off to Hawaii, is this a sick joke? This will be the end of you Gary, Nick will fire you for sure on this one!' Gary replied 'Just pass him the message that I am not going off on a jolly and I will bring back the biggest story the Bromley Mercury has ever run.' Sarah's voice was now at a frequency usually reserved for dogs and bats, 'Don't you dare Gary, you come back to this office this instance, do you hear....' Gary did not hear the last bit as he had pushed the end call button on his mobile and cut off the shrieking harpie. He had hoped that she would have wished him well and to go follow the story, but he should have known things like that might happen in Hollywood films but don't happen in the Bromley Mercury offices. By now Gary imagined, she would have been in Nick's office telling him a pack of truths about where Gary was headed, or at least where he said he was headed. They would both have agreed it was time for him to be fired before Nick would have pushed Sarah up against the filing cabinet for a late afternoon grope. Whilst it did not instil any confidence in his current employment status at the newspaper, the call had distracted him from the terrors of the drive. Just as he got back into the fearful rhythm and was considering bailing out at the next traffic lights, the car sped over a small bridge in the docklands area before screeching to a halt outside a very posh apartment block overlooking the River Thames. 'Do you want to come in?' she asked him 'No, I will just sit quietly for a moment if you don't mind.' he shakily replied. 'Okay, I always have a case packed for work so I will only be two minutes' she said, before she got out of the car and disappeared into the lobby of the building. He watched as she was greeted by the security doorman before getting into the lift. It was suddenly very quiet as both Gary and the Hillman Imp both sat catching their breath like racehorses after a race. Gary reviewed the day's events. This morning he just had a simple hangover but to cure that he had undertaken to steal a source from an ex-girlfriend who worked for a major television news channel. He had been manhandled by security, driven around town by a madwomen and had been told the world was going to end. Now, to cap it all it seemed like he would not have a job for much longer and he was flying off to Hawaii. Gary had accomplished all this in a few short hours and he still had something of the hangover, so none of those things had cured it. Suddenly Gary did not feel quite as clever as when he had started the train of events this morning. He considered all the options and if he got out of the car now and ran away from the crazy Prof, then he could spend all day tomorrow grovelling to Nick in the office and still keep his job. It suddenly seemed the best of the no other options left to him and he put his hand on the car door handle to get out and claim his shitty life back. Just as his hand hit the cold metal to open the door the driver's door was flung open and Emma threw a suitcase in at him 'Shove that into the back will you, the boot is already full of junk' Gary struggled to push the compact but heavy suitcase over his shoulder into the back seat and was still half turned when Emma found a gear she liked and the car tore back towards the little bridge. He was just turning back to the front, so his eyes could not warn his brain that they were about to cross the bridge for the second time. The first Gary knew of it was a sickening sense of weightlessness, followed a second later by the impact of the car hitting the road again and his head the lining of the roof. Emma laughed out loud and would have continued to do so had the events of the day and her driving not suddenly caught up with Gary. Infuriated by nearly everything that had occurred that day and now with a sore head, Gary saw red to add to the stars was already seeing. Without thinking about the consequences, thereby missing the irony of that being that was what had got him into this position in the first place, he reached down between the two seats and pulled the handbrake fully on whilst screaming 'STOP' at the top of his voice. The effect was immediate as the rear wheels stopped rotating and the back of the little car hunched down towards the road. The rest of the car was still operating under the laws of momentum but without the support of the rear end it started to screech and skid across the road. Both Emma and Gary started to scream in unison as they were now both no more than interested parties in the vehicle and its immediate future. It may have seemed like hours but in fact was only a few seconds that they skidded uncontrollably along the road. Whatever the time frame, it took a few years off their natural life expectancy. The car stopped with the front wheels on the pavement, just inches from a large ornamental iron railing. 'FUCK! They both said together, except Gary had a comma on his so he continued the sentence by shouting. 'Stop, stop stop this fucking madness. The whole crazy day thing: The crazy driving thing: The crazy nearly losing my job and nearly my life thing!' Emma sat stunned and silent staring straight ahead through the windscreen. The silence was broken by Gary's mobile indicating a message had arrived for him and to fill in the awkwardness he pushed the button to read it. 'Oh fucking great' he said in a slow deliberate manner. 'News just in Prof. I haven't nearly lost my job, I have actually lost my job' There was another bling noise 'oh and there is more good news, they have suspended my company credit card, game, set and fucking match'. Neither spoke for about twenty seconds before Emma started to speak 'G..' was all she managed before Gary held up his shaking hand with one extended finger. He breathed in deeply three or four times before saying 'go on'. Emma looked across at him 'Gary, I am sorry about your job, I really am, but if I am right about all this then your job won't matter anyway. If am right you will be the first reporter on the planet to know about it and you will be able to work anywhere because Gary Barnet.. 'It's Barnes' he interrupted 'Sorry, because Gary Barnes will have the skinny, the story and in fact 'the' biggest news story ever' Gary liked what he was hearing 'go on' he said quietly. In a voice that a mother might use to on her child at the sweet counter she continued 'And, if it makes you feel any better I will drive a little slower, okay? The effort, explanation and voice were not lost on Gary, and he smiled as he now let go of the handbrake. The rest of the journey to the airport was relatively sedate, with Emma keeping to her word and Gary to himself. He mulled over and over in his mind the sentence 'biggest news scoop ever' If she was right Gary would go from being a lowly hacked off hack to the most sort after guest on a morning chat show ever! He was feeling warm and smug about the situation when Emma reading his mood interrupted his musings. 'I don't want to burst your warm and cosy bubble Gary, but of course you will only be the best reporter on the planet until the planet comes to an end, sometime next year!' It made them both laugh out loud in a lovely warm shared moment of certain doom and destruction. Having arrived at the airport and booked the car into the long term car park, they caught the shuttle to the terminal. Once inside the shiny new British Airways terminal Gary looked around in awe, like a tourist on his first visit to New York. 'Have you not been to this terminal before?' Emma asked 'No' he replied, I usually fly from Gatwick. Whilst this was something of the truth, the usually in this instance meant once. Gary had flown just once before from anywhere and that once was from Gatwick. Emma elegantly pulled her classy luggage along on its four finely engineered wheels. Gary carried his Nan's old tartan suitcase which had never been designed with wheels, although once it had been attached to a shopping trolley for ease of use on her coach journey back from Brighton. Scanning the many information boards as they walked Emma guided them to the correct check in area, where there was already a large queue for their flight. Gary sucked his teeth 'Well you might get on if you have booked but I can't see them having room for me after this lot' Emma looked at him 'I phoned ahead whilst you were collecting your bag and it should be all sorted' Gary was impressed and said 'lead on then' Skirting the masses Emma found the empty first class check in lane she was looking for. Ignoring the sly envious looks from the queuing hordes, she led Gary along the empty lane to the dedicated check in. Gary whispered to Emma 'we will get rumbled you know and it is a long walk back there to the end of the queue'. She ignored Gary's comment and approached the smiling girl behind the desk. Emma produced her credit card and both their passports 'You should have reservations for Miss Rowlinson and Mister Barnes? I amended the booking by telephone a couple of hours ago' After some keyboard punching and screen searching the girl replied 'ah yes Miss Rowlinson I see your booking but the gentlemen's name here is down as Barnett? 'No' Emma quickly countered hoping that Gary didn't hear it. It is definitely Barnes, it must be a mistake at your end?' Given that this was the first class checking desk the assistant knew it was definitely going to be their mistake no matter who had cocked up, so she simply said 'No problem Miss Rowlinson, I'll amend right now for you' and began changing Gary's surname. Gary whispered again 'I heard that'. After some minutes of typing and amending the assistant continued. 'So Miss Rowlinson, that's two first class fares to Hawaii via Los Angeles, which comes to twelve thousand, six hundred and thirty eight pounds please. Gary's leg buckled momentarily and he swallowed hard. Even if his company credit card had not been cancelled there was no way he could afford this on any or total available credit of the other cards in his wallet. Emma handed over a sleek black credit card without a murmur and quickly entered the pin number when prompted. Gary was speechless, but for the first time it was a controlled 'best keep my mouth shut' moment and not just stunned silence. Once the paperwork was completed and the passports checked, the check in girl summoned a waiting minion. First class travel includes not handling your bags again until you are at your destination, so the minion picked up their cases and deposited them on the weighing scales at the desk. The minion even maintained an air of professionalism as he lifted Gary's Nan's case, despite the ripe smell emanating from it. Emma retrieved their passports and was then given directions to the British Airways first class lounge. With Gary following like a nervous puppy, she then walked back past the sneering proletariat who were still queuing for circus class seats on the flight. Waiting till they were clear of the crowd Gary said to Emma 'You have just spent half my yearly salary on two seats on a plane, I can't afford that sort of outlay' She did not break stride 'As I said Gary, if I am right then money will soon be irrelevant, so better to travel in style and die happy right?' This was not the sort of decision that Gary had to consider in his daily life, or even in his past life as it now was. They moved through the terminal following the signs to the security search area and airport gates. As they neared the long queue for security, Emma guided Gary into a swift left turn towards a door marked 'By Invitation Only' The guardian of the door asked to see their boarding passes, with only a hint of surprise that Gary actually had one he ushered them through. The First class security area was screened off from the economy area and was very different to what Gary had experienced in air travel in his previous life. There was no queue, only personal security screeners holding hand held devices, all of whom were polite and full of smiles. If they had the need to open your hand held bag then one of the British Airways personal staff packed it for you. Gary thought this was wonderful and something he could get used to. They were through security in moments before the one of the BA staff introduced himself as David and asked them if they wanted to shop in the airside duty free area or go straight to the first class lounge. 'I think I could do with a drink, what about you Gary? Asked Emma. 'Yes' he replied, 'a drink, why not?' wondering what other surprises would be in store for him today. David ushered them to a waiting electric cart and they set off through the airport. They eased through the walking herds of economy passengers, their warning beeping clearing a path. Emma felt a bit conspicuous but Gary felt like the Pope and couldn't help himself waving papaly at a few of the less fortunate flying refugees. He was a little surprised that none of them waved back and even a little hurt that someone from Essex offered him a middle finger salute. They arrived at the discreet entrance to the first class lounge and were taken straight past the receptionist into the huge area reserved for the rich, famous and downright lucky. Gary was so in awe that he imagined he could hear a great harp glissando as they entered the first room. Whilst he was still taking it all in the David served them both a chilled flute of champagne and pointed out the various facilities on offer. They included a shoe shine, a hairdresser's, a massage and as much to eat and drink as they liked. Wishing them a pleasant journey, the obsequious David turned on his heel and was gone again, to meet, greet and generally bum lick other privileged travellers. 'So Gary, what do you think so far, do you like travelling in style?' He held up his champagne and looked through the glass in mock admiration 'I could certainly get used to it' he said and the both laughed. They found a comfortable lounge seat with a designer coffee table arrangement in front of them. Gary was quiet for a moment prompting Emma to ask 'Penny for your thoughts?' 'Well' he said looking at his watch. 'It's now nearly seven o'clock in the evening. At seven o'clock this morning I had a hangover, a job and the rest of my life in front of me. Now I have none of those of things. Instead, here I am sipping champagne, waiting to fly off to Hawaii, with the life expectancy of a fruit fly. It's been a funny old day' Emma nodded in mute agreement 'Sorry Gary, most of those things are my fault aren't they? But if I am right then the future is not very bright for any of us' 'So you are not 100% sure we are all headed for certain death?' Gary asked in a far lighter tone than the question really needed. She looked over at him 'Well, let's say if things continue as they have been then it is only the when and not if, so shall we leave it at that for now?' Gary breathed in to reply but she held up her hand 'That was rhetorical Gary' and he breathed out again. To lighten the reflective mood they were now in, Emma suddenly said. 'How about some food, I'm famished!' She quickly craned her neck and scanned her eyes around the room looking to find the buffet or dining area. Almost instantly a red waist coated waiter appeared, who must have been hovering nearby waiting for them to show interest in some food, more drinks or anything at all. He offered them a menu of fresh al la carte meals or pointed them in the direction of the buffet if they preferred a lighter snack. All the while he spoke he continued to expertly refill their glasses from an expensive bottle of champagne. 'Mmm this Moat is very nice 'said Gary. The waiter ignored the ignorance and merely replied 'Good, I'll leave the bottle', as he pulled up an ice bucket next to their table. 'Thank you' said Emma before whispering to Gary 'its pronounced Moet' Noting she had embarrassed Gary she quickly changed direction 'Actually I think I will try the buffet' The waiter nodded 'If madam changes her mind or requires more champagne, then just catch my eye and I will arrange everything' He slipped quietly away to offer his services to a couple at the bar. 'I could get used to this Moet' said Gary with emphasis, before finishing his drink and topping himself up from the bottle. Emma put her hand over her glass and declined a refill 'It will be a long enough flight without also being tipsy' she said. The both walked to the buffet and looked over the many hot and cold dishes on offer. Catering staff hovered behind the counter waiting to serve up whatever the customer chose. When they had both chosen their food they sat back down to find the waiter had placed cutlery and fresh linen napkins at their table. Gary looked at Emma's salmon and vegetable gratin which looked nice. Emma looked at Gary's burger and chips, complete with two raw Oysters on the side. Her look was noticed by Gary 'I have never tried them' he offered by way of excuse. After a few mouthfuls Emma watch as Gary attempted his first ever raw Oyster. He slid the mollusc into his mouth as he had seen countless people do on television. Emma stopped eating to see what his reaction was going to be and how he would deal with both the flavour and texture of the raw seafood. It was soon clear that Gary was not going to be a lifelong lover of raw seafood. The Oyster now partly swallowed began to seek an escape and along with Gary's Adam's apple began to bob up and down in his throat. Gary desperately looked for a way out of the embarrassing situation now arising. He couldn't swallow and he didn't feel he could spit in front of Emma, so had more attempt at chewing the oyster before his body completely rejected it. Just as the inevitable chunder was about to occur the all-seeing waiter appeared. Standing in front of Gary to shield the moment, in one deft movement he placed an open napkin in front of Gary's mouth and said 'If I may take that from you sir'. Much relieved, without any thought he spat the offending fishy chewy stuff into the napkin which was quickly whisked away and replaced with a glass of iced water. Gary quickly drank from the glass and then quietly thanked the waiter. 'No problem sir, I don't think anyone noticed' he replied quietly before quickly wheeling about and marching off with the full fishy napkin. Emma had looked on in stunned silence during the short episode. 'Are you okay now?' 'Yes' he replied' It just slid or rather didn't slide down the right way' Once he had regained what little composure he had, they continued eating their food. Emma was then surprised to see Gary's fork hovering over the second Oyster. Just as he poised to strike she said 'Really?' Unaware she had been watching him and now embarrassed, Gary used the fork to push the oyster to the far reaches of the plate away from his Burger & Chips. Once they finished their meal they left the table, nodded thanks to the waiter and walked off to see what else was on offer in the world of the first class traveller. 'So' Gary asked, 'do you always travel like this?' 'No, mostly business class if I am paying' she replied, 'but sometimes conference organisers or potential clients will treat me to first class if they want to impress' The sign on the flight information board repeated the information that due to the strange weather happening around the world, all flights were delayed and theirs would be for at least one hour. Emma suggested they use the spa and showers to freshen up after their long day. Gary followed along, not wanting to commit another first class social indiscretion, he vowed to watch and learn from the prof. As they checked into the spa reception area they were given towels, white robes and a selection of bathing costumes to choose from. Emma asked the middle aged receptionist if she could arrange for Gary's suit to be ironed whilst they used the facilities. Obviously thinking this was way below her station she started to explain how this might be better done down back in the lounge, before Emma cut her off and asked her 'What is your name? I don't see your name badge anywhere? 'The woman flushed a little and in a strong South African accent said 'My name Madame is Oranga and I seem to have lost my name tag' Emma pursed her lips 'Well Oranga, I would hate to be the one to have to bring that to management's attention. So, why don't you sort out the suit and I will forget your little name badge Faux pas' Reluctantly she replied 'Yes Madame, I will arrange it straight away' Gary & Emma moved through the main door bur before splitting into the male and female changing rooms Gary gave her a smile and said 'Yes, I can see you have done this before' Emma replied 'A tip Gary, always ask their name, then you have where you want them' before giving him a wink and walking through the female changing room door. Gary emerged onto the small poolside area first, very self-conscious in the very tight Speedo's which had been provided for him. There was no one in the pool so he strutted his stuff to the hot tub and slowly climbed into the still hot water. He sat very still enjoying the warmth and running through the events of the day in his mind. The adrenalin fuelled drive, losing his job, the champagne and of course the end of the world news all caught with him and he slowly shook his head and closed his eyes. He opened them a few seconds later as a shadow passed over him. He looked up to see Emma silhouetted against the bright lights of the pool. She looked very different with her hair up and wearing a skimpy yellow bikini that showed off her curves and shapely figure. Gary sat up 'I almost didn't recognise you ....' 'Without any clothes on?' she finished the sentence for him. She sat opposite him in silence and let her head rest on the back of the tub, it had been a long day for her to. Somewhere a timer ticked over and the bubbles suddenly came to life, turning the hot pool in a human washing machine. Gary gave out a little 'what the fuck' as it caught him unawares which amused Emma. The bubbles filled his borrowed swimming costume and his crotch floated upwards, pushing the outline of his manhood above the water. He pushed it down and tried letting some air out but nothing would save his blushes so he resigned himself to sitting upright to hide what little assets he had. Emma floated effortlessly, with her head laid back and her breasts and all points south sitting on top of the water. Gary was the perfect gentleman in that he did not look until he was certain her eyes were closed and he could not be caught. With her eyes firmly closed against the light and chlorine Emma spoke. 'I can see you Gary' which of course she couldn't but she knew that Gary didn't know that but now she could relax. After the fifteen minutes on the timer ran out the bubbles stopped and they both enjoyed the quiet moment it brought to them. After a minute she spoke first 'Right, I had better start to get myself ready, see you in reception Gary in ten minutes.' He nodded and watched her climb out of the tub, safe in the knowledge she could not see him this time. She was he thought, under that crazy professor, idiotic driver, end of the world forecaster, quite an attractive woman. He left it there as one final bubble reached the surface of the tub, leaving the feint smell of Oyster in its wake. Once dressed he waited for Emma in reception with the stroppy South African Oranga. She gave him a forced smile but offered no other conversation as she busied herself with her computer screen. The main door opened and in flounced the BA meeter and greeter David, who had seen them from security into the first class lounge. 'Ah Mr Barnes, is Professor Rowlinson with you?' Gary was both stunned and impressed that this guy had made a point of remembering both their names. 'He replied 'she is just getting dressed. The David nodded 'Oh good, I do hope you have both had a good stay at the lounge and everything was to your satisfaction?' 'Yes thank you, everything was to our satisfaction and beyond' said Gary, using what he thought was an amusing Disney space character voice. This reference was lost on David but who was too professional to show it. David produced a very slick looking business card and offered it to Gary 'And if sir finds himself flying back this way then please let me know and I will take care of you and the professors requirements personally' 'Why yes, thank you David, I will be sure to do that'. Emma appeared from the changing room causing Oranga to suddenly sit up straight and put on her most attentive face. 'Sorry to keep you waiting Gary, my hair needed drying. Hello again David' David struck his best camp butler pose 'Ah professor Rowlinson' to which Emma raised a finger 'I am incognito today David, its Miss Rowlinson'. David tapped the side of his nose in a conspiratorial way 'Of course Miss Rowlinson. I have come to tell you your flight boards in thirty minutes and I shall be pleased to drive you to the gate myself, once you are ready of course. 'Thank you David. She replied as they followed David out of the spa reception, leaving Oranga pulling a sour face. Once more on the electric buggy and back amongst the ordinary walking public, David drove them carefully through the airport walkways towards their allotted gate. Gary resisted the urge to wave this time but moved his bum around as something made him uncomfortable. He slid his hand behind him and pulled out a red covered UK passport. In far too good condition to be his own he showed it to Emma. She shook her head and said 'look inside and see who it belongs to' He flicked though many pages of stamps and visas before finding the picture and name page. Gary recognised the picture immediately but still read the name out loud 'Paul McCartney'. Emma looked at the picture and confirmed the name. Hearing the name mentioned David looked over his shoulder and said 'Oh did you manage to get a glimpse of Mr McCartney? I just dropped him off before I collected you. Such a nice man' Gary lent forward and wafted the passport under David's nose 'Nice man or not, he won't be going anywhere without this will he?' The buggy came to a halt as David's eyes came out on stalks. He took the passport and carefully checked the information page. 'Hold on' is all he said as he changed the quiet beeping to a loud claxon and pushed the accelerator to the floor. The buggy set off like a scalded cat and David set off in a high speed through what was a relatively busy area full of the flying public. Gary had a flashback to Emma's driving earlier in the day and looked over at her only to see her grinning manically. David offered some over the shoulder apologies and continued his manic journey across the airport, only missing a whip and a team of horses to complete the scene. They arrived at the New York boarding gate where there was some animated conversation happening between the gate staff and some of the entourage associated with Mr McCartney, who himself was standing quietly by with his arms folded. David approached him and triumphantly produced the passport like a magician produces flowers from a sleeve. Emma and Gary could not hear the conversation but the body language told that there was much relief and thanks being given. David bowed slightly and offered Paul McCartney one of his cards, which was ignored by him but accepted by one of his group with good grace. David climbed back aboard the buggy and full of apologies set off again at a more sedate pace towards the Los Angeles boarding gate. As they approached he used the buggy to part the human waves of queuing passengers and drive them right to the first class entrance. David introduced them to the staff manning the gate and told them to take good care of these special passengers. Even though it was a superficial and well-used line, it still managed to make Gary feel special. To David and Emma's horror, Gary started patting his cheap suit pockets as if he were looking for a tip to give David. They need not have worried as this was a favourite ruse used by Gary when he felt a tip was required. It was always followed by 'sorry fella, I am out of cash will catch you another time'.

The relief on the faces of David and Emma was evident as this played out. Emma did the correct thing and said quietly, making sure to use his name 'David you have been a star. I will make sure someone hears about your work and attention to detail today' David grew another inch as this is what he lived for, customer satisfaction and feedback to his bosses. Had this been Germany in the 1940's he would have clicked his heels and bowed his head, but in keeping with the times he just limply shook both their hands, wished them a pleasant flight and flounced back to the buggy. After their boarding passes and passports were checked again they were led straight to the waiting plane. Once aboard they were turned left and escorted through the magic curtains into the first class compartment. If Gary had been awestruck at the lounge then he was gobsmacked at the combination seat, sofa and bed compartment that was all his for the flight. Emma was sat opposite him but facing the other direction so they could chose to talk if they wanted or have the privacy screens raised for a more secluded flight. They were offered more champagne as soon as they were seated but Gary was more interested in pushing the myriad of buttons that turned the seat into a bed and then the bed into a sofa. He managed to operate the overhead lights, raise and lower the privacy screen and call the stewardess all at the same time. Her name was Debbie and she was a very experienced and patient stewardess, something that would be tested time and time again on this flight. Having got Gary's seat back into a configuration suitable for take-off, she continued to walk around the cabin meeting the needs of the other ten or so first class flyers on the flight. The cabin could take twenty passengers, but since the weather had started to change many people had cancelled flights so today her workload was halved, or with Gary aboard probably more than doubled. Since they were some of the first people to board they also had to wait the longest whilst the other passengers boarded. This was not really an issue since they were kept liberally supplied with champagne by Debbie and Gary still had a number of button functions to discover. Debbie had discovered long ago in her career that giving away company champagne was the way to a passenger's heart, compliments and eventually sleep, so she did not hold back on the refills. Another thing she had learnt was when a first class passenger asks what time dinner will be served it was sure to be their first time up front. Gary annoyingly grabbed her sleeve as she passed by 'Debbie, what time do you serve dinner on this flight?' 'Why sir, whenever you want it. If you look at the menu and want something then just let me know and I will have it prepared and served fresh'. Gary tried to look non-plussed but once Debbie moved off he picked up the menu and looked through the extensive range of meat, fish, steak and vegetarian options on offer. Debbie had just reached the galley section when the customer call bell chimed and she turned back to who she knew it must be, Gary. He smiled as if in apology 'I am a bit peckish, can I have a fillet steak now please? 'Debbie falsely smiled back 'I am sorry sir, when I said anytime I meant when we are in the air and the captain has given us permission to cook in the galley. How about I get you some more nuts and snacks, and then bring your steak as soon as we are airborne? Gary got the hidden message and agreed before looking over at Emma for support. Her support came in the form of her pushing a button on her arm rest and raising the privacy screen between them. The flight finished boarding and after the usual safety briefing and talk from the captain the flight took off without incident. Gary had settled down to watch a film and was busy laughing to himself when Debbie appeared with his meal. He now had food, was half drunk on champagne and a cartoon on the TV. He was as happy as a sand boy, but a sand boy with a flute of champagne and a filet steak, what more could he want? No doubt Debbie would be the one to answer that question to after the long flight. Once the aircraft was established in the cruise, the captain's voice once more came on the public address system. He told them once more about the strange weather around the globe and how that might affect their flight across the Atlantic tonight. He advised them to remain strapped in whenever not moving around and because of the danger the first class stand up bar would be closed for safety reasons. With a full belly, a tiring day behind him and the cabin lights dimmed for night time flying, Gary easily drifted off to sleep on the converted bed. He slept well and long but had a vivid and disturbing dream about jolted about in his seat as the aircraft was tossed about in a storm. A vivid dream that is until he was jolted awake as the aircraft really was tossed around in a storm. He awoke to the sounds of the captain's reassuring tones telling everyone to remain seated and the aircraft was in no immediate danger. The word immediate was poorly chosen as it hinted at a disaster in the near future and did reassure as it might have done. Gary rearranged his bed back to a seat and looked over at Emma who was also sat upright, looking a little nervous whilst washing down some tablets from a medicine bottle. To help himself feel better Gary reached out and touched her hand, which Emma mistook for a warm and comforting gesture, so she smiled over at him. The cosy moment was interrupted as Debbie lurched through the cabin carrying a full sick bag, causing Gary to quickly withdraw his hand, which for some inexplicable reason he could not summon the will to replace after Debbie had passed by. The movement of the plane gradually grew less violent and finally settled back into normal flight, which Emma took as a cue to attempt some drug induced sleep. With normal service resumed in the cabin, Gary ordered another yet drink and was just in the process of sipping it when the plane fell like a stone for about five seconds. The freefall left everyone hanging in their seat belts, all except for Debbie who was momentarily pinned flat against the roof of the cabin until the freefall suddenly stopped and she fell heavily onto the floor. Having been caught unawares but not having lost her professional demeanour, she stood, quickly patted her skirt flat and arranged her hair. She took a deep breath and was just going to get herself a cheeky stiff drink from the bar when Gary once again grasped her arm 'If you are going that way I could use a refill please Debbie'. She took another deep breath, the deepest she had ever taken and there and then decided her flying career was at an end. The captain came on the PA system and made a further apologetic announcement, blaming the errant weather conditions for the clear air turbulence and hoped it had not been too traumatic. Emma had raised her privacy screen and had managed further sleep, but Gary had remained awake for the remainder of the flight, unable to switch off and trust the same freefall thing would not happen again. Gary was slightly miffed that Emma's privacy screen remained firmly in place, which he at first took as a snub. However, peeking over the top he could see she was in some sort of deep sleep, oblivious to the turbulence and dive bomber plunge of earlier. Gary distracted himself by watching a selection of TV shows on the entertainment system, along with frequent requests for drinks and snacks from Debbie's replacement stewardess. The flight continued without further incident through the night, until the sky slowly lightened and the dawn caught up with them. With the light came the sound of passengers slowly rising from their slumbers in the beds, accompanied by loud stretching and quiet farting. There was much ordering of bespoke teas, infusions and breakfasts from the first class passengers. Some of them were quite smug in the knowledge that economy passengers were being served rubbery scrambled eggs and a non-descript meat like sausage something, so low in meat content that a vegetarian could have eaten it. Gary was on his second breakfast and third coffee when Emma's head slowly appeared above the edge of the privacy screen. She yawned, stretched her head from side to side before realising Gary could see her and smiled over at him. She lowered her screen and said 'Good morning Gary, did you get some sleep?' 'A little' he replied, but the rings around his eyes told a different story. 'I would have got a lot had it not been for the hand of Satan throwing us around the sky and pinning the stewardess to the cabin ceiling like some haunted house horror movie!' Emma scrunched up her face 'Oh Really? I did take some tablets to help me sleep and they must have really worked!' 'I'll say' he replied, 'it was a near death experience and you slept through it' Pushing her hair back out of her eyes she replied 'I must have really needed the sleep. With my work I have hardly slept at all this last week' 'Well you made up for it last night' he answered jealousy. Emma got herself organised, visited the bathroom and got breakfast ordered. She found a live feed news channel on the inflight system and updated herself on the effects the weather was currently having round the globe. She was going to discuss what she had seen with Gary but when she looked over she saw that he was watching a cartoon of some kind. He had a coffee in one hand, a breakfast doughnut in the other and a big childish grin on his face. She decided she would leave him in his happy baby bubble a little longer, as there was going to be plenty of bad news in the near future and he was the one that was going to be breaking it. Looking over at the giggling man-child that was Gary, she thought to herself '*Is he up to the job?*' However, she decided it was already a bit too late to have those kind of thoughts, as she had already got him fired and had practically abducted him from his natural habitat. Gary, she rationalised, regardless of his eating, drinking and cartoon watching habits was still a reporter of sorts, and besides, she needed a reporter she could control. Once all the breakfast things had been cleared away the cabin returned to an air of normality, but a normality with most people in first class keeping themselves to themselves in their little first class bubbles. Gary and Emma spoke together over more coffee, with Gary trying to ask what he thought were intelligent questions about the impending weather of doom, as he called it. Not wishing to alarm other passengers, Emma deliberately steered the conversation away from the weather for the third time before Gary eventually took the hint. 'Gotcha' he winked.

He briefly asked about her father, which she found touching enough to give a complete, lengthy and detailed answer to. Gary did not regret asking the question but he regretted being alive for the answer, or at least the second hour of it. He found himself with knowledge of her father's schooling, childhood and career, each reported in agonisingly minute detail. Gary really did not care that her father had once kept a pet spider called Cecil, or that he preferred porridge to cornflakes, especially with a Mickey Mouse cartoon playing through his headphones. It transpired that her father was also an eminent scientist who had doted on little Emma and prepared for every facet of professional life as a scientist. He not only pushed her through her early scholastic examinations, he also taught and guided her through her first degree at the age of fifteen. He then quietly mentored her through her other academic achievements, research posts and doctorate, all the while using his influence to ensure she got the jobs and accreditation for swift advancement. Emma was quick to point out that she did have the ability to achieve, just that father's help got her there quicker. Gary briefly saw her breathe in and tried desperately to change tack a little or a lot, he really care which. 'So, what about your mother and you? Your relationships, boyfriends, husband?' Emma visibly winced and looked down biting her lip 'my mother left us when I was six and away at boarding school. She ran off with the Spanish gardener, saying that father neglected her as he was always tied up with his work or some scientific conference or other.' 'Oh, I'm sorry to have brought it up' Lied Gary. 'It's not your fault and I don't blame my father. Apparently she was always a little bit flirty and a party animal, which is what attracted my father in the first place.... opposites attract and all that. The good that came out of it was that my father took me out of boarding school and spent all his time and effort into giving me the right sort of upbringing' She went quiet 'and then he died suddenly two years ago and I was alone' Her eyes watered a little but Gary could see she was fighting hard to keep a lid on it, so without thinking it through he blurted out 'Well now at least you have me!' in an attempt stop her crying. They both heard the words at the same time and both put quite different interpretations on them. Gary burst into nervous laughter and Emma burst into nervous crying. He found his used breakfast hanky stuffed into the side of his seat and offered it to her. She sniffed and wiped the tears from her face, replacing them with red ketchup from the napkin. 'Gary' you are funny' she said as sniffed as she came down from the emotional outburst. 'And so are you' he replied, taking the tissue and wiping the ketchup off her face, but pausing to show her what had happened. It made her laugh again but this time not at him, but with him. 'I had better visit the bathroom and get cleaned up' she said and left Gary to his thoughts and cartoon. She was gone for some time and as Emma returned to her seat the captain once more spoke on the PA system. He gave them the weather in Los Angeles, which was good and told them they would be landing in forty minutes. He apologised again for the turbulence and the weather, unaware that at least one of his passengers knew a lot more about it than he did. Without a solution to the problem Emma secretly wished she did not know herself the full extent of the problems facing them. Debbie, their original stewardess was now back on duty. Having been comforted by her fellow crew members and taken herself off to rest in the crew rest room, she was now feeling a little better, not least of which was because of the cocktail of sedatives and vodka she had self-administered. Doing her best to work the cabin normally but smiling inanely at each passenger, she moved unsteadily as she moved around. She convinced herself that she had a firm grip on things and happily dealt with the passenger's needs. With notice to land she had nearly made it through the trip before she made the mistake of passing Gary's seat one last time. Gary used the moment to ask for 'one more drink for the road' before landing but it was to prove to be the last straw across the last camel's back. Debbie's eyes widened as she slipped the surly bounds of reality. 'Drink! Another fucking drink you lard ass, go get it yourself you you fuckwit'. Suddenly seeing the other passenger faces all turned towards her she then turned on them. Pointing her finger at each of them in turn she slurred 'And that goes for the rest of you... you rich fat assed bitches and bastards... you can go fu..' The last word was cut off as one of her colleagues cupped his hand over Debbie's mouth and with the help of another dragged her back behind the galley curtain. There were further muffled shouts before they subsided and were replaced with quiet sobbing. Various senior cabin crew moved around cabin offering personal apologies and dealing with the terminally affronted, but for some the matter was something only to be dealt with by their solicitor. Emma took an understanding viewpoint, whilst Gary tried to laugh it off with the male steward called Jerard. However, Jerard had taken Debbie's outburst as breaking the secret code of cabin crew and could do little to hide his camp angst at her behaviour. Emma and Gary both ended up uncomfortably comforting Jerard instead, as it had all got too much for him. With great joy and relief all round, the flight eventually landed and taxied in to the allotted gate. As usual, the first class passengers were invited to exit first, whilst the economy hoards were held back by a line of smiling cabin staff. Even the middle classes in business had to suffer the superior and snide glances of first class as they trooped off first. The Business class knew that the law of air travel would not permit them to look down on economy passengers whilst first classers were still aboard, so they waited impatiently for their moment in the sun. Emma & Gary followed the signs to the baggage carousel. Due again to privilege, Emma's designer case was the second to appear on the conveyor belt and moved towards where they were stood. Gary's was not to be seen until a look down the line of waiting passengers showed a Mexican wave of people pointing and laughing. The object of derision was Gary's tartan suitcase, previously owned by his Nan and gifted to him on her death. With his pants sticking out of the sides and the handle hanging loose, it was something to be amused by. As it advanced towards Gary the potential for embarrassment grew and people were looking to see who the poor owner would be. It had actually reached Gary and was on its way around the system again before he broke ranks and quickly snatched it up. With the not so silent giggling ringing in his ears he pushed through the crowd towards Emma, who had secured an airport luggage trolley. With the first class portion of their journey now behind them, Gary found the come down hard as he was now back amongst the crowds of ordinary travellers. Emma found the adjustment easier, especially with Gary's case on display atop of the luggage trolley. 'Listen Gary, getting into the States can be quite tricky at the best of times, so best you let me do the talking at the immigration desk, okay?' 'Sure thing' he replied in a poor and highly racist accent, 'I'll leave it all to momma to sort out'. The queue for the immigration was lengthy but moved along at a reasonable quick snail's pace until they were next in line for one of the immigration booths. Emma spoke 'Now remember Gary', but he interrupted her using his poor taste accent 'I'll leave the talking to yall, momma'. An official who had failed the final immigration exam and was now forever destined to manage the queues, sent them off to an empty booth at the far end.

There, the big black immigration officer called Errol Blackman watched them approach. His face exchanged the standby benign sneer to the narrowed eyes scowl he had learnt after many years of dealing with those who dared try and entry his beloved United States of America. Emma saw him watching them and used the last few steps to start a warm smile of greeting and flirtation. Gary also realised they were being watched but this only made him nervous and caused a change to his already ugly body language. He found the steady gaze made his walking gait change to a clumsy shuffle and for no good reason he averted his eyes. 'Good morning Officer Blackman' said Emma in a cheery and uplifting tone, offering both their passports together. 'One at a time Mam' he drawled and looking at Gary he said. 'You wait behind the line back there' pointing to a yellow line drawn on the floor a few feet back from the booth.' Gary had a nervous reaction to being sternly told what to do and trying to copy Emma's lead he blurted out 'Yes Blackman, I mean Errol...sir', unfortunately still with a hint of the southern accent he had used on Emma. Officer Blackman bit on his lip and just starred at Gary whilst he backed up towards the line, running his foot over with the trolley in the process. 'Behind the line!' he shouted causing Gary to look down at his feet and move back a few more inches. 'What brings you to the United States Miss Rowlinson?' he asked Emma. 'It's Professor Rowlinson actually' replied Emma, hoping it carried some kudos, as it had many times before. Officer Blackman's mind was thinking '*I don't give a rat's ass if you are a professor or Mister Spock from the Starship Enterprise*' but his professional outward demeanour did not change at all. 'And what is the purpose of your visit to the USA....professor?' Emma detected the slight upwards cadence in his voice but chose to ignore it. 'I am, I mean we are, transiting through to Hawaii to do some scientific work at one of the big telescopes on the Island' He nodded 'Length of stay?' She pretended to think about it 'probably two weeks work and another week down on the beach, so three weeks in total' Motioning towards Gary he asked 'And him, is he with you, another scientist?' Emma tried to answer both questions with one answer 'Yes, Gary Barnett, I mean Barnes is part of my team' Errol thought for moment before starting a stamping frenzy of her entry card and passport before waving her through. 'Have a nice stay' he said, without meaning one word of it. As Gary took hold of the trolley to step forward, Errol's mind started a little rhyme he often recited. '*Two, four, six, eight it always pays to make them wait. Three, six, seven, nine, it's good to make them wait in line.*' He got to the next delaying line in his head when Gary appeared in front of him. Errol took a depth breath 'I didn't call you forward yet' 'Really' replied Gary, I could see your lips moving. This took Errol aback a little, could he have been leaking body language whilst reciting his rhyme? He would need to check himself on that' 'Okay Sir' Looking at Gary's passport he asked 'name?' Gary's nerves were still evident as he mumbled 'Gary Barnes' Errol looked at him and testing him said 'Are you sure now, because your colleague there didn't seem too sure either? 'Yes, erm No, I am definitely Gary Barnes, British citizen and newspaper reporter by trade' this raised some curiosity in Errol and he started to type Gary's details into his computer. 'So, you are not a scientist like her' 'Oh no', replied Gary and for reasons known only to himself added, 'and I have only known her about twenty four hours, so no wonder she gets my name and job wrong' Errol was already interested in the mismatch of answers he was getting from the two of them when his computer screen flashed up an amber banner. Something in the system had also raised a suspicion, namely the last minute name change from Barnet to Barnes when Emma had booked them in at Heathrow. Errol used his knee to activate a small pressure pad under his desk and delayed matters by typing in a few notes on his computer keyboard. Gary waited patiently but was suddenly once again aware of having two large and menacing people standing either side of him. Errol spoke to them, 'It's an orange flag on the system with a name anomaly and questionable job employment details.' 'Got it' the larger of the two uniformed large men answered. 'If you would come with us sir, we need to clear up a few matters'. 'But what?' said Gary, I've told the Blackman everything I know' His mistake in the use of Errol's surname did not go unnoticed, as was his questionable accent. This was taken as a personal slight by Errol and the two officers stood either side of him. Taking a firm hold of his elbows Gary was guided through the gate and towards where Emma waited. 'Officers is there a problem?' asked Emma. 'Please stay back Miss, we just have to ask this gentleman some questions about his identity' Gary jumped in sarcastically 'yes momma , once again yo unfamiliarity with my name has cause confusion!' The two officers, one of whom was also black, took further umbrage at Gary's use of the word 'momma' as though it were a personal racial slur. Their grip tightened slightly on Gary's arms. 'Well can I at least take my own case off the trolley?' asked Emma. 'Sorry Mam, it's in his possession so we must treat it as belonging to him.' They started to walk Gary off towards a locked security door with Emma half running behind to keep up. 'But that is my stuff in there and I...' she stopped as she realised it was useless and shouted to Gary 'I will wait for you in the coffee lounge over there. Gary did his best over the shoulder sarcastic smile, before being led through the door which clanged shut behind him. He was led along a corridor to a room that had the most obvious two way mirrors along two of its sides. They could have only been more obvious had they had a sign underneath saying 'smile, you are being watched' He was told to sit on a particular small stool, leaving the two larger chairs for the security men. The positioning and size of the chairs were clumsily meant to impart a sense of hierarchy and superiority over any suspect, but was so obviously done as to negate any advantage. 'So I suppose this is where the rubber hoses come out and you boys beat the confession out of me?' Gary joked. Unfortunately it was a one man joke as the two officers both frowned at him before one of them spoke 'We'll ask the questions sir' and the other added 'Which might make this go a little easier and quicker for you' The menacing tone was not lost on Gary and neither was it meant to be. There then followed a lengthy and repetitive series of questions about Gary's surname being changed on the ticket. Also how Emma who was travelling with him, had bought his first class ticket but did not seem sure of his name or occupation. The same questions with the same answers continued for nearly fifty minutes before a light bulb flashed twice above one of the two way mirrors. Whoever had been watching had made a signal which was noted by the two officers. 'Right sir, we now need to look through your cases, if you could open them please' Gary easily obliged opening his Nan's tartan case by pulling open the one working zip. He was silently amused as the two officers rifled through his less than designer luggage and less than clean underwear with some obvious distain etched on their faces. Emma's case was next to be searched, leaving the two of them trying clumsily not to notice the lacy underwear, three if you add Gary who was looking over the top of the case. Gary stood up as if ready to leave 'Well gentlemen, if you are quite done then I will be on my way' the two officers looked at each and then Gary. The black guy spoke 'There is one more formality we have to take care of sir' as he pulled a pair of latex gloves from a box on the desk. The other officer also gloved up and offered by way of an amused apology 'It's the rules sir, we don't make the rules we just follow them' Gary thought for a moment and took a deep breath. Even he knew better than to resist, knowing the best he could hope for was to keep what little dignity he had and get it over as quickly as possible. Which was possible the same mind set he had used during his sex with Joanne Graymond all those years ago. 'Now sir, if you would turn around, drop your pants and bend over please? Gary did so slowly, retaining what dignity he could, but any dignity retained or imagined soon went out of the window when he bent over in front of the two officers. Whether it was a nervous reaction, trapped wind from the flight or just the position he was now in, Gary farted long and hard and long again. The initial loud report settled into a lengthy rasp as his bum cheeks appeared to be applauding themselves. After the initial shock of the noise came the feint brown mist and the smell. Both officers registered the smell of seafood, but one of them was instantly able to identify the unmistakable odour of oysters. Although a favourite of his, after today he would never be able to eat them again. Within one second of Gary's involuntary indiscretion there was coughing, spluttering, eye watering and some gagging from the two officers, whilst Gary looked apologetically over his shoulder at them. They motioned for him to pull up his pants whilst covering their mouths with tissues and dabbing at their watery eyes. Gary pulled up his trousers and started to apologise but the officers were not interested in apologies. They were both engaged in spraying the room with a fragrant smelling chemical from an industrial business like container, whilst holding their free hands over their faces. The light above the two way mirror was now flashing rapidly and without need of explanation they ushered Gary out of the room. They slid the room tag from 'in use' to 'unusable', hinting that perhaps Gary was not the first person to commit a foul act whilst being searched, even if he would be remembered the longest. Now satisfied that Gary was both genuine and bad company the officers wanted rid of him as quickly as possible. Still not quite recovered from their gas attack they marched him down the corridor and to the security door. There were no explanations, apologies or goodbyes as the door slammed shut behind Gary and he found himself back in the airport concourse. Looking around he spotted a generic branded coffee shop just beyond the immigration hall exit and pushed the trolley solemnly towards it. Emma had been keeping a keen lookout and waved him over as he entered the coffee shop area. 'How was it?' she asked nervously biting her lip. Gary flopped down in the booth seat opposite and was silent for a moment. 'mmm how was it' He mused out loud 'Let me tell you how it was Prof. I have been manhandled by two paid thugs for the second time in twenty four hours. I have been treated like a drug dealer, interrogated, generally abused and very nearly thoroughly searched, all because you didn't get my name right Prof. That's how it is!' Emma nodded sympathetically' Yes, I am sorry about that but when I booked the tickets I wasn't completely sure of your surname. But tell me, what do you mean when you said nearly thoroughly searched, as I thought these people were very thorough?' Gary looked at Emma and in a mischievous way quietly said 'Let's just say they didn't quite get to the bottom of things' Emma thought about the reply and spoke quickly 'It was the oyster again, wasn't it?' Gary's raised eyebrow was all the answer she needed. A waitress appeared with the coffee jug and filled both their branded mugs. There was little talk as they drank their coffee, both of them running their own version of recent events through their minds, neither version of which was very appealing. They gathered their things together and made their way to the checking area for their next flight out to Hawaii. As they walked Gary threw in a little aside 'You didn't exactly get away Scott free either, as they had a good look through your case in general and underwear in particular' Emma was shocked 'Didn't you try and stop them?' 'I was hardly in a position to stop them doing anything' he replied but took a moment to reflect on what he had seen in her case. They found the Northeast airline information desk and Emma left Gary with the trolley whilst she collected the pre ordered tickets. He could see there was something of a discussion happening between Emma and the airline staff but after fifteen minutes of haggling and phone calls Emma returned triumphantly holding two boarding passes. She proudly gave Gary his, taking great care that he could see it had the correct surname on it. 'Is that what the holdup was?' asked Gary. 'Yes' she replied 'but I have now sorted it all out and same again for the return flights, so no more mister please bend over sir' in what she hoped was a soothing voice.' Their flight was due out within the hour so they had to rush to get to the gate in time to queue again. As this was an internal US domestic flight there was no first class and the best seats she could get them were in the business section, which consisted of leather seats and a curtain separating them from the economy. Once seated and Gary had got over his newly acquired first class travel snobbery, the very white toothed smiling cabin crew made them as comfortable as their ticket class would allow. Once airborne, Gary got that been-awake-all-night-feeling because as he rightly reasoned, he-had-been-awake-all-night. He took his shoes off to be more comfortable, put his head on the small leprechaun sized airline pillow and remembered nothing else till Emma gently nudged him awake four hours later. 'We are landing soon' she said 'I thought I had better wake you to freshen up and have some coffee' 'Thanks 'he muttered through sticky teeth and baited breath. The stewardess brought them both coffee. 'I ordered it a little a while ago so it would be fresh for you' Emma said. 'Thanks again' he muttered, sitting up and taking the hot coffee. Through the window the Hawaiian Islands started to appear, just as the first officer made an announcement about landing times and the weather in Hawaii, which apparently was good! Having landed and collected the luggage without incident, Gary started to get nervous as they approached the security checkpoint. Noticing his change in demeanour Emma reassured him 'We are, or rather already were in the United States when we landed in Los Angeles, so this is just normal security, just a formality'. Gary was in no way reassured but had little choice but to shuffle forward in the queue until it was their turn. A grumpy, overworked and unhappy female official sat behind the counter, but after a cursory look at both passports and their faces, waved them through. Somehow, in a strange way Gary was disappointed.

CHAPTER SEVEN: ALOHA

As they excited the airside of the airport into the public area they were greeted by members of the Hawaii tourist association dressed in native garb. Each visitor was presented with a garland of artificial flowers and a traditional greeting. Everyone it seemed who came to the islands was warmly welcomed, everyone that is except for Gary. The dozen or so natives had to be selective so avoided what appeared to be locals or businessmen, concentrating their efforts on the bona fide tourist or honeymooners. Maybe it was the cheap suit, unkempt look or just the smell of oysters, whatever the reason despite Gary's smile he was ignored. Emma on the other hand was festooned by flowers and greeted and kissed by both the male and female natives as if she were family. Like piranhas devouring an injured fish, the natives finished with their group and quickly moved on to the next party coming through the arrival doors. 'My how sweet' Said Emma, admiring her new floral necklace. 'Yes' replied Gary sarcastically 'How fucking sweet' Emma was just going to chide Gary for his bad language when she saw someone waving from the card holding meet and greet section. She led Gary through the crowd and warmly greeted the tall tanned good looking Adonis that had come to meet them. 'Gary, this is Doctor Mike Stevens, a good friend and colleague of mine from time at NASA' 'Hey you, less of the doctor amongst friends. Nice to meet you Gary, just call me Mike' Gary extended his hand and mumbled 'Yeah, pleased to meet you too' although his lack of enthusiasm was noted by both Emma and Mike. 'Thanks for picking us up Mike' said Emma and added 'so you got my emails with telescope time slot requests?' 'Mike scratched his head 'Yeah, but I could have used some more detail to push you into the schedule. You left out more than you put in!' Emma smiled 'I still have some work to do on the theory before I can go public and besides, I knew I could rely on you to get me time on the telescope at short notice' Mike cocked his head 'Well I did my best and managed to get you some scope time, but then yesterday someone else higher up the food chain issued a decree that you get all the university scope time you need this week. Have you been calling in favours?' Emma shook her head, 'No. That's curious as you were the only one I emailed with the request'. Mike held up his hands 'Well whoever authorised it from the faculty has also underwritten the cost, so you obviously have friends in high places. I will do some more digging once you are settled in' He led them out of the building to the waiting zone and help load their luggage into a large yellow people carrier with a University Of Colorado crest and name on the doors. Mike drove whilst Emma sat in the front passenger seat with Gary between them but in the rear. 'So Gary' what's your specialty' asked Mike, trying to include Gary in the conversation. 'Well I can knock up a pretty good chicken madras' Gary grumpily replied to which Emma and Mike laughed. 'No' Mike tried again 'I meant your scientific field of study' Sensing a trap Gary prepared a sarcastic and cutting reply but before he could speak Emma jumped boldly in. 'Gary is not a scientist Mike, he's a reporter' There was a slight lurch of the vehicle as Mike reacted physically to that news and then silence. Gary rather enjoyed the feeling that the Adonis Mike was feeling a little uncomfortable 'welcome to my world 'he thought. 'Is that a problem Mike' asked Gary. 'Well no, it just kinda caught me off guard a little.' said Mike. 'I just assumed as this is an earth changing event we are going through, then your focus would be on solving the problem, not reporting on it. No offence Gary' 'None taken Mike' said Gary. Emma spoke 'If my current thinking is correct Mike and I can prove the end game is disastrous, then we will need the press on-board, and what better than our own tame reporter Gary to move things along' It almost sounded like a compliment thought Gary and given the current climate he would take whatever he could get. Mike nodded thoughtfully 'Mm okay Professor, you are in charge. I assume then that since Gary is not technically minded you will need some help on this, preferably from an up and coming young stud like myself?' Emma laughed, unaware that Gary was mimicking her in the background, who was also equally unaware Mike could see him in the rear view mirror. 'I thought you would never offer' she laughed. Gary also started to mimic these words then caught Mike eyes looking at him on the mirror and tried to make it look like he was trying to remove something from between his teeth. They drove onwards and steadily upwards, leaving the airport and city behind them. Mike had tried to raise the subject of Emma's theory but she told him she was tired and wanted to start with a fresh mind in the morning. Then she would bring him up to date on what she knew or at least thought she knew until it was proven by study and observation. Mike accepted this and the rest of the ninety minute journey was made with small talk and catching up on mutual acquaintances. Gary did not join in unless he was asked a specific question, preferring to give the air of a disinterested third party. He also wanted to discourage questions about his reporting experience, preferring that Mike not know that he was very much a local reporter for a regional newspaper. 'So' Mike asked no one in particular 'How did you guys meet. Who chose who? Emma answered first in a matter of fact way, 'Well Gary was trying to blagg his way into a TV station to try and get an interview with me. When that failed he sabotaged my car and then bought me a coffee whilst it was being fixed. His boss didn't like that so fired him, so I brought him here with me to work with us on the biggest story to ever hit the human race. That's right, isn't it Gary?' She said it in such a matter of fact way that it made all three of them laugh out loud, but for different reasons. As they climbed higher Gary saw in the distance the unmistakable shape of one of those big telescopes that you might see on a BBC science programme. 'Is that we are heading' he asked, pointing towards the shape through the front windscreen.' 'No, ours is much bigger and is another three thousand feet up the mountain yet' replied Mike. They continued the climb until they cleared a final false summit and the real summit of the mountain was revealed. 'There it is' said Emma as they rounded a bend in the road and revealed the large Lindars telescope and radio array. No sooner had they spotted it than Mike turned the vehicle off the main road onto a smaller off shoot asphalt track. This led them into a small cutting in the hillside which widened out into a bowl shaped space containing an accommodation block of apartments and offices arranged around a central courtyard. Mike spoke 'So I have booked you into apartments one and two and arranged for the refrigerators to be filled with some basics to get you through the next few days. The students up at the 'scope have been given their marching orders and will vacate the 'scope and other apartments tonight, so from tomorrow morning the mountain and all the facilities are all yours' 'Thanks Mike. You will be staying for dinner right?' asked Emma. 'Sorry but no, I have a long standing engagement for tonight, and since you also need to sleep off that jet lag I will keep that date and see you in the morning' Mike helped them with their cases and opened the number lock door to the main block. 'Just remember it's the first moon landing 1969 to get this door open and here are the keys to the apartments. Gary had got over his initial misgivings over the good looking Mike, and now realising he also had a date somehow meant he was less threatening. 'Thanks Mike' he grudgingly offered. 'Hey no problem Gary, See you tomorrow professor' said Mike. As he backed out the door Emma grabbed him and gave him a hug and kiss goodbye. Gary suddenly hated him again. Once inside, Gary looked around the well-appointed apartment that looked more like a high class time share. Looking out of the back window he was even more pleased to see where a decent sized swimming pool and hot tub sat beckoning him. Pleased with his room he went across the hall to where Emma was staying and knocked on the door, it swung open and calling her name he stepped in to tell her about the pool. Emma stepped into the living room from the bathroom wearing only her underwear and trying to undo a stud earring that would not budge. She saw Gary and screamed a little before gathering up a scatter cushion to cover her blushes. 'Sorry' said Gary 'I did knock honest' Emma was flustered and annoyed at being caught out 'Just go Gary, get out whilst I shower'. Gary make apologetic facial gestures as he backed out of the room and returned to his own apartment feeling slightly embarrassed, a feeling that that was unusual for Gary. He unpacked the rest of his clean, creased, new and old clothes and decided to have a shower himself. The high pressure shower head felt good as it cleansed his body of the travelling grime he had accumulated. With the fresh towels provided he dried himself, then wrapped another one about his body before looking around the kitchen to see what food and drink there was.

The fridge was full of instantly consumable and cookable items, along with a stash of weak flavourless American beer. He found some chicken breasts and a jar of a nondescript white sauce, and decided he could knock up a dinner for them both and perhaps make a recovery from his earlier faux pas. Putting the radio on, opening a beer and singing along to Hotel California, he quickly combined some opinions with the chicken and sauce and put the dish into the oven to cook slowly. He was in full flow singing 'but you can never leave…' when he turned around and was horrified to see Emma stood in the doorway smiling whilst watching him. 'I came over to apologise for shouting at you and the door was open. I did knock honest' she said mimicking his earlier excuse. It was now Gary's turn to feel exposed and he said 'How long have you been there?' 'Oh' she said 'Just long enough to see you crying over the onions and for me to cry over your singing'. 'Well it won't be ready for a while' he replied, not quite forgiving her for catching him singing. 'No problems' she said 'look it is well past three o'clock and the sun goes down quick here. Do you want to check out the pool before it gets dark? We can eat later?' Gary sensed she was teasing him in some way but was not worldly wise enough to know how. 'Okay, he said. 'You go on down and I will change and see you down there'

She thoughtfully bit her lower lip before turning and left, leaving Gary posing in his towel. Gary found some shorts in his clothes that he thought would also pass as swim wear and got changed. He found Emma had pulled up two sunbeds and an umbrella to protect her from the sun. He noted that she looked quite shapely in her one piece black costume but that she also looked very pale in comparison. She looked up at him from under a huge sun hat as he approached across the hot concrete floor. Wearing his cheap nylon shorts, Gary found himself pulling his shoulders back and his beer belly in as he became aware of her gaze. He settled on the sun lounger next to her and stretched out, enjoying the warmth of the late afternoon sun. Emma picked up an A4 folder and was leafing through the pages, ticking mathematical formulas as she went. She stopped momentarily to say to Gary 'Hey be careful not to burn, we are so high up there is not much protection' Gary nodded 'Thanks but I'm fine with the sun' he said before turning over and letting the tropical sun warm his back. Emma's eyes had done all they could on the bright sun reflected pages in front of her, so she decided to swim and relax with fifty lengths of the pool. Once in the pool her body enjoyed the refreshing cold water cursing over her and her mind enjoyed the release from thinking about the problems facing her. She started swimming and simply switched off, leaving just enough brain function to count the amount of lengths she had swam. Whether it was jetlag, the actual travelling or the emotional rollercoaster of the last thirty six hours Gary didn't know. The other thing Gary didn't know was that he had fallen asleep in the sun. A part of Emma's brain told her fifty lengths had been reached, but she was so enjoying both the exercise and the down time that she carried for another twenty five lengths. That was good she thought as she finished the seventy fifth length and hung on the edge of the pool. As she relaxed she formed a plan of action for the morning and wanted to share it with Gary, 'GARY! Oh God, Gary, please don't let him still be laying in the sun!' She shouted his name as she climbed from the pool and quickly walked over to him still face down on the sun lounger. His back was as red as two lobsters, except for one small portion where the umbrella had partly shaded him, giving him an interesting scalloped white patch. She called his name but he didn't answer so she roughly shook his foot. Gary moved and in a half delirious voice croaked 'what, what's the matter?' She shouted 'you, you are the matter, you are burnt to a crisp. Quick get in the pool and cool off your back. He tried to turn around but the tightened burnt flesh on his back resisted and caused him some pain. He slowly managed to get to a seated then standing position and guided by Emma walked slowly to the edge of the pool. 'I told you to be careful' she said in a motherly kind of way. 'I was careful' he replied in an equally childlike way 'but you know I was also asleep!' He walked down the steps into the shallow end of the pool, each step taking him deeper in the cool water, which both soothed and agonised his burnt leg flesh. He tried to keep some semblance of manliness but all was lost when the water reached his back and he cried out in agony 'Oh my fucking god that hurts!' Emma led him further into the pool where the water might still help but he would also be out of the sun, which although was now setting behind the buildings was still capable of burning. 'Couldn't you have woken me?' he asked pitifully, whilst both burning up and yet also shivering. 'I was swimming' she replied in a less than convincing excuse of a way. 'But whilst I was swimming I figured out where to start the program of work tomorrow' she added in an upbeat tone. 'Well whoopee' he replied sarcastically 'you save the Earth but I die of sunstroke two weeks early' There was nothing she could say really, so to stop him shivering she suggested they get out of the pool and go indoors. Once back in the apartment Gary started to feel a little light headed brought on by his over exposure to the sun and chilling air conditioning. Whilst he slowly made his way to the bedroom and laid himself face down on the white cotton sheets, Emma searched first his apartment and then hers for some sun cream. In a small bathroom cabinet she did find some left over blue gel after sun, which claimed to contain a cocaine pain killing ingredient. She also found some strong Co-codamol tablets for generic back pain. She got Gary to take two of the tablets with plenty of water and then applied the blue gel to his back. This was both ecstasy and agony for Gary as the gel was soaked up by his dry burnt flesh. It did, as the label promised, provide some extra form of pain relief with the added ingredient, but this was offset somewhat by having to touch the area in the first place. His mild sunstroke, combined with the strong Co-codamal pain killers sent him off into a fitful and nightmare inducing sleep. Emma patiently and dutifully sat with him for the first full ten minutes of his incoherent ramblings and shivering, before she then decided there was nothing more to do but leave him to sleep. It was now getting dark outside, so she left the blinds open and stopping briefly to turn off the oven in the kitchen returned to her own apartment.

CHAPTER EIGHT: CRISPY CRITTER

The early morning sun had just appeared back over the buildings and was starting to peek through Gary's bedroom window. Even that small amount of morning heat caused his back to twinge and the pain signals awoke him from his nightmarish sleep. It only took a few seconds for the events of yesterday to come flooding back to him as the crispy tight flesh on his back reminded him of what he had done to it. Putting the back pain aside for a moment, he was glad to be awake as the vivid dreams brought about by the sunburn and strong painkillers had been truly terrifying. He carefully sat up and felt the tight skin on his back crunching and burning still, so decided a cold shower might help. The cold water did offer some comfort but being the absolute pussy he was he could not stomach it for more than a few seconds at a time. Drying his painful back with the towel was also something he could have done without this morning, with some of the skin sloughing off and falling to the floor. He felt like some sort of snake exchanging its new skin for old. He was wondering in what to do next when there was a knock at the door. He expected Emma but it was Mike, stood there all waggy tailed and Adonis like. 'Oh, come in' said Gary as he turned around and led Mike to the living area. 'Ouch' said Mike, seeing the raw and red flesh on Gary's back. 'The sun bite you huh?' Mike said, over stating the obvious. 'Well, you could say that' replied Gary, with more than a hint of irony. Ignoring the barb, Mike looked thoughtful 'I have the very thing for that outside in the van, stay here' Not that Gary was going anywhere right now, but he might have stopped Mike scurrying off if he had been quicker. Gary was not best disposed towards Adonis Mike and certainly did not want to be indebted to him. When Mike returned he was shaking a small clear bottle containing a pink looking liquid, which Gary assumed was some sort of exotic calamine lotion. 'Lay down on the sofa crispy critter' said Mike, 'I get this from a chemist friend of mine and it is really good stuff. It contains all manner of soothing compounds that you can't buy over the counter' Gary protested a little but his back protested even more, so he lay down on the sofa for a quick application and hopefully some respite. As it happened, years of academic work had left Mike with soft and gentle hands. The magic pink potion combined with the gentle application started to work and Gary started to feel some relief from the pain. Whatever it was in that bottle it was so good at numbing the pain that Mike was able to add a little pressure and make something of a massage of the rubbing action. This brought both painful and pleasurable moans from Gary in equal measure. Mike had left the door open and through it came Emma all dressed and ready for action. Gary suddenly didn't feel quite so comfortable having his back rubbed by another man with Emma watching, but it was medicinal after all he rationalised. After greeting them, Emma went to the kitchen and put the coffee pot on and whilst it was bubbling away came back to the two men. 'So Mike how was your date?' Mike rolled his eyes 'Well, as usual not nearly as nice as his profile picture on the website' Gary tensed up, did he just say 'he'? He listened intently until Mike once again used the male vernacular for his date last night, confirming Gary's idea that Mike was more than just kind to other men. Gary quickly pushed himself upright and away from Mike, rolling his shoulders in mock stretching and indicating the massage was officially over. Emma laughed, 'Wow, I think Gary has just worked out that you are gay Mike', causing Gary's face to blush the same colour as his back. 'Oh sweetie, did you not know' said Mike 'How do you think I got the magic in these fingers!' Now the two of them were laughing at him, the two being Mike and Emma. Gary replied rather too quickly, instantly regretting his comment 'Of course I knew, I could tell by the relief his hands were giving me'. Emma and Mike exchanged knowing and overtly camp gestures, which only added to Gary's growing embarrassment and red flushed face. Emma looked at Gary's back 'Is it any better this morning?' Reluctantly, Gary admitted the Mike's lotion had certainly eased the pain, but stopped at further commendation. He couldn't quite get over the fact he had willingly taken a massage from a gay guy and enjoyed it. *'No, that was something new and something to be quickly forgotten'* he thought. With three steaming mugs of coffee sat on the table, Emma got all business like 'Right guys listen in. The plan is to spend the daylight hours down here at the lab gathering data from other sites that I can access through the internet. Mike, I would like you to call up telescope images from coordinates I will supply once the data is crunched and also book us telescope time tonight. I also want access to the radio telescope array on the island and that to be aligned with the big scope for tonight. Frequencies and bands to scan will be detailed later as data comes in from the London laboratory. Mike nodded enthusiastically and answered 'No problem, the Uni have given you carte blanche on the big scope for at least a week and everyone else has been cleared out. The radio array is not part of the University's assets on the island but I am sure I can arrange sometime each evening to coincide with the big scope. They do owe us a favour or two over there. Emma nodded 'Good' 'and what about me?' asked Gary feeling a little left out. Emma and Mike exchanged knowing glances. Emma spoke 'Well Gary, without a scientific background it would be difficult to incorporate you into any detailed research.' and to make the point further Mike added 'and without a day's training you probably wouldn't even be able to open the telescope doors' Gary visibly winced at that last remark. Emma tried to be comforting 'Gary you are very much part of this team but your role will become more important once we have something to tell the world and then the emphasis shifts to you. So, why not come to the lab with me today, establish yourself on a computer and start recording the events as they happen?' Still smarting from Mike's 'not being able to open the doors' jibe, Gary gladly accepted the designated role, especially since it was well within his comfort zone. 'Yes, I will do that and it will be the best recording of events in the history of recorded events' he said triumphantly. 'Well that is exactly what history is, recorded events' added Mike, once again not endearing himself to Gary or the overall working atmosphere in the room. 'Right, let's get to work then' said Emma before the mood could sour anymore. The three of them left the accommodation and walked across the forecourt to the low office and laboratory block. Mike opened the doors using the same key code and switched on the lights and power to the buildings. In the long office Emma sat herself at a desk that had six computer monitors arranged before it in three banks of two. She wasted no time in powering up the computer and getting logged onto her remote webpage and office cloud so she could start work. Mike got busy on the phone organising Emma's requests whilst Gary investigated the building. He was still stooging around ten minutes later when Emma gestured to an empty desk that had a single monitor and computer for him to use. Gary logged on to the system and with the ordinary internet available to him started to trawl the web. He started by looking at the newspaper's website where he worked, or rather where he used to work, but there was nothing about him or anything interesting other than local stories. He progressed then to live streaming the NCN news station coverage and pleased to note their level of technical and back story news had significantly decreased since Emma had left them a few days ago. Joanne *fucking* Graymond, with nothing new to add it seemed, was now having to make do with re running graphics and charts from the previous week. Now with a task that he was familiar with, Gary started to chronicle the events of the last few weeks as knew them, leaving space for the technical science stuff when and if Emma fed it to him. He also included his own involvement, abduction and relocation around the globe, just in case some future reader should doubt his part in saving the world. About an hour into the process Emma said a loud 'WOW, come and look at this', summoning Mike and Gary to her computer. Two of the monitors displayed various weather and science web pages and another just emails, but the mid top one had a clear photograph of the whole Globe. 'What are we looking at?' asked Mike 'It's the Earth' replied Gary, garnering nothing but dirty looks. Rolling his eyes Mike replied 'I can see that, I mean what's the significance' Emma tilted the screen a little to allow less light to shine on the image. 'This is an image for a geostationary weather satellite sat 150 miles out in space. I just downloaded it from the WETSAT site. Mike and Gary looked but saw nothing out of the ordinary. 'Look here' she said, using a pen to point 'See the faint drift of cloud, the whole worlds weather is being drawn around the globe and upwards into space at this point' with that she pushed a button on the keyboard and the picture became a series of images that produced a short animation Showing the clouds slowly moving around the globe and then whisping off at one point on the north American continent. The last picture in the series was more dramatic as they could clearly see the clouds being drawn up in a slowly moving vortex pattern. 'It's like the world has got a little hat' Gary casually suggested. 'Well not a very technical appraisal Gary, but that about sums it up in layman's terms' said Emma. 'So' said Mike, 'for some as yet unknown reason or reasons, the Earths cloud based weather systems are being drawn off the face of the planet in one place by some force?' Emma nodded 'Yes, it was what the maths model was already suggesting but I didn't want to believe it until I could confirm it either with other data or visually, but now it seems certain' 'We are losing a lot of moisture there, do you know how long it will take at the rate of loss to be irreversible? Asked Mike. 'No, but now it is confirmed I can set someone else back in the London lab to do a more detailed math model to see how much time is left' Gary spoke again 'Just where is the point we are losing all this stuff? Emma called up another screen and typed in Google Earth. Copying the coordinates from the weather picture she typed them into Google earth and hit the enter button. The Globe slowly started to turn, stopping over the North American continent before then zooming in on a body of water called Lake Michigan. 'Well there it is guys, the egress point is Lake Michigan in the United States of America' said Emma. 'Do you think the fact it is a lake has any bearing on the situation or is just a coincidence?' asked Mike 'No idea as yet Mike, but it is a starting point.' Gary had an epiphany, a sudden realisation that all this was really happening.

There had been a small part of him that suspected this was a load of old tosh, thought up by Emma to self-serve her scientific credentials and get some new funding. He had been happy to go along with it so far because this new life of Gary's was far sweeter and more interesting than that his old one, which he assumed at some point he would go back to. But now he saw the images it looked like it really was going to be the end of the world and somehow he had a part in it. With some slight anger in his voice he spoke 'Well congratulations prof, you were right all along. The world is ending and you will go down in history, well just down in history for the next few weeks, as the women who broke the world. So, what actually can you do about it prof? Emma was quiet for a moment 'Nothing Gary, at the moment absolutely nothing'. Gary instantly regretted his accusatory tone as he watched a single tear ran down Emma's cheek and fall onto the computer keyboard, whilst another ran down her face and sploshed onto the desk. 'Please, don't shoot the messenger Gary' she softly added. Mike grabbed a tissue and wiped his own eyes before passing them to Emma. They both hugged and over her shoulder Mike passed the tissues to Gary. He managed to avoid letting the others see his watery eyes by turning his head away. Caught up in the touching moment, he put one hand on Emma's shoulder and reached out towards Mike with the other but awkwardly shied away at the last moment. To mark the end of the shared moment Emma sniffed, took a deep breath and said 'Well cannot do anything unless we know the cause, so we had best get on with some work. I will pass this on to the London lab to work on for any anomalies in the weather over the Lake Michigan area. Mike, please arrange for the big scope and the radio array to also be looking at space straight above Lake Michigan. I'll take anything they pick up from the radio straight away and we will be ready to go up the hill to the big scope as soon as it is dark okay?' 'Yes mam' said Mike. 'And Gary' 'Yes' he replied expectantly 'Some coffee would be nice… please?' 'Yes mam' he replied, copying Mike's overly enthusiastic voice. Gary had already found the small kitchen area during his earlier exploration and soon had the coffee machine in action. Although still sore and heady with sunburn, he was still Gary enough to want to eat. He remembered the chicken he had cooked yesterday evening and went back to the apartment to see if it was still edible. It was cold and no longer a dinner dish unless you had consumed eight pints of lager, but by some careful slicing and dicing, along with some tomatoes he put together three presentable looking sandwiches. Emma and Mike were both at their separate work stations working away when Gary reappeared with a tray full of food and drinks. They were both overly appreciative of Gary's efforts when he delivered them a sandwich garnished with crisps and some hot coffee. Gary realised they were over compensating but was happy to take any compliment from the team he could get, even patronising compliments over yesterday's chicken. He nodded mutely before sitting down at what was now become his desk. He diligently started searching for weather related stories, partly to be able to better understand what was going on, but also to cut and paste and decent copy that would save him a lot of typing later. Gary was nothing, if he was not still Gary deep down. Despite being actively engaged, Gary's mind soon began to wander from the task. He started day dreaming, and looking around the lab started to relate the office to the deck of the Enterprise from Star Trek, the first and best series of course! He saw Emma as the Captain, leading the team towards salvation. Then was Mike, who surely assumed the role of the diligent Executive and logical thinking science officer. However, Gary did find Mike's sexuality leaked into his day dream and somewhat spoilt the image, as he imagined Spock with a very camp and flamboyant personality. Finally he considered his own Enterprise bridge job description. Would he fit in as Chekov or Sulu, the steady and reliable helmsman, or the redoubtable engineer Scotty? He even sat himself in the chair of Lt. Uhura for a brief second before realising he was just *'not that in touch'* with his feminine side. This narrowed the field and left him with very few savoury choices. He certainly did not want to be the unnamed and destined for certain death anonymous crewman, so in a rare moment of candid reflection he ordained himself as Dr. Leonard 'Bones' McCoy. Without fully realising it, the doctor's character of always missing the point, challenging authority and spitting his dummy out when ignored, fitted Gary's perfectly. Absently mindedly Gary suddenly spoke out loud 'You can't be serious Jim!' which caused the Emma and Mike to look up, which caused Gary an embarrassed smile and to look down. Now rudely awakened from his daydream and bored of looking at weather stories to help solve the imminent world crisis, he turned to his own religion, pornography.

His fingers genuflected across the keyboard as he quickly typed out the incantation of instant gratification, dot com. As it was foretold in the scripts, in an instant his old friend and companion appeared, bedecked in very little and soon offering to be bedecked in nothing at all. If Gary had been religious he would have prayed, if an alcoholic he would have had a drink, but pornography was both Gary's weakness and strength. Weakness, in that it took up so much of his time, even on occasion making him late for work. This occurred because whilst Gary slept, pornographers in the USA were making more porn, and he felt obliged to review and rate their work before he could leave for the office. A strength? Well Gary considered himself one of the world's leading experts on a tiny sexual deviancy that involved dressing up as Star Trek characters before, during and after fornication. This not only explained his daydreams but also most of his night dreams, with the exception of the one about being chased by a large cat past rows of endless stone Roman columns. Deep down, in fact not so deep down Gary was still Gary.

CHAPTER NINE: WHAT PRICE THE TRAVEL, WHAT REASON THE JOURNEY?

As the entity now slowed it began to consider its wants and needs. It could do this across its whole intelligence in a flash, but preferred, in fact enjoyed reducing the process to a relatively sedate and organic process. It would be the equivalent to a man buying the most specialised and expensive algebraic calculator, but still taking some pleasure in putting in numbers that spell 'BOOBS'. Using it's intellect to interrogate itself was both challenging and rewarding. It was an experience from a bygone era of its development, but one it periodically used as a check and for the simple enjoyment of doing so. Having washed the discussion around itself several times it came up with the same answer. It wanted information to digest, facts to feed on and fresh new things, especially some new emotions that is no longer has within its intellect. This was its motivation for travelling vast incomprehensible distances across space and now it was nearing the time to feast. It would not, and did not have need to eat, all of its energy needs were available to be simply drawn from the media it travelled in. What it craved was stimuli, raw and fresh stimuli to be savoured as a delicacy.

CHAPTER TEN: IT'S NOT GOING, IT'S COMING!

After Mike and Emma had much complimented his sandwich, coffee and general cooking ability, Gary was starting to feel like he had a role and was a part of the team. Emma was busy crunching data and exchanging emails with her colleagues across the globe, whilst Mike was busy down loading more weather satellite images and making the arrangements Emma had asked for. Gary had progressed onto boobs and all manner of pornography south of there. He justified it in his own mind by rationalising that at least he would be on hand when they needed anything and besides, his time, if nothing else, was coming soon. It was also too easy, because the way they were sat in the room no one else could see his computer screen. After another hour had past, Gary guilt tripped and offered to make them another drink, which they both accepted. Having gone to Emma's desk to collect her dirty coffee cup he glanced up at the last screen which had not been activated earlier. Onscreen were silent jiggling boobs and porn of good quality, in fact it was the same porn Gary currently had playing on his screen. He tried not to stare but without looking up Emma spoke 'Yes Gary, well spotted. That is a repeater screen so that we can all share information across the computers. Whilst we were are striving to save the people of the world, you are striving to watch some of them having sex. Gary, hoping that Mike could not hear the conversation glanced across at Mike. He also did not look up but said 'Yes, I have been getting it to Gary thanks, and I am not even a little bit straight'. Suddenly caught out, embarrassed and stumbling over his words Gary said 'Oh why didn't you say anything' 'Well apart from admiring your endless capacity for porn, it seemed a shame to interrupt you' said Mike with a smirk before Emma added 'and it kept you quiet for an hour or two' before they both began laughing, most definitely at Gary. Gary grabbed the cups and red faced walked towards the kitchen, stopping briefly at his computer to prematurely bring to the Star Trek dressed shag fest that he had been watching to an end. The rest of the afternoon passed slowly for Gary but quickly for the other two, as they were totally absorbed by the data and number crunching they were engaged in. They did swap information when needed, but for the most part it was a solo work, each working their own area of expertise. Gary, wary that his efforts were being monitored made sure there was plenty of weather related news reports passing across his screen, to the point that he surprised himself by actually learning some things hitherto unknown to the group. The requested radio array data came in late in the afternoon in the form of attached zipped files. Emma was able to examine the numbers before playing the transcribed sound through the speakers. She at first played samples for comparison of other space noise, including background static and deep space pulsar stars with their distinctive and regular patterns. She then played what the radio array was picking up in space above the area around Lake Michigan and it instantly became a solid continuous tone. Gary and Mike stayed at their own desks as the speakers were loud enough but the sound was unfamiliar to either of them. 'It sounds like someone playing a wine glass' offered Gary, and in the lack of any scientific explanation was accepted as a reasonable layman analogy by the other two. Emma zipped it back up into a data file and sent it off for further analysis back at the UK office, asking for an immediate reply if they had any ideas about the mysterious noise. That done, she sat back in her seat and rubbed her eyes. It had been a long day and most of it had been sat at a bank of computer monitors looking at data, images and of course thanks to

Gary also boobs. It had started to get dark outside causing Mike to check his watch before suggesting 'we can head up to the big scope whenever you want but the darker it is, the better it will be, especially for long exposure photographs for comparison' 'Okay' said Emma 'It would also be useful to have some answers from the UK which might help us how to best to use big scope tonight. Shall we give it another hour before heading up?' Mike nodded in agreement 'Shall I get some pizza sent in? It will save us having to cook!' Both Emma and Gary agreed, although Gary was unsure a pizza delivery boy would come all this way up a mountain to deliver. Mike got on the phone to a number that was obviously on speed dial, then promptly announced dinner would be served in thirty minutes or it would be free! Much to Gary's surprise but liking, the mini pizza delivery van did show exactly on the thirty minute mark. He had just started his pocket-patting-poor-man routine when Mark just jumped in with a fistful of green US cash and told the driver to keep the change. They sat in Emma's apartment attacking the huge amount of pizzas and chicken wings Mike had ordered. 'I ordered extra so we could graze through the night if it turns out to be a long one' said Mike. They finished eating in silence, the only sound being

Gary's mouth chomping and a twenty second near death choking on a chicken bone. With dinner over and with the time being 8pm, they agreed it was time to head up the hill to 'bigscope'. It was still quite warm as they left the accommodation and headed back along the track to main road but Gary had taken their patronising hint and took along a coat 'for later'. They also all had a long black metal torch each, as without streetlights or light pollution of any kind, the mountain was black, very black. They stayed on the road as they could feel their way by the tarmac underfoot but as their eyes slowly adjusted more details of the mountain and stars above them became clearer. The walk was only about four hundred meters uphill and they could see the silhouette of the bigscope telescope domed building ahead of them. As they neared the door a dim automatic red light came on to allow them to see the number door lock. Mike opened the door and once inside pulled a large electrical switch into the on position. It seemed to Gary that nothing much had happened except for a low hum and the distant whine of some hidden equipment. Mike said to wait a moment until the lights warmed up but even as he spoke many dull red lights came on all across the inside of the big dome housing the telescope machine. Mike explained the lights were to help retain their night vision and help make using the telescope easier on the eye. Slowly adjusting to the dim level of light they slowly followed Mike to one of the back rooms that served as the control room. Mike moved around the room activating switches and bringing more machinery and computers into life. At the rear of the room were several ordinary workstations that Mike indicated they could log onto whilst he continued getting the equipment ready and calibrated.

Emma sat at a desk and after logging in retrieved her recent emails, including one from the UK scientists she had working for her. 'Gary' she called 'you might like to see this' indicating the bottom part of an email. Apparently Joanne Graymond had been constantly on the phone to Emma's office, at first asking, then demanding to speak to her. Various emails had followed, all of them pleading, begging or just demanding more information. It did make Gary smile to see the shoe was on the foot 'That'll teach the smug bitch' he said out loud causing Emma to raise an eyebrow and Mike to purse his lips in mock gay shock. Emma read the rest of the email before opening and playing the compressed file that her team had worked on and returned by email. 'The guys in the UK have run that sound through various filters and programs and have come to two conclusions. Firstly, that the continuous sound is not solid or made up of waves, but originates from millions of small pieces' there she paused. 'And the second?' asked Mike. She read it again to herself just to be sure 'They are saying that there is a constant shift down in the frequency, which they think means the sound beam is heading towards us?' she had read that last piece in a questioning way as if trying to make sense of it herself. 'It's the Doppler effect Gary' she said, 'like an express train horn passing through a station, noise is relative to the listener and appears to change tone. This effect can be used as a measurement.' This simple explanation made sense to Gary, but what was also not lost on him was that if they were right the beam was headed for the planet Earth, which is where he currently lived. Whilst they now had more information about what was happening, it was not enough to help with the problem they were originally working with, namely the weather systems leaving the globe. The sound or beam was just a complicating factor and whilst it must somehow be involved, how it was involved was still a mystery. Mike asked Emma where she wanted to start and she said the area again roughly over Lake Michigan, where the sound was emanating from. Sat at a huge console comprising of both ancient looking electrical dials combined with modern computer equipment, Mike inputted various coordinates via the keyboard. He then started on the older dials and switches, setting each one in turn. He then pushed a big green lit button and a deep rumbling commenced. There was a movement of air and as Gary looked through the control window he saw the big domed roof begin to slide open. Once slid fully back Mike moved another dial and slowly the whole roof and telescope rotated onto the required heading and azimuth. 'Ready when you are Emma' Mike said, so Emma left her computer to go into the main domed room. The three of them climbed a small spiral stair case to where there was a small seat positioned under the eyepiece of the scope. Emma settled herself into the chair and got comfortable, adjusting the seat height and eyepiece so she could view what the scope was seeing. 'Well' asked Gary excitedly 'can you see anything?' 'No, and neither is she likely to' replied Mike. 'At least not at the first look' Emma added 'I can only see a very small piece of the sky Gary, so it will take hours and hours just to cover the area that the radio data suggests we should be looking at' Gary was confused 'then it is hopeless isn't it, why bother?' 'Well firstly because we do have to bother Gary, we know that. And secondly viewing by eye is not the only or most efficient way of searching the sky. It was just a hunch to see if we might get lucky.'

'So what is the most efficient way of searching the sky? Gary asked. Mike answered 'photographs Gary. Thousands and thousands of photographs taken at timed intervals then compared for movement or disturbance' Gary got the basic concept 'But that will still take an age to compare thousands of photographs wont it? 'Not exactly an age as we have computer programs that will do the comparisons for us and flag up any anomalies, but it will take some time' replied Mike. 'Talking of which I had better go and get the cameras set up and calibrated for the movement of the dome' Mike went to another desk and started the process of engaging the digital cameras and recording the images to run through the computer. 'Emma, you will have to come off the eyepiece whilst we are in photo mode or you could distort the images with just the slightest of vibrations' shouted Mike. 'Yes I know Mike, remember I also have an astrophysics doctorate' she replied with just a hint of sarcasm as she climbed down from the telescope. 'Oops, sorry I forgot' he replied in a fake British accent. After a few minutes the process had begun and Mike monitored progress at the console whilst Emma went back to the computer where she was logged on. She managed to log on to another satellite site and find similar resolution pictures from space of the area she was interested in. Comparing several pictures together and flicking back and forth she spotted something that caught her eye. A little tired with the whole day of looking at computer screen she was feeling the eye strain a little so called Gary over. 'Gary, what do you see that is different between these two pictures?' She flicked back and forth between the two pictures whilst Gary looked over her shoulder and compared the two. 'Well' he said 'to my untrained eye it seems like in this one the clouds are being drawn off as you thought, and in this one they are being pushed down, compressed almost' 'That is what I thought I was seeing, but if you look at the time stamps the picture with the clouds being compressed is dated later, today at 6 pm GMT' They both looked, agreed and then called Mike over for a third opinion. 'This is either a strange turn of events or just a mistake on the time stamps' Emma added. 'Can you get further update pictures from another source?' asked Gary 'Good idea Gary' said Mike leaning in and patting Gary's sunburn shoulder. 'Sorry Gary,' he quickly said as

Gary winced in mock man pain. 'I will try the other WETSAT download for comparison. They always update their website pictures on the hour, so in thirty seven minutes we will have fresh images to compare.' The time passed slowly whilst the bigscope cameras did their slow methodical scan of the sky, whilst Emma waited for another source of photographs to compare with. At two minutes after the hour Emma managed to log on with her account details and take the latest weather space photographs off the site. A quick look by all three confirmed the first result. The clouds that had for weeks been thinly streaming off into space had stopped and were now being pushed back down towards the surface of the earth. 'How can this be?' said Emma in thought. 'But surely this is good isn't it? Said Gary 'the clouds are staying, the weather will get better and the earth is saved...hoorah yes?' It was quiet for a moment 'It's not quite that simple Gary. Whilst it seems in the short term we have a reprieve we still need to know what is causing this. As a scientist I want to understand it, but we also have to be prepared in case it happens again' said Emma. Mike agreed 'yes, we must know the cause of this phenomenon, the reversal may only be temporary or cyclical' 'Like a tide rolling in and out? Asked Gary 'Possibly Gary, possibly' Emma added thoughtfully thinking over Gary's words. 'You have given me some food for thought there Gary with your tidal suggestion' 'Did I. I did?' Gary asked even more surprised than the others. 'So' said Mike, 'you are considering the possibility that this is a tidal flow back and forth event that has just not been recorded before, or just a one off?' 'Well given what we are seeing we have to include it in the list of theories to be explored' replied Emma. She rubbed her eyes and rolled her neck from side to side 'what's the time now?' 'Just coming up to midnight' said Gary yawning. 'How about we call it a night and get some rest' suggested Mike 'Nothing has been found by the program monitoring the cameras so far, and we can leave it running whilst we sleep and review it in the morning' Emma thought for a moment 'Well the UK office has gone to bed and there is nothing else to do until we find an anomaly from the pictures or more data is sent over from London. Certainly some sleep might help in thinking through the problem. Okay, let's call it a night and get some rest' Mike quickly went around the work stations making sure they were running the programs automatically and backing up any data at regular intervals. They left everything on except for the red lighting and exited the building, locking the door behind them. A full canopy of stars was visible in the clear dark sky causing Gary to look up in wonder 'wow' he said 'what a show' 'yes, it's something isn't it. You get a great view up here because we are so high and there is so little pollution, plus your night vision will now have fully adjusted' offered Mike. They walked carefully back down the hill with Mike leading the way. Emma came next with her head down in deep thought, followed by Gary. His head was swivelling round as he looked up at the full horizon to horizon spectacle of the night sky. He saw a shooting star which came and went in a brief micro second before he could point it out to the others. It was a fantastic sight and made Gary feel very small as he considered just what might be up there. They reached the accommodation blocks in a couple of minutes and went inside. After refusing more coffee they agreed to all turn in and meet at eight in the morning to begin the day. Mike wished them goodnight and went to the upstairs apartment, leaving Emma and Gary in the hallway. 'You were very quiet on the walk down the hill' said Gary 'Mm yes, I am a bit tired but also something bugging me about this sudden reversal we have seen. Just when I thought we were getting somewhere the goal posts have moved and we have to reconsider what we thought we knew' Gary reached out, touched her arm and in a mock authoritive voice said 'Try and switch off. Sleep is what you need young lady, off you go' causing Emma to smile weakly before going into her apartment and closing the door. In their separate apartments they all prepared for bed in their own way. Mike, unusually for him decided to have a bath and unwind a bit before sleep. He turned on the taps whilst he checked his Facebook page for messages from his last date. Gary appeared to be wrestling with himself as he tried unsuccessfully to apply sun cream to his own back, whilst Emma just lay on her bed trying to stop her mind running the facts over and over. 'What am I missing?' she thought as she tried to stop thinking and prepare for sleep. Mike was both pleasantly surprised by the messages waiting for him from his last date, and even more intrigued by a new message waiting for him from the next one. He quickly switched over to his instant chat program and invited the intriguing new man called Jack to chat live with him. His laptop binged as Jack entered the chat screen and they began an animated exchange over matters that gay men liked to discuss. The innuendo filled chat and picture of the hunky man completely took over Mike's mind, erasing all memory of the bath he was running in the other room. Their conversation soon turned to a prospective date, with Mike knowing timescales were limited making most of the running. Downstairs Gary was still trying to smother his back in cream to alleviate some of the pain and itching he was still feeling on his sun bur. In desperation he found a way to apply the cream was to smother it onto the bathroom mirror then rub himself up and down against it. The cold mirror added something to pain relief and he shimmied against it as best he could. At one mid rub he stopped and listened to a strange noise coming from the ceiling, but as he couldn't place it, he just assumed it was just Mike in the apartment above moving around. He had just managed to cover most of his back when the noise increased in volume again, causing him to look up. It seemed as if the ceiling was bowed down in the corner causing it to sag. Gary's brain was trying to make sense of what he was seeing but just as he reached the most logical solution, the corner of the ceiling suddenly gave way and a deluge of water cascaded down onto him, knocking him backwards. Emma had nearly succeeded in switching off from the problems facing her and was just in a pre-sleep state. Her world was suddenly rocked by a loud crashing noise coming from outside her apartment. Grabbing a dressing gown she ran out of the door and found Mike running down the stairs. In some sort of panic he tried to quickly explain by shouting a series of words 'BATH, FACEBOOK, DATE, WATER, GONE ,GARY! He shouted. They both carefully entered Gary's apartment and not seeing him made their way to the bathroom. Gary was laying on his back in his own bath with a coating of wet plaster and dust covering him. The slippery coating of sun cream on his back made it impossible for him to right himself or get out of the bath and he was cursing loudly as he floundered and fought to get himself upright. Relieved to find that he was not hurt, both Emma and Mike began to laugh at Gary's predicament, which only drew more cursing but this time directed at them. Mike reached in and with one had supported by the wall he managed to pull Gary upright and out of the bath. 'What happened 'asked Emma 'Isn't it obvious' said Gary sarcastically 'one minute I am in the bathroom getting cream on my back, the next a fucking tsunami comes through the ceiling and splosh, suddenly I am a tortoise floundering on my back!' Mike stopped laughing long enough to speak 'I am really sorry Gary this is my fault. I let the bath overflow and it obviously got into the false ceiling before crashing through into yours' Gary could not believe what he was hearing, a grown man letting a bath overflow 'How the fuck did you manage that?' he said but the sheepish look on Mike's face told him he probably did not want to know the answer. 'On second thoughts don't answer that. Now if you have all quite finished laughing at me I would like to get cleaned up and into bed before the walls start attacking me!' Emma and Mike bit their lips, once again said their goodnights and returned to their own rooms. The distraction, even though painful and embarrassing for Gary had succeeded in taking Emma's mind off world events and she was soon asleep. Gary and Mike were not as fortunate as there was still some housekeeping to be done before they two also managed to get into their own beds and find sleep. Emma's alarm went off at seven fifteen as planned and she awoke fresh after a good six hours sleep. She sat up and smiled as she quickly recalled the late night antics in Gary's room 'A tsunami fell on him' she said out loud 'a tsunami' She stopped and bit her lip, the word tsunami created a series of thoughts that flowed over into the weather problem. There was one missing part of the puzzle she had so far missed! She quickly showered, dressed and went to find Mike and Gary. Neither were in their rooms but she soon found them in the morning sunshine down by the pool. Mike was swimming his usual fifty morning lengths and Gary was using the poolside shower as his had been broken in the ceiling collapse. There was a pot of coffee that Gary had made and she poured herself a cup whilst calling the guys together. Morning greetings out of the way she stood smugly in front of them. 'I recognise that look, what have you done?' Mike asked. 'Well not me, but Gary really' Emma replied. 'Me, how?' asked Gary. 'Tsunami' she said 'last night you said the tsunami fell on you. That is what you actually said last night'. Gary was confused 'yes, but it wasn't funny then or now for that matter' he said. 'No, not funny but pertinent' said Emma getting into her stride, 'just before a tsunami hits a coastal area the sea gets drawn out leaving everything exposed. People then rush into see what's happened, then bam, the sea rushes back in bigger and badder than before' 'So' said Mike 'are you suggesting that the clouds being drawn out were like the sea just before a tsunami hits and we are now seeing the process in action but very slowly?' 'It's certainly another theory we have to explore, but it does fit what we currently know' she replied 'But' said Gary 'if you are right, doesn't that mean something big is coming and might swamp the earth?' 'Yes possibly, but it is great to have an understanding isn't it?' said Emma excitedly. 'Well it would be if it also didn't spell out just a different end of the world to the one we were expecting. Sorry if I can't quite share your enthusiasm for a different catastrophe' Gary replied. Mike stood up 'well at least with the overnight data the scope and the radio array have been collecting you should be able to prove or disprove that theory in very short order' Yes' Emma replied 'Let's get cracking' The boys went to their rooms and dressed, before meeting at the lab block. Emma was already at work sharing her ideas by email with the UK scientists back in London. Mike went to work logging onto his computer and then the bigscope system so they could view the images taken overnight. He also checked to see if the photograph comparison program had spotted anything of interest. As soon as his computer booted up and settled down he ran the program and was instantly shown a dozen alerts, each indicating movement anomalies in the area of space they were interested in. He allowed screen sharing with Emma and Gary's machine on the local network and put them up one by one. The oldest ones showed light distortion around a small cluster of distant stars. For Gary's benefit he explained out loud 'these two photographs were taken a short time apart but the light from the stars appears to have been moved or distorted in the second photograph' 'Couldn't they have just moved?' asked Gary. 'No, the telescope and software allow for that. It has taken thousands of photographs during the night and compared them for movement or light distortion by another body, then flagged them up for us' Mike replied. Emma finished the explanation 'to get an alert of that kind means something must have passed in front of the star or so close that the light from it has been distorted, which is why we are seeing it' Mike flashed up another pair of photographs and then another and then a third, all showing similar changes between the two photographs. The fourth set of pictures had similar differences but with the addition of a speck of light that appeared in the second frame. The fifth set showed the same speck in the first and second frames and the sixth showed it again but slightly longer. 'Now we really do have an anomaly' said Emma 'what is the time scale of these sets of pictures Mike?' Mike looked down at the running program and said 'all taken between three and three thirty seven this morning. The photographs and the measurement data that came with them gave Emma plenty of new material to work with and she set about updating her spreadsheet and computer program. She also sent the new data to the UK office for when they came online. Mike also appeared busy, so Gary went to the kitchen to make yet more coffee, he knew his role and took some pleasure in it. Delivering the cups to each of them he asked 'Just for the record and my benefit, can we just go over what we already know please' 'Sure, it wouldn't hurt to clarify things and stimulate ideas' said Emma. 'Well let me say it as I see *it* in layman's terms, and if I have got *IT* then anyone can get *it*' said Gary. 'Go ahead' encouraged Emma as she sipped her coffee. Gary began speaking slowly and deliberately 'So a few weeks ago the world's weather clouds were all being slowly dragged around the planet to somewhere near Lake Michigan and then off into space. Mike went to speak but Emma held up her hand 'go on' she said. Gary continued 'about the time we found this out, we also find a mysterious sound signal coming from somewhere in space, which as it happens also appears to be slowing down in frequency, like the train sound Doppler thing. But suddenly the clouds start to reverse direction and that crisis is over, but then we find pictures of stars being moved and realise instead there might be something big coming this way, like some interstellar tsunami…. is that about it?'

Mike and Emma looked at each 'I think Gary, even by excluding every known scientific term or principle, you have summarised that very well' said Emma, Gary was pleased an a little smug 'well thank you profs and docs, I do have my uses other than making coffee. Since it is me that will have to write this up for the public I do need to get the core facts straight. It strikes me though that somehow your science is not the exact science you might have thought it was'. Mike looked a little anxious and paused before speaking 'If we are right, then there is the small matter of the large moral question of when, how or even if we going to break the news to the public. It might cause mass panic and rioting if people thought their days were numbered'. Gary found himself getting a little angry 'what! That's the whole fucking reason I was hijacked by missy there and brought into all this in the first place. I was to be the bearer of bad news to the world'. 'And so you shall be Gary' jumped in Emma 'once we have confirmed the cause, effect and hopefully some sort of plan to offset the loss of life. But that will be once we know what is actually coming this way' Both Mike and Gary started to speak but she cut them off. 'This is not the time for that discussion boys. When we have all the facts we will consult and decide how to proceed, but until then let's not get caught up in any moral dilemmas that might cloud our judgement, okay... OKAY?' 'Yes' both men mumbled and went back to their respective screens like told off schoolboys. A computer Bing rang out which prompted Emma to look back at her screen. The program that had first suggested the beam had been slowing down in frequency had been fed a lot more data from the radio array overnight. It had been crunching the numbers for several hours and at last had completed its computations. The results once again showed either a lowering of the frequency, which confirmed that whatever it was out there, it was definitely slowing down. Emma shared the news with the other two and ensured it was updated to the UK team. Unknown to her, this latest piece of data fitted perfectly into the model the UK team were working with. They had recently received all the images she had, but they also some more gravitational lensing time lapse photographs from another telescope, so they had four way data to compare. Combining all the photographs and radio array data into a computer model they were able to produce a computer generated image of the events unfolding before them. The results were compressed and emailed straight back to Emma in Hawaii. After the minor argument between Mike and

Gary, and with Emma head down busy working hard, the mood in the lab was a little quiet and subdued. The miserable bubble was rudely burst by the loud ping of an incoming email and seeing it was from London Emma opened it at once. The short message said *'Important. See attached computer generated imagery and then discuss:'* It was short, to the point but also dramatic enough to get her excited. She double clicked on the attached file which then searched her computer for the correct decompression app to open the data file. It assembled the program, loaded the data which produced some graphs and a static pictorial animation screen. Emma clicked on the run button and started the animated simulation sequence. She then paused it and told Gary and Mike to look at the shared information screens. On screen was a pictorial computer image of planet Earth which revolved once to stop over the now familiar Lake Michigan. The computer view then rotated 180 degrees away from Earth and headed off into space, getting quicker as it did so. In seconds it had passed through our solar system before encountering the nearest stars, each with a name tag or number. The view swung back to show Earth briefly but it was now no more than a named speck on the screen. Once more heading at computer animation speed into space, the computer image did flybys of many unnamed stars and constellations before slowing down and heading for one bright spot of light. They all watched in silence as the computer image first approached the enlarging spot before swinging off to one side of it. From this angle it could be seen that the spot was actually a tube shaped or possibly a beam of some sort. A numeric graphic indicated the tube to be approximately ten kilometres in length, and about half a kilometre in diameter. The graphic then travelled along the top of the tube back towards Earth, increasing sped to a blur before impacting the Earth in the area over Lake Michigan. There was silence as no one spoke but this was shattered a few seconds later as the phone on the desk rang loudly making them all jump. Emma composed herself and answered the phone. From her tone and words it was obviously the London team who had sent the file to them. They had timed it just right to make a dramatic entrance, albeit by phone. As she put down the receiver she looked in turn at Gary and Mike. 'So, if what we have seen can be believed, a ten kilometre long radio wave, beam of light or something is heading towards Earth. It is slowing down but who knows if it will stop or just crash right into us, possibly destroying the planet and everything and everyone on it! Mike took a nervous

drink of water and Gary swallowed the rising bile that he felt in his

throat.

CHAPTER ELEVEN: WILL IT STOP?

The three of them watched the one minute ten second simulation several times over. They had already accepted they were in a bad situation, but at least that situation had been full of theories, maybes, but with a strong hope that it might just be kind of alright in the end. This visual representation diminished that hope and brought the problem into sharp focus. Gary was the first to speak 'KABOOM! So where do we go from here?' Emma and Mike were silent so Gary tried again 'Anybody?' Emma spoke 'well, firstly we need to continue monitoring the signal as that will give us a clue to its speed and when it will contact Earth' 'and secondly?' asked Gary, hoping for some better news. Emma sighed and pursed her lips in thought 'actually, there is no secondly as such, it is now pretty much a gathering more data game until we know enough to predict exactly what will happen and when' Mike looked up 'while we are waiting we could have the have the moral discussion on whether to release the news or keep it to ourselves. And, since we are in the United States whether we inform the government first.' To Gary this statement briefly carried a moral question about human kind's right to know, but more importantly to him, the means to completely keep him out of the game. He tried to hide the selfish part of his personality and spoke 'Are we the right group to try and decide on what people should know? To keep them from saying their goodbyes, to stop mothers seeing their loved ones for the last time? He looked at Mike and Emma in turn but there was no reply only thoughtful looks. Gary was about to start on another round of guilt laden diatribe when Emma spoke 'I have been thinking about this, and the one conclusion I have come to is that the decision if far too important to be kept to such a small group such as ourselves. We need to widen the scope of who should know and who can help map out the moral and ethical path to either telling people or letting them live their last days in blissful ignorance. I suggest we all give some time to making a list of who should be privy to this information, but my list will not include any government agency' It was a short but complete speech and seemed to satisfy all parties in the short term. Emma went back to her computer whilst Mike deep in thought chewed on a pencil before writing some quick notes to himself on an email. Gary made yet more coffee. Emma was aware through her emails that as a leading expert on the world's weather she was in increasing demand in her absence. Everyone from Joanne Graymond, the world's media, various governments and in particular her own university wanted to cash in on her, their prize investment. The media were easy to deal with as all she had to do was delete their emails and ignore her public work cell phone. However, several of the governments were becoming more persistent in their pursuit, sending people to knock on doors and calling on people she was known to. The university faculty had a good idea where she was, as using her remote computer access to log in to her office accounts, emails and work stations left a trail. There had at first been a series of polite and then increasingly terse emails from the university's Dean Groombridge, as he requested both updates on the weather situation and her location. However, it was not difficult for one of the technology department to track her computer movements and soon the Dean was informed of her whereabouts. Under ever increasing pressure from the faculty, various agencies and government officials, the Dean decided to fly out and speak to her in person. For all his faults, of which there were many but most of which he was not aware of, Gary was not a complete fool. One of his few skills included a good intuition where people were concerned, especially where it concerned his own well-being. He had noted Mike's pensive face during their previous discussion and then how he had furtively typed away on his computer. His curiosity was further piqued when Gary delivered Mike's coffee to his computer desk and saw Mike quickly change screens and move to another computer window. Gary had used this method himself whilst working in the newspaper office and viewing pornography at his desk, so was well versed in the technique. Later in the day Mike went back to the accommodation to get what he said was 'some moisturiser', which Gary no longer found strange, which in itself was strange. Emma was suffering from some eye strain and needed a break from the computer screen, so rubbing her eyes she excused herself and went to the small kitchen area that served the complex. Now alone, Gary thought about Mike's behaviour earlier and decided to surreptitiously have a look at Mike's computer for clues as to what he was thinking. After a quick check to see if he was alone, Gary went to Mike's desk and saw the bronzed hunk of an early twenties surfer dude grinning back at him as the screen saver. He moved the mouse and the main window popped open to reveal many open windows and programs along the bottom of the screen. Gary noted that the main email was not opened so double clicked and the windows outlook un-express whirred into life. As expected there were many thousands of emails on his system but the top three were bolded, virginal, new and unopened. Gary opened each one in turn, finding a copied reply from the London office, one from a gay dating agency with a prospective date and the third from the FBI. Despite being curious about Mike's new date, Gary read the FBI email first. It was short and to the point 'Hi Mikey, thanks for contacting me about your concerns, please contact me in person to discuss ASAP.' It was electronically signed Special Agent Searle FBI, and then went on to give details of phone numbers where the special agent could be contacted. Gary scrolled quickly down to where he could see Mike's original message and read 'Hi Mark,

Mike calling here from sunny Hawaii. Hope you are well? I have a bit of sticky problem regarding my work and a small matter of national security. Can I have an off the record chat to you about it when you are available please? Thanks Mike x'

The significance of the little X kiss at the bottom of the email was not lost on Gary and neither was the content of the message. It seemed Mike's loyalties were being tested by the moral discussion they had had this morning and now he was seeking to snitch on them to the FBI, or at least ask their advice, which basically amounted to the same thing. Gary heard one of the outer doors slam shut, so he quickly forwarded the FBI email to himself before right clicking all three emails, marking them as unread again. Yes, that can be done! He then quickly padded back to his seat on the other side of the room. He had just picked up his own mouse when Mike walked into the room smelling heavily of rose petal, which Gary took to mean he really had gone back for moisturiser and found it. He smiled and greeted Gary before going to his desk, but was surprised not to see his screen saver waiting to greet him. Mike thought for a moment and looked suspiciously over at Gary, but Gary had played this game many times before and ignored the stare in his periphery and concentrated on his own screen. When he deemed it safe to do so he looked across at Mike 'Everything okay?' 'Oh yes, considering everything that is going on I'm just fine and dandy' replied Mike. Gary thought *'Well dandy might be the name of your screen saver surfer dude, but you are not fine'* Emma came back into the room looking tired and red around the eyes where she had been rubbing them. The two men looked up at her and she said defensively 'What?' Mike spoke 'You look like you could use some rest' before Gary added 'and you do look like shit!' 'I think I put it better, but in general terms Gary is right' said Mike. Gary spoke' Look, there is nothing new happening right now and you still have to be fresh for tonight when the telescopy thing can be used again, so let's all take a break' She looked at both men defiantly before taking a deep breath and sagged her shoulders. 'You're right. I'll be no good to anyone if I can't think straight' 'Great' said Gary 'We can have some food and catch an hour around the pool before the sun goes down' Mike nodded then said 'You guys go on, I have a couple of things to clear up here' Gary was ready for this, there was no way he wanted to leave Mike alone with his thoughts or his email until he had worked out what his game plan was. 'You too Mike' said

Gary, 'we need you to order in the pizza and I could do with some of more of your cream on my back' The three of them froze awkwardly for a moment, each of them evaluating what Gary had just said and putting their own spin on it. Mike spoke slowly 'Okay, I guess a break wouldn't hurt me either'. The awkward spell broken, the three of them quickly gathered up their few personal belongings and walked back to the apartment block. Gary quickly changed and went to swim in the cool water before the late afternoon sun quickly went down over the horizon. He then chose a sun lounger with cover overhead before laying down to dry. Gary's mind was racing as he evaluated this latest turn of events. It not only seemed that Mike had divided loyalties about who should break the news, but that he also had a contact in the FBI who signed his name with a kiss. They were living in liberal times but Gary could not imagine that a Special Agent of the FBI signed all his emails in this way, so why only to Mike? He was tired so at first thought he missed the obvious but a few seconds later the rest of his brain caught up. GAY! That eureka moment was rudely interrupted by the plop of cream spurting over his still red back. He at first froze, then remembering his earlier request to Mike started to spin around to sit up. A hand pushed him back down onto the sun lounger and a familiar voice said 'whoa stay there, I haven't rubbed it in yet'. Something did not fit the horrible scenario Gary had instantly imagined in his mind when the cream had hit him. There was something wrong with the voice, wrong yet familiar. He craned his neck around and squinting against the sun looked at the silhouette of the person perched on the edge of the sun lounger. Emma laughed out loud. 'Oh Gary, don't panic, it's not Mike again, it's me' she said as she gently rubbed the sun cream into his shoulders and back. 'I thought that given the given the awkward silence as we walked back I had better get the cream from Mike for you' Gary slumped back onto the lounger, resting his head on his crossed arms. 'I wasn't panicking at all' he replied 'I am completely at home with gay men, in fact some of my best friends like Lady Gaga music and drink sparkling water, so there' 'Really' said Emma in mock surprise 'Shall I give him a call then to finish you off?' she said in a teasing voice. 'No, you are doing just fine' Gary said and breathed deeply as Emma finished covering his sunburn before surprisingly wiping her cream covered hands on Gary's swimming trunks and slapping him playfully on his ass. This provoked the second awkward silence of the afternoon as both the slapper and slappee pulled surprise faces, for different reasons. Emma clumsily apologised 'oh sorry, I didn't mean, em to em…' Gary helped her out by interrupting, 'Who could blame you. I have always been told I had a cute ass, just never had it slapped by a professor before'! The joke broke the tension and allowed them both to relax again. 'You do make me laugh Gary' said Emma as she made to get up off the side of the lounger. Gary felt the springs move and said quickly 'Don't go' Emma hovered caught in between standing and sitting. Gary was aware he created yet another moment, one that in a cheesy film would see the music rise to a crescendo and Gary kiss Emma passionately. Emma was also expectant but unsure of what exactly. She too had seen her share of cheesy films but in that particular instant the thought of Gary kissing her did not cross her mind. In a millisecond she realised he must have something difficult to say, so she encouraged him 'what is it Gary, something you want to say?' Gary turned around to face her and completely missing the vocal queues she had just given him, decided in a moment of madness and sunburn that she was in the same cheesy film moment that he was. Gary leant forward to kiss Emma in what he thought and hoped would be a romantic and poignant moment. It well might have been all those things, had not his creamy sweaty hands not slipped on the lounger springs, slipping his hand through the frame and his head towards Emma's chest. Emma had watched in slow motion as Gary appeared to be making an attempt at a kiss before crashing through the springs of the sun lounger and forcing his head onto her breasts. She was not sure which of the two things were more likely, but she was sure he was stuck in the springs and touching her breasts. Gary was floundering, both physically to untangle himself and orally to excuse himself. She tried to both help him out of the springs and also to keep his head away from her breasts, but the two things were not simultaneously possible. They struggled alternatively between springs and breasts for a few seconds, and were nearly separated when they heard Mike's voice. 'Well my O my, you two have become close pals haven't you?' he teased, allowing some gay campness to creep into his voice. Both Emma and Gary were both embarrassed, and talked over each other in an attempt to excuse the scene, or nearly scene that Mike had witnessed. Mike laughed and continued the tease 'well at least I know you are off the menu Gary and the lovely professor does have real blood in her veins' He waited till their protestations died down before continuing 'Well, if you lovebirds have quite finished making out, I am cooking my famous pasta, which will be ready in ten minutes' He gave them a knowing wink and a wag of his finger, before he turned and walked back across the pool area towards the accommodation door. 'I slipped' Gary quickly said offering an excuse. 'Yes, I know' said Emma, letting him off the hook whilst adjusting her top and recovering her composure. She knew there was more to it than that, but was also surprised to find that she was not entirely horrified at the prospect. She thought to herself *Was Gary going to kiss me? Would I have let him? Was the world coming to end?* Oh yes, the small matter of the world coming to an end dismissed all other thoughts. 'Shall we go eat before you slip again?' she asked. Gary sighed 'yes, let's go eat'. They went up to Mike's apartment on the first floor and knocking went in through the open door. Since Mike was on the permanent staff at the telescope he had the choice of accommodation and was able to make it more homely. The apartment looked nice with some personal decorative touches that matched his style, and he had taken the trouble to lay the table for dinner. 'Take a seat, dinner will be just a minute' Mike shouted from the adjoining kitchen. They sat opposite each other and both looked around the room at the pictures, lamps and tastefully scattered cushions on the sofa. Gary smiled and pointed to a picture of Lady Gaga in a full skimpy wedding dress ensemble. Emma stifled a giggle as Mike entered the room carrying two bowls of pasta and a block of parmesan cheese. He deftly and with flourish grated some onto their meals before setting back off into the kitchen. 'You guys go ahead before it gets cold' Mike shouted from the kitchen. Emma and Gary nodded at each other and started to blow on and eat the ribbons of creamy pasta. 'Mmm' said Gary, 'it tastes like the sun cream you put on my back' Emma laughed again, enjoying the respite from worrying about the obvious thing hanging over them. Mike returned 'How is it?' he asked 'Just like my mother used to burn' Gary teased before Emma chided him 'Take no notice Mike, it is delicious'. Mike gave a little bow than sat at the end of the table with his meal. From the window they could see a wonderful sunset in the Hawaiian horizon and for a moment they enjoyed the meal, the view and the shared silent company, all deep in their own thoughts. Mike was the first to speak 'at the risk of upsetting the lovely reflective mood, and if we can discuss it like adults, have you given any more thought as to who we might giving our finding to?' Although it was primarily directed at Emma, it was Gary who replied first. 'My thoughts are the same as earlier, namely that the people should know what is coming. They can then prepare, say goodbye, travel to visit loved one and a thousand other things that will not be done or said if they are left in the dark till boomsday' Although his motives were not entirely selfless, Gary had managed to convey his statement with a sense of compassion and caring that did add weight. Mike nodded, the premise of disclosure suited his argument, but as a patriotic American he felt duty bound to do it via government channels. He spoke 'I think the US Government are the right people to inform. They have the resources, diplomatic connections and security to see this is handled correctly' His words were spoken passionately, but everyone including himself could hear the Hollywood movie culture pervaded the sentiment. They both looked across expectantly at Emma for the casting vote. She was just finishing her last mouthful of pasta and dabbing at her lips with a napkin. She paused for thought, running her tongue around her teeth whilst contemplating how to phrase her sentence. She opened her mouth, but just as she started to speak there was a loud ringing from the hallway doorbell 'What the fuck!' exclaimed Mike 'we are not expecting visitors, right?' The three of them left the table, rushed into the hallway and towards the stairs to see just who the visitor was. As they descended the single staircase they could see a smartly dressed middle aged man trying to peer through the glass of the outer door. They slowed their pace as they walked in single file down the stairs, whilst they each tried to work out who it was. Gary was immediately suspicious that given Mike's earlier email and recent question over dinner, that he had jumped the gun and already informed the authorities. However, although not an expert on the FBI, gay or otherwise, the guy beyond the door did not match Gary's expectations. Before they reached the door Emma surprised them 'I know who this is, leave the talking to me guys' She pushed past Mike and opened the door. 'Hello professor' said the man in a polite but formal way. 'Dean Groombridge, what a pleasant but unexpected surprise' she said 'to what do we owe the privilege?' 'Professor, I would have thought given the state of things in the big bad world, that question is really quite redundant. Are you going to introduce me? He added, indicating towards Mike and Gary. Emma briefly introduced them both, but Gary duly noted his profession as reporter was not mentioned. Both of them shook his hand as Emma explained that

Dean Groombridge was in charge of her University, job and funding, and was in affect her boss. Introductions over, Mike invited the Dean upstairs to join them for after dinner coffee and the group returned to his apartment. The Dean declined the offer of food as he had eaten on the flight but accepted coffee and some sparkling water. Once the four of them were all seated again around the table, the small talk of pleasant flight and airline food ended and there was an expectation of an explanation for the visit. Emma already knew why he was here but Gary & Mike were somewhat in the dark, prompting Mike to ask the question. 'So Dean, we don't many visitors, at least unannounced visitors. What brings you to this neck of the woods?' Emma's shoulders sagged and her body language gave away her dread in both the question and the answer. The Dean answered, 'well the professor here has been playing a game of international hide & seek, and given she works for our faculty I thought I ought to pay her a visit and check on her welfare' Whilst the answer was technically accurate, it left out a lot of detail and was said in such an understated way as to leave everyone in no doubt Emma was not flavour of the month. Gary tried to help Emma out by offering 'Well Dean, she has been rather busy trying to save the world. It's not every day the sky comes tumbling down' he added in a jokey fashion that no one found funny 'oh, tough crowd' he added. 'I would have preferred to do this in private professor' said the Dean 'but since your colleagues here are already in the loop and appear to know more than me, I will get to the point'. In a most deliberate and head masterly like way, the Dean slowly set out his list of disappointments in Emma's behaviour and lack of contact over the last week. He pointed out her research funding, salary, and departmental grants were all in place to allow her the freedom to conduct research, but that major findings or discoveries were contractually to be shared with the University. He finished with a small aside about how he was personally disappointed given he had sanctioned her appointment and further grant funding. It felt like a very civilised telling off, which was exactly what it was with each word carefully spoken to add impact and weight. In some sort of professional deference to the title of Dean, Mike said nothing whilst Emma looked into her coffee and slowly stirred the cream in. The Dean, smug and satisfied that he had made all his points waited patiently for a reply, and raised his coffee cup to his lips. 'I am a reporter' Gary suddenly blurted out in a moment of social

Tourette's. He meant well, in that he hoped it would take some of the heat off Emma in a kind of 'I AM SPARTACUS' kind of moment, giving her time to compose herself. What it actually did was to cause the Dean to involuntary cough and spurt his coffee out over the table in front of them. Emma dropped her spoon and Mike put a hand over his mouth to stifle the 'oh fuck' that came to his lips. 'Was it something I said?' asked Gary in mock innocence. Wiping coffee from his lips and dabbing wildly at the front of his jacket, the Dean's composure was completely lost. His voice no longer measured and restrained, he exclaimed 'A reporter, A REPORTER! What professor in god's name were you thinking!?' A scientist yes, one from another university just maybe, but a reporter!? His coffee spittle words added invective to the point he was making. Like some southern states evangelical preacher, he raised his voice and banged his fist on the table causing the coffee cups and the three of them to all jump. In his apoplexy he struggled to find words to continue and sat wide eyed waiting for answers, none of which would be good enough, so no one tried. The only noise that could be heard was the strange sound Gary made when thinking. It was a sucking inwards of his bottom lip with his tongue, making a strange tuk tuk tuk sort of noise, which by any measure and in any culture became instantly annoying. The three of them looked at Gary who stopped his lip tuking long enough to speak. 'Dean, perhaps I can explain' he started. Emma froze in horror, Mike leaned forward in anticipation and the Dean's rising blood pressure was shown in the colour of his face. 'A week ago I was the reporter on a small town newspaper. I have been twice manhandled by burly men in cheap suits and been scared shitless in a Hillman Imp. Now, through various circumstances, most of which I have to say were my own work, I find myself here in the tropical paradise which is Hawaii. Am I enjoying a vacation, do I still have a job? No, instead I am shacked up here on the top of mountain contemplating not only the end of the world, but whether or not I should tell someone and get the newspaper scoop of all time' They still looked at him, all uncertain as to the point he was making or hopefully was going to make. He went on 'In all this, the Prof here has done nothing that hasn't been in the interests of the whole human race, not herself or her family or her country...THE WHOLE OF THE HUMAN RACE!' Gary stopped, he was not expecting a round of applause as British movie culture did not allow for that, which was good as no applause was forthcoming. Whilst his point was not in any way scientific, it was heartfelt and not lacking in emotion. Perhaps more importantly it was one of those speeches that could not be argued against without looking like a complete bastard, which in itself bought some time. The Dean weighed up his options: He had travelled a long way to find the professor and so far so good, he had achieved that aim. He now needed the latest information on the world's weather situation and then he could decide on how to proceed, with or without the presence of the scruffy reporter creature sat opposite him. 'Right, here is what is going to happen' he said in his most authoritative way. 'Professor Rowlinson and I are going to have a private chat, where she will bring me up to date on all and every salient fact' He paused for effect then looked at Mike 'You will then assist me in accessing my own university's computer's facilities, where we can compare material and data' He looked firmly at Gary 'And you mister, mister? Gary helped him 'Barnes, Gary Barnes'. 'You Mister Barnes are to say nothing, do nothing and to speak to no one until I say so, is that perfectly clear?' Gary surprised everyone by replying 'Yes Dean that is perfectly clear' but no one had noticed that Gary had crossed his fingers, which in his schoolboy days completely invalidated his promise.

CHAPTER TWELVE: FINAL APPROACH

The entity's constituent parts were all now fully awake and working again as one. It was just one being but could close down parts of its intelligence on long transits to conserve energy and avoid the tedium. Now approaching its goal it wanted to be fully functioning for the task ahead. It knew which part of the planet it wanted to alight on and had sent out sensory markers as a precursor to ensure the landmass had not changed too much since it was last there. It was the path of these markers that in close proximity to the Earth had caused the strange weather experienced by the inhabitants. The entity's curiosity and interest were rising as it anticipated seeing how the planet and life had evolved in the intervening eons since its previous visit. It had long ago done away with emotions as an unnecessary waste of resources, so the interest it felt was refreshing in itself, replacing some of the sterile pure thinking it was used to. Intuitively it slowed even more as it made a slight correction to line up with the markers that were showing the way to its final destination. As it turned, the tube shape of energy bent onto the new course but in a fraction of a second was straight again and aligned with Earth. It knew where it wanted to be on the planet, but was unaware that the current inhabitants had given it the name of Lake

Michigan. Whilst still a long way off in terms of humankinds method of measurement, at the speed and distance it had travelled it was relatively close. It was now aware of passing through some primitive radio waves that were emanating from the direction of the planet. It quickly sampled them for useful information or clues as to the originators, but found nothing to suggest anything like a higher intelligence. It felt something akin to disappointment but once again the stirring of an extinct emotion was more interesting than the actual disappointment itself. It knew so very much about the universe it roamed that nothing could really surprise or threaten it. In its long search across the millennia of grand space, the slightest new thought, discovery or emotion was stimuli for its massive intelligence. Even with that low benchmark it could find nothing of interest in the radio waves that mankind had been leaking into space for the last one hundred years. It stopped processing them as worthless, what it needed to know it would find out first hand, very soon.

CHAPTER THIRTEEN: LEATHER & HANDCUFFS

Gary and Mike quickly cleared the table before leaving the apartment so that Emma could brief the Dean. He had insisted on a private meeting with his professor so that he would get the full story, but also so he could impress on Emma that she still worked for him. Gary and Mike sat outside in the still warm air enjoying the evening and open skies. Gary thought he would use the time to test Mike and asked him 'So, I guess working here for such a long time you have plenty of friends in high places?' Mike cocked his head 'Well, yes, I suppose I have met quite a few high flyers here, some of whom have gone on to have stellar careers' The slight joke was lost on Gary, not least of which because he was really looking for information, not humour. 'Government people come here a lot? He asked. 'Yes' replied Miki 'sometimes on a fact finding mission, sometimes for a briefing and sometimes just to look through the telescope' with a smile he added thoughtfully 'actually a few of them turned to be interesting characters and became friends' This was where Gary hoped the conversation would lead so he tried one more push. 'What about law enforcement, Secret Service, Police, FBI.....? He tailed his voice off as if he was not really interested and just making conversation. Mike's expression changed from the far away happy memory look to one of suspicion 'why do you ask that Gary?' Gary looked hurt and held up his hands 'just making small talk Mike, nothing else' he lied. Mike folded his arms defensively

'Really Gary? Or is it because I am gay and you think I have screwed my way through the visitor's book and every Tom, Dick and William that has come up the mountain!' This is going better than I could have hoped for thought Gary 'Whoa, steady there tiger, no offence meant. I wasn't asking if you preferred to ride a cycle side saddle, just whether you had met some interesting and influential people whilst working up here'. Mike seemed satisfied by Gary's genuine but overacted display of hurt, and took a deep breath. 'Sorry Gary, I get a little defensive sometimes where my sexuality is involved' Gary nodded 'I can understand that' he said but seeing the door open he gave one more push. 'Still, now you mention it, I guess you do get a little action from time to time?' Gary asked, ending the sentence with that annoying Australian upward inflection. Mike relaxed and smiled thoughtfully as he remembered some of his liaisons 'well let's just say I have had my moments' Although Gary was not as comfortable discussing gay sex as he was currently portraying, he needed to check out his theory, so continued. Cringing inwardly at the question, Gary pursued his theme 'So, any uniform rough and tumble that would really add a little zing to the festivities?' 'Gary!' Mike said 'are you one of those greedy bastards that swings both ways kind of guys?' 'Oh No,' said Gary quickly, 'I was just wondering what floats your boat' Mike smiled and bit his lower 'Well you know, there was this one time last summer when some government officials were on the tour of the hill. They had some security with them, one of whom got a little fresh once he realised we were on the same page' Gary nodded in an encouraging way, 'Interesting, go on' Mike rose to the challenge and was enjoying reliving the experience 'Well he was a big blonde guy, very straight looking but of course he would have to be, given that he is an FBI agent' Mike paused for effect. 'Jackpot' thought Gary before replying 'wow, sounds interesting, dangerous and exciting' Mike nodded and sighed deeply 'yes, it was. A whole night of the leather and handcuff thing, it was quite some session' 'So' Gary asked nonchalantly 'still in contact?' 'Oh yes we stay in touch by email but I haven't seen him since' replied Mike, but even as he spoke a little alarm bell started to ring in his head as he realised he was perhaps giving away a little too much information. 'Gary, you are quite the curious one aren't you, drawing all that out of me in one go. It must be the reporter in you or perhaps you are more than just a little curious?' He teased. Gary now felt really uncomfortable, coughed to lower his voice to a more manly level and stood up. 'No, just passing the time' he answered unconvincingly. Needing to distance himself from the slightly strange atmosphere he had created with Mike, Gary made an excuse of needing the bathroom and went into his apartment, leaving Mike on the stairs. He had unknowingly raising questions in Mike's mind, the first of which had Mike looking Gary up and down as he walked back towards the door. Once inside Gary leaned against the inside of the door and took a deep breath. Yes, he had got the information he wanted and confirmed Mike's link to the FBI was something less than formal, but at what price. Perhaps a shower would help him focus and clean his mind of some of the dodgy images that were now hot seared into his memory. He stood under the warm power shower and let the water run down his head and down his body. His mind was running through the knowns and unknowns of the current situation. Having come this far, he realised that bizarrely he was more concerned with being the one to release the end of the world news to the world, than the fact the world was actually coming to an end. Somehow, by careful rationalisation of the facts to date, he was able to make the actual situation fit in with his own version of reality and warped sense of purpose. He had just managed to clear his mind of leather bound men handcuffed to beds and convinced himself that his conversation with Mike could not have been misconstrued, when there was a gentle knock at the door. He put his head outside of the shower and froze as he heard more knocking and Mike's voice through the letterbox 'Gary, I have made some cocktails and brought you fresh towels from the store...hello Gary, can you hear me?' Glad that he locked the apartment door behind him, Gary ducked back under the shower and slid the shower door closed to keep Mike's plaintiff voice from reaching his ears. He realised that somewhere in his carefully planned but clumsily executed machinations, he had created enough doubt in Mike's mind to see him as a future leather clad handcuffed participant. Gary was not sure how the next few weeks would pan out, but he was one hundred percent certain that his last few weeks on earth were not going to be sullied with kinky mansex of any kind. However, the word sex did strike a chord and he used it as a springboard to move his thoughts on to something other than two penises touching. Was the world going to end and if so was he, Gary Barnes, going to die without having sex, with a proper woman, one last time? It was a rhetorical question but one that bothered him and one that would hover in the back of his mind for the next few days. Through the sound of the water he caught the continued knocking at the door and the occasional snippet of Mike's voice urging him to open the door. Never mind the fucking end of the world he thought, just getting through the next few hours without being man fucked would throw up its own challenges.

CHAPTER FOURTEEN: RUN FATBOY RUN!

Dean Groombridge and Emma had finished their sometimes frosty private meeting and she went to tell the boys what had transpired. Coming down the stairs she was surprised to find Mike bent over calling through the letterbox of the apartment that Gary was using. 'What's up Mike?' she asked. 'Oh nothing, I just got a few things for Gary but it sounds like he is stuck in the shower and I can't get him to answer the door' Curious, Emma joined Mike at the door and bending over called through the letterbox. 'Gary, its Emma. Everything alright in there?' Instantly the door opened and Gary's head appeared, with the bottom half covered by a towel. 'Can't a fella not even have a shower in peace?' asked Gary. Mike looked a little surprised and hurt but Emma just looked a little surprised. 'Sorry' she said 'Mike thought you might be having a problem' Gary flashed a look at Mike, 'No, I am fine, just freshening up and doing some thinking in the shower' said Gary in what he hoped would be a very macho and most un-gay type of way. 'Okay' Emma replied 'When you are dressed, can the two of you come back up to Mike's place as Dean Groombridge wants to talk to you both?' 'Okay, I'll be ten minutes' said Gary as he closed the door and locked it, noting as he did so Mike's gaze looking down at his bottom half. He quickly dressed and went upstairs to join the others in Mike's apartment. The three were sat around the table with the Dean sat at the head of the table, holding court and smoking a big fat cigar. Emma and Mike seemed horrified at the smell and kept waving their hands around to move the thick blue smoke that was swirling around the room. It was obvious that the Dean saw himself as top dog in this four way meeting and was starting as he meant to go on. Clearly, smoking in someone else's apartment was more about making a mark, more like a dog pissing on another dog's tree than really needing to fill a room with smoke. Before he sat down Gary tried to recover a bit of the high ground by opening the sliding doors and wafting some of the smoke out. 'Have a seat Mister Barnes' said the Dean, pointing with his cigar at a carefully arranged seat. 'Call me Gary' said Gary as he reversed the carefully placed chair and irreverently sat on it cowboy style. 'What?' said the Dean, confused and not liking the changes being made to his set piece 'I said, just call me Gary, If we are going to be working together then just call me Gary' The informality threw the Dean off stroke so he reluctantly nodded a mute agreement and spoke. 'Now, in my meeting with professor Rowlinson, I have made it quite clear that she is still contractually working for the University and comes under my jurisdiction whilst 'WE' sort out what is going to happen. He emphasised the 'we' with bunny ears, making the point that we really meant him. He continued 'My University is also paying for the telescope time you are using, so that means you doctor' pointing his cigar at Mike 'also come under my authority. 'Well I don't work for you Dean, unless of course you are putting me on the payroll? Gary joked, but no one laughed. 'No mister… Gary, I won't be employing you directly, but if you want a piece of the story when it breaks, then you will do as I say, or I will have you removed from this property and have another reporter flown when we need one. Is that clear Gary?' the Dean added with heavy emphasis on the words 'removed' and 'another' Gary was angry inside but for he knew there was a bigger picture, and that bigger picture meant him staying on the mountain, at least for the time being. Gary physically and metaphorically bit his lip and then smiled at the Dean 'I think we understand each other Dean, you have a deal' Emma raised an eyebrow in surprise at Gary's quick capitulation but she did notice his fingers were crossed behind his back. Having made his points and in his mind had the three of them in his pocket, the Dean now took on a more generous and inclusive tone. Using both hands in an open gesture he said 'Good. Now the ground rules have been sorted out we can go back to playing happy families. Just think of me as the visiting rich uncle you have to be nice to and we will all get along just fine. Okay? They all nodded in moot agreement. Now released from the formal part of the meeting, the continued smoke desecration of Mike's apartment became too much to bear for him. Mike leapt up and ran to the kitchen, returning a few seconds later with a can of air freshener which he liberally sprayed around the room. The Dean took the hint, grunted and casually tossed the cigar out of the open window before continuing. 'Now, as I understand it the good professor here wants another night's observations from the telescope tonight and also the radio array to confirm the data we have so far. It will give us fresh ideas or confirm what we already know. You techy people can get on with that tonight whilst I placate the faculty and some government departments about your disappearance. I will stall them for another twenty four hours and then in the morning I will make a decision on how to proceed, which is where you may or may not become involved Gary' Gary nodded slowly, apparently in complete agreement, although once again, his fingers were firmly crossed. Gary was nodding slowly because his brain was working quickly. The Dean, along with the FBI becoming involved was yet another complicating turn of events that threatened his involvement. His mind looked at the two problems facing him and he considered if there was one solution to both. The meeting over, Emma and Mike began gathering up their things to make the journey up the hill to the telescope. The Dean asked Mike to get him into the computer system before he left but Gary interrupted and suggested he could do that, so Mike and Emma left. Across the courtyard to the smaller computer room, Gary showed the Dean where the lights and switches were and got him settled at a screen. Whilst he was logging on Gary assumed a subservient attitude and said 'Can I get you a beer Dean?' The Dean liked this new at heel obsequious Gary and replied 'Well Gary, it has been kind of a long week, do you have anything stronger? 'I'll go and see' said Gary, and smiling as he turned he walked back to the apartment. There was nothing in his mini kitchen but a quick check of Mike's apartment soon found the hard liquor. He poured one extra-large whisky for the Dean and an equal sized Ginger ale for himself, but to the casual eye they were both whisky. Taking the bottles and glasses he juggled his way back to the computer room and carefully put them down. 'I found a ten year old malt' said Gary 'will that wet your whistle?' 'That will do nicely Gary, but perhaps I had better have a splash of that ginger ale to dilute it as I do have to keep a clear head'. Gary splashed some into both the glasses, thereby just giving himself an even larger ginger ale and the Dean a large whisky with just a splash of ginger. The Dean took a sip and smacked his lips in appreciation 'Good job Gary, I think we are going to get along just fine, cheers'. They clinked glasses and drank a long mock toast. The Dean logged on, and muttering to himself starting reading and replying to some of the many emails that were stacked up. Gary surreptitiously topped up the Dean's glass with whisky, and did so again after the Dean had taken a few gulps. Gary continued adding to the Dean's glass whenever he could and when he was once caught he simply also pretended to top his own glass as well. He didn't want the Dean drunk, he wanted him comatose, because unlikely as it seemed, Gary actually had a plan.

Up at the telescope Mike was both busy setting up the equipment for another photographic run. Emma was downloading emails and data from the London lab and adding their results to her computer program for studying later. They both quite some preparation work to complete, but by ten o'clock they would be ready and then could relax whilst the images and other data were processed by the computers. They would have their pictures and any flagged up anomalies no earlier than two a.m., so there would be no early to bed tonight. Back down below, Gary and the Dean were having a good old whisky filled time of it, or at least the Dean was as Gary was only drinking ginger ale. The whisky had done it trick, with the tipsy convivial Dean now actively filling his own glass when it neared empty. After the Dean had finished his admin and emails, he settled down to enjoy a few more drinks with Gary whilst waiting for news from Emma up at the telescope. As they were getting through the whisky at a rate of knots, Gary had needed to find more alcohol keep the Dean's solo party going. He returned to Mike's apartment and like the Police with a search warrant proceeded to rummage around for more booze. Whilst there he also searched the bathroom cabinet and found all manner of pills and potions to cover a multitude if not all ills that could befall a man. Quickly reading through the medicine labels he found some sleeping tablets, which he figured might just help him with his plan. Using two dessert spoons he crushed a half dozen sleeping tablets into a fine powder. He took a deep breath as the realisation kicked in that he was about to drug a senior head of a university. He Gary reasoned that it was like date rape but without the really bad bit. Either he continued with his plan to get the Dean to sleep with a cocktail of drink and drugs, or he would have to stop at the whisky and hope the loud and demanding Dean fell asleep of his own accord. 'Fuck it' said Gary out loud and poured the sleeping powder into the newly opened whisky bottle and gave it a good shake. With the corrupted golden potion in his hand, he triumphantly entered the office where the Dean was sat drunkenly at the desk. Gary was just quick enough to notice that the computer screen being quickly closed by the Dean contained a mass of writhing naked bodies, which put him up in Gary's estimation but also made him think *something else to store for later use if needed*. With the fresh bottle of whisky now in play and the Dean's glass once again topped up, Gary sat at another computer screen and logged on. He searched through his recent emails, deleting the Nigerian lottery winner and penis enlargement offers straight away. After a few moments he found what he was looking for, the email from the FBI guy that he had forwarded to himself from Mike's machine yesterday. His hands worked expertly over his keyboard and mouse as he cut and pasted various pieces of the email and signature into a blank email that he could use. Now happy with his work and with a convincing looking FBI blank email before him, he assumed the character and began to type.

Emma and Mike had both completed their work and she was now sitting at her computers checking daily weather reports from around the globe. Mike took the time to look in on his own personal emails to see if anything interesting had come in, in particular if his Grinder dating account profile had been viewed by anyone recently. It may well be that the end of the world was nigh, but Mike was still keen for some final action if he could get it. With nothing on either of the dating websites he used, in some hope and a little desperation he gave his email send and retrieve button one more try. 'You have mail' announced the sexy male voice he had assigned to the computer as the top mail appeared as an unread message. He caught his breath slightly as he saw it was from Steve, the blonde FBI hunk he had emailed recently about the unfolding events. In truth that was only part of the reason, the underlying reason was a desire to see him again and the email a method of contact. He double clicked on it to open the message but as he did so he looked around to make sure Emma could not see the screen. He quickly read the message and his heart skipped a beat.

'Hi Mikey, thanks for the email and intriguing message. Do you really have something important to discuss or is this just your way of getting me back on the island, lol? Either way I couldn't pass up the chance of seeing you again, so I am combining business with pleasure and flying in to Honolulu tonight at 7pm. I am staying at the Holiday Out Express on Seventh Boulevard. If you can make it down from the mountain tonight then I will be back in my room from 10 o'clock and would love to see you. If you cannot make it then do not worry I can use the time to look up old friends.

Stevie x

PS I brought the handcuffs!

Mike's head was spinning and his heart pounding. Not only was the FBI hunk back on the island he was actually setting up a date, and a hotel room date at that. He re-read the message several times over, savouring each unsubtle nuance and the action it inferred. If it had been a letter in a movie, as the music swelled he would have clutched it to his chest and then smelt the paper, but he had to settle for 'SAVE AS' on the computer. Had he not been quite so intensely pleased and excited by the contents, he might have noticed the email had been forwarded and not sent directly, but his mind set would not allow the discrepancy to register. He was still enjoying the euphoria and mind sex when the crashing realisation hit him that he could not possibly leave the Emma, the telescope or the mountain, especially tonight of all nights. He was consider any and all of his options when the door opened and in walked Gary. 'Ah there you are Mike, Houston we have a problem'

'Problem, what kind of problem' asked Mike. 'Well it seems the pious Dean has got himself good and drunk, and now has a bad attack of the munchies, demanding pizza of all things' 'really' said Mike 'he doesn't seem the pizza sort of guy' Gary shrugged 'I know what you mean Mike, but hey, whatever the big guys wants the big guy gets. But we have a further problem. The Dean tried ordering the delivery himself, but in his drunken state pissed the guys off at the pizza place so much they are refusing to come up the mountain to make the delivery. So, the big guy wants you to go into town and collect it for him' Mike rolled his eyes and started to protest but then saw a window of opportunity opening. 'I couldn't really take the time right now with everything going on, could I?' he asked expectedly. 'Why not, you seem to have everything ready and are just waiting results right?' said Gary before turning to Emma 'Prof, you can spare Mike for an hour can't you to nip into town on an errand for the Dean?' Keen to keep the Dean off her back Emma spoke 'No problem Mike, it's a waiting game anyway, go ahead' Mike could not believe his luck. His favourite lover was in town and he was being given leave, in fact a definite instruction to go down into town on an errand. If the Dean was as drunk as Gary said, then he would not be under any pressure to return in a hurry as the old man would probably be asleep soon anyways, he rationalised. Trying not to look too keen, Mike made a show of getting the order written down and getting his things together. He took the trouble to make some pre excuse about the bad traffic recently downtown before he slowly left the building. Once outside and alone he ran all the way down to his minivan to maximise his shagging time in town. The Dean vaguely heard the bang of a car door and the squealing of tyres as Mike sped down the mountain. He was already too drunk to care who it was, but not so drunk that he could not pour himself another drink from the newly opened whisky bottle. This particular single malt had a very peaty taste which appealed to the Dean's palette, to the point that he did not notice the slightly cloudy colour, courtesy of the sleeping tablets Gary had added. Now alone with Emma, Gary spoke quickly 'right prof, I need to talk to you urgently and I need you to talk to me' 'Why Gary' she joked 'this is all so sudden'. Suddenly all business and with a no nonsense attitude Gary continued 'there is no time for joking Emma. What is the current state of play with the data?' Emma also got all business like 'Okay mister stroppy pants: the situation is exactly as we thought after last night night's observations. Something impacted on the Earth's weather systems and started to tug them into space. Then we realised that it had been reversed and something was now heading towards the planet. The data we had showed a computer generated image of a tube like structure tearing through space towards us. And, tonight the figures show that whilst it is slowing, it is still heading for us in General and Lake Michigan in particular, but we still have no idea what it is or what will happen when it arrives. Satisfied? She finished. Gary looked at his watch then at Emma 'Right then, your turn to listen to me'. This was a new more authoritative Gary that

Emma had not seen before, and whilst she was slightly taken aback she was also slightly impressed. 'Okay' she said slowly. Gary coughed 'The Dean wants you, me and Mike to meet his own ends and has no interest in the public good. Mike has his own agenda and I have seen emails that show he has been in contact with a former boyfriend in the FBI. He is on his way to meet him right now, or so he thinks. If you stay here, either the Dean, the FBI or both will soon have you completely wrapped up and held to do their bidding. Everything you do will be for the Government or the Dean's financial interests, and not as you would like for the good of mankind.' Emma nodded and sounding melancholy replied 'I had thought it could go that way which is why I thought the mountain the best place to be. But now the Dean is here and possibly the FBI, what choice do I have?' Gary pursed his lips and held both her hands 'You do have a choice prof and one that I have created. The opportunity has unexpectedly arisen for you to get out of here tonight, now, with me, and leave them to find someone else to do their dirty work.' Emma thought for second. She'd already had similar concerns but had pushed them to the back of her mind so as to concentrate on finding scientific solutions to the problems facing them. Gary's black and white view of things did actually make some sense. Also he was laying things out in a non-scientific but common sense way, something she rarely had the luxury of.' She spoke 'If, and I mean if I agreed to this, how could we possibly get away from the Dean and out of here before Mike gets back. Gary could not stop the smug look spreading across his face 'The Dean is already drunk as a lord and just started on his second bottle of whisky, one with an added vitamin supplement' Emma's hand went involuntarily to her mouth 'you poisoned the Dean!' 'Poisoned is such a strong word' replied Gary 'I prefer the term assisted him into a deep and restful sleep' Shocked Emma replied 'and what about Mike? Have you arranged a hit man to take him out from a grassy knoll?' 'No' said Gary in a mock hurt fashion 'Mike is on his way to a fictitious date with an FBI gay hunk, whilst also collecting the Dean's pizza' Emma was amazed and in truth more than a little impressed 'Well my o my, haven't you been busy. You have put all this together in the space of one evening, but have you forgotten that we are on the top of a mountain without transport' Gary looked at his watch 'That prof, is why you only have exactly thirteen minutes left to pack before your carriage arrives to whisk you off' Incredulous, Emma shook her head and asked 'and whisk me off to just where exactly Gary?' He smiled, 'Where else prof, Lake Michigan'

Emma's mind was made up and she quickly gathered up some papers and memory sticks she had been using to transfer data. They both quickly made their way back down to the accommodation block. Gary had already packed his case, so whilst Emma packed hers he went to check on the Dean. He found him lying on his back on the computer room floor, snoring like a chainsaw and completely comatose. He was still trying to turn him over into a safer position when Emma came in. 'What have you done to him!' she said, not a little worried. Gary produced the pill bottle he had used to drug the Dean and showed it to Emma 'Just a little sleeping tablet from Mike's collection' Emma took the trouble to read the whole of the label before telling him 'this is ketamine, a horse tranquiliser' Gary gulped 'horse! What the fuck would Mike need a horse tranquiliser for?' Emma answered him 'it can be used as recreational drug or perhaps Mike has a horse. Either way let's hope you haven't killed the Dean. Help me turn him over' Together they both heaved and managed to turn the large whale shaped Dean onto his side. Emma gave him a cursory look over and raised his eyelids. 'Is he okay' asked Gary. 'No idea'' said Emma, not my area of speciality, I just saw that once in a movie' Headlights cutting across the courtyard outside cut short their conversation, so they left the sleeping snoring Dean and went outside. The bright red garishly lit pizza van sat there ticking over as the driver walking cheerfully towards them carrying the boxed pizzas. Gary spoke to the driver 'There has been a change of delivery address. How much to take this to the airport? The driver looked confused and not a little annoyed. 'Let me rephrase that said Emma 'How much to deliver us to the airport with a fat tip?' The young driver quickly got the message and rolling his eyes quickly said 'one hundred bucks' 'that will do nicely' said Emma as she tossed the pizza boxes into the bushes and got into the car's rear seat. Gary started to complain that he did actually want the pizza but it was now lost in the bushes so he just grudgingly got into the car. The driver needed little encouragement to make quick time to the airport and being a delivery driver and not a taxi driver, the journey was both exciting and scary in equal measure. They arrived at the airport in a shower of dust and pizza crusts as the driver hit the brakes. Emma paid him with a pile of green monopoly looking money that passes for cash in the USA. Without so much as a thank you the spotty young driver simply took the cash, hit the gas and sped off. Gary had only just retrieved their cases from the boot and was left coughing in the dust and questioned the birth right and mental status of all pizza delivery drivers everywhere.

It was exactly midnight when they approached the ticket desk for Merican Airlines. The ever cheerful clerk wanted to improve her commission rate and two late night walk in flyers would add greatly to her target for the month. Since Emma had the money and credit cards Gary had to let her take care of the booking but he stood very close to ensure she got his name right this time. He did not want another run in with airport security or the police just because his name was misspelt. As it was an internal flight across the states, buying the ticket was surprisingly easy and accomplished with the minimum of fuss. Having noted Emma's Professor Title on her card the clerk even bumped them up into club class free of charge. She told them the flight was very under booked and wished them a pleasant flight. They had just over an hour before the flight checked in so they made their way through the security gate and having been searched without incident went to the airside food retail area. As they sat drinking coffee and eating doughnuts, Emma began to smile. 'What's funny' Gary asked. 'Oh, I've always wondered what it would be like to be on the run and now I know. It's really quite exciting.' Gary joined in the upbeat mood, carefully looking around as if he were watching out for the police' He put his hand into his jacket and using a fake Middle Eastern accent, declared his intention to hijack the plane. Emma laughed out loud and looked over at Gary in a slightly different light. She had never actually disliked him and initially had just used him for her own devices, but somehow over the last few days he had become more important to her. Was it his humour, his simplistic way of looking at and dealing with problems, or maybe just because the world may be coming to end, she just didn't know. From their seats they could see through the glass to the arrivals lounge and security area. For different reasons both of them were drawn to one passenger in particular who stood out from the crowd. Emma was admiring him for his good looks and sweep of blonde hair. Gary was also watching him but not because of his obvious physical appearance but because instead of succumbing to the pat down at the screening gate, he discretely produced an official looking ID badge and with a deferential nod was waved through. He walked towards them on the other side of the glass, passing within a few feet of them as he made his way to the exit. For a split second he made eye contact with Gary but it was too short to tell if it was deliberate or just casual. 'Wow' said Emma 'Shit' said Gary 'I think the fictitious FBI blonde date for Mike has just shown up' 'What?' said a confused Emma 'are you sure, but how?' Not only did she not understand, she really did not want that blonde hunk to be the same gay hunk of Mike's past and Gary's email. 'I have no idea how or what he is actually doing here. I certainly didn't summon him up like a demon, but whatever the reason it can't be good news for us.' They quickly finished their coffee and made their way to the gate number displayed on the information screen. Gary was now on edge as he imagined his plan unravelling and himself soon to be face down on the airport floor being handcuffed yet again. Emma told him to relax as they got to the gate and joined the small queue for the redeye overnight flight to Chicago. As the queue moved shuffled forward towards the final gate, Gary was aware of two men behind them who were stood uncomfortable close, certainly closer than his British upbringing was used to. Resigned to the inevitable and wanting to minimise the pain he immediately put his case down, dropped to his knees and put his hands behind his head. 'No need for any rough stuff guys, I am being compliant' Emma, the two men

and nearly everyone else in the queue looked curiously down at Gary

as if he were quite mad, which of course by some people's standards

he was. The two men just walked straight by and hearing Gary's

statement made the common American mistake 'must be Australian'

one said in casual explanation before they presented their boarding

passes to the checking gate staff and moved on. Gary realised his

mistake and quickly stood up, trying to make it look like it was a

deliberate joke, but it was obvious to Emma that he had been a little

jumpy and completely misread the situation, or lack of one. Emma

slowly shook her head at him before turning back and leading them

both to the desk. 'He's a nervous flyer' she offered to the checking

staff by way of an excuse for his behaviour. They were not totally

convinced but after a few words of silent mouthed apology from

Gary, and that they liked Emma's very British accent they allowed

him to board. It wasn't lost on Gary that talking in a posh British

accent could, if needed, defeat the last security barrier to boarding a

US aircraft, hopefully something not known to any terrorist

organisation. The flight was undersubscribed being only about half

full, so finding their seats and getting a drink from the stewardess was easy. Emma cautioned Gary against drinking too much but not knowing what the next twenty fours would bring he wanted to induce an alcohol fuelled sleep for the night flight. They were fed and watered before the stewardess optimistically settled the passengers, cabin and lighting for the eight hour flight across the night sky. Gary found a pillows and a blankets in the overhead locker and gave one set to Emma. With the cabin lights now dimmed they both settled down to try and get some sleep. Gary had some mellow jazz music playing through the headphones and had just closed his eyes when he was aware that Emma's pillow was now on his shoulder and she was leaning across the arm rest resting against him. He couldn't tell if it was deliberate or that she was just making herself comfortable in her half sleep. He looked down at her for some clue but she gave none. He breathed deeply before enjoying the bodily contact and once again closed his eyes. Emma had felt the need to touch something or someone for comfort, like her teddy bear when she was child or her dad when she was frightened. She had neither, so that someone tonight would be Gary, at least for the flight. Her last thought before she fell asleep was how comfortable she felt with Gary and somehow a bit safer. Gary snored. After the stresses of the last weeks, and now in a relatively safe environment, they both managed a good few hours' sleep. Emma awoke to find she had moved even closer to Gary whilst she had been sleeping and had even curled her arm around his under the blanket. Gary had woken fifteen minutes earlier but finding himself entwined with Emma had not dared to move for fear of waking her. She awkwardly removed her arm and sat upright, stretching and moving her head from side to side. 'Sorry about that Gary, I hope I didn't disturb your sleep' 'No' he replied 'The drinks knocked me out and I really didn't notice until you moved just then' he lied to save any embarrassment. Emma found herself a little miffed with Gary's comment. Even if it had been a comfort cuddle, it should still have been important. Why she had thought that it mattered she really didn't know, or more likely she deliberately hid the real reason from herself. The lights in the cabin were slowly turned up as passengers began to stir from their slumber, as the crew started servicing their needs. The cabin crew efficiently served everyone breakfast with Gary asking for, and getting a second portion. He tried rationalising having two breakfasts by saying he did not know when they would next be able to eat. Emma countered his rationale by pointing out they were flying into mainland America, where the streets were paved with fast food joints, all you can eat meat restaurants and the most greasiest of spoon diners. The remainder of the flight passed comfortable before the crew secured the cabin for landing. The pilot made the usual arrival weather announcements but Gary was caught off guard when he announced that Chicago time was four hours different, so they would be landing at five a.m. local time. Gary had not taken that into consideration when planning their great escape and now looked pensive. 'Something bothering you Gary?' asked Emma 'Oh just arriving here at five in the morning will make our next bit of the journey a bit more difficult' She looked at him 'Oh, so you have not got the next already planned, no waiting helicopter, no limousine? She teased. 'No' he said flatly whilst still trying to fill in the gaps of his plan. Absent mindedly his eyes roved across the seat in front of him and he saw sticking out a magazine showing an advertisement for visiting the Grand Canyon in a mobile camper van. 'A campervan' he said out loud 'sorry?' Emma replied. Gary spoke confidently 'We will hire a campervan and drive down to Lake Michigan, then we will have both transport and somewhere discreet to sleep in case they are looking for us'. He spoke as if it had been his plan all along. The more he thought about it and the more he spoke about it, the more sense it made. Emma was not totally convinced but since his escape and evasion plan had worked so far she decided she had little choice but to go along with it, and really what alternative did she have. Whilst Gary and Emma were discussing their next move, back in Hawaii events were going to take a turn in their favour. Mike was in the middle of a heated argument with the camp gay desk clerk at the Holiday Out Express. Not only was he being outgayed, the clerk would not tell him Steve's room number or even tell him if he had checked in as a guest. Getting nowhere fast and having exhausted his gay credentials, Mike decided to call Steve on his mobile phone and get him to come down to the lobby. The phone rang twice before Steve answered. They exchanged greetings and then Mike explained that he was waiting down in the lobby but that the reception clerk would not release his room number 'Well, that's because one, I am still on my way from the airport in a cab and two I am booked into the Marrott Hotel down on the beach' said Steve. Mike was confused but with his prey nearly within grabbing distance he decided to leave the questions till later. 'Okay then, I will see you in the lobby at the

Marrott instead 'said Mike, before giving the clerk a hard stare he hard leant from Paddington Bear books as a child before flouncing out of the hotel. Mike drove to the Marrot Hotel, which he knew well as its bar was a favourite gay haunt amongst his friends. He parked in the car park and then took a seat in the lobby where he could see taxi's arriving outside the main door. The third taxi that stopped caused the doorman to leap forward, casually saluting as he opened the door. Out stepped Steve, who quickly paid the cab driver and strode into the lobby as if he owned it. Getting halfway across the lobby he saw Mike and altered course to greet him. Aware of being in the public eye, Steve extended a hand for a formal handshake, and hello. Mike couldn't quite match Steve's restraint and warmly used both hands to grab his hand. 'Great to see you again Steve' said Mike. 'And you too Mike 'replied Steve, before physically taking his hand from Mike's grip. 'Let me quickly go check in, then we can catch up, okay? 'Okay' said Mike. Steve walked briskly up to the checking desk and quickly completed the formalities. With his key in his hand he motioned for Mike to follow and they made across the lobby to the elevator and pushed the call button. Once alone in the lift Steve spoke first. 'So tell me Mike, how did you know I was arriving?' 'Well the email you sent me of course, did you forget?' Steve looked confused 'No, I have not sent you an email. In fact as you mentioned in your email it was a matter of national security only my boss knew I was flying out. I was going to ring you when I arrived to arrange a discreet meeting'. The conversation was brought to a halt as another passenger joined them at the third floor. On the fifth floor they disembarked and looking at the room signs made their way along the corridor to room 501. Once inside the macho façade was dropped and he gave Mike a quick hug. 'Now, I need to freshen up with a shower Mikey, so whilst I get out of these things, you get into these things.' Mike was a little confused but saw that Steve had produced a set of handcuffs from his belt loop and threw them on the bed. The pizza mission now forgotten, Mike's legs turned to jelly as he realised they were going to pick up their relationship exactly where they had left it last year. He picked up the handcuffs and tried them on for size.

At 35,000 feet over America, Gary and Emma were discussing the next phase of their journey. Gary was convinced that either the Dean, Mike, the FBI or any number of governments would be looking for them. His sole focus was on getting them to Lake

Michigan without being caught, after that it was all down to Emma. 'If I can get you there without us getting captured by the feds, will you be able to do anything to save the planet? Gary asked Emma. She drank her coffee before answering 'This thing, whatever it is, has never happened before in the history of mankind. I know, in fact you know just about as much as anybody does about what this event is. We could get there and find a hole in the ground or arrive in time to see the end of the world close up. But, since I already have all the scientific data available, the only thing left is to observe and record it first-hand. Does that answer your question?' It was more of an answer than Gary had wanted 'I was hoping for a simple yes from you. I get you there, you save the planet and we all go home for tea and medals' 'Sorry Gary, no promises on this.' After a few seconds thought Gary spoke again but with a slightly embarrassed tone in his voice 'have you given any thought to the idea that this might be an alien invasion of some sort?' Emma smiled 'Gary, you really have been watching far too many science fiction films. Everything we do know points to a ninety nine percent chance this a natural phenomenon, just one we have not witnessed or recorded before' 'and the one percent?' he asked. 'Well, that one percent is the X factor Gary. Could it be aliens, gods or beings from another dimension riding unicorns across space, who can say? But, the odds are very much stacked in favour of a natural event of some sort. '

Gary was not comforted by her choice of reply and wildcard additions, as none of them would allow him to be the one to break the story. It was selfish but he rationalised that if you couldn't be selfish in your last days on earth, when could you?'

Mike and Steve had completed their second bout of sweaty naked man wrestling. It had been an energetic and fun packed session, helped along by a large bottle of white wine and a small bottle of amyl nitrate 'poppers'. For differing reasons they had both had tiring days, and now topped off with an emotional reunion, a heavy drug and alcoholic sexual workout, sleep came to them both quickly. In Chicago Gary and Emma had landed and had cleared security. Gary was still a little paranoid and could not relax until they were out of the terminal and heading towards the row of hire car offices. They passed two offices before coming to one that had signage indicating they had all manner of vehicles for hire, including RV vehicles, or as Gary called them campervans. Gary had given the international game of hide and seek they were involved in a lot more thought on the flight. He had convinced Emma that an English couple hiring an RV vehicle in the early morning would attract attention and be memorable to someone. So, his plan was for her to keep quiet and for him to use his much requested at parties 'American accent' to hire the vehicle. Emma was not totally convinced but in the absence of an alternative she acquiesced and let him run with it. They entered the office and found the clerk looking absently through his screen at something on the internet. It could have been anything but the speed at which he closed the window hinted at something far more interesting. As Gary spoke Emma could not believe what she was hearing. In an accent that no American had used ever, she heard Gary speak. 'Gud mornin yawl. Do you kindly have an RV campervan motor home you could rent us for a week or so? Me and the kinfolk is heading out west and be wanting sum good old wheels'. The bleary eyed clerk was confused enough at this time of the morning, without some crazy trying to pull his chain. He looked unsmilingly at Gary. 'And just what part of Australia you from sir?' Gary was taken aback, hurt and almost angry that his American impression had not even got them past the hello stage. He struck a pose but before he could speak Emma jumped in 'Don't pay any attention to him, that's just his little joke. He does it all the time'.

The clerk smiled 'No problem mam, we see some strange things in

here but nothing recently so strange as that accent he just pulled'

Emma and the clerk laughed together whilst Gary pouted. 'What can

I do for yall on this bright and early morning?' 'We would like to

rent a reasonable sized, two berth, all singing and dancing RV

vehicle for one week please' said Emma. 'I like a gal who knows

her mind' replied the clerk. Turning some pages of a brochure on

his desk he showed them a range of vehicles but added that if they

wanted it right now he only had two available. The first one was a

giant Winnebago that would sleep ten, and the other a four berth that

included a shower, TV and a kitchen area. Emma opted for the

smaller vehicle and showed Gary the picture, but he was still a little

hurt, so just grumpily grunted in acknowledgment. Emma started

completing the paperwork and payment whilst the clerk called one

of his team on the radio. It took him several minutes to raise his

counterpart on the radio, who from his eventual reply had no doubt

asleep somewhere, probably the motorhome. He eventually

answered the call and confirmed the vehicle was ready for use. The

clerk gave them instruction on where they could meet him and collect the RV in another part of the airport, before copying Gary's accent and saying 'and have a safe trip yall'. Emma said 'thanks' and Gary replied with a grumpy 'yeah whatever'. He was so miffed that he wished he had told the clerk about his impending doom and in fact if Emma had not been with him would have done so. At the passenger drop off and pick up point they found the RV and delivery driver. He gave them a brief tour of the inside, not because he was particularly interested but because he believed in working for his tips. He was sorely disappointed in the British in general and Gary in particular when his outstretched hand merely collected a sweaty handshake. With the steering wheel on the wrong side for driving in any civilised country, Gary mistakenly got into the front on the right side, thereby allowing Emma to assume the driving seat. He was not overly concerned as he considered they would probably share the driving, but Emma's terror drive of last week had been put to the back of his mind. It was firmly brought back to the front of his mind as she hit the gas and launched the large RV away from the kerbside. Amidst dust, squealing tyres and shouted curses from people she barely missed, the motorhome quickly accelerated. Gary hung on to the strap over the door as Emma rounded the first bend at nearly fifty miles an hour, whilst they were still in the car parking area of the airport. Seeing they were approaching an exit toll booth he braced for impact, but somehow Emma screeched the vehicle to a halt just in time and started searching for cash to give to the shocked booth attendant. She threw a generous handful of money at him and after realising he was up on the deal he quickly lifted the barrier. As they drove another fifty meters before Gary spoke calmly 'prof, just pull over there a second would you please? Emma complied and waited whilst Gary got out of the vehicle and walked around to her door. Once opened he began pushing her over and yelling 'If you think I am going through several hundred white knuckle miles with you at the wheel you had better think again. Move over crazy professor!' Emma complied, again liking the strong Gary type when it reared its head. With Gary at the wheel and Emma reading the map the clerk provided, they eventually found the interstate they needed towards Lake Michigan and began what might be their final journey. Back in the Hawaiian hotel, it was Steve who awoke first just before seven a.m. He looked around the room at the empty wine bottles, the strewn clothes and the small bottle of poppers on the bedside cabinet. He smiled when saw Mike still sleeping on top of the duvet and recalled the evening of cuffing and grunting of the previous evening. Trying not to disturb his sleeping lover, he quietly got up and closing the door behind him went into the bathroom. The light noise of the rushing water through the shower behind the door was enough to slowly rouse Mike from his deep and satisfying sleep. His first moments awake were a little confusing, but when he moved his hand and saw he was still wearing one handcuff he smiled as the events of last night also came flooding back to him. Steve opened the door wrapped in a towel, with another he was rubbing his hair. They smiled at each other and made the slightly awkward morning afterwards conversation. Steve was convinced the Mike's security fears were just a ploy to get him back on the Island, so suggested they had breakfast and discussed whatever it was that Mike was concerned about. 'Yes' said Mike to the idea before thinking *'breakfast, food, pizza.* 'PIZZA, O MY GOD!' he said out loud. 'What is it?' asked Steve. Mike tried to explain but was getting flustered 'Dean Groombridge, Emma, Gary, the end of the world, Pizza' 'Whoa, slow down there tiger' said Steve 'take it slow' Taking a breath and getting his thoughts in some sort of order Mike continued 'I was supposed to be downtown collecting pizza for the drunken Dean but used it as an excuse to meet you, and you know how that ended up!. The Dean, Emma and Gary will all be wondering where I am and the end of the world is approaching, get it?' Steve scratched his head, worried that Mike was losing the plot. He started to ask a question but Mike cut him off. 'No time. Get dressed and I will fill you in on the details on the drive back up the mountain' Mike started searching for his clothes which were strewn crazily all over the room. He managed to gather enough clothing together to dress himself, albeit that he could only find one sock, the other he vaguely remember having been used as a gag during the rough and tumble the night before. Ordering and cajoling Steve into moving quickly, he ushered him out of the room and down to where his car was parked. Driving as fast as his limited ability and current mind state would allow, Mike took the forty minute drive to tell Steve exactly what was, what is and what had been going on. Steve now switched into formal FBI mode and started to process the overload of information he had just been given. He had learnt nothing in FBI school or from life's many experiences of what to do when the end of the world is announced to you. Once he had questioned Mike enough to accept it was definitely not a joke, then that left the possibility that either Mike was quite mad or that this world ending thing was possibly happening. He thought he would accept it on face value but not act on it until he had spoken to the Dean, Gary and Emma, who might clarify the situation that Mike was babbling about. Steve did have enough experience not to go crying wolf about something that your government does not know about until you have all the facts. A thing like this could get a man fired or at least stifle a career if mishandled. He decided to wait until they arrived back at the telescope facility, then perhaps this Dean, Emma and Gary, whoever the hell they were, could add some information that might help him decide on a course of action. The FBI were in the game but Steve would decide what part, if any, they played. Gary drove for just over an hour and then decided to stop for some breakfast and to find Wi-Fi for Emma to connect to her computers. The typical American roadside diner had all the hallmarks of a greasy spoon, complete with some real grease on the spoons. But, the sign proudly announced free Wi-Fi, so they stopped for a while and used the facilities. Gary ordered what the yanks call a breakfast muffin, which was like a complete greasy breakfast in a stale bread bun. Emma could not be tempted into eating as the place was so dirty, so she settled for a coffee but she insisted on pouring it into one of the mugs she fetched from the RV. No matter what the situation Emma was always surprised at Gary's ability to eat, day or night. 'Anything new?' his full mouth mumbled, as grease ran down his fingers and ketchup ran down his shirt. 'Well nothing new as such, but further confirmation that it is still heading this way and it is still slowing down. The Wi-Fi is too slow here to download the updated graphic but the numbers speak for themselves' She turned the laptop towards him to show him the figures. It looked like exactly what it was, a mass of numbers and maths that made no sense to Gary, so he just nodded sagely. 'Doesn't slowing down imply that it is under some sort of control? He asked, wiping his greasy fingers on a non-absorbent cheap paper napkin, which just spread the mess around his hand. 'Well as we discussed before Gary, that is a frankly a remote option that at the moment I am not considering. As a scientist I prefer to look at all the available data, discard the unlikely and discover the scientific answer, rather than just guessing or fantasising about aliens. There could be a thousand reason why the thing is slowing down' Gary looked at her 'but, one of those reasons is that it could be aliens, could it not? She shook her head in frustration 'yes, if it suits your childlike and Hollywood induced view of the universe Gary, then it could be aliens. Happy now?' He chomped away the last of the muffin before wiping his greasy mouth with the back of his greasier hand. 'Yes' he replied through a mouthful of food, 'aliens are much easier to write about than the weather, mathematics or scientific formulas' Much too tired to correct his grammar or discuss aliens yet again, Emma rolled her eyes and went back to looking at her numbers for inspiration. Mike stopped the car dramatically at the accommodation block entrance before running towards the computer room with Steve close behind. Not sure what reception he would get, Mike's mind was still working on delivering his excuses when his eyes saw the figure laying on the floor. He was horrified to see Dean Groombridge face down on the floor, hog tied and apparently not moving. Mike gasped a gay learnt behaviour gasp, putting one hand over his mouth in mock shock as he froze to the spot. However, Steve's training kicked in and quickly knelt down by the Dean and started looking for a pulse. Even before he found a pulse, the Dean's booze filled breath told him he was still alive and still very drunk. 'How long as he been like this?' asked Steve. 'Well, he was already drunk when I left to collect the pizza and that was ten pm last night' replied Mike. Steve nodded 'help me get him up'. With some help from Mike they got the Dean into a sitting position propped against the desk. The Dean briefly battled to open his eyes and tried to focus but having lost that battle he quickly closed them again. 'What the hell happened?' he croaked. Steve answered him 'well it looks like you have had a helluva night and got tied up' 'Didn't we all' said Mike, glancing cheekily at Steve, who shook his head disapprovingly. Admonished by Steve and remembering what he should be doing, Mike said 'I'll leave you to look after Dean Groombridge whilst I find Emma and Gary. Once I have broken the news about you being FBI, then you can talk to them, okay?' Steve nodded 'okay but don't be long, I will have to ring the office and bring my boss up to speed. Mike padded off to the apartment block, calling Emma & Gary's names as he went. He checked all three apartments that they had been using and then the pool area, but without success. Starting to panic, he then ran up the steps to the telescope at the top of the hill. The door was open which gave him hope, but a quick look around showed that no one was there either. Now he really was in a panic and ran back down to the apartments. Hardly daring to look, he opened the wardrobe doors in Emma's bedroom and this time really gasped as he saw the empty row of clothes hangers. He opened the drawers and saw they were also empty before running to where Gary had been staying and doing the same. Everything was gone, either they had left him or had been taken. When he returned to Steve had untied the Dean and helped him onto a chair. The Dean was rubbing his head, eyes and anything else his stubby fingers could reach. 'They have gone!' Mike said. The Dean and Steve both looked confused before Steve asked 'Gone, are you sure?' 'Yes' replied Mike, their clothes, suitcases all gone' 'and what about their toiletries' asked Steve. 'And just what difference would that make?' slurred the Dean. 'It means' replied Steve getting into FBI mode, 'that they left here voluntarily and have not been abducted. Terrorists, Mexican cartels and your average kidnappers tend not to pack perfume or shower gel when taking hostages. No, they left here because they wanted to.' The Dean's banging hangover was momentarily eclipsed by the knowledge that he had been well and truly done over in more ways than one. He tried to stand but it proved difficult and unlikely to succeed so he sat down again. Steve spoke to Mike 'you stay here and look after this guy whilst I go and phone my office.

We need to get after them pronto' Steve left the room and recovered his cell phone from the car. The Dean asked Mike 'who is that man?' and Mike replied 'oh just a friend', before adding 'from the FBI' 'What!' shouted the Dean 'The FBI here!' This news only added to the Dean's misery and did somewhat put his hangover into perspective. He had travelled all this way to contain and control the professor and the information that everyone needed, but now she had gotten away and was soon to be hunted by the FBI. All his immediate planning and personal wealth were tied up in having her and her information to hand when the foreign government agencies wanted it. His plan was to sell the information to the highest bidder, not to have it scooped up by the Americans just because the professor just happened to be in the United States at the wrong time. He fumbled in his pocket for his mobile phone. Whilst the Dean felt sorry for himself and tried to plan some sort of recovery, Mike noticed the pill bottle on the desk and picked it up. He recognised it was from his own cabinet and in horror remembered what it contained. He put and two together and came up with the answer ketamine. Either the Dean had willingly taken a horse tranquiliser or been given some and that is why he had slept for long. Mike could not envisage the Dean rifling through his cabinets for drugs, let along taking them, so how could? He stopped in mid thought at the only feasible explanation, '*Gary had done this!*' The reason Gary would have drugged the Dean would have to wait, he was only happy that the drugs had not killed the Dean, which he put down to his great bulk. What he could not have known was that the Dean had not always led such a sheltered life and his previous recreational drug use had left him with a little immunity to such things. Not wishing to complicate matters or explain why he illicitly had them, Mike quickly slipped the drug bottle into his pocket. Steve came back into the room. Whilst not entirely believing all he had been told so far, find the Dean all trussed up added some credence to Mike's story but also some mystique of its own. He looked at Mike. 'Well there is no way of telling how much of a start they have other than working backwards from the time you left here last night' They mutely both knew that their late night sexual antics and sleep would have added to the time available for Gary and Emma to get away, but apart from a knowing glance it was not mentioned out loud. Steve had one immediate question that he aimed at both Mike and the Dean 'So, do either of you have any idea why they would run away, especially since if your story is right they might hold the key to solving this problem?' The Dean simply lied 'no' but Mike was a little more honest. 'We have had our little differences about how, when and who to tell the news to. The Dean here wanted the university to control it. I thought the US Government should have first call, but Emma had a different view and wanted to gather together an international council of moral thinkers to discuss the whole issue. I guess either Gary agreed or has his own agenda, so thinking they could not trust either of us, have run away'. In that brief sentence Mike had clearly set out the cause and effect of both his and the Dean's involvement. Steve thought for a moment and asked 'So where could they be heading to? Mike pursed his lips thoughtfully and ventured a guess 'Well it could be either her London office where she can gather more data or the area of impact around Lake Michigan' 'Why on earth would she go there? Asked the Dean grumpily. 'Because if she is right and there is nothing more that can be done, then the last thing a scientist would want is a scientific observation of the phenomenon' offered Mike. The Dean shook his head and angrily spat out the words 'No, there will be another reason, and that reason will be that reporter, Gary fucking

Barnes!'

CHAPTER FIFTEEN: ARE WE THERE YET?

Still millions of miles away in space, the entity was now preparing for the final phase of its long journey. Its markers or precursors that it had sent ahead were now sending ever more detailed information back about the planet. These miniscule and much smaller parts of itself had been detached long ago and went ahead of the main body to scout and inform. They had reached the Earth and having sampled various elements of the atmosphere and makeup, had then found a suitable place for the main intelligence to settle on the surface. The being gave itself the briefest of thoughts about slowing down, which had a dramatic and immediate effect on its speed. It had no measurement in miles per hour to consider, or light years to worry about, just an intuitive knowing of how fast it should be moving for any given situation. The markers sent an image of an area that contained an open body of water, which was considered a suitable and discreet arrival point. The entity could survive in any atmosphere or medium, but a flash of consideration instantly caused it to move the landing away from the water as it would want to examine the surface of the planet first. Some millions of minute particles crossed a path to other minute particles and that not simple act made the thought complete. It would land on the planet near to where it had landed before, but this time use the surface. Although the number meant nothing to it, in earth time it would arrive there in twelve hours. The thought or best described of as more of a feeling intuitively made it slow further and also draw itself into a longer and a sleeker shape. This would allow it to arrange its constituent parts into the correct order upon impact and be able to function immediately as a whole. Now stretched out thinner over many thousands of earth measured miles, the entity prepared itself to land. It did not know, need to know or really care that its chosen landing site had been named by the inhabitants. The indigenous Indian people who first lived there called it Menominee, but modern settled Americans now called it Rothbury.

CHAPTER SIXTEEN: GOD'S ARRIVAL?

The newly christened by the Dean, Gary 'fucking' Barnes, was now sat with Emma overlooking Lake Michigan. They were both unaware that right at that moment, back in Hawaii the starting gun had just fired, signalling the start of the hunt for the two of them. Other than when he had been eating, Gary had been paranoid about being followed and had constantly checked his wing mirrors since they left the airport. But now they were parked in a car park with a wonderful view of Lake Michigan reaching out as far as they could see. 'I didn't think it was this big' said Gary. Thinking back to his childhood and the local boating lake he said 'the name lake implied a smaller pond of water than this' Emma nodded 'I know what you mean. Looking at the map it seems to drive around the outside would be about an eight hundred miles round trip'. 'So then' said Gary starting the engine 'where are we headed, or just tell which way around the lake are we going, clockwise or anti clockwise? Emma looked down at her laptop for inspiration. She ran one of the computer simulations that she had just added the data to from last night. Overall it looked the same with the cloud mass moving outwards from a central point over the lake, but then for clarity she changed the resolution. Using the plus key she scrolled in and was surprised to see the centre point move away from the lake and onshore as she zoomed in. With that small scroll of the keyboard she had managed to narrow down the bulls' eye to a point on the eastern side of the lake. 'Voila' she said proudly 'anti clockwise Gary, we are heading for a place called Rothbury, about two hundred miles away'. 'Aye aye captain' replied Gary as he swung the RV out onto the main road. Back in Hawaii Steve's mobile phone rang and he answered it to the head of the FBI office where he worked. From the much one sided conversation it was clear that the head had a series of short questions and long instructions for Steve. Once the call had ended Steve held the phone in his hand and thought hard about the conversation he had just had. Both the Dean and Mike waited for news but the wait became too much for the Dean who blurted out 'well, what is happening?' Steve slipped his phone back onto his belt hook and looked at the two before speaking in short clipped sentences. 'Right. This has now gone Federal, right to the top. They are not as yet totally convinced by me that the end of the world is nigh, but then again neither am I as yet. But neither are they prepared to take that chance, so, my neck is firmly on the line and a national manhunt is has been a lunched. It has been declared a matter of national security. National assets have been mobilised and the pair will be tracked down. Local law enforcement officers are on their way to look after the Dean and then local FBI officers will debrief him for further information. He paused. 'And what about me?' asked Mike. 'As you know them better than anyone else, you are coming with me' Mike looked surprised 'with you, but where?' Mike stood up 'Chicago, so quickly go pack a bag' The Dean stood up 'Chicago! Not without me you're not!' he said in an authoritative way that he assumed would somehow keep him in the loop. He would be proven wrong. With national resources in place, it did not take the FBI long to find that Emma and Gary had boarded a flight to Chicago airport the previous night. At Chicago airport records were checked, CCTV was examined and their path tracked through the airport concourse to where car hire offices were located next to each other. Local FBI officers went to all three rental offices one after the other, but drew a blank because the bleary eyed clerk of the night before was now at home asleep and the day office worker was completely incompetent. Having got nowhere, they regrouped in the office and re-examined the information they had. Their coffee and joke telling session in the office was rudely interrupted by their boss, who having taking some heat from above now handed it out in person to his men. Left in no doubt not to return without information the three young FBI officers went back onto the airport concourse to continue the investigation. Other than the grief from their boss they did not know just how important their work was today, hence their previous lack of enthusiasm, but they now had a wasp up their asses and needed results. There was no doubt the couple had made it to the car hire offices but then the trail went cold. They went back to the rental offices but with their boss's words still ringing in their ears, this time insisted on speaking to the night duty clerks right now! Despite being annoyed at being rudely woken from his sleep, one clerk perked up at the mention of the FBI and got his head together. Yes, he clearly remembered the two Brits and gave the officers, confirmed their descriptions and details of where the RV details could be found in the office. Now with something to tell their boss they felt smug enough to return to the office and report what they had found, although each of them tried to take the most credit. What had been a small rocket up the ass and a lesson in being persistent had added about an hour to the investigation, but to Emma and Gary this hours grace meant they were another fifty miles closer to their destination. Steve and Mike left the protesting Dean in the hands of the local police who had arrived when commanded to by the FBI. Having shown his ID, Steve whispered a few words of instruction to the local officers who then turned their attention to the Dean. He told them he did not need any assistance and just needed to pack his bag for the journey to Chicago. They in turn told him he was being taken into protective custody and would be going into town with them for his own safety. At this unwelcome news the Dean turned a bright red colour and raised first his voice and then his finger in protest. This perceived aggressive act was all the officers needed to spin the Dean around and onto the ground where he was handcuffed, all the while shouting their well-used justification for roughly handcuffing any suspect 'stop resisting'. This was widely but unofficially taught at sheriff schools across the country, as it not only provided the justification needed for violence but also covered up any of the suspects own protestations that they were in fact complying. With the wait of the two officers on his back and firmly cuffed the Dean could do little but moan and complain about the weight of the two men on his back. They assisted him to his feet and walked him out of the building to their police car. It was unfortunate timing in that Steve and Mike were also in the courtyard loading their cases into Mike's car and the three of them momentarily came face to face. The Dean's face contorted and spittle came from his mouth as he shouted at them 'you haven't heard the end of this!' as he was pushed into the back seat of the police cruiser. He was still yelling at them as the car pulled away and headed down the mountain road. Emma used the provided RV tourist map to keep them off the main dual carriageway roads but still heading towards Rothbury along the quieter scenic route. It would have been a great way to spend the time if it weren't for the great unknown being visited upon them in the next few hours. She looked out across the lake and took in the view. It was mostly a sunny day with just a few clouds moving quicker than they should do over the lake. Having enjoyed the changing shapes for a minute she realised that the clouds were actually following a pattern and rotating around a point somewhere in the distance. When Gary stopped at some traffic lights she showed him first her laptop screen and then pointed out where the clouds were rotating somewhere on the horizon. Instead of the normal jumble of figures and graphs she had previously tried to explain with, the laptop image combined with the real clouds ahead provided a clear picture of what was happening, allowing even Gary to grasp Emma's point. 'Wow' said Gary as the penny dropped. 'So, you are thinking that the computer model and cloud formation are pointing us towards the actual impact point?' asked Gary. 'That is how it is looking Gary. All that science, maths and technology and now we are being led by some swirling clouds' she replied. 'Like the bible story where they followed the star to Bethlehem?' asked Gary, surprising them both with the religious reference. 'Where did that come from?' said Emma 'Not sure' replied Gary 'perhaps it is this three day beard growth making me look like Jesus, or maybe it may have come from a primary school nativity play, where for some obscure reasons I was playing the bongo drums in the stable' They both laughed at the ridiculous and unrelated image, but Gary stopped laughing first at the ancient memory. Not only had he enjoyed playing the bongos that year, it had led him to a lifetime of playing drums badly and a trail of annoyed neighbours. He shook his head to clear the image and forget the unpleasant memories. They had been driving in the general direction of the cloud mass for nearly three hours when Gary declared he was hungry yet again. He convinced Emma into stopping with the bolt on promise of more

Wi-Fi for data and stocking up with some food for the trip. They pulled off the road onto a dusty forecourt which housed a combination petrol station, shop and diner. Whilst Gary refuelled the vehicle Emma went to pay in the fuel station shop. Having topped up the fuel Gary signalled to her he had finished, and then drove the RV around the back of the diner in case it was spotted. No sooner had the back end rounded the corner than a police cruiser pulled into the forecourt and parked near the door, before the single officer went inside where Emma was. She was third in the queue and was so engrossed in her own thoughts she had not seen the police car drive up, so was surprised when the police officer walked passed her straight to the front of the queue. He tipped his hat and apologised to the Emma and the others as he queue jumped 'scuse me folks, official police business' as he approached the till and clerk. 'Have you seen a small Bailey's RV come through here, driven by a British couple?' he asked 'No sir, nothing since I been on duty here since nine this morning' replied the clerk. 'Okay thanks' the officer replied 'but if you see 'em then ring 911 immediately, got that?' The clerk nodded 'got it but are they dangerous?' 'Yep' replied the deputy, 'damn near killed some college president with drugs and been acting suspicious at airports. Probably radicalised religious nuts, so keep your eyes peeled' 'Will do sir' replied the clerk. The deputy walked back down the queue and said to them all 'same for you folks too. You see a Baily's RV on the road then give us a ring and we will check it out' They all nodded in agreement, including Emma as the deputy tipped his hat again and left the building. Once in his car he turned left out of the petrol station thereby missing their RV parked behind the diner. Emma legs were shaking from the shot of adrenalin the police officers visit had caused. The other customers had now been served and she found herself stood in front of the till 'yes mam?' enquired the clerk. He waited but Emma froze 'mam? He tried again but still she could not speak. The clerk was confused but before he could ask again Emma heard her own voice in an American accent say 'hell yeah sorry man, fifty dollars of gas on pump six and give me some gum will ya?' She waited to be called out for the phony accent but the clerk merely took her money and said 'yes mam' He gave her the chewing gum and some change before adding 'yall have a nice day' before turning to the person in the queue behind her. She smiled and made herself walk slowly and calmly out of the door and around to where Gary was waiting. 'Strange accent?' said the person who had been stood behind her to the clerk 'yep, sure was' he replied 'she must have been from the East some a wheres' Gary was scratching at his unshaven face and rubbing his hands in anticipation at some more food, but was surprised when Emma hissed at him 'get in and get going' Recognising she was serious Gary quickly got the RV out onto the road and moving before asking her what the problem was. Emma recounted the story and how she had engineered their escape by pretending to be American and using an accent. Gary pursed his lips and was surprisingly quiet given their lucky escape. 'You okay?' she asked. 'Not really' he replied 'not only am I still hungry but somehow your American accent is somehow better than mine, I don't think so!' It was a strange outburst given their current circumstances, so strange Emma could not stifle a giggle that soon developed into a full blown laughing fit. Gary went from surprised, to annoyed, to joining in the laughter in three seconds. They both enjoyed the shared moment, although each of them had their own view on whose accent was better. Mike and Steve made it to the airport and were met by local FBI officers. As a measure of the importance placed on their getting to the mainland, senior FBI officials had arranged a private jet to get them back from Hawaii in the shortest possible time. Within thirty minutes of arriving at the airport their plane was rolling down the runway and heading towards the mainland USA. 'Well this is nice' said Mike 'I could certainly get used to this as the solo stewardess served them champagne and snacks. Steve replied 'don't get the wrong idea, I don't travel like this all the time'. They chinked glasses in a mock toast to absolutely nothing other than sharing the experience together. Mike spoke 'I am not complaining, but why did you insist I come with you?' 'Well it was not difficult to convince my boss that you were important to this investigation. Firstly, you know exactly what they look like and know them better than anyone else in the US. Secondly, when we do find them we will need some technical advice on whether they are telling us the full story or not, and that's where you will come in. Thirdly, well I haven't seen you for a while and forgotten how good you looked in handcuffs' Mike blushed a little and with the memory of last night running through his mind, his only response was yet another chinked toast, but this time for a reason. Emma used the map to take them onto a series of even smaller roads where there was less chance of them being spotted by regular police patrols.

They were still heading roughly in the right direction but the dusty rough road make progress slower than she would have liked. They came to a cross roads and saw a small mini market on the opposite corner. Gary was now claiming his hunger to be life threatening, despite having eaten a breakfast muffin and French fries earlier in the day. However, his argument that they should stock up on food and supplies to cook in the RV for a few days made sense and Emma acquiesced. It only remained to decide who was going to do the shopping. In the end it was decided they would both go but Emma would do the talking as much to Gary's disgust her yank accent had a proven track record. They bounced to a halt outside the shop and walking as casually as they could went inside. Taking a basket they moved up and down the two aisles, Emma carefully selecting food and drink items, whilst Gary gathered cakes, cokes and crisp based carbohydrates a frenzy. Emma wanted quality so shopped carefully but he wanted quantity, so stuffed the basket with everything in arms reach. With the basket overflowing they went to the till and found a brown skinned Asian man smiling and ready to serve. He greeted them in a north London accent with just a hint of the Punjab associated with his forebears. Gary was pleased to hear a familiar accent and was desperate to engage him in conversation, but a stern look from Emma stopped him. She kept her words to a minimum, just nodding and smiling as the shopping was totalled up and placed in those awkward to use brown American grocery bags. In his best mockney cockney, the clerk told Emma the amount. He himself was a little bit miffed as usually the yanks were curious as to his accent, but this couple had little to say and less to enquire about. Emma paid in cash and with a quick 'thank you sir' left to leave the store. In his time in America the Indian clerk had been called many things but sadly never 'sir', which served to make their visit more memorable than it should have been. This only added to his intrigue and cause him to give them more thought than he would have normally done. Back on the road Gary drove whilst eating crisps, or as the packet called them potato chips. He was happier now that he was eating and they good progress along the relatively deserted but poor maintained road. As it was now mid-afternoon Gary suggested they look for a place to camp overnight before it got dark. There were plenty of official campsite marked on the map but they both agreed to avoid them for fear of being found. Emma estimated they were about twenty miles south east of Rothbury, so were in easy driving distance when or if and wherever the event happened. Over to the right of the road she spotted a dirt track that headed towards a collection of low hills and told Gary to follow it. After fifteen minutes of bumping around they came out on top of the middle hill, about one hundred feet above the surrounding country side. Gary switched off the engine and they both enjoyed the sudden silence and the view spread out before them. Emma pointed to the cloud formation just a few miles ahead. It was not violent or striking in any way and a casual observer might have missed the subtle changes, but Emma could see the rotating mass was the eye of some event as yet to happen. Once it had been described to Gary he too could see how the denser clouds were rotating slowly and outwards from a central point but quicker than a cloud formation would normally move. Emma stretched her legs whilst Gary wound down various the various legs to stabilise and level the RV. In his best cowboy voice he told her to 'gather some kindling for the fire', which made him feel all rugged and outdoors but the humour was lost on Emma as she stumbled and cursed amongst the insect ridden logs. Gary thought the fire would be a nice to sit around when it got dark but didn't intend to cook on it, especially with the RV being so well appointed. He opened a pack of half pound burgers and began frying them on a pan in the RV kitchen, along with some onions for smell and flavour. Gary had learnt long ago that most food, and by that he meant hangover cure food, could be made better with the addition of fried onions. The smell wafted out of the extraction system and caught the nose of Emma, who dropped the wood by the fire pit and came up the steps into the RV. 'That smells surprisingly good' she said both annoying him and confirming his onion theory in one bold statement. 'I'll save you the recipe for another day' he replied 'if you look in the fridge that wine should be chilled by now, glasses are up there and plates under the sink.' Emma saluted 'sir, yes sir' and began collecting the items as ordered. Gary left the RV and began fumbling around in one of the side lockers before finding two large folding camping chairs, which he set overlooking the view. When he returned Emma had poured them both a glass of a Californian Chardonnay and passed him his glass. 'Well fellow partner in crime, here's looking at you' and they clinked their glasses. 'I am not sure we are partners in crimes 'said Gary 'Just runaways'. 'Well you did drug and rope the Dean, so let's call it being fugitives from the law, it sounds much more exciting' He nodded 'I suppose if this does end badly then at least we ended it on our terms and not working for the Government or Dean Groombridge' Emma put her hand to her face 'Dean Groombridge, I hope he is alright?' 'I am sure he is' Gary lied, the lie made all the more convincing by hiding his lips behind his glass and crossing his fingers behind his back. He turned and flipped the burgers once more before placing them on the buns and adding a slice of possessed cheese, his mild dyslexia missing the letter R and getting him wondering just how cheese could be possessed instead of processed. They took their plates and wine and went out to the comfortable camping chairs Gary had set out. They ate in silence for a minute, both enjoying the view, the food and without speaking each other's company. Emma was glad Gary was with her. She had slowly warmed to him over the last week as he provided a comfort not afforded by the scientists she normally worked with. He said what he thought, even if he didn't always think about what he said. He had also shown a thoughtful and caring side to his character when he had planned their running away together to save her from the authorities. This had come to a head on the flight, when in need of physical contact she had feigned sleep to be able to hold his arm and rest her head against him. Gary was having the man version of these thoughts 'Now can I get her drunk enough to sleep with me before the end of the world?' he mused in the way most men would do. He allowed his dick led man mind the freedom to explore the possibilities, and a smile slipped across his face as he imagined getting to second base with Emma under the open skies. His thoughts and the moment were shattered as he jumped at the touch of Emma's hand on his arm. 'You were smiling, what were you thinking about? She asked both in hope and curiosity. Caught unawares or at least caught at first base in his mind, Gary was embarrassed. 'Oh just admiring the view' he said which brought a frown to Emma's face, to which Gary added '…and the company' Emma smiled again and slid her hand down Gary's forearm and squeezed the top of his hand in what was even to Gary's thick skin a romantic gesture. He had been caught unawares thinking his sexual fantasies, so to go suddenly to actually holding her hand somehow did not sit well together. He made the excuse of needing to move his from her so as to pick up his glass and take a drink, but tried to offset the action by raising his glass. She copied him but with a confused and thoughtful look on her face. She had made a move and been rebuffed, albeit in a small way, but what did that mean. She went back to being quiet and looking at the view whilst she re-examined her feelings and Gary's clumsy ways. The rest of the dinner was punctuated with polite conversation, interspersed with talk of the events that might or might not happen sometime out there tonight. It was just getting dark and quiet, with only the crickets breaking the silence. American crickets have a posh name that Gary did not know, so they were just crickets. Gary took a gap in the conversation as an excuse to get some yoghurt type desserts from the RV fridge, but whilst inside and out of Emma's view lent on the sink to take stock of the unfolding situation. He opened another bottle of wine and poured himself a large glass before taking a gulp. Here he was possibly on his last day alive, alone with a pretty intelligent woman and he had recoiled from her touch because of, because of? He could find no answer other than maybe because it should have been himself making the moves and not Emma reaching out to him. She obviously needed contact, he obviously needed contact and tomorrow might be too late. He finished his wine in one swallow and refilled his glass. The decisive Gary from a few days ago was back and now ready for action. He was going straight back out there and was just going to lean over and kiss that Emma, 'you just see if I don't! He said out loud in self-affirmation. Whilst Gary spoke those courageous words, just a few thousand miles above his head the entity was ready. It had landed on countless planets over the millennia but each landing was always different. Depending on the chemical makeup of the planet it could shoot straight through a gas giant or destroy a frozen moon without even slowing down. The markers had sent back enough information for it to know what density of surface to expect and it also had a distant memory of what the planet had been like on its first visit. Now just a couple of thousand miles from reaching the landing place, it thought itself down to a modest speed of a few hundred miles an hour to reduce the impact on the planet and any life forms, if indeed there were any. The stewardess approached Steve and gave him the telephone that was patched into the aircraft's system radio systems. He listened more than talked, indicating it was his boss or if he had not been gay his wife. Finishing with a curt 'yes sir, will do' he turned the phone off and sat back in his chair. 'Trouble? 'Asked Mike. 'well it depends on your idea of trouble' Steve replied ' 'It seems that having passed on the information you gave me, NASA and the Air Force have been scanning the skies in the area you suggested. An hour ago they picked up an object travelling at thousands of miles an hour heading for earth in general, and Lake Michigan in particular.' Even though he had been part of the project Mike was still astounded that this was actually happening. It was the most exciting thing to happen in his scientific career but also possibly the last thing. He grabbed Steve's hand and squeezed. 'Are we still going there?' Mike asked. 'Yes' Steve replied 'headquarters wants us both there in case we find the professor or in case there is something that can be done to lessen the damage. The one good thing to come out of this is that had you not made the report, then the Air Force would have assumed it was a Russian attack and retaliated. As things stand the NASA findings were able to stop the Air Force reacting. You Mikey, might have saved the world today! 'Great, but for how long?' Mike replied. With his newly acquired mission in mind, Gary strode purposefully down the steps of the RV carrying his wine and the fresh bottle. He approached Emma from behind and leaning over to kiss her suddenly lost his confidence and swung away at the last minute. He changed his action to filling her glass. 'Thanks' she said distractedly. Inwardly cursing his lack of action, he swigged at his drink, took a deep breath and again bent over towards her. Time seem to stand still as he slowly approached her with his lips. He did not want to go crashing into her but also wanted her to have time to object if she wanted so that he could offer some feeble excuse. The approach was good but seemed interminable as he closed from the side. With nothing to stop him, his lips eventually landed on her right cheek. The both froze, she in shock and he in anticipation of being challenged or slapped. Nothing happened, but this time nothing happened in real time. They were frozen together, neither of them daring to move in case something changed or something was lost. Gary couldn't read the signs as there were not any being given out, as Emma sat in silence staring straight ahead. Gary undocked, and slowly moved back, withdrawing outside of Emma's personal space. He walked slowly around to his chair and sat down, watching Emma out of the corner of his eye. She still had not moved or spoken. Now starting to wonder if she was still alive after his display of passion, he looked directly across at her. Her mouth was slightly open and her eyes stared as she raised he hand and pointed to the sky. He followed her outstretched hand and looked into the darkened sky. He could still see the feint outline of the clouds as before but now they had formed in a swirling mass, with a clearly defined centre. Just as his eyes adjusted to the gloom and made sense of the image, his ears started to pick up a feint sound in addition to the natural ambience. The high pitched tearing noise was descending in pitch as it slowly increased in volume. It took a few moments for them both to recognise that it was an unearthly sound and the beginning of the event they had come to witness. Emma reached out and grabbed Gary's hand tightly and this time he did not move his but gripped her hand tighter. They were transfixed, staring wildly at the hole in the sky, without knowing what to expect, but anything less than death would be a bonus. The cloud lightened briefly as if a bright light was above it before an explosion of light appeared through the hole and in a flash reached down to the ground. Down poured a solid tube of iridescent light, accompanied by a loud roaring sound as the air was torn. The light was so bright they both used their other hands to shield their eyes, whilst still squeezing their held hand tighter together. The event lasted for thirty four seconds before briefly the tail of the light appeared in the cloud and disappeared down to the ground. The noise continued for a further fifteen seconds and then suddenly stopped as if a tap had been turned off. Without the light the landscape was instantly plunged back into darkness, exaggerated by their eyes readjusting to the lack of light. The lack of sound was also accentuated by the fact that the crickets had stopped chirping and there was no other ambient sound. After about twenty seconds Emma spoke 'Wow' she said. 'Fucking hell' said Gary 'and we're still alive, was that it? 'I have no idea Gary, I have never been to an end of the world event before' she quietly replied. Fascinated by the unique event they had just witnessed they continued to scan the horizon for any other connected event. As their eyes slowly adjusted to the darkness it was Gary who first spotted that there was a glow in the distance. It was hard to judge how far away it was but certainly seemed to be in the region of where the light had made contact with the surface. 'It is about three miles away' said Emma 'How can you be sure of that?' asked Gary. 'Because the sound continued for fifteen seconds after the light stopped and at sea level sound travels at a mile every five seconds, ergo, three miles' said Emma. 'Really Emma!' said Gary 'There we were waiting for the death and you had the thought to count the seconds off to calculate the distance?' he asked incredulously. 'It's the scientist in me' she offered apologetically. She was aware of some slight discomfort in the palm of her hand where Gary's nails were still biting into her palm. 'Can you ease up on the hand squeeze Gary, it is hurting me a little' 'Oh sorry about that' he said and tried to release his grip, but once the pressure eased she stopped him from taking his hand back completely. She looked across at him 'I couldn't have done this without you Gary' which made him a tad uncomfortable but then she added 'and thank you for the kiss' He gulped and looked back towards the light before speaking 'I didn't think you had noticed'. 'Oh yes, I noticed and then the whole world lit up' she said, trying to make a joke but making the discussion even more awkward than it already was. 'Right then' said Gary letting go of her hand to clap his hands together 'what's the plan?' Ema thought for a moment. On the air came the sound of sirens and they could see blue and red flashing lights rushing along the main road in the distance. 'I suppose we had better get over there and see what all the fuss was about before the police arrive and seal the site off' she said. They quickly packed up the camping chairs and threw the plates and glasses into the sink on the RV. Gary got into the driving seat and as he started the engine was aware that Emma was behind him. As he turned his head she leant down and copying him earlier, she gently kissed him on the cheek before smiling at him and taking her seat. The entity had arrived just as it had planned and taken up a position just below the surface. It did this from experience, giving it time to assess the situation and also to avoid causing undue alarm amongst whatever lifeforms may have evolved. It blended itself into a compact shape beneath the surface, leaving only a dome of bright energy above ground protecting its entry point. It did not displace the earth it settled in, it just occupied the same physical space but in a slightly different dimension. The dome of light above ground also served to allow it to gather initial information on the planets structure, atmosphere and native life. Although it did not have or need a name for them, it sensed the minute electrical activity that suggested electro/chemical life of some sort. It would complete arranging itself into the shape it preferred for exploration and then commence the examination of the planet. Time was not an issue and the anticipation was still being relished. The RV bumped and shook as it crossed terrain it was never designed to drive over. Gary tried to keep to the roads but when they went off at a tangent he just turned back towards the glowing light and went cross country towards it. With the contents of the RV, including Emma in danger of being shook to pieces, they were both relieved to eventually find one dusty track that headed roughly in the right direction. They made comparatively good progress along this track until it swerved to the left slightly leaving the light on the right side. From Emma's side window she could not only see the light glowing upwards, but also through the undergrowth some tantalising glimpses of what was causing it. The brushwood and small trees suddenly became a clearing and she could now see the source of the light, which was formed by a shimmering dome. 'Stop Gary, Look!' The RV stopped moving and Gary did a double take out of Emma's window. Without taking his eyes off the dome, he automatically switched off the engine and they both sat there staring at the light. Emma went to open her door but Gary grabbed her arm 'we don't know if it safe to out there yet' he said. 'And we won't know unless we get out there and have a look, will we?' she Emma said before adding 'Whatever it is, it has travelled millions of miles to get here and it has not killed us yet, so I am betting it will not now' Gary whispered a reply 'have you not seen any science fiction films? They always come here to kill us, that's what they do'. 'Well we don't know yet if it is a thing, an it, or a natural occurring phenomenon, so I intend to find out.

Coming?' said Emma as she opened the door and got out of the RV. Gary folded his arms as his scaredy cat gland cut in 'No way am I going out there' he thought, but as Emma took a few tentative steps towards the object Gary realised he would soon be left alone, so panicking slightly he opened his door and went after her. 'Wait' he hissed, looking around for the bug eyed creatures he was sure were watching their every move. 'Shsss' she said, let's use all our senses to investigate' said Emma. 'Let's just use our fucking common sense and get back in the RV' Gary whispered with more than a hint of urgency. Emma took no notice of his protestations and continued walking forward. The dome was about fifty feet across and appeared to be sat in the middle of a crescent shaped clump of bushes, some of which appeared to be under and protruding from its edges. The light from it was bright but not so bright that you couldn't look at it. It had an opaque luminescence that seemed to shimmer and change shape beneath the outer surface. Emma moved to about ten feet from the edge of the dome and took in what she was seeing. Gary was two paces behind, stealing glances at the dome whilst still looking frantically around for aliens of the worst kind. Emma scientific mind registered there was a feint humming sound mixed with a random ticking noise as you find with static electricity. Emma held her hand up to feel if there was any heat but as she did so the feint hum and static noise increased slightly. She put her hand down and the noise reduced, so she experimented by repeating the exercise. Gary was getting cross, hot and frightened that she might be waking up some evil alien beast within. His heart rate and blood pressure went sky high as he produced a physical reaction to an emotional situation. This increase in vital signs would have an enormous life changing impact on Gary in the next few moments. The entity had a protocol when it arrived on a planet for the first time, but this planet was different as it had been here before. It had the capability to examine a planet from an overall global position down to an atomic level, but generally it started small and worked its way up. It had already sampled its immediate surroundings, and stored the information. Part of its intelligence shared the fact that there were two life forms just beyond the edge of its dome on the surface. Something akin to excitement flashed across its intellect as it passively scanned the two beings. It formed a picture of their carbon based structure and interrogated their ability to form intelligent thought. As yet it could not understand the thoughts it sensed within the warm bodies or to what intelligence level those thoughts were operating on, so it decided to take a sample. Gary now moved alongside Emma and with a rare show of bravery held up his hand as he has seen her do. As with Emma the noise increased slightly and Gary enjoy the slight tingling it produced. His confidence and bravado changed places several times and he started to enjoy showing off what he was doing. He was about to make a prophetic statement to Emma, when a beam of light shot forth from the dome and completely encompassed him in the same shimmering light. His whole body was bathed in the light and the static sound grew considerably louder. Emma covered her mouth in a quiet scream, hoping that Gary was safe but not daring to put her hand into the light which had Gary frozen within it. Frozen was the right word because Gary was very much alive within the light, just unable to move or think straight as the beam closely examined him in minute detail. It lasted for three minutes and twenty one seconds, before as quickly as it shot forth the beam quickly retracted into the dome. Gary sank to his knees and began hyperventilating and incoherently tried to speak. Emma tried speaking to him but got no response, just a jumble of words, heavy laboured breathing and some definite swearing. She pulled at his hands to try and get him on his feet before in desperation she slapped him twice to get him back with her. She was just bringing her hand back for the third slap when Gary spoke 'stop, please don't hit me again' 'Thank goodness, I thought you were gone forever' she said. Holding her arm Gary remained kneeling and shook his head. 'Wow' he said 'What was that? It was the most incredible few seconds of my life'. 'Seconds?' said Emma 'but you were in there for three or four minutes. I was just going to leave and go and go and get help'. Gary was confused, in his mind he had seen the flash coming at him, felt a warm electrical type tingle run through his whole body. He had been mentally aware but confused inside the glow, but also frozen to the spot. When the beam released him he found himself kneeling on the ground next to Emma. She must have made a mistake in the timing. Before he could explain further there was a loud voice from behind them 'both of you kneel down and put your hands on your head' Even with his head still buzzing from his far too close encounter, Gary knew better than to argue or resist and he reached up and pulled Emma down to kneel beside him.

The Entity had gathered some information from the being it had just scanned. There were two of them but it choose that particular one because there was more heat and electrical activity emanating from it. The lifeform seemed to have some rudimentary intelligence and communication abilities, as it had exchanged sounds with the cooler being next to it, but was this simple lifeform the pinnacle of life on this planet? Making contact was always the most interesting part of its mission, and it always hoped to find greater intelligence, but perhaps there would be better examples somewhere else on the planet. It would need confirmation before proceeding with the synthesis, as there would be no point in communicating with the less than highest life form on the planet. It stored the imprint of the being within its vast memory in case it was needed. It extended its thought process to send out markers as scouts and report back on what other life existed on the planet. These small parts of its intelligence left the dome invisibly and began encircling the globe in search of life more intelligent than Gary. Given the markers worked remotely and also the thickness of the planet's atmosphere, they would take nearly a day to complete their survey and report back.

Gary was still buzzing but was now focused on the threatening voices behind them 'stay calm and do what we say and you will not be hurt' the voice behind them shouted. Gary whispered to Emma 'just stay calm and do what they say and we will not be hurt' which drew a withering look from Emma. The voice continued 'stand up and walk slowly backwards'. They both complied, walking backwards side by side until they reached the edge of the bushes. The voice told them to stop before they were grabbed and handcuffed with their hands behind their backs. They were quickly patted down before being spun around to face three local police officers, including the one Ema had seen earlier in the petrol station. On his uniform shirt his name tag announced that he was called Sheriff Tanner. He was obviously in charge as the other officers deferred to him. 'Who are and what is that?' he demanded to know, jabbing a finger towards the glowing dome behind them. 'We are just plain simple tourists' offered Gary, to which Emma readily agreed. The police officer cocked his head at the sound of the accents and smiled, 'tourists? No, I don't think somehow. You will be those two Brits from the FBI most wanted list we been hunting, and I am guessing that is the reason' again pointing to the dome.' He looked very pleased with himself as he told one of the other officers to call in and report finding the FBI fugitives. As he did so a fourth officer appeared out of the dark and told him 'I found the

Bailey RV over there is the bushes. It looks in a bit of a mess' Sheriff Tanner looked at each of them in turn and in a threatening voice growled 'Now, you 'd better be straight and tell me what's going on, or I am gonna lock you up and throw away the key' 'We can't tell you anything Sheriff Tanner' said Gary. 'Oh and just why is that smartass?' said Tanner. Gary saw his chance to big up their part and put the sheriff firmly in his place. Emma and the Sheriff both winced as Gary cockily said 'because sheriff, this is a matter of national security, in fact international security, and you just don't have the security clearance needed. Best you get them FBI people down here pronto and we can fully brief the people who need to know.' Sheriff Tanner turned red, angry and then red again. He had not ever been spoken to like that before by someone in his custody, at least not without being able to beat the crap out of them after they resisted arrest. But this mouthy Brit was wanted by the FBI and he would have to explain any damage to the feds when they arrived. He looked down and spat on the floor, well actually it was on Gary's shoe. It wasn't much in the way of retaliation but it would have to do for now. Gary looked down 'a bit of spit of polish sheriff?' he said casually. Struggling to keep his cool he took a step forward and prodded Gary in the chest to emphasise each word, 'you and me boy are going to fall out, real soon, real hard' He considered giving Gary a quick dig in the ribs but was stopped as the officer suddenly returned from the police car, running and breathing hard. 'Sheriff, when I called it in I was told to wait, then I was put through to the director of the FBI. 'What?' asked the sheriff, incredulous at what he had just been told 'Yeah sheriff, it's true. The director said these two are the most important assets in the country right now and we have to guard them, with our lives if need be' he emphasised the last bit 'with our lives'. Sheriff Tanner was beside himself, in the last few minutes he had found the most wanted people in the US, been given a load of lip by the man and was now being told to look after them by the FBI. 'Then what? Asked the Sheriff.' 'He said they were sending people to take charge and we are to retreat to a safe distance and wait for them' said the young officer. The Sheriff thought about his options which were few, and his future career, which would be short if he did not comply with the FBI directive. He turned to Emma, 'now missy'. Emma cut him off 'Its professor, my title is professor'. Running his tongue around his mouth, he took another deep breath and tried again 'Now then professor. I am guessing you are the brains behind this little outfit of yours. So tell me, since you are the expert, just what might be a safe distance from that that thing over there?' Emma thought before replying 'Sheriff, whilst I am a professor, my first and only contact with that thing was a few minutes ago. Gary here has physically touched it and might have a better idea'. The Sheriff hated this nearly as much as Gary loved it 'Okay smartass same question. What is a safe distance do you think?' Since no one actually knew what a safe distance was and that Emma could not give an answer, Gary realised he had acquired some power to wield and some control over the situation. Using his best air of superiority Gary spoke 'Well Sheriff, given my vastly superior knowledge, I would suggest we all pull back two hundred yards in that direction'. The Sheriff looked down at Gary's foot once more but thought better of decorating the other shoe. He turned to his deputies and making as if it was his decision said 'Put these two in the car and let's move that way a couple of hundred yards to wait till the Feds arrive'. Emma and Gary were placed carefully in the back of the police car and they set off across the rough scrub. They were in a convoy of three police vehicles and their RV which was driven by one of the police officers. They arrived at another natural clearing and the sheriff ordered them to park up alongside each other. Gary and Emma were allowed out of the car but remained handcuffed. 'Can you undo these please?' asked Emma to the young officer but he shook his head and said 'sorry mam, need the Sheriff's say so to do that'. The sheriff finished talking on his phone and then got from his vehicle. His face was red and his demeanour different, giving a few clues to the fact he had just been given a major bollocking from the state governor. He had called his office to seek further clarification and powers to lock up the two under local laws, but the federal authorities had already briefed the governor and he was firmly on the side of the feds. In the distance there was the faint sound of a helicopter but as it increased in sound it became clear there were three of them flying in close formation. They flew a low circuit over the police vehicles before setting up for a formation landing fifty feet from the group. Everyone shielded their eyes with their hands from the dust storm blown up, everyone except the handcuffed Gary and Emma who could only turn away to protect their eyes. With the rotor blades still turning on the helicopters, eleven persons disgorged themselves from each aircraft. Most of them were uniformed, wearing gas masks and carrying weapons.

This group formed a defensive perimeter around the aircraft and assumed a fighting position, but against what they seemed to have no idea. A third group consisting of two men in civilian clothing and two military officers ducked under the rotor blades and ran towards the Sheriff's group. The Sheriff started to introduce himself 'I am Sherriff Tanner and this' but he was cut off by the first civilian 'I know who you are. I am the FBI east coast supervising officer' as he flipped open a leather wallet containing a large and impressive badge of office. 'This is now a federal matter and until higher authority arrives I am in charge, you got that Sheriff?' 'Got that sir' the Sheriff replied, noting the look of satisfaction on Gary's face. The civilian turned to Emma and Gary 'Don't worry, I am here to look after you until back up arrives. This is just the first response, the full team and facilities will arrive soon. In the meantime is there anything you need?' Gary wasted no time 'yes, we need to be out of these handcuffs' turning to show the FBI agent. His eyes widened and he shouted 'Get those cuffs off them now!' to which the Sheriff and his men quickly reacted. The helicopters turbine engines had cooled enough to be shut down and one by the engines and blades slowly wound. Now it was quiet the FBI guy spoke 'That's better.

My name is special agent Morgan, this is Special Agent Rose and this is Colonel Fitts United States Marine Corps. The other FBI man and the Colonel both nodded in acknowledgement. Morgan continued 'I have been told to look after you and the colonel here is to secure the immediate area until back up arrives. So some questions. Where is the point of impact and is there anything we need to know in the way of contamination, explosion, gas exposure, or radiation dangers? Emma and Gary were both taken aback. Having been on the run from the US authorities they were not really surprised at the Sheriff's attitude and expected more of the same from the feds when they arrived. What they did not know was that Steve and Mike had given a lot of input to the government authorities even whilst they were still in the air. They had made it clear that Emma was by far the leading authority in the world on the phenomenon currently facing them and was an asset not a threat. Mike had explained that her running away was in fear of the Feds containing them and keeping it a one nation secret. But the landing event was so widely recorded and documented by worldwide scientific technology that there would be no way of keeping this a secret and no need to regard Emma and Gary as hostile. Whilst

Emma carefully thought about her reply to Morgan's questions, Gary had seen enough Hollywood movies to know how he should act. Giving little thought to the actual content he started issuing orders and details. 'It is over there about two hundred yards. It is a glowing dome of light sitting on the ground. There was no explosion and we have not seen or smelt any gas but when I got about ten feet away from it a beam of light shot out and surrounded me. Got that?' 'Got it Sir' said the US Marine Colonel, who saluted and doubled away to brief and positon his marines. There were some shouted orders before the sergeants amongst them took charge and they headed off in line abreast towards the dome's location. Everyone was clearly impressed with Gary's forthright and clipped report, even Emma who although was technically was the expert, could not have given a more succinct or detailed reply. She looked approvingly at Gary who just winked back in acknowledgement. Morgan spoke to them both 'Thanks for that information' then looking for assurances he went on 'and can I assume that given this is now out in the open there will be no more running away?' 'Our place is here at the event and we will do whatever we can to assist' said Emma. 'Yes' added Gary 'we are only too pleased not to have witnessed the end of the world, all this is now a bonus' Morgan raised his eyebrows 'It could have been that serious?' 'If you call serious the destruction of the planet, then yes' said Emma. She had now established her credentials and importance to the authorities, whilst Gary had established his self-importance, which for the time being had also impressed the feds. With the enormity of what he had just heard, Morgan made a decision 'given the sensitive nature of all this we will use your RV to meet if you don't mind? It will only a temporary base until headquarters arrive' Emma and Gary both nodded. Morgan issued some orders to the waiting Sheriff 'get your men to clear some more space near the choppers as more will be arriving.' Yes sir' said Tanner. 'Oh and Sheriff, make sure your men speak to no one about this, not even each other, got it?' 'Sir, yes sir' said the Sheriff. Emma and Gary went up the steps into the RV followed by the two FBI men. Morgan turned to the second agent as he reached the door 'You wait outside agent Rose' before closing the door. He turned to Emma and Gary 'There is just one more question I have been approved to ask you. Are we dealing with a naturally occurring event or this a thing, or an it? Gary lifted his finger as if to speak but no words came out. He tried again but realised he was way of his depth, far too deep to bullshit, so turned and looked at Emma. She paused to consider what she already knew from her research, combined with what she had seen today. 'My considered but early opinion is that it is a naturally occurring phenomenon, but with some interactive capabilities. That is all I can say until I study it in detail' Despite being deliberately vague and somewhat contradictory, this statement was written down by the FBI agent as if it were gospel and would be transmitted first to his superiors and then the government. He put his notebook away 'can I suggest you stay here for the moment as there will a lot of personnel and equipment arriving, along with some of our scientists who will want to speak with you. Plus there is the security issue, so will need to get you some identity passes made up so there is no more confusion with the local law enforcement or the marines. Is there anything specific you need, equipment or selected people from your teams? Emma nodded, 'I will make a list' she said. Special Agent Morgan nodded and left the RV leaving Emma and Gary alone. 'Right prof, what's the plan, steal one of those helicopters? Asked Gary. 'I think Gary, having got this far and not been vaporised or sent to Guantanamo Bay in an orange jumpsuit, we might just stay and see this through. Besides we might actually be of some use and we seem to have been given ringside seats for the main event.' she replied. 'Well you might be of use, but it seems like my part in the proceedings is definitely over. Gary Barnes, reporter and breaker of global world news has blown it' he said defectively. Without regard for his self-pitied statement, Emma looked at him and completely out of context she said 'I did enjoy it', which confused Gary. 'Enjoyed what, the running away, the RV cross country trip, the what? He replied. She cut across him 'The kiss Gary, your demonstrative, two day old stubble, wine breathed kiss. I enjoyed it' Gary physically and mentally rocked backwards. His mind raced as he desperately searched his brain for the right thing to say under these particular circumstances, but there was no precedent to draw on and no film line deemed appropriate. For some bizarre reason the only line that came to mind was from the film Zulu, where Michael Cane said to the bugler 'Spit man, spit!' Even Gary could not put that sentence into any meaningful perspective. At the time of the kissing incident, in the perceived romantic moment he kissed her everything seemed to make sense. The shared experience of running away and being together twenty four seven had added to the feeling, and so that moment it seemed just the right thing. In the excitement of seeing the heavens open and something spectacular come crashing through the clouds to land in front of them, he assumed that one moment had been lost and forgotten. Now, they were back in the real world, with real people and being reminded of it made it seem somehow silly. For perhaps only the second time in his life but twice in the same day, Gary was caught off guard and without a reply. Emma moved across to him and lent over to kiss him gently once on the lips. He closed his eyes and enjoyed the moment but she suddenly pulled away as the door opened and agent Morgan came into the RV. 'Our field resources unit have been mobilised and will be here soon, so we will have office, communications and laboratory support. NASA are sending a team and we will have more military on scene soon' More military?' asked Emma. 'Yes, the marines were always kept on standby for immediate security alerts, but if this gets heavy we will need heavy armour and attack aircraft to keep the nation secure'. 'But we are not yet sure if it from Earth, a natural happening or an alien, and even if it is then there is currently no threatening behaviour' she said. 'Agreed' said Morgan, 'but we have protocols in place for circumstances such as this, so these measures are being insisted on by the Whitehouse. But, only in the event they are needed for defence, not an offensive operation'. Emma gave a look that suggested she did not completely believe in or have trust in that statement. There was the sound of further helicopters approaching the site, which Gary watched from the window of the RV. Two of the first figures from the helicopter appeared familiar, even at that distance. He watched them move towards the vehicles and speak to the other Special Agent who pointed towards the RV. They moved closer and then the penny dropped, it was Mike and Special Agent hunky blondie Steve. As a warning Gary said to Emma 'standby for trouble, we have visitors'. The door opened and in came Special Agent Steve, followed by Mike. 'Mike!' said a surprised Emma but Mike held up his hand in a most camp way said 'well if it isn't Bonnie and Clyde, international fugitives'. Emma offered an apology 'Mike I am so sorry we left the way we did, it was just we were not sure of your motives in contacting the FBI' Gary spoke up 'well we had something of an idea' looking Steve up and down and winking at them both. This one comment broke the ice as it allowed Steve and Mike's relationship to be a mutely accepted part of the discussion. Realising some of his own motives were now obviously out in the open, Mike immediately changed his tone and hugged Emma. 'Don't apologise. I have been giving a lot of thought to the moral issues we discussed but really I should have waited to talk it through with you first before going off half cocked'. Given the elephant in the room circumstances they were all thinking about but not discussing, this expression caused Gary to stifle a smile. Mike pretended not to notice and continued 'I should have realised that just one hint and the Feds would be all over this' Steve jumped in 'Hey, a little less of the Feds if you don't mind, we are people too'. Up to this point Special Agent Morgan had considered that he had done a good job in the initial part of the containment operation and done everything by the book. Now there was more FBI on scene, one of whom was obviously very much more in the loop and overly friendly with the main players. He could sense there was some hidden agenda he was not privy to and was starting to feel a bit uncomfortable. What really irked him was the informality leaking into this formal operation, an operation that was deemed to be of national security. Having checked Steve's ID and credentials he said 'well I see you all know each other, so I will leave you to all catch up whilst I get the camp and facilities set up' before he left the RV, slamming the door slightly harder than was needed. Steve, shook Gary's hand and as he did so he lent forward and said quietly to Gary 'I gather it must be you I have to thank for getting Mikey off the mountain to meet me downtown?' There was an awkward silence as Gary wondered if Steve was being ironic, but Steve laughed and winked at Gary, signalling his comment had been genuine. Since peace and goodwill appeared to have broken out all round, Gary decide to cement the arrangement by offering everyone coffee and proceeded to crank up the coffee machine. Stopping to look out through the RV window Gary could see a hive of activity taking place. Vehicles of all shapes and sizes, porta cabins and communication equipment were arriving and being set up, like some technological circus By the time coffee was finished the area around the RV already resembled a small military base, with armed soldiers, technical vehicles and many technicians aligning satellite dishes and aerials. With coffee and the social niceties over, Gary suggested he show them big event, the glow from which could be seen a few hundred yards away. They had taken just a few steps outside the RV when they were challenged for their passes by two marines patrolling the newly setup camp. None of them had been issued a pass yet and it was only the production of Steve's FBI identification that allowed them to disengage from the marines and return to the RV. 'Well this is a real fuck up' said Gary 'we have come all this way to save to save the world. We found the fucking thing and now we are not even allowed to see it without a pass, like some fucking show at SeaWorld'. Emma spoke 'This is just the kind of thing I was worried about, the military taking over and the science being pushed into the background.' 'I think' said Steve 'that this is just the initial response to lock things down and ensure security. Once things have settled down and the threat assessed, I am sure you guys will be allowed to do your thing'. 'I hope so' said Mike, 'It is the sort of thing us scientists have been waiting and praying for all our careers and Emma might be the planet's only hope of getting through this'. The weight of what Mike had just said was not lost of the other three. 'As my badge seems to still carry some weight I will go and talk to Special Agent Morgan about getting us all badges valid for this area. Okay? Said Steve. They all nodded in agreement and Steve left to find Morgan. Two hundred yards away the entity continued to gather information of the chemical makeup of the planet and some of the life forms that it could scan. It knew that a number of the lifeforms had formed a circle around it, which suggested some sort of order and intelligence of a kind. It did not feel in any way threatened, and although it had been threatened in the past it could not remember the emotion of fear. Frightened was perhaps one of those emotions that its ancestors may have known, along with a thousand others, but it had long ago transcended such things. In fact it was feeling these emotions through other lifeforms on its travels that made its existence more interesting. It shut down most of its thinking self on long space transits because there was little to interest it in deep space anymore, but now on a planet again it was keen to investigate, reap and savour feelings and emotions long ago redundant in its own species. The exploration of the planet was the meal, the emotional capture was the spicy sauce that added to the flavour. The markers it had sent out reported back with a wealth of information on other varied lifeforms and species existing around the planet. It experienced a sense of disappointment that none were significantly more intelligent than the sample he had taken from the nearest life form, or as his mother called him, Gary. It decided to proceed to synthesise a copy of the lifeform it had sampled, perhaps then it could communicate and experience the thoughts and emotions of this native dweller. It used its essence to collect carbon and other elements that it knew the lifeform to be made up from. It reproduced what it needed and matched them against the scan it had taken of Gary, making sure it copied every cell structure the scan had captured. It now had a ready store of building materials within itself, ready for when it assembled the copy it needed. Having had first gone within fifty yards to identify the threat the marine Colonel backed off a little to set up his forward communications base. He established communications with his superiors in the Pentagon and also the FBI back at the RV base. One of his sergeants came running up and reported that there had been a slight increase in the frequent flashes moving across the dome and also the static noise the dome produced. He passed this information back to the Pentagon who were organising the military response, and then the FBI who were currently setting up the local camp and scientific studies. The Pentagon ordered an increase in both manpower and security at the site, which in the short term suited Special Agent Morgan. Still as the local commander he was still in charge and issued orders that everyone should stay within the camp boundary until further notified. He was in his mobile office when Steve approached him and after the usual greetings said 'Morgan, my group of scientists want to go visit the site but have been told they need special passes'. 'That is correct' replied Morgan, 'the director himself has taken charge of this operation and whilst he is briefing the president those are his instructions. The marines are keeping close security on this thing until we can get our own scientists down here to start their examination. Once we are assured it is safe and either no threat or benefit to the United States, then the site will be opened up to other specialists like your group'. Steve was not entirely happy and as an FBI man himself knew the power plays that were being used. He also knew the others would be angry at being denied access and this would play exactly into the predictions that Emma and Gary had made, which had made them run away in the first place. He tried to negotiate with Morgan to allow them to at least move about the camp but again this was denied 'at least for the short term' said Morgan 'once I get further orders, or we know what we are dealing with locally then I will review the situation'. Seeing he was getting nowhere, Steve left the Morgan and returned to the RV, being challenged twice on the way by marines wanting to see his ID. He tried to sugar coat the news to the others but as predicted they did not take it at all well. Gary, keeping to type immediately suggested an escape but as Emma pointed out, 'this is actually where we need to be, so running away would be counterproductive'. Reluctantly Gary agreed but he did what he always does in times of stress, he started looking in the cupboards to see what he could find to eat. Steve saw a chance to divert their anger and stall for time, so told Gary he was also hungry. Reluctantly they all agreed to wait and eat, which led Gary too busy himself preparing some frozen ready meals for all of them. Outside yet another large truck arrived towing a portable laboratory with the words NASA on the side. It was accompanied by a large American style people carrier with a dozen scientists and assistants, who got out and quickly set about getting their lab up and running. Once the head of this American scientific group had met with Special Agent Morgan, the whole team were issued identity passes on straps to wear around their necks, giving them free reign around the base. Looking out of the RV window whilst eating Emma's team could see all this happening, which only added to their mounting frustration and Gary's anger. It looked like someone else was going to get to the science data first and Gary was already resigned to the fact that the news story was already blown wide open. The entity had now gathered enough information about the planet and the living beings on it to proceed with its plan. Based on the tiny electrical activity that evidently passed for some sort of intelligent process, it deduced that the one lifeform it had sampled earlier was comparatively more intelligent than some of the other lower species it had found. Whatever level of intelligence that Gary's brain electrical signalled, the entity decided it would suffice for an initial point of contact. It knew from experience that this electrical activity did not always represent the highest intelligence but it was a starting point and another species or specimen could be chosen for sampling if required. Calling up the memory of the lifeform's DNA, molecular make up and atomic structure, it proceeded to manufacture another one. It was making a copy of Gary. This was a relatively simple process for the entity, combining chemistry, physics and atomic manipulation that would be unknown to the scientists of earth. Using a large amount of power, the entity created the atoms it required, then out them into molecules and structures, before finally piecing them together into a human like form. It suspended this yet inanimate shape in a gaseous fluid held within the dome. It would soon be ready to animate the object and begin interacting with other lifeforms and the planet. It had found that one of the most effective ways of gathering detailed information was to become one of the lifeforms on the planet. This allowed it to collect minute details that might be missed in a purely technology based examination. There was also another reason, that being it gave the entity some personal experience of what the local lifeforms actually felt. The acts of feelings, emotions and physical sensations had all long ago been lost to it as it evolved over the countless millennia, but it was something that could still be sampled, analysed and vicariously enjoyed when it used a local surrogate body. The synthesis was complete and now needed to be inhabited to become as one. It would animate the copy using part of its own life force, thereby remotely controlling and using the shell. Just sending it forth onto the planet as an extension would give a presence but this would simply be a sterile version of the lifeform. It needed one last thing to complete the human shaped form it had created and that was to contaminate it with the actual electrical and chemical activity from the donor it had sampled. It ideally needed Gary's thoughts and emotions as this would ensure a smooth transition, or it could use

take those things from another compatible donor, if it could find one.

CHAPTER SEVENTEEN: CONTACT

At three PM, there was a knock on the RV door before Special Agent Morgan walked up the steps and stood in front of them. The four of them all started speaking at once, each complaining about being kept from their own particular part of the unfolding saga. Steve seemed the angriest, as being a bono fide National asset FBI agent and the one who broke the story, felt he was now being kept out of the limelight by the local FBI. Morgan held his hands and waited till they all stopped shouting. 'Thank you' he said 'Right I have some news to share with you, but these decisions have been made at the highest national level, so please don't shoot the messenger' He looked at Steve 'You Special Agent will be issued a pass for the base and will work with me but under my jurisdiction.' This satisfied Steve's honour and he nodded in agreement. 'The Professor and Doctor here will both brief and be briefed by our scientists before our people begin their initial study down at the landing site. Once our people have established there is no immediate danger then you will be allowed access to the laboratory to assist where and when they see fit.' Emma and Mike were now both happy to be included in some shape or form, albeit from the back seat for the moment. 'And what about me? Asked Gary, although he already knew he would not like the answer. Morgan pursed his lips as if trying to hold in bad news, which it was. 'Gary, our checks have confirmed what you have told us, namely that you are a reporter, and in a situation like this that makes you about as popular as a turd in a lucky dip. Now, I am not saying you do not have a role in this, just that there is no role for you right now. So, I have been directed to keep you close in case you are needed'. Gary knew a fob off when he heard one and he also knew what 'keep you close' meant when coming from a police official. 'So what you really mean is there is bugger all for me to do and I am under arrest until you work out what to do with me' Gary replied sarcastically. 'Well, if that is the spin you want to put on it Gary then so be it. But for now stay in the RV until I call for you' said Morgan. 'Okay, if we are done, I will send our lead scientists over to meet you professor soon' and with that Morgan left the RV. Steve, Emma and Mike all showed Gary various amounts of sympathy over the situation he was in, but this was soon overshadowed when two NASA scientists arrived at the RV along with an armed US marine. The guard handed over Steve's newly printed pass which he hung around his neck and then went with the guard to meet Morgan in the command post. The scientists introduced themselves. Professor's Brown and Carter were both eminent in their own field of study and known to Emma from various scientific papers and conferences. There was a plethora of introductions, discussing mutual scientific acquaintances and an exchange of what each other knew about the dome and how it had got there. Brown & Carter were both apologetic about the current security situation but promised to feedback information as it became available and to push for them to be fully included in their research team as soon as possible. Once they had left, Mike excused himself to use the RV toilet. Emma sat down alone with Gary and put her hand on his 'I am really sorry about how this has turned out for you' He nodded and patted her hand 'Don't worry about me, at least you now have a role to play, and rightly so' he said, and then added in a more mysterious voice. 'I did notice though that Brown and Carter were quite straight with you but you were less than totally upfront with them' Emma looked to see the toilet door was still closed 'You mean the bit about you getting zapped out there. Well, one of the things I have learnt from you Gary Barnes is to not give too much away in one go' They both smiled at the shared confidence, before Emma lent forward and kissed him. It was short and to the point.

Something about Gary's calm demeanour also bothered Emma, so she asked him 'I would have thought you would be spitting feathers after being told by Morgan you have to stay in here, especially with two marines guarding the door? Gary's eyes shone and he raised one eyebrow as he spoke 'But they aren't Royal Marines though are they?' leaving a silent question hanging in the air as the RV toilet flushed and Mike came back into the room. Mike had given up being petulant about being left in Hawaii and was in fact was most grateful for the excuse to get back with Steve. Yes, he had a sore bottom, but on the other hand '*YES, I HAVE A SORE BOTTOM!*' he mused in quiet satisfaction. In a caring and sharing moment Mike poured more coffee for everyone, but they had just at the table to drink it when there was a knock on the door and Morgan appeared. 'There has been a development and Professor Brown requests you attend the laboratory for an update please'. All three of them stood up, Gary more in hope then expectation. Morgan gave Emma and Mike printed passes to wear 'sorry Gary, not your time yet'

With an apologetic look, both Emma and Mike squeezed Gary's arm and left, leaving Gary alone with his thoughts, something dangerous the FBI had not taken into consideration. Morgan escorted Emma and Mike across the quickly expanding base. They were amazed at how many resources had been put in place in the few hours since the dome had landed and they had been captured. Mike managed a quick hello to Steve as they passed the guarded FBI command trailer before they arrived at the joined mobile units that formed the laboratory. Professor Brown welcomed them and showed them through to the far end of the second unit which had several CCTV screens in place on the end wall. An assistant was remotely operating the cameras which had been elevated by means of telescopic poles, giving a good overview of the dome and surrounding areas. Professor Brown proceeded to brief them 'About an hour ago the marines at the dome reported an increase in flashing and noise levels. By zooming in we were able to pick out the changing patterns and are analysing them in case they mean anything' Emma spoke 'so you do think this is a living thing?' Brown paused, hardly believing what he was saying himself 'well it is just speculation at the moment, but as you know nothing like it has ever been seen before. We are trying to confirm or eliminate natural phenomena, but failing that this could be life. Also, with the FBI and military being very jumpy about national security we are equally keen to show them that whatever it is, it does not pose a threat' Brown then spoke quietly in a conspiratorial tone. He tapped the white coated assistant on the shoulder and said 'replay those shadows and lights again from mark minute thirty seven please'. One of the screens went blank before coming back on with a recorded time in the corner. It showed the camera zooming in as the dome flashed. It soon became clear that there was an increase in the light activity, along with a fleeting glimpse of a shadowy something suspended just below the surface of the dome' Mike spoke 'It seems like the dome is filled with some kind of liquid or gas and has something floating around in it. Is that how you are reading it?' 'Yes' replied Brown, 'it looks like a gaseous fluid but flashes and acts like an electrical event, like a storm on Jupiter'. Emma asked 'Have you actually been down to the dome yet professor?' Brown shook his head 'No, not yet. The military have control of the dome site itself and will not allow us access until the President and staff are all in their secret bunker. They did set up the cameras for us but closer inspection will not be allowed until we have the all clear from the Whitehouse and FBI'. Emma and Mike looked at each other in amazement. Of course they assumed the President would have been told but to have him and the government moved as a precaution seemed something of an overreaction. Brown then said 'We do have some air samples from around the dome and also some sounds that are being analysed in the lab next door, if you would like to come though and see the tests being conducted? Emma had not forgotten Gary, but this opportunity had arisen and her scientific mind was hungry for more information about the dome. One way or another it had been a part of her life for the last seven months and her scientific mind desperately needed to know what it was. Brown's assistant gave Emma and Mike new white lab coats and they went to work. Gary was not lonely as he had himself to contend with and talk to. A small part of him was suggesting that he relax, have some more food and wait patiently till they called for him. There was after all still a story to be told, and amongst the circus of equipment that had showed up he had yet to see a TV channel satellite van. Then there was the other side of Gary's brain, the part that made him drink, be late for work, blag his way into TV stations and run all the way around the world following a crazy professor. This was the part of the brain that did not want to sit around the RV waiting, although it mutely agreed with the other bit that perhaps some food might be in order first. Gary cooked some of the beef burgers they had bought yesterday and for good measure fried some onions. The smell was an international nasal tease and Gary was pleased to see the two marines outside the RV tantalisingly sniffing the air from RV vent. He opened the RV door and one of the marines said 'Sorry sir, orders are you stay inside' 'I know' said Gary 'just thought you guys could use one of these each?' as he produced a plate with two good looking cheese burgers on them. The gesture caught the marines off guard and they exchanged glances as they silently conferred as to the legitimacy of taking food from their captive. The lance corporal in charge quickly weighed up the risks versus the outcome and nodded to the marine. They were always told in training to eat and sleep whenever you can, so with a quick mumbled 'thanks' they both took a burger each, impressing even Gary with their speed eating. With their mouths full and eyes full of appreciation, Gary winked and went back into the RV closing the door. Part one of his plan was in place, getting the guards to like him could be ticked off his imaginary check list. *'At worst I have fed two marines, at best it might stop them shooting him!'* he thought. Emma and Mike worked with the NASA and FBI teams, examining the few samples they had taken and throwing around ideas and theories about what they were dealing with. Having spent four hours but still with no definite conclusions, Mike suggested a short break might be in order, to which Emma agreed so that she could catch up with and more importantly check-up on Gary. On the way back to the RV another new feature of the whole circus was a canteen serving hot food everyone on the site. To show some consideration Emma thought it would be nice to take some food back for Gary, so ordered a baked potato covered in chilli sauce and some fries covered in cheese. 'That ought to please him' she thought. Mike ordered a salad and with their takeaway boxed meals they returned to the RV. The marines gave looked in detail at their ID hanging around their necks and opened the door to the RV for them. The strong smell of frying and onions did not please Emma, especially as she had gone to the trouble of bring food for Gary. However, Gary was seldom satisfied when it came to eating so he tucked into the chilli and French fries as if he had been prisoner in a Japanese prisoner of war camp. They sat around the small table eating and updating Gary on what was happening at the lab and dome, including the curious object that could be seen within the dome itself. Gary appeared to be listening intently as he opened a bottle of ketchup, but as he squirted it in the clumsiest way possible he managed to get it down the front of Mike's newly issued white lab coat. Both Mike's gay and scientific minds were horrified at the mess, made worse when Gary got a paper towel to dab at the red stain but only succeeded in making it only worse. Gary apologised profusely as Mike sat quietly, obviously annoyed but carefully holding it in. through pursed lips. Gary apologised again 'I am really sorry Mike, clumsy ol me. Take it off and I will wash it through for you and have you looking like a snowman again in no time.' Emma laughed but Mike did not. Amongst his many gay attributes was one about always looking at his best, and so a ketchup stained lab coat would not do at all. He took it off and thrust it at Gary who with a last apology put it carefully in the kitchen area. 'Don't worry Mike, they have boxes of those and I am sure will give you another' said Emma. Mike nodded and went back to eating his salad. Having eaten, had coffee and spent some time with Gary, Emma thought they ought to check back in at the lab to see if there had been any results. Mike wanted to try and check in with Steve, so they both made their excuses and apologetically left Gary alone for the second time that day. He was starting to feel like a housewife, cooking, cleaning and now if his story was to be believed, hand washing Mike's lab coat. Yeah right! At the laboratory professor's Brown and Carter had finished running multiple tests but with no positive conclusion about what the dome was. There was a limit to what they could do from a distance and so the next step was to see if they could approach it to make some first-hand notes and samples. Brown had approached Morgan again, who then sent the request back up the chain of communication for a decision. Brown was discussing the way forward with Carter when Morgan appeared 'Now the President is safe and there has been no hostile intent, I have received approval for a small scientific team to approach the dome and obtain more samples' Brown thanked Morgan before speaking to Carter 'I think you and I should make the initial approach and see what samples we can collect. We can share that with the professor later' He said this in a way that Carter fully understood. Although they were working on the same side there was still an underlying competitiveness to be first with any scientific papers that might be published from this unique situation. With the help of their assistants, Brown and Carter were dressed in full hazard protective suits, with a completely enclosed hoods and visors. Carrying their sample equipment like astronauts, they were driven in a golf buggy style vehicle to where the marines were set up in a defensive ring around the dome. Leaving the vehicle they walked slowly towards the pulsating and ever changing light, breathing heavily through their supplied air and communications equipment. Despite this being live and very serious, they had both been brought up watching Hollywood movies and television, so had a degree of learnt behaviour in how they thought they should act. This was confirmed by the reciprocal actions of the lab team, who also played their part. They were still some distance away but both stood and waved at the cameras before speaking into their microphone 'testing communication channels' said Brown. One of the assistants spoke into the microphone linking them with the two scientists 'we are receiving all your vital signs and telemetry professor, you are good to go'. His voice was transmitted direct to the two suited men but also broadcast over the speaker system around the base so that everyone could hear in case of an emergency. This added to the dramatic theatre of the events unfolding onscreen for the team, but suddenly for made things very real for the two suited scientists, each of which were now doubting their decision to be first at the scene. The two scientist's nervousness could be heard as they spoke through the radio microphones in their suits. Emma and Mike had just returned to the lab and after Mike had got himself a new lab coat they went looking for the Professor Brown. They found most of his team huddled around the CCTV screen and were both surprised and dismayed to see the two figures entering the dome area. One of the assistants looked up and spoke 'the professor said to apologise for going ahead, but permission had just come through so they were keen to get some samples' It was a poor excuse for an excuse, and a shared Mike look between Mike and Emma confirmed they both thought the same. The entity itself was now ready for the next phase of its plan. It had assembled the synthesised being, and could at the merest thought inhabit it and move the body itself. However, this would not achieve its aims. It could of course already go where ever it liked, the purpose of recreating one of the lifeforms was to be able to feel it, to be it, to understand it. It needed to know what level of intelligence it had reached, how far it had evolved and the best way of knowing all these things was first hand, but there was still something missing. Yes, the entity had created the empty vessel but now needed to fill it with something, the very essence of the being it had copied. Only then would it be able to fully communicate and understand the subtle nuances and emotions behind that communication. It could use another lifeforms thought but ideally it would prefer to fill the brain storage area with the electrical activity of the actual form it had copied. Experience had taught it that it would make an exact fit and not a forced combination. It now needed Gary.

In the laboratory everyone's eyes were on the screens watching Brown and Carter approach the dome. Morgan was there, as was a newly arrived United States Air Force General, who had assumed control of the military assets and had the authority to use them if needed. Since he had arrived at the exact moment Brown and Carter were approaching the dome, the General had yet to be introduced. Having slowly, deliberately and warily approached the dome, the two scientists were aware that each step closer brought a resulting increase in electrical static noise. Once they were within six feet Brown held up his hand and they began by taking samples of the earth around the base of the dome and Carter roamed around the perimeter to visually inspect the dome and to measure the circumference. They conducted these small tests as a way of putting off the inevitable big one, the big one being someone had to actually touch the dome to measure its density. The atmosphere in the laboratory was tense as they all watched the two figures conduct their tests and report over the radio what they were doing. With the limit on their air supply getting low it was now time to finish by using the probe to physically touch the dome and obtain the final readings planned for this initial inspection. Brown told Carter to pick up the probe whilst he held the recording device. Carter briefly considered suggesting it should be better the other way around but thought better of when he remembered they had an audience and Brown was technically in charge. The probe was to test the dome for density, temperature and chemical makeup and therefore needed to make actual contact. Carter picked up the probe and removed the protective covering of the sensor on the tip, before slowly edging forward. There was a build-up of tension in the CCTV lab as the onlookers held their breath in anticipation. Brown found himself edging slowly backwards an inch then a foot as Carter went equally slowly forward. The entity knew there were two lifeforms just outside its outer dome but it did not have any fear, or need of any fear. What it did need was to fill its newly created form with the thoughts, knowledge and imagination of the donor subject, and so needed to know if one of these two forms was actually it or at least compatible with the vessel it had created. At the same time as Carter tentatively brought the probe towards the dome, the entity sent two intense beams of energy to interrogate and identify the life forms. Having not been warned by Emma that this had occurred earlier to Gary, the light shocked and horrified both the scientists and those watching the CCTV screens. They watched as the two were held firmly in the fingers of light, seemingly unable to move or react. Since neither of them were what the entity needed the examination lasted only a minute before it quickly stopped, retracted the light and the two men were released. It had looked at the electrical activity in the brain of the two samples and Gary would have been deeply offended to find that it had rejected these scientist because they appeared to have much more electrical activity than he did, which corresponded to intelligence and knowledge. It would have been like trying to fill an egg cup from a pint pot. Gary's exact copy simply did not have enough capacity for the intellect of either scientist. Watching the men caught in the beam, the tension became too much for the General watching the events unfold on the CCTV screen. He grabbed the microphone and shouted to the two scientists to 'get the hell out of there' Once the beam had retracted, like Gary earlier they were both freed and were able to move again. Not needing any encouragement, once he regained his senses Carter dropped the probe and closely followed by Brown ran away from the dome and out of sight of the CCTV cameras. As they reached the cordon of marines they were gently grabbed and held whilst they calmed down and recovered their breathing. The experience had been life changing and neither one of them could speak for the moment and just stood looking at each other in wide eyed amazement. The entity was not disappointed as it did not have need of that emotion. However, what it did need now for the original lifeform hardware it had synthesised was to copy the software intelligence that it required. Gary would have preferred to keep his thoughts, emotions and limited intelligence to himself, but he would soon have little choice in the matter. Gary was getting fed up with being side lined and left in the RV. Everyone else had a free run of the camp and access to whatever that thing out there was and he wanted in on the action. As always, Gary had a plan, and as always that plan had not been thoroughly thought through to the end. If successful however, what the plan did allow was his release from the RV and some freedom of movement around the camp. If it failed he discounted being shot by the marines as he had just fed them, so for Gary the worst case scenario was being caught and locked up in the RV again, so no major gamble he wrongly reasoned. Gary went to the well-appointed RV toilet room and sat down on the seat. It was not his time for number two's or 'plop plops' as he called them. Generally he was a morning person, but he persevered and after much grunting and groaning he soon added a considerable contribution the toilet reservoir cartridge which was held within the vehicle. This cartridge system was designed to hold all the waste from the occupants and be emptied daily at a campsite, but in the excitement this duty had been neglected and consequently it was very nearly full. Gary needed to move the two marine guards away from the left side of the vehicle so that he could exit the door. However, since asking them nicely was out of the question, Gary plan called 'operation dump' was put into action. Having read the RV operating manual supplied by the rental company, he lifted the floor inspection hatch. Below him was the top of the toilet cartridge which would normally be slid out from the outside, but there was also a screwed bracket which could be undone for complete removal of the box. Gary went to work loosening the fitting, becoming more aware of the increasing smell as the box came away from the underside of the toilet and started to sag away from the underside of the vehicle. He struggled on and after a minute of unscrewing and retching the retaining nut finally came undone releasing one end of the box. With one hand over his nose and mouth he kicked at the loosely hanging box and was pleased and relieved to see it slide out towards the side the two marines were guarding. He replaced the hatch and returned to the main RVG lounge and sat down, whilst his work was rewarded with a cacophony of swearing and cursing as the two marines were now stood in the lava flow of urine and smelly excrement. One of them opened the RV door and asked Gary what the hell was going on. Gary looked at him innocently whilst rubbing his belly. 'Sorry guys' Gary said 'It must have been that Mexican food I ate' he offered in mock apology. The marine shook his head and left, slamming door behind him. Gary could hear their conversation and was pleased to hear them say they could guard him equally well from the other side as 'the limey wouldn't be going anywhere soon with a dodgy Mexican ass' The two marines moved out of the festering puddle and shaking what they could off their boots moved around to the other side of the RV. They took up positions on either side of the right hand door, reassured that Gary's gastronomic issues would keep him near a toilet. Gary was pleased with himself and set about phase two of his plan. He opened the dishwasher and on each end of the spinning washer arms he attached a small pan. He gave the arm an experimental spin and was pleased to see and hear the pans swinging out and hitting the inside of the dishwasher with a loud clump. He set the machine on a cycle and stood back to admire his work as the now noisy and unbalanced machine made a row. He peeked through the curtains and could see the marines gesticulating and discussing the commotion he was causing. They wrongly assumed it was more stomach trouble but were comforted to hear their guest moving about the RV. Ready for the final phase Gary now out on the white lab coat he had acquired from Mike when they had eaten earlier and he had deliberately spilt food over. He produced from his pocket a fake ID card that he had made from a corn flakes box, leaving the chicken emblem in the corner where the photograph would belong. He inserted the card into the plastic sleeve from the vehicle handbook and hung it around his neck. Other than being the about right colour the ID would not pass any inspection closer than six feet, but it might just pass at a distance, especially if the owner was a chicken. Finally he picked up a bundle of papers. If there was one thing a lazy office worker learns early on it is to always carry a stack of papers with you at all times to give the appearance of being busy and to dissuade people stopping you enroute. Gary was a master of this technique, having carried the equivalent of a small forest around his office over the years. He took a final deep breath before quietly opening the left door of the RV and quickly exiting the vehicle. He stood silently in the smelly puddle for a few second, waiting to see if he would be challenged, but nothing happened. Pushing his shoulders back Gary assumed the posture of a man on a mission and walked deliberately away from the noisy RV, the uneven dishwasher doing its job covering for him. He walked at right angles towards a line of vehicles and then turned right so he was out of sight of the RV and his guards. He was pleased with himself for getting away with such an audacious plan, then came the crushing realisation that having unexpectedly got that far, the plan had come to an abrupt end. Professor's Brown and Carter were sat in the mobile laboratory being helped out of their cumbersome bio hazard suits by the lab assistants. Once their one head piece head was unzipped and removed the gathered throng could see they were bright red in colour and still had a look of shock on their faces. 'What happened?' asked the General but neither of them could formulate a sentence. Emma offered them a plastic bottle of water each, from which they both took a long drink' 'take your time' said Emma. Brown licked his lips and took a deep breath 'I have never known a feeling like it' he said 'there was an increase in the static noise, a flash of light and then for a few seconds we just could not move' 'Actually, according to the CCTV time clock it was nearer a minute' said one of the assistants. Both Brown and Carter looked surprised 'I was aware but I couldn't really function' said Carter 'it was like being conscious but in a state of limbo' he added to which Brown nodded in agreement. The group continued asking detailed questions but there nothing meaningful the two could add. Mike suggested 'perhaps it would better to let the professor's gather their thoughts and write their notes whilst we look at the data they collected? The group nodded agreement on this and whilst their assistants finished getting the suits off the scientists Emma and Mike started examining the data that had collected.

Gary was now out of ideas. He had successfully escaped the RV and the attentions of his personal US marine guards, but he did not know where Emma was, what was happening at the dome thing or what he should do next. Since Emma would no doubt be in company of the FBI and military he reasoned he would go down and check out the dome first, although this time from a good distance. Rather than try and sneak around the camp he decided to continue with his brazen '*Gary owns the world*' walk, which had served him well just now and in his office past. He arranged his papers to cover most of his fake ID and set out towards the area of the dome. The camp had changed significantly since he had secured in the RV, with dozens of vehicles and trailers providing full support to the military and scientific missions taking place. He got lost and took several wrong turns before he found the last line vehicles and began walking across no man's land towards where the inner cordon was being manned by the US Marines. They had formed a ring around the entity and were clustered about twenty yards apart in groups of two. There was a larger separate group to Gary's right about a hundred yards, which Gary assumed to be the forward headquarters containing the US marine colonel. Gary made for a gap between two of the other units and walked briskly and with purpose in the direction of the dome. The marines saw him coming and two of them moved out of their position to meet him and check him out. The taller of the two was a corporal and as he approached Gary he looked for and glimpsed the edge of his ID card, but could not see the detail. Since they were the inner ring of defence and part of an expanding twenty mile exclusion zone, had no reason to suspect that the guy in the white was not a legitimate scientist. 'Hello sir, can we help you' he asked politely but firmly 'No thank you corporal, I am just gathering some more data to run through the computer' said Gary in his best British accent, which had the desired effect. 'Okay sir. Are you a British?' asked the corporal. 'Yes' said Gary 'I am indeed 'a British', as you so quaintly put it. And you boys are from?' 'Well I am from Boston sir and Miller here is from Milwaukee, but we are marines to the core OORAH!' Miller repeated the corporal's cadence 'OORAH!' Gary laughed 'of course you are, I haven't met a marine who isn't' HOORAY' he mimicked, but got it completely wrong. Marine Miller was still trying to get a look at Gary's ID, not that he didn't believe Gary was legit but he was curious to this guy's name now that he had heard his accent. The corporal quietly asked Gary a question 'can you tell us anything about the dome sir? They ain't telling us nothing and rumours are rife. Some of the guys say it's an alien, is that right sir?' Gary was on the spot but he realised he knew a little more than the marines so gave them his best bullshit answer 'Yes corporal, it is an alien life form. We think it has come here to feed and so are keeping everyone away until we defeat it or it is full' Gary was pleased with his quick reply, even if it was completely pulled out of thin air. The shocked look on the marines faces told him he was being believed and so he embellished a little more 'It eats metal, so keep you guns behind you and take any loose change from your pockets. Now in full flow, Gary was going to deliver the final lie and hope to scare the marines into letting him past, but as he breathed in there was a sudden increase in the static noise from the direction of the dome. The entity had plenty of time but having had such a long period of little to do whilst transiting space it wanted to proceed with the more interesting aspects of the visit. It used its senses to look for the compatible life form it had copied and quickly energised parts of its dome to assist. Almost immediately it found what it was looking for amongst the groups of lifeforms which were formed in a circle around it. It exponentially increased the power and thought being used to form the dome and caused to suddenly expand and grow. The edge of the dome suddenly moved out in all directions until it encompassed the groups of marines ranged around it. They were all temporarily enclosed and incapacitated by the energy surrounding them until just as suddenly the light receded and left them all stood shocked but otherwise as if nothing had happened. But, something was different and as the marine corporal gathered his senses he realised that where before there were three of them talking, now there were only two, Gary had disappeared with the light. Gary's view of events differed very little from the marines apart from one important aspect, he was no longer stood next to them. He had heard the increase in static noise and was just going to begin a tactical retreat when there was a blinding flash and he was for the second time bathed in that strange blinding light. He was then vaguely aware of moving but without actually moving. It was more like his position had been adjusted somehow. This all took place in what he thought was a fraction of a second but in fact was quicker, certainly quicker than the eye could register. He had enough cognitive function to recall that last time the light had suddenly stopped and released him and he hoped for the same, but this time it felt different. He still had the bright light around him but he felt he was more a part of it instead of being outside and it coming to him. It was like being contained in a bright swirling liquid, where he could see little and feel nothing, but was still aware of his surroundings. He was able to think a little but could not complete complex thoughts as something was interfering with his thought patterns and confusing him but he could not identify what. The entity had found Gary amongst the marines and physically drawn him to it. It now held him within and using its very essence started the process of gently getting into the brain of Gary, where most of the electrical activity was taking place. It knew from experience that forcing itself upon and into another being did not always have a good outcome, so it had learnt to take this part slowly so as to not damage the lifeform it was examining. It looked into the brain in minute detail, looking into each neuron and finding it was connected by synapses to yet another. It was able to ascertain the overall low intelligence capable to a being with such a relatively simple brain. Delving to a deeper level it was able to ascertain stored memory, simple thoughts and complex feelings that this being had accumulated in its lifetime. It did not take the time to try and understand these in real time as it would be much easier once it completed its own synthesised version, so if concentrated on collecting them. It would then use them use them to boot up its own synthesised body, enabling a much higher level of communication and understanding. This first hand understanding it considered to be far more valuable than just sampling the indigenous life alone.

In the CCTV lab after the light event had encompassed the whole camp including them, there was stunned shock. No one moved or spoke but just took a moment to gather their thoughts and check they still possessed the correct number of limbs. The first to recover were Brown & Carter, who having already experienced the event earlier were not quite so utterly in shock as the others but could have done without a repeat performance. Within a few seconds the others in the room began looking at their limbs and moving their heads to ensure everything was where it should be and working. 'So now we know what it's like' said Mike whilst rubbing the back of his neck. There were no after effects but it felt the right thing to do and others were similarly clicking necks and stretching limbs. 'How long were we out for? Snapped the General, sending one of the assistants into a keyboard frenzy as he rewound the recording. Having got an answer he spoke 'data from the recording shows the light expanded from the dome a distance of one kilometre, sat there for fifteen seconds before returning to its previous dimensions'. Emma spoke 'just fifteen seconds? It felt a lot longer' which the gathered group agreed with. The General lent forward and activated the base PA system microphone 'This is General Baxter of the United States Air Force. I am the military commander of this base. I want a full report on all casualties if there are any and written reports from commanders on any activity that seemed aggressive during that last event'. The microphone went off with a click, quickly followed by the military radio bursting into life 'This is cordon commander calling base commander on secure' The military radio operator answered and passed the headset to the General. 'Base commander, go ahead' said the General. 'Sir, all my men felt that last light episode, but apart from the mental confusion it caused it appears no one has been physical injured' he paused but held the mike open, not sure how to tell the General the next bit 'Go on' said the General 'Sir, some of my men were checking out one of the scientists who came down to the cordon. They were just confirming his ID when the light episode happened and like everyone else they were in limbo for a while. But, once they were released the scientist had disappeared' 'What!' said the General 'How can that have happened?' The commander answered 'No idea sir, one minute the British scientist was there, the next he was not'. At the mention of 'British scientist' both Emma and Mike looked at each other and quietly mouthed the word Gary!' The General issued some generic be careful and on guard type orders before signing off the radio and turning to the scientists 'Well professors, you need to do a head count and let me know which of your team is missing so we can start a search' Professor Brown answered him 'General, all our American team are here and the only British scientists working is stood in front of you 'indicating towards Emma. 'Well you all heard what the colonel just said, a British scientist was down there and now isn't! Emma decided it was time to air her theory on the mysterious white coated scientist 'I think General, unless we have an intruder then that person must be Gary Barnes, our tame reporter' The General shook his head 'That can't be so professor, my understanding is that we have Mr Barnes being held securely by our marines' Emma shook her head and meant to say under her breath 'but they are not Royal Marines' but it came out loud enough for the General to hear

'WHAT!' he shouted. Emma continued 'It's just something that Gary said to me several times. They are not British Royal Marines, is what he said, and he has shown himself to be quite resourceful' 'Professor' said the General in a most patronising way 'for your information, our U.S. marines are every bit as good as your British marines. And, that besides, this was a simple task of guarding one man in an RV, so there is no chance of him giving them the slip!' Emma and Mike exchanged glances as the phone on the desk rang. The assistant answered and quickly passed the phone to the General 'General Baxter, go ahead' There a series of 'yes', 'how' and 'dammit' questions, as the General got increasingly redder in the face before he finally shouted 'Find him!' before slamming the telephone back on its cradle. He took a deep breath and rubbed his fingers around his uniform collar 'It seems professor as if Mr Barnes has indeed managed to leave the RV and is loose somewhere in the camp. Any suggestions?' Before Emma could answer, one of the assistants operating the cameras pointed at the screen and shouted 'look there he is!' As they all gathered closer to the screen they could clearly see the Gary Barnes they knew. He was stood facing the still shimmering dome with his arms outstretched, but seemed to be frozen to the spot and with a slight sparkle to his clothing. As they watched there another increase in the domes light activity and a bulge began to appear in the side of the dome facing Gary. The bulge steadily increased in size, growing like a blister moving slowly towards where Gary stood. It continued to grow in size and just when the observers thought it must burst a portion suddenly separated from the dome and became a separate shining entity. They watched the screens, mesmerised as the glowing mass slowly started to settle into a distinct shape. Within a few seconds the overpowering shimmering light had started to diminish, allowing them to see the shape that was forming, and that shape was familiar. It was clear that a humanlike outline had begun to emerge and was getting more defined by the second. It seemed to increase its resolution quickly, going from a vague human shape to a complete human form in around ten seconds. There was a gasp as the now clearly human being could now be seen on screen standing and facing Gary. There was plenty of confusion over what they were actually seeing but no confusion over what they actually saw. Before them onscreen there were two Gary Barnes, one facing the other. Whilst both their faces had the identical and unmistakeable stubble face of Gary Barnes, they were dressed quite differently. One was wearing a stained laboratory white coat with cereal packet ID card, which any casual observer would say was the 'real' Gary Barnes. The other figure was wearing shimmering clothes which seemed to be made of materiel similar to the light coming from the dome, but less intensive. It gave the appearance of having a glowing aura around its body. It stood facing Gary, mimicking his outstretched arm stance. All six people watching the screens broke the silence at the same time 'Jesus Christ!' said four of them except for Emma and Mike who both said 'Gary Barnes!' Once the words had broken the spell the first person to react was the General. He reached for the red phone on the desk, which without having to dial was answered immediately by someone at the other end. The General took a deep breath and using prearranged code words he slowly spoke 'CONTACT. CODEWORD LAZARUS, I recommend immediate DEFCOM ONE'. He repeated the message then slowly put the phone down again without taking his eyes off the screen. Special Agent Morgan was busy trying to raise his superiors on his mobile phone when the General pulled an envelope from inside his jacket and without looking at him handed it to him. It bore the seal of the

President of the United States of America and the label was signed. Morgan hung up the phone and opened the envelope to read the short letter it contained. It told the reader that they, and every one of their staff were now under the military command of the General until further instructed. It was signed by the President himself and counter witnessed by the secretary for defence. Morgan went to ask a question but thought better of it and just nodded to the General.

CHAPTER EIGHTEEN: HE LIVES, HE SPEAKS, HE WALKS
AMONG US

Although Gary had not been fully unconscious, neither had he been
fully aware of what had happened or where he had been for the last
few minutes. He now started to have the realisation that he was stood
up and slowly coming round from a very vivid dream. He blinked
his eyes as his arms dropped to his sides and he looked down at his

hands as he moved his fingers. He slowly began coming to terms with the confusion that comes when waking from a bad dream. He moved his head and cricked his neck muscles as more and more of Gary's consciousness slowly came back to him. He was part way through rotating his head a second time when his eyes became aware of someone stood in front of him. Given the events of the last few days and with childhood memories of scary films in his mind, he was wary of suddenly looking up in case he did not like what he saw. Starting with his eyes he started at the bottom of the apparition and seeing shimmering human shaped feet of sorts, he slowly made his way up the body. By the time he had reached the midway point and could see some hands his confidence had grown a little and he felt assured the top half would reveal a kindly face and not a bug eyed alien. He raised his whole head to see face to face who or what was standing in front of him. There were many thousands of possibilities going through Gary's mind at that point but none of them came close to the actual reality of what he saw. Less than six feet in front of him stood a glowing aura shrouded man, but a man wearing Gary's face. As the recognition hit him Gary physically jumped and started to scream out loud in one continuous breath. The other figure had not up until this point not moved but now its mouth opened, copying Gary's action but in a silent scream. Gary ran out of breath and stopped screaming but still stood with his mouth open gasping for breath, his shoulders moving up and down. The other Gary again copied this motion with its mouth open and its shoulders also moving in mock breathing. The entity was copying Gary's moves with good reason. Based on experience, it knew that to mimic its host's actions might help reassure it, whilst it went about the task of learning how to finely animate the body it had created, and also learnt how to communicate. Although it was using Gary's image and looking through the eyes it had created, its main essence was still in the dome, and this was to all intents and purposes was a remote controlled body it was using. Despite being petrified to the spot, Gary somehow found looking at his own face shouting silently back at him and not that of a monster to be mildly reassuring. He put his hand to his mouth to try and stop himself screaming again and then saw his copy also make the same movement. He tried the other hand and was again amazed to see his actions copied and without any obvious threat. With his confidence slowly building, Gary started to make other movements with his hands, which to the people looking at him through the CCTV screens seemed most odd behaviour at a time like this. 'What is that fool doing dancing in front of Jesus Christ?' said the General angrily. 'I don't think he is dancing' said Emma 'Look at his doppelganger, it is copying him, Gary is trying to communicate with it!' Communicate might have been stretching the meaning of the word but Gary certainly was experimenting, if only to see how much movement it had and if could he outrun it. Gary had recovered sufficiently to have thoughts on self-preservation, which in this situation meant running away. Taking a breath he thought, then commanded his legs to turn around and get him the hell out of there. There was a slight delay which Gary put down to nerves, but as the seconds passed and Gary was still stood there it became clear the problem was not his nerves. Somehow, Gary was simply not able to command his legs to run away. Everything else worked why then could he simply not implement the much over hyped second part of the natural 'fight or flight' reflex? His legs appeared to work but his feet would not move as commanded by him. Special Agent Morgan and the General were having a heated discussion at the rear of the CCTV unit. Morgan was trying to restrain the General from ordering the Marines to open fire on the Gary copy. The General was both clear in his military duty and also a little punch drunk on holding the Presidential letter of authority. He was on the verge of giving the order to fire when several things gave him good cause to have second thoughts. Firstly, Morgan reminded him of their 'Jesus Christ' outburst when Gary two had appeared 'what if this is the second coming?' asked Morgan 'or just the first ever alien contact, we cannot be the aggressors who start an interstellar war'. Morgan's voice of reason caused the General to pause and reflect on his hastily reached decision. Whilst he was doing so there was a murmur from those still gathered around the screens and he looked to see what was happening. Gary having discovered he could move his knee joints and seen those movements copied by his other self, decided to try and sit down and crawl away. Bending his legs he slowly sat back down before momentum took over and he fell the last few feet onto his bottom. Now sat with his knees drawn up in front of him he used to his hands to try and move his feet, but they were still immovable and stuck to the spot. The entity continued to copy Gary's movements whilst it worked away inside the copy of his Brain looking for the communication area. Now sat opposite Gary it started experimenting with the full range of facial expressions allowed by the simple muscle groups in the face. Gary was both reassured and terrified in equal measure as he first saw the grinning, smiling and then angry grimacing face staring back at him. Unable to fully deal with the sensory overload of circumstances, frustration and adrenaline running through his body, Gary shouted 'STOP IT WILL YOU, STOP TAKING THE PISS!' As words go, for the first ever contact between mankind and a being from another world it ranked well below that suggested in nerdy science fiction books. Having released his pent up emotion Gary's head slumped, as he tried to think of a Gary way out of this situation. He would have settled for the Marines, whom he knew were close by to start shooting, anything to release him. His thoughts were suddenly stopped as a sound emerged from his copy and startled him 'STOPITWILLYOU. STOPTAKINGTHEPISS'. The entity had found where communication was stored in the Brain it had used the sounds it had heard Gary make to established a link. Those noises were an audible communication of some sort and it followed its own protocol in copying and repeating them. It noted Gary's response and dedicated more of its remote power in identifying other speech patterns. In a dark and lonely part of the brain it found what it was looking for and a jumble of new sounds, words and language became instantly available to it. It still had to make sense of it all but it now had the toolbox, it just needed to know what each tool did. Allowing the mouth to vocalise its newly found store of words, it started to slowly say out loud words and sounds that Gary himself knew and that it had copied. 'Beer, industrial, espionage, algebra, helicopter, wine, comestibles, burp, allotment' Gary's eyes widened as he heard his own voice speaking random words back at him. At first they were said slowly and deliberately but as the entity gained more control over the thinking and mouth function it speeded up. Gary was amazed as his copy now spat words at him quicker than anyone could speak them. It became a machine gun staccato of continuous words and verbalisation of every word that Gary had ever used and had stored in his memory from childhood through to now. Having reconsidered his position, the General took a mental step back from ordering the Marines to open fire. This was validated a few seconds later when the two Gary's sat opposite each other in what looked like a American Indian pow wow seating posture, and not at all aggressive. This was further confirmed in his mind when he could see that 'Jesus Christ' appeared to be talking to Gary and whatever he had to say must be important because he appeared to be talking without a pause. The General reached again for the red phone, which when it was answered he said 'Get me the President' There was a pause, a click and the General puffed up his chest out as he recognised the President's voice. He must have been waiting for his call. Gary sat silently listening to the stream of words, sounds and not infrequent swearing tumbling from the mouth of his double. Of course he did not know that it was like a printer with a new cartridge, doing a calibration test page with all the lines, letters and symbols that it knew. The entity could have course done all this easier and quicker using its main self within the dome, but the whole purpose of creating a remote Gary was to enable communication, so it had to work with the capacity of its host. It eventually exhausted the entire contents of Gary's lexicon and came to the very last word. The last words it said, without knowing the full meaning of them was 'cunty fuckface', an expression that Gary had used to his editor during one of their many rows. Being the last words spoken and then left hanging in the air, it momentarily struck Gary just how effective a swear word it actually was. It interested Gary to hear his own invented swear words, expressions and curses read back at him aloud but he frantically struggled for an explanation of why it would be doing so. The entity spoke slowly 'Gary, you, are Gary. Gary you are, are you Gary', arranging the words in its first attempt at communication. It now had all the words and phrases, now it just needed the rules and context to use them and gain experience. Gary was stunned at now hearing his own name being used and tried to reply but nothing came out. The entity presumed it had made a mistake since Gary had not replied, so correcting itself it tried again but used an upwards inflection at the end of the sentence like an annoying American teenager girl 'Gary, you are a Gary?' It waited. Gary nodded slowly before making his tongue and throat form words from his dry throat. 'Gary, yes I am a Gary' he replied, not knowing what action this would bring. The entity nodded in response 'Gary good. Gary hello' Which had the effect of allowing Gary a moment to reflect that perhaps he was not going to die right at that moment. Gaining just a modicum of confidence, Gary breathed deeply and dared to ask a question. Stumbling slightly over his words he said 'who, who are you?' The entity processed the words, instantly matching them and their meaning. It took heart from the fact that the question was one of curiosity, which implied some level of thought above that of self-survival. It was also one of the most difficult questions to answer, especially using a primitive language that it had only just been equipped to use. Drawing on experience it chose a simple reply which would satisfy until it had better knowledge of the planet and beings it was communicating with 'I am not from here' it replied. It was surprised when it saw that its reply made the being called Gary express a short laugh and spoke 'No shit!' It examined all uses of the words but as yet did not have the subtlety and comprehension to put it into the correct context. It replied as politely as it could 'No, be assured I will not'. Gary took a few moments to consider this reply and having worked out that this imposters English was not its first language, decided he had better be careful in case any communication could be misconstrued as aggressive. They sat staring at each other for a few moments as Gary considered his next move and the entity continued to run Gary's complete lexicon through its mind as it pieced together words and grammar and swearwords. The General was suddenly in two minds as to whether he wanted this job or not. This role of dealing with National unusual and unforeseen events was part of his command, and was handed over each year to a new recipient. Whilst he relished the challenge and power that it gave him, he was thinking carefully about how he should brief the President. The President's voice came through loud and clear on the direct secure telephone 'Go ahead with your update General, you are on speakerphone and the secretary for defence is listening in' said the President. The General coughed before speaking 'Well mister President, the situation here is that we do have an unusual and unforeseen event of national importance' he said, using the very words in the document of authorisation. 'Well we gathered that much General, that is why we took your recommendation to go to Defcom one. The Russians are pretty jumpy about this and the Europeans allies want to know what the hell is going on. So General, what the hell is going on?' the President asked, with a little amount of frustration edging into his voice. 'Mister President, we either have a one being alien visitation or...' he paused not wanting to say the words ''spit it out' he heard the President mutter down the phone 'or, we have the second coming of the lord Jesus Christ'. There was silence at the other end of the phone as the other parties digested what had been said. 'Did you get that mister President?' asked the General. 'Yes General, we heard you but it kinda takes a bit of getting used to hearing' said the secretary of defence's voice. After a pause the President spoke again 'Okay General, I want live video feeds over a secure network to my command bunker as soon as possible. Now General tell me what threat you identified to warrant going to Defcom one?' 'Well sir, the threat was the unknown circumstances surrounding the appearance of the apparition. I can say at this time it appears to be non-aggressive and I can recommend standing down from high alert'

'Noted General and I will discuss that option with the secretary of defence after we terminate this call. It seems you currently have things under control there General so well done, but we must keep this away from the public and the media until we can fully assess the threat and security implications to the USA. So, tell us what is happening right now?' 'Well sir, the being has appeared in a human form and has modelled its appearance on one of the staff here at ground zero. The General hoped that the generic description of staff would suffice until he could get Gary Barnes out of there. 'Staff General?' asked the President 'what member of staff is down there and is he trained for this in any way?' There was a very long pause as the General carefully considered his answer and thereby his future career. Could he really lie to the President of the United States he thought rhetorically. 'Sir, the ah staff member is one of the Brits we were searching for, the one with the female scientist from Hawaii'. His sentence fell off at the end as heard his own words condemn his career. He could hear some muted discussion on the other end as the secretary for defence brought the President up to speed on the recent hunt for the Gary and Emma. The phone was snatched up from the desk and he could hear a quiver in the President's voice as he tried to keep control 'General, I sincerely hope you are not telling me that this once only alien visitation, God's return or Jesus Christ's second coming, that has happened slap bang in the middle of the United States, is currently being presided over by a British reporter!? It was more a question based on hope than on the actual facts to hand. The General swallowed hard 'Yes Mister President that is technically correct, although we are in control of all other facets of this operation'. The line went dead but not before the General could hear swearing and the phone being slammed down onto its base. He winced at the noise before slowly putting his phone back on the cradle. Special Agent Morgan already knew the answer by looking at the General's face but he asked the question anyway. 'So, how did it go?' Gary was now reconciled to the fact he was somehow stuck to this apparition of himself and that for the time being it was

not going to eat or kill him, which allowed him space for more

rational thought. He had heard the words it had uttered but so far,

but they had either been regurgitated variations of things Gary had

said himself or was trying to communicate. He was mid thought

when he jumped out of his skin as something touched him on the

shoulder. He looked around to see a few feet away a rope lying next

to him. A further twenty feet away was a group of marines, who had

been tasked by the General with getting Gary out of there. In hushed

tones and miming, they indicated Gary should tie the rope around

his body and they would pull him clear. Knowing how he was firmly

held he tried to dissuade them but their actions were being urged on

by the General shouting at them through their earpieces. Gary

decided he at least ought to try and reaching back he took the rope

and secured it about his middle. The marines gathered themselves

along the rope as if in a tug of war competition and when ordered

began to gently pull. Having taken up the slack, the rope tightened

around Gary and started to pull the top of him backwards, but his

feet were still anchored by some invisible force. As Gary was forced

to lay back the few inches gained gave the marines the impression of success, and motivated they pulled all the harder. This now left Gary laying straight back with the rope slowly sliding up his body under his arms and towards his neck. He started to shout, but the marines were used to being shouted at, which only served to double their efforts. Within a few moments of blacking out or being horizontally hung, Gary was saved by his poor feral childhood. Never one for clubs and organisations, had Gary joined the scouts in his youth then his self-tied rope knot would have held and he would most likely have been hung or pulled in half. As it was, his misspent childhood and lack of rope tying technique allowed the knot to slowly slip through and release him and the marines from their uneven tugging match. Gary rubbed at the rope burn around his neck, whilst the marine sergeant shouted at him to tie the rope around him again. Gary was incredulous and mouthed his reply 'FUCK OFF!' He looked back towards the entity, trying to decide if being sat with himself, with the slight possibility of sudden death was preferable to being pulled in half by the US Marine Corps. He decided it was. The shimmering form beamed at him across the few feet that separated them. He studied the face and there was no mistaking his own face looking back at him, complete with a nearly a week's beard growth. The entity, whilst it was sat quietly beaming was not sat idle. During the few minutes of Gary's love tugging with the US Marines, and despite the limitations of the brain it had copied, it had managed to complete processing of Gary's version of the English language. 'You are Gary, correct?' it suddenly spoke, in a much more fluid way than before. Gary's eyes widened, as not only did it use him name it was also using Gary's voice, which it had copied along with the rest of him. 'Yes, I am Gary, how did you know my name?' he replied slowly, but 'I know everything that you know Gary, I am just do not know yet how to access it'. Gary was confused, and with his brain having so many questions, although his mouth moved nothing came out. 'You will want to know who I am?' asked the entity, again using the American upward inflection. 'I suppose so yes' said Gary, but since nothing was offered he asked the question 'so who are you, what are you, a Martian, some god, a ghost or, or what…?' Gary trailed off as he heard himself asking such prophetic questions. Still getting used to the language and the audio way of communicating, the entity took a moment to process the question. Unfortunately it was using a copy of Gary's dictionary, so whilst it knew every word, just like Gary it did not fully understand the meaning of all those words. 'Gary, I cannot answer that until I have processed more of your information' was its considered reply. It hoped it had managed to convey the message but it found using such a slow and inefficient method of communication frustrating. A cheap torch bulb of light began to come on in Gary's mind as he strung information together into an actual thought 'Wait a minute. My information, my face, my voice, are you using me? He asked. Again there was a pause as the entity remotely manipulated the Gary it had made 'Not using you directly Gary, I have made a copy of you so that I may communicate with'. The words all made sense individually but combined into a sentence they overwhelmed Gary, adding little to his understanding. His face contorted as he struggled to grasp the meaning. Whilst this information was being processed in Gary's mind he struggled to formulate another question. 'Gary you will have many questions for me, and I will have many of you, but I first I need more information about your planet and a better understanding of how you communicate' This simple benign statement to Gary this sounded a much more pleasing prospect than being torn in half by the marines, who were still behind attempting to get him away. They had now resorted to trying to lasso Gary, which only resulted in him being periodically hit on the head by the heavy rope. At the third hit Gary turned and half whispered, half shouted to them 'Go away!' The entity by now had a better understanding of the language and a basic understanding of what Gary wanted the marines to do. In what it thought would be a helpful gesture it also repeated Gary's comment to the marines to 'GO AWAY'. The difference being that the entity had raised the volume of its voice by many factors, causing Gary and the marines to physically recoil in the face of the horrendously loud audio onslaught, which could be heard back at the laboratory and for several miles around. Gary put his hands over his ears 'whoa, stop that' he shouted, as he shook his head to clear the pain. 'The other beings appeared not to hear you Gary, so I was trying to help you.' said the entity in a normal voice. 'Well that much volume causes us pain and hurts our ears, so keep it normal please' said Gary. Aware that he was now chiding whatever 'it' was, Gary tried to return the conversation back to what had passed for normal a few seconds ago, so asked a question 'So whilst you are learning the lingo and asking questions, what should I call you. What is your name?' This was easily understood by the entity but not a question easily answered as it had never had need of a name before 'I have no such title or name like yours Gary, but if it helps us to communicate then you can choose a name to call me?' Several things struck Gary at the same time. Now relieved that through he realised that he was no longer in danger from this being or god, Gary was able to relax slightly and give some thought to a name for 'it'. Still without any real idea of what 'it' was but with his head full of many possibilities, Gary ran a few ideas through his head and mentally applied them to the vison of himself sat opposite. He discarded most of the science fiction monster names from his childhood and moved towards other famous names for. Given that the entity figure was sat calmly and benignly beaming across at him, he did for a second consider calling him Buda. However, Gary realised part of the reason for being drawn to that name was that the entity also appeared to be a little overweight but that would reflect badly on Gary's own self view. Given the unique nature of the event and there still being the possibility of divine intervention, Gary came up with a name he hoped the simplicity of which would be simple and tongue in cheek, but the name he chose would have far reaching consequences. 'JC' he announced triumphantly 'I will call you JC.

How does that sound to you?' The entity searched Gary's limited vocabulary and finding only the letters JC without any other reference decided it was suitable 'Yes Gary, call me JC' In the CCTV cabin the events thus far had been witnessed from many camera angles but witnessed silently as Gary was not wired for sound. The exception was when the words 'GO AWAY!' were blasted from the entity at ground zero, causing the marines to all clasp their hands over their ears and drop the rope. The General had given specific orders to the marines to remove Gary so that he could regain control of the situation and report back positively to the President. They could all see the efforts the marines were going to and were relieved when none of them seemed hurt by the extremely loud 'go away' instruction. Now faced with the possibility that this British journalist was somehow in the driving seat and communicating with the being, the General needed to exercise some control or at least be able to hear what was happening. He spoke into the radio handset held by his aide and told the marine colonel to get a microphone near enough to 'that damn Brit' to hear what was going on. As with all military operations, the colonel sent the order down through his chain of command until it reached somebody who knew that they were doing. In this case it was a tall, skinny, nerdy looking marine called Mandy, who maintained and operated the encryption radio equipment. Not only was he the right man technically for the job, but also because the other marines held a not so secret grudge against. This mainly but not wholly stemmed from the fact whenever they were out living in the mud, he was always with his sensitive equipment in a tent or vehicle in the warm and dry. The other reason was that he was called Mandy, which they felt did not reflect the proud traditions of the US Marine Corps. The shit now having travelled right down the chain of command landed at his vehicle doorstep within two minutes of the General giving the order. 'Mandy' said the corporal 'Get a microphone and some audio recording equipment down at ground zero ASAP. Got it?' In the time honoured tradition of marines everywhere, Mandy replied in the affirmative before he had really thought the order through. He had witnessed his fellow marines attempting to get a rope around that guy and even took a little pleasure at watching them get knocked back by the loud noise. He was something of a loner but not a stupid one, so gave the problem some more thought until he had a solution.

The General was getting impatient. It had been ten minutes since he had ordered 'ears on' to the target and every minute that passed bore silent witness to that Brit conversing with America's greatest threat, greatest ally or greatest God. He had just picked up the microphone to start issuing a rollicking when something moved across the edge of the screen. It was small compact and weaved about as it made its way towards where ground zero. Gary was faintly aware of a slight buzzing noise from behind him, but before he could turn his head something ran into his back. He looked around to see a red radio control pick-up truck nudging him and tooting as if to get his attention. In the back of the truck was a headset and small radio pack, complete with a hand written note. 'Sir, the General requests that you wear the microphone so we can monitor the situation and protect you if required' Gary read the note with a slight smile. He didn't know much about what was happening but what he did know was that there was little they could do to protect him if this went wrong and he really was in danger. But he reasoned that apart from the General, Emma and Mike would also be watching and listening, so a microphone would give him a chance to big his part up and play to the gallery. Donning the headset microphone and earpiece he spoke into it 'testing one two, you getting me out there? The General grabbed the table mike before anyone else could answer said tersely 'yes you limey bottom feeding reporter, we are getting you loud and clear. Now what the hell do you think…' was the start of a question that Gary quickly interrupted 'whoa, steady there honcho. Admittedly I may not be the most qualified person at the site but at the moment I am all you've got, so can I suggest you play nice or I will turn the mic off!' This came out over the speakers in the CCTV lab and the camp, bringing a smile to those listening, especially Emma and the marines. Realising Gary did indeed hold the 'benny left right' of trump cards, the General took a deep breath and a big mouthful of humble pie 'Mister Barnes, I have personal authorisation from the President of the United States to take whatever action I deem necessary to protect the security of our nation and that includes military action if needed. Do you hear that?' 'Yes General I heard that, but luckily for you JC here did not' There was a gasp in the lab and around the base camp as the word 'JC' rang out from the speakers. It may have seemed an off the cuff name to Gary but in the context of the situation they were in it seemed to ring out like a bell to the faithful and doubters alike. The General assumed the worst or best in equal measure, and in fact could not decide if this really was Jesus Christ whether it would be a good or bad thing. Only Gary knew the much simpler explanation for the name at that point, unknowing as to what he had done. The General was lost for words. Having been brought up to believe that 'in god we trust' and every man written word of the god bible, he never thought he would ever see the much written about second coming. 'Are you communicating with others Gary?' asked JC. 'Yes JC' Gary replied 'Some of the military people were getting anxious about your motives and wanted to hear our conversation. That is what this sophisticated equipment is doing' JC smiled benignly. Actually having operated the clumsy body for a while it was getting used to some of the subtler movements and expressions. It recognised that the thing called a smile was the least threatening facial expression and used it in between all its sentences. JC continued beaming its newly learnt perma smile, and holding out its hands in an open gesture said 'I mean them no harm'. The name JC that Gary had chosen, along with these words were now clearly picked up the microphone and transmitted back to the CCTV lab, along with the pictures to the President's office. JC's shimmering appearance, words, arms held wide posture and JC title, all contributed to feeding the religious expectations of many of the people watching the CCTV live feed. The General felt his knees weaken as he now assumed that he was watching and hearing the voice of Jesus Christ for the first time ever. The same feeling came over everyone authorised to hear the words, especially those with religious convictions. There was a small contingent of other religious beliefs, who whilst fascinated by the unfolding spectacle also started to have nagging doubts about their own choice of god's. The one thing that did keep some people's feet on the ground was that although the shimmering and benign being seemed to offer no threat, its voice and face were unmistakably that of Gary Barnes. It caused enough doubt to stop most people falling to their knees in supplication, with the exception of the military padre at the base who was already on his third rendition of the Lord's Prayer and whom had broken his crucifix by gripping it so tightly. The General started to speak but in his shock had not really formulated any complete questions only thoughts that he aired before filtering them 'Can you ask him or it, is he, Is this, is he really?' The questions tumbled nonsensically from his mouth, with even his voice now lacking any air of military authority. Whilst Gary was also still in awe, he was also a few minutes ahead of everyone else. Now fairly confident that he was going to live through the next few minutes he had time to use of his recently regained composure to consider what was best for himself. Using his position to his advantage, Gary presumed, presupposed and guessed a great deal as he spoke through into the microphone. 'General, remember I am only one step ahead of you so far. However, it seems I am the chosen one, the conduit for communication and that is why JC is using a copy of me. I do not have any answers as yet but JC here is slowly getting around to filling in details, but this is breaking ground for everyone, okay?' Gary's use of the expression 'chosen one' and again use of the name JC, only reaffirmed the religious thoughts going through most people's minds, not least the atheists amongst the listeners, who were also starting to worry a little about their not so entrenched positions. 'So JC' said Gary 'Could you release my feet so that I can move a little?

'Yes Gary, of course' replied JC. The shimmering lights that emanated from JC and surrounded Gary's feet immediately withdrew. Gary rubbed his feet as if to restore circulation, but this proved to be just a reflex action that surprisingly to Gary was totally unnecessary. The fact his feet were fine came as a surprise, as later would be to find the miraculous disappearance of his lifelong fungal nail infection that Gary lived with. Gary stood up and just for a split second considered running away, '*but running away to where and from what?* He thought. *'After all, wasn't this what he wanted? Chasing the mad professor across the world in the vain hope that he would be able to break the biggest news story ever?* Ridiculous as this sounded in his head, now here he was stood in front of JC or ET, but whatever it was. Gary Barnes was now world centre stage, '*so sod it no*' he thought, '*Gary Barnes was not running away anytime soon'*

CHAPTER NINETEEN: THE LEARNING

Emma and Mike looked incredulously at each other across the CCTV cabin. They were not sure what they were actually seeing but whatever it was it was causing them to have serious doubts about every known universal scientific law and principal they had lived their lives by. The only thing keeping them both grounded was the fact that Gary was involved, and that must in part account for what was happening. Several of the staff were quietly muttering prayers under their breath and crossing themselves, as the General laid his hands on their shoulders in support. The atmosphere was suddenly shaken by the loud warbling noise made by the red secure telephone.

The same phone might have at some point passed orders for a nuclear strike, a declaration of war on another country or told of the assassination of a President, but now it needed information. On answering the phone the General spoke quietly and reverently to the President of the United States. There were obviously many questions being asked and many assumptions being given as answers. To those listening it was clear and not unreasonable that the General was confirming to the President, which at this time, given all available information that this was indeed the much vaulted second coming of the lord. Bringing himself to attention he ended the conversation 'Yes Mister President, I will' before hanging up the phone. Everyone in the room looked at him expectantly 'Ladies and gentlemen, at this time we are to assume that this is indeed a religious visitation and we are to continue monitoring and conversing with JC to confirm this. The President will visit ground zero in the next twenty four hours. That is all carry on'. With a curt nod of self-importance, the General and left the lab and went to the motorhome that had been put at his disposal. Once inside he took off his braided Air Force cap and went across to the bureau where he poured himself a large whisky. Sitting on the edge of the sofa, his mind whirling with facts, assumptions and years of religious dogma, he stared confused into the tan coloured glass. He could smell the whisky but did not drink it, instead he watched as the tears running down his cheeks plopped into the glass, dissolving into the overpriced Scottish liquid. Even this simple thing only served to confirm some deeper value to the events he had just witnessed. Emma watched the General leave and then taking Mike's arm she led him away from the CCTV monitors towards the back of the room. In hushed tones she said 'Well then Mike, what do you make of that. Alien, God or some figment of Gary's imagination that he had drawn us into?' Mike shrugged his shoulders 'I just don't know anything for sure anymore. Everything I thought I knew has been moved sideways or made irrelevant. And even Gary could not have set this up' They both seem to take mutual comfort in agreeing that whilst Gary was good, innovative and a damn good liar, he could not have put all this together' 'No you are right' Emma said 'Gary has got himself very much at the centre of all this but he is not the cause, this is real'. Besides, it was me that dragged him away from his job and life in England when I thought I needed a journalist' Mike managed a smile 'Yes, well it seems like your plan to catch a journalist went a little too well. Not only has he now got your story, am I right in thinking he has also got your heart?' Emma blushed and tried to dismiss Mike's suggestion out of hand, but it was clear she was 'protesting too much' so having run out of steam she added 'well perhaps I do have a soft spot for him, but that mostly because he is vulnerable and I got him into all this' Mike's eyes widened 'Vulnerable!' he laughed 'That's like saying Hitler was in touch with his feminine side!' Emma's laughed at the clumsy but accurate description and mutely accepted Mike's point. She started to smile and was about to verbally agree with him, but before she could answer there were a gasp from the camera assistant so they returned their attention to the monitors. Gary was feeling more confident by the minute. Since he had been released physically by JC, all the residual fuzziness in his head had disappeared. He was nearly functioning normally except for an abundance of adrenaline that was coursing through his body. In truth, having thought they were all going to die over the last few weeks and then narrowly missed death himself at the hands of the creator, Gary was feeling quite smug. Somehow, either because the creator of the entire universe wanted it to be, or through his own Gary Barnes self-belief, he now appeared to be in the driving seat of the greatest story ever to be told. There was of course a third possibility which as had not yet occurred to Gary. He decided the time was right to ask some questions, not just to get some answers but also to get information that would continue to keep in the front row of the grid. Gary had decided to release whatever information he could find in small chunks, thereby making his own role more important. Standing in front of the shimmering JC and in a much more confident tone he spoke, 'so JC, I have the big three questions for. Everyone is really curious as to who you are, where you are from and what do you want? There was no immediate reply from JC who just sat contemplatively with his eyes closed. After a few seconds his eyes opened and the beaming face returned, reassuring Gary and giving JC a little more facial muscle practice. JC spoke 'Gary, I know that you must be curious and have many questions to ask me, but I cannot answer your questions until I know more about you and the species that live here'. Gary nodded 'Okay, I can understand that JC, so go ahead, what do you want to know?' JC closed his eyes again and after a twenty second gap opened his eyes and spoke.' Gary, I already know most of what you know, I am just having some difficulty finding and arranging it in an order that

I can readily understand and evaluate. Your capacity appears to be lower than some of the others I have sampled but since I have made already made a facsimile of you then I will persevere with what I have. However, I do need to have a full and complete understanding before I can answer your questions. It is a protocol I must follow' Gary was slightly hurt but not entirely surprised to hear that he was not the cleverest person on the planet, he just did not expect to hear it spelt out for him by an intergalactic visitor. He took some small comfort from the fact that it was actually him stood there in front of JC and not some dry crusty professor who wanted to discuss scientific formulae. Gary Barnes was here by guile & strength of mind, not because of some framed degree scroll hanging on a wall. Skipping over the unintended insult, Gary continued 'I have seen you close your eyes before talking, is there a reason for this?' The eyes closed again but only for a few seconds 'Yes Gary. When I close the eyes it is because I am looking at the language area of your mind that I copied and comparing words, thoughts and emotions. It sometime takes a few seconds or many if I also have to refer back to my main essence which is still inside the dome to clarify something. It is not too disturbing I hope and my communication is getting better?' 'No' said Gary 'that is not a problem now that I know and yes, your language is getter better'. By answering both a yes and a no in the same sentence, Gary had caused JC some consternation and the eyes closed. It took another fifteen seconds for him to find the words, translate them to its higher intelligence in the dome and then reverse the process. JC beamed again 'Good Gary'. Gary was at a loss what to ask next, since he had already been informed by JC that he need a fuller understanding of everything. 'Then how can I help you understand all that you need to know?' asked Gary. JC replied almost immediately as this level of language was already understood. 'Is there someone here who answer all my questions Gary?' This was an unexpected turn of events that Gary did not like, as it could take him out of the loop if there was a third party that could easily take his place. He was getting along just fine with JC but on the other hand he did not want to feel he was replaceable by a scientist or worse a politician. Of course there were any number of educated egg headed boffins who could be sat here in his place, but how would that benefit Gary?' Thinking quickly, Gary came up with an idea that might still leave him with some sort of control. 'There is no one person that could answer all your questions JC, but there is one place'. He left the words to hang for effect, which apart from being completely lost on JC only added to the time to reply. 'So Gary, there is a central reservoir of information that I can access which might meet my requirements?' Gary nodded 'Yes JC, I can get you access to the most powerful system, it is called the internet.' Back in the CCTV lab the people were again edging closer to the screens for a better look. The slight gasp that had brought Emma and the others back was because two things had happened. Firstly the shimmering bonds that secured Gary has suddenly vanished and he was now able to move around. Secondly they had lost the audio feed from Gary's mic, so were back to pictures only. A few seconds after this had happened the red phone warbled again and Special Agent Morgan answered it. Having explained who he was and that he General had stepped out for a moment, he was quickly dismissed to find him and get him back on the phone tout suite! Hanging up the phone, he scuttled down the steps of the cabin and ran through the maze of trucks and cabins to the one reserved for the General. After knocking twice, he tentatively open the door and called the General's name. He was surprised to see the General knelt in the corner of the motorhome, rocking back and forth and apparently praying. He coughed once 'General Sir, General?' At the second attempt the General did respond by slowly raising his head, showing his tear stained cheeks where he had been crying. 'He has come back' was all he seemed to be saying over and over. Morgan approached the General and helped him get to his feet. In truth he did not like the General much, especially since he as now technically in charge, but an order from the President was an order, and beside perhaps when he saw the state of the General control would revert back to him. After several attempts at reasoning with him Morgan felt time was slipping away, so in desperation he slapped the General across the face and shook him by the lapels. 'General, the President wants you on the hotline, NOW!' Whether it was the physical shock or the mention of the President's name was not clear, but certainly the combination had the desired effect and the General started to shape up. 'Yes' he said unsteadily as he regained his composure and balance 'Thank you Special Agent Morgan. Tell the President I will right along'. Now looking like he was in a position to be 'right along' Morgan nodded and left the General to tidy himself up before returning to the lab. It was precisely three minutes later when the phone rang again and was answered by Morgan. There was a terse exchange of views, or at least the President sharing his single angry view that the General should be on the phone by now. The President had just finished listing the things that would happen if he did not talk to the General right now, when he entered the lab. Everyone was shocked at the dishevelled state of the General, to say nothing of the faint smell of alcohol that pervaded the room. Morgan took the phone from his ear and held it out to the General. 'It's the President' he said needlessly. The General dragged his hand across his face, then taking a deep breath took hold of the phone. 'General Baxter here. Go ahead Mister President' he said. The next minute was a painful one to witness as the General was subjected to a one sided tirade as the President vented his anger. Once he had run out of steam and the President sensed he had made his point, he turned to the matter in hand. 'Now General. The security lockdown we have in place has caused a lot of questions to be asked. The state governor, senators, congress and the press are all pushing me for answers. I have even had the Russian President on the phone demanding to know what we are up to. What I need from you now is some sort of answer as to what we are dealing with here. I need a definitive proof that this really Jesus Christ, an alien or some sort of clever commie scheme to undermine the United States. You hear me General? The General stood staring straight ahead. His whole childhood, Sunday school and church upbringing mingled with thoughts of his mother and her last words to him 'son Jesus Christ will return'. This whole situation had played heavily on his mind and that combined with these thoughts and the whisky had led him to a conclusion. 'Mister President, as you know we have been tracking and preparing for a cataclysmic event for the last two months. None of the scientists could tell us what to expect and no one could have predicted what has actually happened. Today sir, I believe we have really witnessed the second coming of the lord Jesus Christ.' There was a few seconds silence before the President spoke 'And you are quite sure about this General?' 'yes sir' the General replied 'Everything about this, his appearance, the power we have witnessed, the location here in the United States and even his name all tell me we have a religious event here, not little green men from Mars' 'Very well General, if that is your considered personal and professional opinion, then we will go with it and God help us. Now you monitor the situation and keep me informed of any developments but be able to be contacted at a moment's notice, do you hear me General?' 'I hear you sir' said the General as the line went dead. Emma had left the cabin for some fresh air and to clear her head. She wanted to start examining the science that she felt sure was there now everyone was talking about god, the science had been pushed into the background. She went around the rear of the cabin into the darkness and was surprised to see two figures huddled in an embrace. They heard her approach and disentangled themselves to reveal it was Mike and Steve renewing their relationship with a hug. It was a slightly awkward moment but Steve seized the initiative 'I was just updating Mikey on the situation with the FBI bosses' he offered. None of them believed it for a moment but it was enough to stave off the slight clumsiness that the situation had created. 'How are you doing?' asked Mikey to Emma. 'Okay I guess' she replied 'No, you are most definitely not' said Steve 'so what is it?' Emma looked at them both 'Well first I was the expert, trying to save the world. Then it arrived, we name it god and suddenly I am not needed anymore. Any science learning is being lost in the religion of the whole thing and also…' she stopped mid-sentence 'and also Gary?' ventured Mikey. Her silent pursed lip was enough of a reply. 'Anything we can do to help' asked Steve.

'No' she replied,' the only one that could help fill in all those gaps would be Gary, and I am not going to be able to get anywhere near him anytime soon' 'Perhaps Steve could help' asked Mike, looking directly at him. 'Sorry, but that is way above my paygrade, but maybe Morgan would sanction it. I see him getting more and more frustrated with the way the military are handling this, so he just might help'.' Well perhaps if you could ask him if I could just have a couple of minutes with Gary, it might just help?' pleaded Emma. With both Mike and Emma looking at him, Steve nodded and acquiesced to the peer pressure but mentally he thought he would put off speaking to Morgan as long as possible. JC opened his eyes, smiled the way he knew how and spoke. 'Gary, how is my language?' Gary nodded 'pretty good considering you have only been at it for a couple of hours'. JC tried to widen his smile to show the appreciation emotion he had recently discovered in a dark recess of Gary's mind, but was hindered by running the facial muscles to their limit. Gary decided to have one more attempt at getting information from JC, both through curiosity and knowing that any knowledge was power. 'JC, I understand your need for further information, but there are some personal things that I am having difficulty with and would appreciate an answer to?' The now familiar eyes close and open routine quickly occurred whilst JC was processing the information, before he eventually he spoke. 'Gary, I have already learnt a lot but there are many things still unknown to me, which I must know before I can give full disclosure to you.' Gary nodded 'I understand, but what is really freaking me out is standing here looking and talking to an image of myself. Can you at least explain that to me please? The eyes were closed a little longer as JC researched the new words he was exposed to but when he understood he spoke 'Gary, my native communication is highly complex and not an audible one, so I need a way of converting my intelligence into your speech. I also need an understanding on the level of intelligence you possess, so creating a facsimile of you and your brain and exploring deep within its recesses gives me that understanding. Its small capacity does limit the amount I can process without referring back to myself inside the dome, where what you would call my brain resides. I also thought an image of you would be less threatening to yourself. Does that help? Whilst once again slapped in the face by the throwaway comment about his 'small capacity' he was pleased to have least managed to get more information. At this moment in time he was the world leader in JC's and their associated copy making. 'Yes thank you' said Gary 'that explains why you copied me and also why you chose to copy the prettiest one on the planet' Gary laughed to indicate it was a joke but the rictus grin on JC's face indicated it had not discovered humour yet. Gary continued 'So, I suggest the first thing you need is to access the internet for information, then you will able to answer all my questions?' Without warning JC began several large mouth movements combined with guttural noises. Gary was at first worried until he realised that JC was trying to perform a laugh. 'Are you okay?' asked Gary. The noise stopped and JC replied 'Gary, I was behind in the language processing and just realised that you made a humour. My understanding is that a response was required from me and I performed a chortle. Was that correct?' 'Wow tough room, a chortle would do but a belly laugh would have been more polite' JC digested this information but also enjoyed the synthetically produced pleasure that the humour had caused. It noted this new emotion. As Gary waited to speak there was a thump as the loud speakers were turned on. A voice that Gary recognised as the General spoke 'Would Mister Barnes please turn his microphone back on and not turn it off again without permission'. Gary wondered how they knew, but of course the CCTV and the lack of sound were two obvious clues. He turned the microphone back on with a definite lack of enthusiasm and respect in his tone spoke 'Got you General. I got you good and proper' 'Good mister Barnes, good. Now as you can imagine we have a lot of questions, so...' Gary held up his hand and cut the General off 'General, I' then corrected himself 'WE understand your need for information but at the moment that is not possible' There was silence before the General's voice returned with a little more edge in it 'Mister Barnes, we have the whole defence network of the United States at readiness and the whole world stood by in anticipation. I am sure you can see why the president needs information urgently?' There was an implied threat in his voice Gary thought, or was it perhaps nervousness? 'General, I think it best if I come and speak to you in person, okay?' 'Yes, that sounds a good idea Mister Barnes. If you would slowly step back towards the lights the marines will escort you to my location'. Gary looked at JC 'I think it best if I go and meet with these others so I can allay their fears about you. I can also arrange for you to have access to the internet, so then you can find all the information you need. Is that okay?' Once he understood, JC smiled and said 'Yes Gary, that is a good idea, but you will come back? 'Yes' replied Gary 'I will come back soon. Gary turned and walked back towards the lights that had been set up at the edge of the clearing. Walking into the light he was temporarily blinded until he passed them and his eyes adjusted. As he blinked he was firmly grasped by both arms and his hands zip tied behind his back. He was also gagged and a hood put over his head as he was roughly manhandled and taken under control. Mumbling and being as uncooperative as he could be given the circumstances he was led away. The only sense that was of use was his nose, and the smell of human faeces told him the same marine guards he had duped back at the motorhome were now exacting some revenge. After a minute or so of walking he was aware of being led up some steps into a moving vehicle. His hood was taken off and he found himself stood in another motorhome, but this time in front of him was the General and Special Agent Morgan. With a nod from the General his gag was removed along with the zip ties holding his wrists. 'That will be all men' said the General to the two marines. Both men saluted and went to leave the vehicle before the General added 'and clean that shit of your boots!' Gary shook himself down 'Was there really any need for that General?' 'Oh let me see Mister Barnes, you took off with the only scientist who had any clues about the bad weather. You evaded capture by the FBI and when we finally caught up with you here, you managed to escape from the marine guards on your motorhome!' Gary listened and could not help smirking like a naughty schoolboy. Ignoring his expression the General spoke 'Now, the President of the United States would like some answers Mister Barnes'. 'Call me Gary' said Gary, causing the General's face to flush 'General, JC is currently not taking any questions or giving out any answers, simples'. Both men looked at each other. 'And why not' asked Morgan. 'Because, he wants information first' Then from somewhere deep in him mind said ' He has made himself in my image to better understand the language and communicate, but he now desires greater knowledge before he can best judge how to answer yours, mine and the President's questions, got it?' The General spoke, 'information? But how and in what format? Before Morgan joined in 'meetings, paper, books, and computers?' 'The internet' said Gary to gasps of astonishment from the two men. 'But that's where people go to play games, show each other pictures of their dancing cat and to watch porn' said Morgan. 'Yes' replied Gary 'and that is exactly what JC wants, the inside scoop, who we are and what we do so he can judge us' Once again Gary's choice of words, namely the words judge and JC in the same sentence brought an overriding emotional response from the General. Speaking slowly he said 'he wants to judge us? He wants to judge us!' Aware that he might be losing the General again to some religious emotional state, Morgan decided to take charge. 'Can we be assured there is no threat from JC?' he asked. Gary struck a serious pose 'Well none so far. I am sure you can see from the cameras he mostly just sits there smiling like a Cheshire cat. It's simples, if we want more from him then he needs something from us and besides if we don't give it to him I think he is capable of getting it himself. This could be a test of our good will'. Morgan and the General were both silent but each for different reasons. The General needed a prayer and a drink, but not necessarily in that order. Morgan needed someone in charge who he could rely on or who would hand over responsibility to him. He offered an opinion, 'General, since the internet is open source anyways, with none of our top secret stuff on it, I suggest we allow this as a gesture of compliance and cooperation?' The question in his voice slowly registered with the General, who in a sliver of lucidness nodded in agreement. 'Right that is agreed then, I will arrange the technical aspect of getting a satellite broadband feed down to ground zero and you Gary tell us how you want him hooked up, okay?' 'That's sounds good' said Gary, happy that he got what he wanted 'but there are two other things urgently needed' 'Go on' said Morgan, ready to take notes and act. 'I need to take a piss and eat some food before I go back down there' said Gary. Somewhat deflated Morgan replied 'The toilet is through there and I will arrange the marines to bring something over from the canteen' Gary nodded and moved to the toilet, but before closing the door said 'can you get two other marines to fetch my food, I think those two outside might have something against me'. By the time Gary had finished his ablutions and eaten his food, he was nearly ready to return to JC, but there was one other thing he needed to do. 'I want to see Emma, I mean professor Rowlinson before I go back' he said. 'What for?' asked the General, wary that there was some ulterior motive for the request 'What is wrong with our scientific team, we have the best in the world?' Moving from one foot to another like a naughty school boy,

Gary replied 'Ah it's not that General, it's a small personal matter'. The General and Morgan both looked at each other in a moment of understanding and nodded in agreement. Morgan replied 'I'll take you over to where she is'.

Emma had her back to the door of the lab talking to Mike as she heard someone coming up the steps. Assuming it was going to be the *efficient and done by the book* Morgan, or the all too flaky General, she did not bother looking around. Looking straight at Mike, she was surprised to his gaze shift from her eyes to over her shoulder and a faint smile start to form on his face. Before she could react everything went dark as someone's hands came from behind and covered her eyes. She gasped a little at the shock of the moment whilst her mind tried to work out who it could be. She was assisted by a familiar and unpleasant smell from the fingers that assaulted her senses, which under any other circumstances would have made her gag. The combination of chilli powder, earth, sweat and a cheap and nasty after shave lotion could mean only one thing, Gary! She spun and looked straight into the face of the man she had for some reason been missing. Gary opened his arms wide in greeting, expecting the music to swell and the woman to fall into his arms. He stood in that position for a few expectant seconds before switching slowly to a slightly embarrassed pose as it became obvious the long lost greeting was not going to happen. Everyone in the lab watching felt for him, it was like watching a spurned marriage proposal at a football game but in agonising close up. Not that Emma did not want to return his public display of affection, it was just that she was still firmly in professional mode amongst her scientific peers and could not simply let go. Trying to lessen the tension she spoke first 'Gary, what are you doing up here? Are you okay?' she asked in what she thought was a caring tone but came across as cold as a *'cough please'* type medical question. His arms now firmly by his side and his face trying to hide deep disappointment, he responded glibly 'Good to see you to Prof. Yes, I am fine thanks for asking, just popped back to make JC a cup of tea'. Nobody laughed or even smiled, assuming that is exactly what Gary was doing. He sighed 'Wow, tough room. It was a joke you bozo's, JC only drinks coffee!' There was polite laughter as the joke permeated but at least it had broken the awkward tension that had been created in the room. Emma realising that her cold reaction had caused some offence tried to make up the lost ground 'Gary, we have been watching you on the CCTV, you are doing great. What it is, who is it and why does he look like you?' The last sentence tumbled from her lips as she could not contain her curiosity. 'Just wait a minute prof.' replied Gary calmly 'I have come up to make some arrangement for JC and to tell you what I know so far. Rather than repeat myself over and over, can I suggest I tell all you boffins about it together over coffee'. It wasn't a question but a carefully worded statement designed to do two things. Firstly, it was to ensure that everyone knew Gary was firmly in the driving seat, and that information would be forthcoming when he deemed the time was right. There was also a small undertone of punishing Emma for her recent lack of enthusiasm, keeping her in line with the others. Even in the midst of the world class events that were unfolding, Gary was still able to be small minded and petty when his feeling had been hurt. Emma of course realised what Gary was doing but also something of an understanding because of the way she had just reacted. Special Agent Morgan spoke 'All the science based participants who have clearance are to meet in the canteen for a briefing in five minutes. Mister Barnes here will update you on what we currently know before returning to ground zero'. 'Emma bit her bottom lip 'you are going back down there Gary? 'Yes' Gary replied in what he hoped was a 'man must do what a man must do' kind of voice. 'I have to see this thing through'. Happy with his reply he turned and followed Morgan out of the lab and through the labyrinth of vehicles to the larger canteen porta cabin. Inside were a group of marines getting some much needed food, along with some of the technical staff. Morgan cleared his throat and spoke loudly 'I am sorry but everyone who does not have Alpha Black security clearance must leave the canteen now'. There was a moments disbelief as the marines had just been relieved had full plates of much needed food to consume. Morgan waited a second before adding another 'NOW!' to his sentence. This galvanised the marines and techies into action as reluctantly they got up to leave. The techie left everything and hurried out but the marines took their time as they gathered up their weapon, helmets and other possessions, before also taking their plates of food. As they walked passed Morgan they avoided eye contact but the two still with human faeces on their boots gave Gary a menacing stare as they passed by. Gary made his way to the serving hatch where the chef was waiting to serve food from the hot plate containers. Morgan spoke to the chef 'You too chef, outta here please'. The chef threw down his ladle in disgust and taking off his apron also skulked sullenly out of the cabin. Gary wasted no time in helping himself to a selection of the chicken, chilli, rice and French fries that were laid out. Morgan looked despairingly at the huge pile of food on Gary's plate 'are you going to eat all that?' with the emphasis on the word 'all'. Gary stopped shovelling food for a moment and looked at him 'Special agent Morgan, it is hard to describe how hungry it makes you feel having yourself cloned and then dealing with outrageous beings from god know where. Do you know?' Of course he did not know and the put down was as obvious as the mound of food on Gary's plate, or at least what was now left of it. He ate in silence for another minute before the door opened and in trooped the American scientific team led by Professor Brown, followed by Emma, Mike and the General. They took up positions facing Gary, most of them horrified at the crab like way he was feeding his face. Gary made them wait till the last mouthful of hot chilli was burning his mouth and sliding south down his gullet before he pushed the plate away and belched loudly. He was holding court and savouring the moment. Gary rang his tongue around the inside of his mouth, on the face of it to savour the taste of the chilli but in reality he was savouring the moment as everyone's eyes were on him expectantly. He judged the time was just right to make the most impact and took a deep breath, but as he did so the door to the canteen was suddenly thrown open. Through the door came four men dressed identically in loose fitting jackets and ear pieces, looking slightly menacing and with purpose in their step. All eyes turned to them as they surveyed the scene and looked at the assembled group. It was clear they were a security team of some sort but not one that had been expected. There was one who appeared to be in charge of the team and who was overseeing the situation. He directed the others to various positions and looked everyone up and down suspiciously. The General started to speak but the man in charge held up his hand to stop him, which surprisingly worked. Once the men had dispersed themselves around the canteen and he was satisfied with the situation, the main man spoke 'Apologies ladies and gentlemen for this unannounced intrusion and security clampdown, the reasons for which will become obvious in a few minutes'. Now if you will just be patient'. The General looked at Special Agent Morgan for an answer but merely got a shrug and 'I have no idea' look in return. Morgan's many years of instinct and training had not been wasted and almost unconsciously he moved his hand towards his concealed automatic pistol under his jacket, '*just in case*' he thought to himself. Fortunately for him, the security team now controlling the room had better training and quicker reactions. Before his hand had even reached his jacket two of them team had drawn weapons and were pointing them at him. The leader spoke 'perhaps I should have mentioned that if anyone is carrying a weapon they should declare it now to avoid any accidents' He emphasised the word 'accidents' and left everyone in no doubt as to exactly what he meant. Morgan was impressed with the professional reaction times but also slightly pissed off that he still had no idea who these men were and that they had read him like a book. 'I would like to see some ID' he said to the leader, who then nodded to the nearest agent to Morgan. Instantly a leather badge holder was flicked open in front of his face. It was not the shiny badge that impressed him but the words written on the small qualifying insert underneath. Morgan raised his eyes and nodded in mute agreement. 'I am special agent Morgan FBI and I am carrying a weapon'. Thank you special Agent Morgan, if you would do me the courtesy of handing it over to my colleague for safe keeping. It will be returned shortly'. Much to everyone's surprise, whatever Morgan had seen in the badge cover had convinced him to give up his weapon. Moving slowly he pulled the jacket open to reveal his weapon, allowing the security team member to reach in and carefully remove his pistol from the shoulder holster. Now satisfied that the room was sterile and ready, the leader lifted his sleeve to his mouth and spoke two code words into the hidden microphone concealed in the cuff. There was then an uncomfortable silence which nobody saw fit to break, except for Gary's body which was noisily dealing with the spicy dinner he had just consumed. The wait lasted a full three minutes before the leader put his hand to his earpiece and nodded as a message came through. 'Ladies and gentlemen, please remain seated and make no sudden movements. The President of the United States'. Perfectly timed, the door was opened and preceded by another security member in briskly walked the President, along with a small entourage of men and women. He nodded in recognition to the amazed team of scientists sat in a row before taking a seat that was quickly organised for him. He was joined by one of the senior men with him, the rest stood at the back ready to do his bidding. Gary, was as amazed as everyone else in the room but still the child in him spotted something he knew from national Geographic documentaries. One of the stood military officers was carrying a briefcase which if the documentary was to be believed, contained the nuclear missile launch information, triggers and codes. Amongst everything else that had gone on in the last twenty four hours, this one small thing seriously impressed Gary. The President spoke 'I must apologise for the turning up unannounced ladies and gentlemen, but given the current situation my security team insisted on it' he waved his hand towards the security team leader. 'Since we are facing a unique set of circumstances, and I was having trouble making contact with my representative here' making an obvious reference to the General 'I decided I must come down and see for myself what we are facing and as leader of the free world make contact'. He looked to the front of the room and spoke to Gary 'I understand you Mister...' 'Barnes' was whispered in his ear by the man sat next to him. 'Yes, Mister Barnes, a British journalist has made first contact.' You could hear in his voice that there was no doubt that the President found it difficult to reconcile just how a British journalist had managed to literally beat literally everyone else in the USA to literally make first contact. He started to speak again but was interrupted by Gary and consequently a slight gasp from some of the people in the room. 'Gary, just call me Gary'. The President was not used to being interrupted and had quite forgotten what it was like. Having been slightly taken aback, after five years of being surrounded by 'yes men' he actually found the experience curiously refreshing and amusing. 'So, Gary. You have made contact and exchanged some conversation with 'it', is that correct?' Gary nodded but answered in a questioning manner, 'Yes..?' as if he wanted to know what to call the President of the United States. 'You call him Mister President, or sir' said one of the aides quickly, very much used to correcting protocols of visiting dignitaries. 'Mister President, sir' said Gary. 'Yes, I am the chosen one, personally selected by, copied by and talking to JC.' The President nodded 'He told you his name was JC?' Gary shook his head and lied a little then lied a lot. He lied partly because he had named JC in a hurry and having given him divine status he now had to see it through. He could have equally called him Dave and that might have been easier in the long run. 'I am not sure sir because there was a lot of things happening at once'. The look on the President and everyone's face told Gary he had their full attention, so he launched into his rehearsed whilst sat on the toilet version of events. 'So, there I was down by the dome checking it out. Suddenly I am frozen to the spot and then face to face with a copy of myself. There is some static electricity noise, my brain refuses to work properly and then wham suddenly I am talking with JC himself. He starts to say random words, getting faster with each word until he is talking in a blur, until he said everything single word that I know and a few that I had forgotten. Once he has done that he tells me he can now speak English and that his name is JC. I have tried talking to him and he makes polite conversation but he refuses point blank to answer any questions about himself until he says he fully understands us better. He wants to make a judgement about us and needs information to do it. He has made a copy of me so he can better understand us and also so he can communicate using our language. So Mister President, that is what I know and that is where we are at!' Whilst this was essentially the truth, it had of course been modified to suit Gary's immediate needs and to protect his future wants. JC's name change was all part of the game Gary thought. Although he himself did have some concerns about what might happen if this really did turn out to be a religious event, but he would deal with that when the time came.

The President nodded thoughtfully before speaking 'Thank you Gary, that is very informative' Turing to his aid he said 'I would like to speak with Gary alone, is there somewhere private we can talk?' The General spoke up 'Ah Mister President, my Winnebago is at your disposal' 'Thank you General and of course after that I will need to meet with you'. The tone is his voice left little doubt that this would be a one sided meeting without coffee, cake or pleasantries. The General led the President and his entourage out of the canteen and through the vehicles to his motorhome. Gary followed on flanked by two of the security team, who for some inner reason really did not seem to fully trust Gary. Once in the motorhome the President dismissed the General but had to tell the security twice to leave him alone with Gary. Their parting words were 'we will be right outside Mister President!' The President spun the front driver's seat around and sat down and sat facing Gary. Thoughtfully he spoke 'Gary, I am in a difficult position'. 'Yes' replied Gary quickly, 'I can see having a limey running the biggest show on earth could be difficult. Certainly some of your fellow Americans don't like it much!' The President nodded 'Well yes, we Americans are very patriotic and no, we don't particularly like having a Brit in charge! However, that is not what I meant by difficult Gary. I am the President of the United States, a country that believes that in god we trust. But I am also the nominal leader of the western free world, some of whom believe in many different religions other than our Christian god. I really need to get this right Gary, I really need to know how to play this. I need the inside track. We have just gotten over the fact that there is no calamitous event about to wipe out the earth but we could equally destroy everyone on it if the religious thing catches fire and it is not the God or Allah or whatever we were expecting. Do you understand Gary?' 'I think I do sir' replied Gary, now feeling a little guilty about the name he had selected for JC. 'But what if JC is not god at all 'Gary ventured, 'what if he is an alien, an intergalactic tourist. Wouldn't that cause just as much chaos and panic?' 'Gary, it might surprise you to know we have spent many years preparing for just such a visitation and we have many protocols and plans in place if that is the case, none of these plans involved a limey reporter' he said with a smile on his face. 'But, what we have not prepared for is the second coming or god himself coming back. So, I need you to keep me informed Gary, because what JC actually is becomes very important, very quickly, you understand me?' Gary nodded, he was now a little more centre stage than he planned to be. He wanted to be in the limelight and sing a song, but he did not want to be singing *Nessun Dorma* solo at the Carnegie Hall. Now it seemed the President had anointed him with the sole duty of finding out what JC was and to get it wrong would be disastrous, not only for the inhabitants of earth but also for Gary personally. Gary decided he liked the President and felt there was some sort of mutual understanding between them. Giving the matter some consideration and experiencing a strange feeling of responsibility, Gary answered positively 'yes sir, I will find out exactly who and what JC is and report to you personally as soon as I know anything'. Thank you Gary' said the President. 'Now, I need to speak to the General about some things but rest assured he will be left in no doubt that you are to get anything you want or need and that you are reporting directly to me, got that?'. 'Got that' said Gary, who only just avoided slipping into an American accent and saluting the President. Once outside he ignored the suspicious looks of the security team as he walked away. As he headed back to the laboratory complex he could clearly hear the Presidents raised voice as the General was given an old school bollocking and succinct orders about the future conduct of this operation. Gary found Emma with the group of American scientists, each of whom had their own questions for Gary. It was unfortunate that some of the questions were too technical for him to answer and the rest of what he knew he had shared during the briefing, so they were left frustrated. He did however confirm what he already told them and that he now had the full authority of the President to continue his personal contact with JC. This obviously did not meet with universal approval from the American contingent but it was no surprise to Emma and Mike, both of whom were not in the least bit surprised that Gary had once again come out of the shit smelling of roses. 'Shall we get a coffee?' he asked Emma. 'Yes, let's take some time to talk' she replied and the two of them left the lab and the moaning bunch of scientists in their wake. As they waited for the coffee to be poured into the Styrofoam cups the made small talk about being surprised by the President. With the hot coffee just starting to burn their fingers they juggled the disposable cups as they walked. Once alone Emma spoke first 'so it looks like you have cracked it Gary, the big number one reporter on the big number one story'. He smiled 'yes, it does look that doesn't it' he replied with more than a hint of smugness in his voice.

'But what comes next Gary?' she asked. The question was said in one way but be interpreted in many. Emma had dropped her professional façade and her body language suggested she was actually referring to the slow burning relationship that had been slowly evolving between them over the last few weeks. Gary either missed the female subtlety or deliberately chose to ignore the real question Emma was posing. 'Oh, I am not sure' he said thoughtfully 'Perhaps I'll be whisked off to Mars, Heaven, The White House or maybe be I will be presented with the Noble prize' he laughed. Having had her romantic gesture missed or ignored Emma became a bit frosty 'Yes, and you will probably die there and it is the Nobel prize you oaf! She said as she crossed her arms defensively. 'Ouch' teased Gary, 'somebody's tired'. She remained silent and looked sullenly at him, her lips held tightly shut. Gary's brain started to realise that something was not right but it was also full of its own self-importance, what with having met either an alien or a god, and certainly The President of the United States. He could not see the wood for the trees, and certainly not the notional emotional axe that was headed for those trees. Emma's moods had swung from longing, to curiosity, to romance and then anger in the space of a minute. In her mind she had clearly set out how she felt and suddenly felt foolish that Gary had either missed the signal or was playing with her. 'Oh Gary' she shouted, 'you are the most infuriating man I know!' as she clenched her hands into small fists and started to quickly pound on his chest. Surprised but with a slow dawning of what was happening, Gary allowed her a few seconds to vent her anger before laughing at her and grabbing her wrists. In frustration she tried to get away but he was much stronger and just contained her whilst laughing. She struggled for a few seconds before realising the futility of the situation and stopped, then just stood looking angrily up at his grinning face. The very thing that Gary found so funny had also managed to push his own self-centred thoughts to the back of his mind for a second, making room to allow another thought in. This time the thought was the right one and drawing her hands towards him Gary bent forwards and kissed Emma's angry mouth. She wanted to pull away and tell him to 'fuck off' but the longing in her quickly won the argument and she responded to his kisses. It was a heady moment of passion, very unlike their earlier kisses which had been exploratory and testing. This time they used tongues!

By the time the first flush of passion had come and gone all thoughts of pushing him away had passed. Their relationship had slowly built over the last few weeks to the point where they had had fleeting kisses and romantic moments, but no real time together to confirm and cement their relationship. '*Maybe this will be our time*? Emma thought as Gary once against kissed her and held her tight against him. She pulled back just enough to be able to look up at his face and smile at him. 'You knew what I meant all along, didn't you?' Gary smiled back, pulled her back against his chest and for only the second time that day lied 'of course I did'. They held their embrace for

a few more seconds, Emma so as to not break the spell and Gary to avoid having to lie to her face again so soon. The romantic moment however was soon shattered as a terrifically loud wailing noise swept over them, with the unmistakeable word 'GARRRRRY' carried within it. They were both shocked at the sudden and loud interruption to their romantic entwinement but it was Ema who recognised and responded first. 'Sounds like you are needed' she said but Gary's reply was drowned out by another call. When there was a second pause between calls Gary spoke 'Yes, it sounds like JC is missing me or has something important to say, so I had better get back'. Kissing her gently on the forehead Gary smiled and they moved back towards the CCTV lab. As they moved between the vehicles there was another plaintiff call and most people they passed had their hands over their ears to protect themselves. As they arrived at the door Morgan was coming out 'Ah Gary, we have been looking for you. It seems...' Gary interrupted 'like the baby is awake and needs feeding? Yes, I have heard and am on my way' Gary smiled at Emma before with all the urgency and grace that years of poor food and little exercise gave him clumsily plodded off in the direction of ground zero and his new friend in need, JC. Gary reached where was JC was sitting just in front of the dome. He had not shouted again since Gary had started moving back towards him, as if he knew Gary was returning. 'You wanted me?' said Gary. 'Yes Gary, I am struggling with the small capacity of your brain's memory and require more information to increase it'. Despite still being in awe at the uniqueness of the situation and JC, Gary decided he ought to try and establish some rules and possibly with it some control. 'JC I have two things to ask you. Firstly, can you please stop loudly shouting when you want something, it hurts our ears. And secondly, can you stop referring to my brain capacity as small as I find it offensive?' Whilst both these requests seemed perfectly straightforward, they both contained new concepts to JC, all of which needed consideration. After closing his eyes and using Gary's lexicon to examine the meaning of the words *hurt* and *offensive*, by consequence JC also found himself examining the concept of guilt. 'Gary, I am getting an understanding of those words but together they also convey to me a new feeling, one of being responsible for hurt to another being?' 'Ah yes, the old guilt trip' said Gary, 'you had better get used to that one, there is plenty of that about. But it would be much better if you could avoid it in the first place by not hurting my ears and insulting my intelligence. Do you understand?' After the briefest of eye closures for consideration JC replied 'yes Gary I understand and will not use the loud voice or discuss your intellect unless I want to hurt or offend you'. It sounded like a considerate answer but Gary was aware it was either cleverly or badly worded, depending on your point of view. 'So what did you want that needed me to come back so soon? Asked Gary. 'Gary I am ready to process more information but the memory I copied from you does not hold all the information I need. I have to know what is important and what is not so I can delete it'. Gary considered his options. It seemed like this would be the first opportunity to shape what JC got to know about him and the earth, which might prove useful later. 'Perhaps' said Gary 'it would help if we were to categorise what I think would need to know then when each subject is finished with you could erase the unimportant bits and keep that is pertinent. How does that sound?' If Gary had been talking to the real essence of JC within the dome, then it would have hardly been able to understand or even recognise the low level of intelligence that Gary exhibited. But by using a facsimile of Gary, JC was able to converse with it on nearly equal terms. 'Gary that sounds a good solution to the problem as then anything I deem important and need to keep can be harvested and sent back to myself and stored indefinitely. Will you make a list of categories for me?' Gary nodded and spoke 'Yes of course, but I will need to give the matter some thought so that you get the best information to work with'. This wasn't strictly true, it was just that Gary needed to give the matter a lot more *Gary* type thought if he was going to make the most of the situation.' That is fine Gary, have you thought of them yet?' 'Yet? No, it will take me several hours to create the list that will benefit you most, but once you have the list you can look at things in detail' 'Yes Gary, I will wait for your list for several hours'. 'Gary spoke again 'I do have some news for you JC. Whilst I was away I met with the most powerful person on the planet, the President of the United States!' Gary said this with a flourish as if JC would be impressed. JC's understanding was increasing exponentially as he learned the language and how to operate Gary's body copy, so his eye closures were getting shorter to the point that they could now be taken as normal blinking. 'And this is a person with whom I should be speaking?' asked JC. 'No, not yet JC, it is better that only you and I communicate until we have a fuller understanding of each other, then you could meet other important people. 'The President does have many questions for you JC, some of which he would like answered soon' said Gary. JC beamed the smile, blinked and replied 'Gary I will be happy to answer what questions I can once I fully understand your species overall level of knowledge and intelligence. Until I know where you are in your evolutionary development I cannot answer your questions as I have a protocol to follow.' Gary nodded 'Yes, you have said that before. I am making preparations for you to have access to the internet, where all you questions can be answered. Once it is in place you can use it to research the categories that I suggest to you, then you will better understand us'. Gary was enjoying his role as envoy, meeting with Presidents and having an input on world issues, so he was determined to keep JC as his own personal property for as long as possible. This would be for the story in the short term but also for the glory in his long term future role, whatever future that might be. He would hold back the internet access as long as possible and control the flow of information both ways, this would ensure he was needed by both parties. Gary unconsciously yawned, which was copied by JC as he looked for new behaviours to ape and understand. Gary laughed 'so you are feeling tired to?' he asked. After a blink JC found the tired reference 'There is a new feeling, perhaps it could be why the brain is functioning slowly' before JC added 'No offence Gary' 'none taken' said Gary, wondering if JC had suddenly discovered his stash of sarcasm. After discussing tiredness Gary realised he had been awake for nearly twenty four hours. Now that the adrenaline had waned and with belly full of belly he could really do with some sleep. 'JC, I will function better if I rest for a while and come to think of it so might you. I am going leave you and go and sleep before returning with your list, okay?' JC used the smile expression and replied 'Yes Gary, of course. How long will you be?' Gary carefully considered his answer, knowing that JC will take his answer literally. 'I will be eight hours JC and then I shall return'. 'Good Gary, I will wait eight hours for you to return' replied JC. Gary went to leave but then quickly turning back he said 'And JC, no shouting please!' JC beamed a smile as something approaching humour flashed across his brain copy 'Of course Gary, I will not shout again'. In the CCTV van there were the usual crowd of people around the screens watching Gary interact. Again there were pictures only as Gary had accidentally *on purpose* not turned it back on when he had gone back down to JC. They watched as he turned his back on JC and walked out of the brightly lit scene. To those watching it was like watching a brave but foolish lion tamer in a circus turn his back on the king of the jungle, but they did not know what Gary knew. It took a minute for Gary to walk from ground zero to the collection of vehicles, motorhomes and satellite dishes that had grown into the small town at ground zero. Even now more vehicles and specialist personnel were arriving, mostly activated by the changing security states but some specifically sent by the President to keep an overview on how the situation was being managed. Gary walked into the CCTV van with the pained and tired look of a returning hero. People moved aside for him and one of the assistants gave up his seat to allow Gary to flop down into it in an over dramatic way. Everyone responded to Gary's act and played their part, offering drinks and sandwiches, all in the hope that he would let some further crumb of information slip. Gary ran his hand through his hair and down his face, pulling his bottom eyelids down and blinking. It gave the crowd the impression that the world weary Gary the hero had either just returned from a spacewalk or saved someone from a burning building, something he was keen to propagate. He was busy milking the adulation when he caught sight of Emma looking at him through the crowd. Her arms were folded and her head was cocked to one side with her lips pursed. She alone was not buying what Gary was currently selling and with just a raised eyebrow conveyed that message to him. Realising he was perhaps overcooking the moment, Gary made eye contact with Special Agent Morgan 'I am knackered, is there somewhere I can crash out and gets some sleep?' Morgan nodded 'Yes, more accommodation wagons have been shipped in alongside some of the other resources. Come with me and I get you fixed up'. Gary stood up and stretched, before smiling at Emma and following Morgan out of the van and into the labyrinth of vehicles. On the outskirts of the ever growing trailer park they came to three large Winnebago type motorhomes, each one bigger than Gary's apartment back in the UK. Morgan fumbled for some keys 'I was keeping this one for myself, but since your needs are more immediate you had better have it. Besides, I have specific instructions from The President to take good care of you, and I want to keep my job on this project'. They went up the steps of the RV and Gary was impressed at the space and luxurious appointments of the vehicle. 'Wow, very nice, I'll take it' said Gary. 'I thought you might like it' said Morgan 'It's all straight forward, bathroom, bedrooms, kitchen etc. and if you want food then we have now set up a VIP catering area for you and the scientific staff to help maintain security. Come find me when you need to eat. 'Thanks' said Gary as Morgan nodded and left leaving Gary alone. Although tired Gary could not resist the urge to look through the motorhome to see what it had that the previous ones did not. It had three bedrooms, a full kitchen, a toilet and a large separate shower room. As he compared the motorhome to his own grotty apartment in the UK, Gary remembered the hours he would spend in the shower plotting and scheming the best way to get one over on his boss at work, with the least amount of effort. In a nod back to those not so distant days he turned on the shower and quickly stripped off his dirty clothes. The hot water felt good as it hit his head and cascaded over his body, loudly splashing and gurgling down the plug hole. It was a wonderful feeling and Gary was in no great rush to leave this warm embracing cocoon. He spontaneously broke into song, or in truth broke into several different songs at one, none of which he knew the correct words to. '*I want to break free, I want to break free, la la da da dum, da da free. God knows, mam killed a man, gun against his head da da dum dum set free*' he wailed, convinced that no one could hear him but not really bothered if they could or not. Outside in the darkness between the motorhomes, Morgan was stood quietly waiting for someone. They should have been here by now and he was getting impatient as he looked at his watch. Suddenly in the gap at the end he saw someone walk slowly and stealthily across. He made the international sign of 'I am here' by hissing in the time honoured fashion of spooks everywhere. The person backtracked and looking down the line saw Morgan beckoning them towards him. As they got near, Morgan held out his hand and pushed something metallic and shiny into their hands. Talking quietly Morgan spoke 'be as quick and as quiet as you can, I don't know how long I can stall them back there in the lab. And, I want no comebacks on me, got it?' 'Got it' came the hushed reply as Morgan turned and looking left and right went back towards what was now the main base area. The person now moved around to the main door of the motorhome and stood listening for a second. There was the sound of running water and the painful screeching of nails on glass as song after song were wrenched apart in agony. *This will be easier than I thought* thought the intruder, as they used the keys given to them by Morgan to slowly open the door to the motorhome and slip silently inside. Gary was on his second attempt at Bohemian Break Free Rhapsody and had started his mindless repeating of the *'mama killed a man, put a gun against his head'* part. He normally repeated this part as it was some of the few words he really knew. In the steam, noise and musical moment, he did not hear the shower room door quietly open or the see the figure now stood just the other side of the steamy glass. 'Trigger now he's dead' he intoned for yet the third time as he was suddenly made aware of a slight draft as the main shower door was opened. Unable to see properly through the lather of shampoo bubbles on his head, he assumed he had knocked it open and reached out blindly to pull the door closed again. As he fumbled to find the handle his hand made contact with something soft and fleshy, something that should not be there. He tried to force his eyes open against the water torrent and soap suds, but he could only make out an indistinct form. Putting two and two together and realising he was no longer alone, Gary screamed and made to exit the shower, but in his haste and amidst the soapsuds only succeeded in slipping and falling backwards into the shower. Now somehow resigned to his face he stopped screaming and wiping the water from his eyes tried desperately to see the intruders face. Through the steam and water he could see that whoever it was they were so determined to get him they were entering the shower cubicle. He put his hand up to defend himself, which also stopped some of the water getting into his eyes, allowing him some a brief glimpse of his assailant. He blinked disbelievingly, as there stood over him in the shower was Professor Emma Rowlinson, and she was stark naked!

Gary's loud and trombone like snoring woke him with a start. It took a few seconds for him to realise where he actually was and then a few seconds more to remember what had happened there. If he had not been laid in bed looking around the well-appointed bedroom of the motorhome he might have thought the previous night's events had been a dream. As if to reinforce the reality he could hear noises coming from the kitchen area and the smell of frying bacon. He half got out of bed to go to the toilet when the bedroom was kicked open and Emma walked in carrying a plate of food and a mug of steaming coffee. Realising he was naked, Gary, leapt back under the sheets and covered himself up, the embarrassment obvious. 'A bit late for that lover boy' said Emma, putting the food and coffee on the bedside table before sitting herself down on the edge of the bed. Although he had not been drunk, the deep seated sleep he was awakening from and the unlikely hood of the situation caused Gary to question if this was really happening or just more of the dream. If what he remembered was indeed reality, then he and Emma had spent their time together rolling, jumping, kissing and fucking their way through the night. Watching the consternation on Gary's face Emma laughed 'Go on' she said 'think your way back through it'.

Gary took her suggestion and re ran the imagery, stopping momentarily to both shudder and inwardly smile in equal measure at the previous evening's activities. His face gave away little signs as each thought was processed and either savoured or pushed to the back of his mind, depending on who was doing what. 'When you have quite finished reliving your exploits and the sexual violation of my body, then you had better eat your breakfast before it gets cold' said Emma. She was obviously ahead of Gary in dealing with the situation 'but then' thought Gary, 'it was her that broke into the motorhome and attacked me in the shower'. He pulled the plate of food onto his lap and put some bacon into his mouth. The smoked crispy meat hit his taste buds and he realised just how ravenous he was. 'Hungry? Emma asked innocently before changing her tone 'because you ought to be!' 'This is good' replied Gary, trying not to act too surprised 'so you can cook as well'. 'As well as what?' teased Emma to her amusement, and to Gary's obvious ongoing embarrassment. 'Gary, there is no need to feel awkward. It's not as if we were drunk and this is the clumsy morning after the night before. We both had an itch and we scratched it, perfectly reasonable behaviour amongst adults'. Gary paused from his food 'Can I just remind the erudite professor that it was she who got into my shower to scratch herself, when I was not even itching!' 'Methinks you doth protest too much' she replied. 'Now you had better get a move on or your intergalactic boyfriend will be wondering where you are and will start shouting the place down'. Gary looked across at the clock, which suggested that the time was 9am, a full ten hours since he had left JC. He bolted down the last mouthful of food and washed it home with a swig of the coffee. About to uncover himself and run for the shower, he paused 'Do you mind, I need to get cleaned up' 'what, and after last night rough and tumble you are suddenly going all coy on me, puulease' she replied. Attempting to call her bluff Gary made a big show of throwing the sheets back but at the last second kept hold of enough of the corner to hide his manhood as he ran out of the bedroom. Once in the bathroom he ran the water in the shower, but just before entering the cubicle, on a hunch he turned back and locked the bathroom door before slipping into the shower. The noise of the running water hid the shower room door handle rattling and Emma walking sulkily back towards the bedroom disappointed. Unknowingly, Gary had created his second monster of the week. Once he had showered and dressed, Gary went through to the living room area of the motorhome and found Emma sat at the breakfast bar. She was writing something, which gave Gary something to say that did not involve their night time wrestling. 'What are you working on?' he asked. 'Oh just some ideas that I have been asked to consider by the American scientists. It seems they accept we are part of the team now and want some input from us'. 'Well that's good, isn't it?' he asked. 'Well' she sighed 'it depends on your point of view. They have realised they might be able to gain more access to you through me, so suddenly I am very popular with Brown and Carter. Also, some of the scientists have been tasked with planning how to attack JC if he turns nasty. Then there is the religious lot who think if he turns out not to be god or Jesus then it is all blasphemous, so they are also happy to have a means to do away with him!' Gary was shocked and horrified. Not only could he lose his place in history, he could also lose JC his life if the scientists were successful in finding a way to kill him. 'That is ridiculous, he means no harm and I am sure will have a lot to give us of scientific knowledge when he is good and ready' he said. 'That's as maybe' replied Emma, but we are in America, where religion, guns and power are all tied up together. If he will listen to you Gary, then I suggest you get JC to spill some beans, before someone spills his!' Although shocked, on reflection Gary did after all have the ear of the President and also some promises from JC about answering questions once he knew more about us. 'I think I may have a more productive and positive use of all your collective science power' said Gary 'meet me in the CCTV cabin in twenty minutes, but get dressed first!' By the time Emma had made herself decent and arrived at the CCTV cabin, Gary had got Morgan to assemble everyone for a briefing. It had been Mike's lover Steve, who when he deemed the time right had spoken to Morgan about getting Emma alone time with Gary. Now entering the already full cabin, Emma's face flushed a little as she realised amongst her peer group were at least two members who knew how her previous evening had gone, three if you included Gary. The American, Professor Brown welcomed her and unwittingly made her blush more by asking if she had been running. The final person to arrive was the General, who slightly put out at being summoned by the 'that damn limey reporter', grumpily took his seat in the front row. Reverting to a more formal approach, Morgan spoke 'I think that is everyone Mr Barnes'. 'Please, call me Gary okay? And that goes for the rest of you to'. A ripple of disapproval ran through the scientists and military personnel seated in the room. They all had rank, degrees or titles and did not like informality being forced upon them, especially from someone without any. Gary hid his slight nerves as he started his not so carefully planned speech, opening with his ace card. 'Ladies and gentlemen, for those who as do not know, the President has appointed me as principal contact with JC'. There was another ripple of shifting negative body language, as the formal group registered their mute disapproval. Gary waited till most of the arms had uncrossed and people under his gaze had visibly relaxed, all except the General, whose mood and demeanour was fixed and obvious to all. Gary continued 'I know this has not met with universal approval' he waited to see if the joke would raise a laugh, then quickly moved on when it did not 'However, for whatever reason and whether you like it or not, JC has also chosen me as his point of contact. This combined with the President's directive makes me the conduit through which all information flows. So, whatever you get to know will come through me'. He paused to let that sink in before he continued 'That to some of you is the bad news, the good news is that I am a team player and see myself as your representative down at ground zero'. 'Like the Pope' growled the General. Like a pissed off teacher Gary challenged him 'you want to share something with the group General?' 'I said, like the Pope' said the General and then to grumpily explain the reference 'the pope is god's representative here on earth and you are saying that you our representative at ground zero! It sounds like a very bad choice of words to us god worshiping Christians mister!' he snarled. 'Thank you General' replied Gary, 'I shall bear that in mind when giving out sainthoods'. The General was not impressed with the reply but several of the scientists warmed to Gary a bit when they saw him poking the General and quietly laughed at the joke. 'So, if you are ready, I shall tell you what I actually know, what the immediate future holds and then try to answer any questions you may have.' Having up till now been kept mostly in the dark, the prospect of getting some information from the horse's mouth impressed the select group of people sat in the room and their body language visibly changed in anticipation. 'So, I will start from the beginning' began Gary 'As you know, I arrived here with Professor Rowlinson, after her extensive studies indicated that whatever was causing the weather anomaly was going to touch down somewhere near here. Once law enforcement and the military arrived and took charge, I found myself held in a form of detention. Having heard the commotion caused by Doctor Brown's visit to the site, I released myself from the custody of the US Marines and made my way to ground zero.' He paused for a second to allow his little joke about escaping to amuse the scientists and annoy the military people. 'Once I neared the site I was drawn in by some sort of presence, who having selected me, then set about creating a replica of me, plain old Gary Barnes' Gary continued, telling the group about his experience and interaction with JC, before finishing with 'Now, JC understands we will have many questions but will not answer them until he has a fuller understanding of us, so he wants access to the internet' At this there was an audible gasp from the room as each group imagined what this might entail for their own research and interests. Gary continued 'So, that is where we are with JC, so any comments or questions?' Unsurprisingly the General spoke first 'So when will we know if JC confirms he is indeed the second coming?' Gary replied 'When he deems to tell us General, if indeed that turns out to be the case. I know there are a lot of people wanting it to be god and equally a lot of people wanting it to be an alien being for the science it will bring, but at the moment he is just not saying'. Any other questions?' One of the lead scientists raised his hand 'How do we know it is not dangerous and giving him access to the internet will not make him more so?' Gary thought for a moment 'Well firstly although he has exhibited a great deal of power which so far has not hurt anyone. Secondly, we give internet access to six year old children, so I can't see how allowing JC access can make the situation worse'. Gary took one last question from one of the FBI team 'You sometimes call him JC and also refer to him as a 'he', is that actually the case?' Having already painted himself into a corner over the name, Gary continued as noncommittally as he could 'JC is what called himself and I use the male term as he modelled himself on me'. Aware that he was in danger of being caught out on the little things that he had embellished, Gary made to bring the briefing to a close. 'I think I will be better placed to answer your questions once JC has what he wants and then gives us some answers, so if you don't mind I will get back to work'. The General however was not done and had a final shot at Gary 'One last thing. Why should we trust you, a Brit. reporter, here in America, telling us what to do?' Most of the military personnel and some of the science team nodded in agreement. 'Because General, like it or not, I was chosen. It could be I was chosen because I do not hold any strong religious beliefs and have no scientific training, but amongst all of you I was chosen, first by JC and then by your President.' Gary let his last comment hang in the air as he looked around the room. Despite never actually given a press briefing before he had been to many and knew that the moment was right to finish, so he nodded and walked out of the room. Outside he stood with Emma and Morgan as the rest of the people left the cabin. 'That was pretty damn good' said Emma, blushing as she realised that Gary's raised eyebrow thought she was referring to last night instead of the briefing 'Today I mean, the briefing' she quickly added, which only added to the obvious embarrassment. Morgan let her off the hook by asking Gary 'So, what do you need us to do Gary?' 'Yes it was' Gary said to Emma in what he hoped would be an abstract reference to the previous night's lovemaking before looking at Morgan. 'I am not feeling the love in the room from the General. For whatever reason the President has given me a free hand, so I need you to stop him interfering'. Morgan nodded 'I saw what you meant back there. The President has authorised you so I will do what I can to keep him out of the way'. 'And what can the science team do?' asked Emma. 'Well firstly there is arranging a heavy feed of the internet to the site' said Gary 'and then start putting together specific questions that you might like answers to for when and if JC decides to spill the beans'. All three of them were surprised that Gary seemed to have a plan and the confidence to see it through. 'I will make a start' said Morgan and with a knowing look left the two of them alone as he walked off. 'When I said pretty damn good, I meant the briefing Gary, not the, the last night thing' said Emma in hushed voice. 'I know, just couldn't help myself prof. but last night was pretty damn good'. 'I have to ask Gary how you are managing this situation so calmly, it's like you were born to it?' 'Gary looked around furtively 'It is all bullshit, smoke and mirrors. I worked out that since no one has ever has been in my position, then everything I do is being done for the first time, with nothing to measure it against. Gary Barnes, chancer, lowly hack and blagger, has blagged his way to the front to the front of the queue and is loving it!' She smiled and shook her head, all her years of science and study, replaced by this grinning oaf and a surge of hormones. 'Sorry, but I do have to go' said Gary 'I have a date with a being and he gets loud if I am late!' After a quick look over his shoulder he bent down and kissed Emma on the forehead, before winking and setting off through the base towards his date with JC. Emma watched him walk away, a rosy glow running through her as you thought back to last night and she wondered about the future. Gary strutted as if he owned the place as he walked out of the edge of the vehicle base and into the open ground. He nodded to the marines guarding the perimeter, and those who had not had the misfortune to meet him before acknowledged him. Their officers had briefed them on who was allowed access to ground zero and Gary was at the top of their list. Once through the inner cordon Gary walked the final fifty feet towards where JC was still sat, shimmering, eyes closed but with his mouth opening and closing. As Gary got closer he realised JC was speaking, but quietly' Come back Gary' he seemed to be repeating over and over. Gary stopped in front of JC 'Hello JC'. Instantly JC opened his eyes and he initiated his broad smile 'Gary, you have returned' 'Of course, I said I would 'said Gary. JC blinked as he processed 'I am glad Gary, as I have counted more than eight of your hours, that is why I was calling you, but I did not shout'. Gary nodded 'yes, I saw that you were calling me quietly'. Gary decided it was not the right time to explain that he could not actually hear JC, and it was just luck that he returned when he did. 'Do you have news for me Gary?' Although Gary was still in awe at being with JC, his inbuilt confidence and planning allowed him to remain calm. It had been the same with the scientists and military briefing earlier, *'walk tall, look tall'* he thought. 'Yes JC, I have news for you. The President has allowed me to be your sole contact and provide for your needs. The scientific team will be providing you with internet access, so you can look at our information. I will be choosing categories that I think will be of greatest interest to you, how does that sound?' The blink this time was a micro second longer as JC briefly connected back to his real self within the dome to see if Gary's news met his needs. 'Yes Gary that would be a good starting point'. 'And then' said Gary, 'in return they would like some answers to questions about you JC. They are very curious about you and what you want here'. 'Of course Gary, they must be curious if an event like this happens. Once I have a better understanding of them I will be able to give them answers that they themselves will be able to understand. Otherwise Gary it would be like giving a highly scientific item to a young child, they would not understand it and might harm themselves with it.' Gary noted that not only was JC forming sentences better, he was now using them to describe abstract thoughts, so figured he must have been busy whilst left alone'. There was a motion behind Gary and he turned to see Morgan and two white coated technicians seated on a small electric ATV buggy type vehicle. Morgan shouted to him 'Gary is it okay to come down with the internet equipment?' 'Of course, come down' Gary shouted back before turning to JC. 'This is the equipment that will allow you the internet access we discussed' 'Thank you Gary, then my study can begin' JC replied. Driving cautiously Morgan stopped the laden buggy a few feet behind Gary and the three of them got out. They all stood with their eyes agog, as other than on the CCTV screen they had not seen JC in person. After about twenty seconds of staring Gary coughed 'Can we make a start gentlemen?' Morgan snapped out of his curiosity based trance and motioned to the technicians to unload the truck and begin setting up. They did so, but whilst setting up their kit they seldom took their eyes off JC for more than a few seconds. When they finished, there sat in this open space was a small computer desk, with a large desktop PC and monitor. They completed the installation by connecting power and networking cables which had been reeled out from a drum on the vehicle as they drove. One of the technicians turned on and tested the system before reporting it was working to Morgan 'Looks like it is ready to go Gary. Should I stay?' Gary noted Morgan's offer but said 'No, you all get along please'. His refusal was as much about retaining power over the situation than any real reason to dismiss Morgan. The vehicle drove off with the technicians peering over their shoulders like curious Meer Kats. Gary sat at the computer terminal and for the hell of it called up the website of the newspaper he used to work for. Even for a parochial local UK newspaper the top story was one of mysterious goings on and rumours of alien encounters in the American wilderness 'If only they knew' thought Gary to himself. 'So where shall we start?' asked Gary 'what is most important to you JC?' After the customary blink 'Gary, I would first like to know how your species has evolved? Gary nodded and with painfully slow to watch typing, stabbed JC's question about evolution into google. The connection was superfast and almost instantly many google answers titles appeared on the screen. Because of the question asked the answers ranged from technical, scientific and religious, as all had a bearing on evolution, depending on what you believed in. Gary started at the top and read the first answer from a Wikipedia page, which was a surprisingly simple explanation of what evolution was'. JC noted the answer and asked him to continue. By the time Gary had read the first eight entries and still only three hours had passed, Gary was getting tired and dismayed as there were still many thousands of answers to be sifted and read. 'I am wondering if it would be more efficient if you read these yourself JC?' said Gary, turning the screen towards him. 'If it is efficient you want Gary, then it would be better for me to accept the electrical connectors directly and for me to absorb the information. Would that be of help?' 'Directly?' asked Gary in frustration, 'you would be able to connect directly?' 'Yes Gary. The facsimile I made of you is produced from within the dome. I can also adapt it accept a connector if you can show me what it looks like.' Gary thought carefully about this. On the one hand having JC direct access to the internet would be easier but on the other hand it took him out of the loop a bit, and how would he filter what JC saw and read? But it dawned on him that he could not spend the rest of his life reading out google answers to JC as there probably was not enough years left of it. Gary fumbled around the back of the machine and unplugged the network cable. Getting closer to JC than he had been before he held up the plug end for him to see. Not bothering to look at it JC closed his eyes took the plug into his hand, which appeared to be absorbed and become one with it. 'Can you do that, is it working? Asked Gary. 'I am just sensing the binary electrical language and comparing it to yours Gary, it is very different but once I have the key I will understand it. Before Gary could respond JC spoke again 'Yes, I have found the pattern and am processing the language. Now I am getting access to information and am able to see words and pictures Gary. Yes, this will be more efficient'. Gary spoke 'Before you begin your studies there is one important thing you need to know before everything else' JC opened his eyes 'and what is that one thing Gary?' 'Our internet covers the whole planet and is used by everyone, who can download and upload information to it. But, not everyone upload or downloads the truth, they sometimes put their own version of the truth on the internet' JC's eye closed for many seconds whilst this difficult concept and possible consequences were considered 'But how will I know what is the truth and what is not Gary?' asked JC. 'It is mainly common sense and experience JC, but in the absence of both those I will be here to guide you'. This caused JC to beam his smile again as he closed his eyes to sample more internet. Gary spoke 'If you start with evolution that will lead to many offshoots of information that we can discuss before you also investigate further'. I have nearly finished the evolution entries Gary and wish to delve more, can this system be made to work faster?' Finished, already? Gary said incredulously 'but how?' he then remembered the speed with which JC had learnt all of his words, so realised perhaps he should not be so surprised. 'How many of those internet connection could you use at once? Asked Gary. Opening his eyes JC spoke 'By porting important information back to my own self in the dome I can take unlimited amounts of data and process it, sending pertinent information back to your facsimile here. Can I have more? Gary nodded 'I will see if it can be arranged. Speaking into the headset he wore Gary asked 'Morgan are you getting this, can we have many more internet network cables down here? Into his earpiece Morgan's voice answered 'sure, how many do you need?' 'As many as you have got' replied Gary repeating 'as many as you have got'. Within half an hour the buggy arrived again with Morgan and techy crew. They reeled out twenty individual network cables behind them, along with one additional thick bundled loom. The technicians presented them to Gary like some ancient sacrificial offering, whilst maintaining their gaze on JC. 'These are what we could muster in short order and the tech guys have also direct linked this large cluster cable if that is any use?' Gary looked at the spaghetti and whilst it made little sense to him he hoped JC could probably make something of it. 'Let's see. Drag it over here guys'. The tech guys were wide eyed as they realised they were going to get closer to JC and were a little nervous. 'Don't be scared, he's not eaten anyone yet' joked Gary, as much as to confirm his power over the JC as well as demonstrate confidence. Under Gary's guidance they pulled the cables forward and placed them in JC's hands. Like Gary they looked on in wonder as the plug ends melded into the shimmering hand and disappeared into it. 'How is that JC?' asked Gary. JC opened his eyes, I have the connection but the data is not flowing any faster' Gary looked at the technicians for an answer. In their current state of shock and awe they had forgotten to activate the new cables. One of them took out a small radio and spoke into 'activate the main network hub cables'. Nothing happened for a few seconds then JC seemed to sit up a little straighter and his face beamed his now familiar smile. 'I am guessing you are getting more now, the information is flowing faster?' asked Gary. 'Yes Gary, a lot of information is flowing and being processed'. Gary watched as JC closed his eyes and appeared to be concentrating on the data now flowing into him from the many cables. Gary spoke to the technician 'Just how much information is he getting?' Doing some mental calculations the techy thought for a moment before answering 'Well he is taking the main feed, along with about twenty fibre optic cables, so enough broadband traffic to supply a small town'. 'Impressive' replied Gary, 'Thanks guys, you can go now' he added. The techies and Morgan got back into the buggy and drove back to the main base area leaving Gary stood in front of JC. After few minutes of apparent inactivity Gary spoke 'You getting everything you want?' But there was no response. Gary tried again but raised his voice a little 'JC, are you getting what you want?' This time JC eyes flickered open and closed several times before remaining open 'Gary, I have now established the overall size of your internet and am now arranging it in some order so that I can begin going through it in detail. I can see there is a great deal of spurious material in the internet that I will need to disregard before I can study the facts that

I need. Using your facsimile to process so much information is difficult, so I will not have spare capacity to engage in conversation. I suggest you go Gary, and when I have need you again I will summon you'. Gary noted a slight change in JC's tone and one that he did not like. 'And just when that might be o great wizard?' Gary replied with heavy sarcasm. JC closed his eyes for a few seconds before answering 'Gary, at this speed and using your facsimile it will take me approximately forty two days of constant study, then I will summon you back to discuss what I have found'. 'Forty two days, that's nearly six weeks!' said Gary not really knowing whether to be impressed or disappointed, but the more he considered the amount of information on the internet the more he considered the former to be impressive. 'Okay JC. I shall come and visit you each day to discuss what you have found.' JC's eyes instantly opened 'No Gary that would be a distraction and a waste of both of our resources and time.' Gary shrugged his shoulder 'well what shall I do in the meanwhile?' 'Whatever you did before my arrival Gary' replied JC, before closing his eyes with the clear intent of continuing his research. Gary was angry and frustrated at this turn of events, being dismissed like the monkey when he thought all along he was the organ grinder. He was considering pushing the point further when he heard the now familiar sound of the buggy approaching from behind. Morgan was alone and called Gary over. 'Can you get away for a while as the President has scheduled a call to you at 1700 hrs?' Gary climbed into the buggy as he replied 'yes I'm free, as it seems that JC is happy surfing the internet'. On the drive back through the base Morgan spoke 'I had better bring you up to speed on what has been happening in the real world whilst we have been here. The security cordon we have thrown around the area has attracted a lot of attention and created a lot of rumours. Actually most of the rumours involve little green men, so they have been easy to discredit but we can't maintain this level of security for ever. Just outside the cordon the press have set up camp, along with the end of the world religious groups, so the story will surely leak soon, which is probably why the President needs to talk with you Gary'. Morgan assumed this news would be of interest to Gary and was surprised when he did not respond but was staring blankly ahead. 'Gary?' he tried again, which brought Gary out of his trance 'Sorry Morgan, was thinking about something'. 'Yes, I could see that' said Morgan before briefly repeating the information again. It was ten to five as they arrived back at what was the ever growing scientific cluster of mobile buildings. Gary looked for Emma amongst the white coated scientists and technical staff that were busy at different consoles, but could not see her. He was aware that some of the new staff were stealing glances in his direction as he poured himself a coffee from the machine. Morgan noticed too 'something of the rock star?' 'More like rock ape' Gary replied in a self-mocking tone. 'If you bring your coffee through to the communication centre I will get you setup on the secure phone for the President's call' said Morgan, as he led the way to an adjacent unit. Having had their passes checked and admitted to the communications centre, Gary was shown to a secure and soundproof booth at one end. He sat down at the single chair and looked out of the glass partition at Morgan and the technician who were talking, although he could not hear a word. In fact the booth was so well sound proofed that Gary could hear himself breathing and his heart beating, always a reassuring sign. The heavy silence gave Gary a weird, yet strangely refreshing experience, adding extra clarity to Gary's thoughts. He quickly reviewed the event of the last few weeks, meeting Emma, leaving his job, going on the run, meeting JC and now waiting for a phone call from the President of the United States, quite something for a small town reporter. He jumped as the phone suddenly warbled into his solitude and he nearly fell from the stool from underneath him. He took a breath, then licked his lips nervously before picking it and speaking 'hello'. There was a female voice on the other end 'Is that Mister Gary Barnes?' 'Yes, this is he' Gary replied, his slight nerves causing him to speak in an awkward manner. 'This is The Whitehouse, I have a call for you from the President of the United Stes, please hold'. There were several clicks and hums as the call was transferred and was digitally scrambled, before one final click and the President's voice was heard 'Mister Barnes, Gary?' 'Yes Mister President, I'm here' replied Gary. The President asked how Gary was and asked a few General polite questions before getting down to business. 'Gary. I have been under increasing pressure at home and internationally since we last met. The security perimeter set up around the base at ground zero was pushed back another ten miles, which has led to all manner of speculation about what is happening there. Some of it close to the truth and some of it wild and speculative. Gary, I cannot hold off the American people and the rest of the world any longer. Tomorrow morning I have to make a televised statement about what is happening down there and I need to know from you what that something is. In short Gary, do we have an Alien, God or the Devil sat here in the USA?' Gary was taken aback. He had considered the first two options but 'the devil' had not even entered his head. It took a second to readjust to the fact although he was in this sterile bubble, he was still also in the 'god we trust, the devil will come get ya' USA, with all the religious connotations that brought with it. 'Mister President' Gary replied 'As you know through the video feed, I have spent a good deal of time with JC and I still cannot give you and answer to that, although to be honest the idea of him being the devil never occurred to me. As to whether he is a god or an alien, well he will not answer any questions until he has finished his research of the internet and understands us better. I am sorry I cannot be more specific'. 'I understand Gary, and it is good that you are being upfront with this. How long will the internet research take and when can we expect some answers?' Gary did not want to say the words but they tumbled out anyways 'Six weeks. JC tells me it will take about six weeks to review the whole of the internet, disregard the crap and find whatever it is he is looking for.' There was sigh at the other end before the President spoke again 'six weeks, I can't stall them for another six weeks Gary! What can I do?' Having recovered from his earlier bout of nerves, the adrenaline in Gary's system started to work in his favour and sharpened him up. He knew that JC did not want to see him for a while, so he was redundant here. Also he knew that tomorrow the President was going live to the world and release the story, something that Gary had always thought would be his job. 'Mister President, I have a suggestion for you. 'Well let's hear it Gary, because I am getting very few workable suggestions from my people here!' Sitting upright in his chair Gary spoke 'Sir, what about playing good cop, bad cop? I would suggest that you broke the good news to the world that whilst we do have an unexpected visitor, the end of the world is not as we first thought imminent. Then I could deliver the relatively bad news that as yet JC has not disclosed his purpose for being here and we do not know who he is, thereby letting you off the hook somewhat. How does that sound?' The President was obviously on speaker phone and consulting with whoever was in his office at the same time, so there was a short delay before he replied 'Gary, nobody here likes that idea except for me. Pack a bag and expect to be picked up within the hour, you should be here by midnight but we can brief together in the morning, how does that sound?' Gary was excited 'Sounds good to me Sir, but just one request?' 'Go ahead' said the President 'Can I bring Professor Emma Rowlinson with me? Her scientific knowledge might help flesh out the good news we have about the world not ending just yet. 'Sounds like a good idea Gary, get her ready to come with you. My aides will make the travel arrangements. See you in the morning' There was a click, the line was dead but Gary was very much alive. Gary may have lost JC's attention but he had certainly got the President's and possibly the whole world's attention when he appeared tomorrow. Rejuvenated he left the booth with a swing in his step and a new sense of purpose. 'How did it go?' asked Morgan. 'Great' replied Gary 'I am off to Washington tonight to brief the President in person, so I am going to pack my things. Oh, and Emma is coming with me' Morgan shook his head 'I don't know how you do it!' He was interrupted by his cell phone ringing confirming that Gary was indeed headed to Washington and Morgan should make the arrangements to get him to the helipad by 8 pm. Morgan finished the call by asking 'and who will tell the General?' before grimly nodding at the answer 'I thought I would get the short straw'. Gary went back to the motorhome he had used last night and the memory of the evening with Emma brought a smile to his face. He made moves as if to pack but realised he only had a few shirts, one pair of trousers and some dirty jockey shorts to pack. The initial excitement over and packing done, he thought he had better find Emma and tell her the news. He found her with Professor Brown in the laboratory, talking about the static electricity readings that were coming from JC at ground zero. It was obvious that neither of them had heard the news yet about their trip, but sensing Prof. Brown would not be too happy about it, Gary avoided mentioning it. 'I was just going to get some food, if either of you are hungry?' Gary asked noncommittally, hoping the Emma would take the hint. 'Well It has been a while since lunch, if that is okay with you professor?' 'Yes, go ahead, I don't eat so much these days' bemoaned the ageing professor Brown, whilst rubbing at his rumbling gastric area. Emma and Gary made small talk as they walked over to the VIP catering unit. They ordered their food and then sat alone in the corner away from the few other diners. Emma was keen to discuss last night to be reassured that it was not a one night stand but Gary had other things to discuss. Once their food had been delivered he cut her off from her more probing romantic questions and in hushed tones told her of their impending trip. 'What, tonight?' she said loudly, causing some of the others in the unit to look at them. 'yes, eight o'clock' he whispered, Morgan is making the arrangements but we have to keep it quiet until the General has been told.' And I don't think Professor Brown and the team will be too pleased either' said Emma 'Exactly' replied Gary. 'So after we have eaten go pack what you need and be prepared for Morgan to come and collect you'. Emma was excited about the trip but also pleased that Gary had arranged for her to go with him, giving her hope that perhaps there was a future in this after all. After they had quietly discussed the trip, despite Emma's attempt at conversation Gary became preoccupied with his own thoughts. 'Are you okay?' she asked 'Yes fine' he lied in reply. In truth Gary was inwardly worried about the sudden change in JC's demeanour once he had got what he wanted, namely access to the internet. Gary has assumed he had built up something of a rapport with JC, especially since he had chosen a Gary looky likey to inhabit, but suddenly the information had taken on a new importance, even more important than Gary it seemed. They went back to small talk and finished their food before Gary made to leave

'You leaving me?' Emma asked in false hurt tones. 'There is something I have to do before I leave and please don't be late for our date' he chided in return and left her sat with her lasagne and thoughts. Gary had just over an hour before pick up, so decided he would pay JC one last visit and tell him he would be away. Taking the now familiar path through the vehicles he nodded to the marines on guard and moved into the brightly lit area where that JC occupied. His approach seemed to go unnoticed, so he took a moment to look deeply at the shimmering likeness of himself. JC was obviously in deep thought as his closed eyelids flickered and there was an ever changing range of emotions flashing across his face. Gary spoke 'Hello JC' which brought no response so he tried again in a slightly louder voice 'Hello JC, are you there?' but again there was no change. Losing patience Gary shouted 'HELLO JC, I AM BACK' to which there was a noticeable difference as the eye and facial motions suddenly ceased. The eyes slowly opened and JC looked down. 'Gary, you have come back before I summoned you. You have interrupted my research and delayed the process of understanding I need'. Once again Gary did not like the tone JC was using. He was briefly reminded of the film The Wizard of OZ, where

Dorothy met the mechanically operated Wizard for the first time. 'Well I am sorry for spoiling your day O great Oz, but I have some news which I thought you might be interested in'. JC blinked in thought 'What news Gary do you think would be interesting to me?' Playing what he hoped would be a trump card Gary replied 'It appears that the President of the United States wants me to go and meet with him in another place and I am leaving soon'. JC processed the words 'and Gary you thought this was more important than my research?' 'Well the President is the most powerful man on the planet and could ultimately be the person who would order an attack on you, if he thought you were a danger to us. In response to Gary's words JC's eyes remained closed for a full ten seconds, which indicated to Gary he was giving the matter his full attention. JC eventually spoke 'Then you were right to bring this to my attention Gary, as any misplaced aggressive behaviour could only lead to destruction' he paused. Gary assumed JC meant destruction of himself until he added 'of the planet and everything on it'. Gary swallowed hard. This was not the way he had wanted the discussion to go, he had just wanted to bring JC back to heel but now seemed to have stirred him up. 'You could do that JC?' Gary asked hesitantly 'If required too Gary either by aggression or protocol, then yes, I am capable of great acts of power and destruction merely by thinking of them. You will be sure to tell your President of this and then perhaps he will give thought to any consequences before acting' Gary nodded and formed a meek 'yes I will'. 'That is good Gary, you are still fulfilling a useful function for me and your species. Now I must return to my research, so you can go and I will summon you in...' there was a moment of calculation before he added 'in five weeks and four days. Good bye Gary'. Even before Gary muttered his reply JC had settled back into the flickering eyes, deep thought routine, leaving Gary in no doubt he had been dismissed. He turned and stomped angrily away. Not only had he not been welcomed, he now had to consider how to break the clear warning to the President. Emma continued her packing, although most of her clothes were sensible working wear and white coats, she did have some nice underwear that might be useful on their trip together. Despite having the credentials of an internationally recognised scientists, she felt like a light headed teenager going on a first date. She'd had boyfriends before and even some sexual entanglements, but nothing previously that had made her feel this way. Her previous partners had all been from her natural peer group, clever, intelligent and careful individuals. Now here she was throwing herself at Gary, a man who had more confidence than ability and who was slippery enough to wriggle under a stone wearing a top hat. That aside, she realised he was essentially a good man trying against all the odds to make something of himself, and also do the best for the planet. She was hooked. It was 7.45pm when Morgan knocked at the motorhome door before entering. 'Ready?' he asked 'Yes, these are my worldly possessions, at least in the USA they are' replied Gary. Outside Emma sat ready in the buggy and with greetings taken care of they headed out of the base in the opposite direction. Having passed several groups of marines in the cordon and produced their ID's, they were ushered though and arrived at the area designated as a helipad. Just finishing refuelling was a Marine Corps helicopter, with the crew climbing over it doing their pre-flight checks. One of the pilots came across and introduced himself as Captain Douglas USMC. 'We'll be ready for you in two minutes, just as soon as we gets clearance from the Whitehouse'. He saluted and ran back to the helicopter where he climbed aboard and strapped himself in. 'How did the General take it?' Gary asked

Morgan. 'We won't know that until he knows you have gone' replied Morgan, causing them all to laugh. 'Is there anything I should know about JC whilst you are gone?' asked Morgan 'Not really, other than to leave him be as he is a little bit tetchy right now. Best keep everyone clear of him until I get back, especially the General okay!' 'Yes, I got that'. There was a low whining sound as the pilot started the first and then the second of the two engines and brought the rotor blades up to operating speed. As it sat turning and burn and the final checks were complete, one of the back seat crewmen ran across to them 'Time to go sir, madam'. They shook hands with Morgan before the crewman back to the helicopter, ducking under the quickly rotating blades. The interior of the chopper was better fitted out than Gary expected, and was obviously used for VIP flights. They were given headsets and when plugged in the crewman gave them a short safety briefing, which he finished by saying 'but don't worry too much about it, when helicopters crash there are usually no survivors'. He told them their flight time to Washington would be about three and a half hours. They watched Morgan shielding his eyes from the downwash as the blades bit the air and the chopper rose slowly into the night. Once they had settled into the trip the crewman served them some coffee from a flask before settling down to fill in his fuel and flight records. The interior of the chopper was quite dark except for a few small lights, and that combined with the rhythm of the machine sent Gary off into a much needed deep sleep. He managed to sleep for most of the journey until the crewman gently shook him and told him to prepare for landing. He blinked and looked across at Emma who smiled at him. He got the impression she had been looking at him for the whole of the flight. It stirred something warm in him but also the natural reflex action of the single man, that to be careful unless you wanted to be caught. The chopper landed gently and the blades started to spin down until the pilot stopped them using the rotor brake. He gave a signal and Emma and Gary were ushered out of the chopper onto the lawn of the Whitehouse. It was brightly lit and Gary could only manage a whispered 'wow'. They were approached by two uniformed officers and two men in suits. One of the men introduced himself 'Mister Barnes, Professor Rowlinson, I am Michael Meads, one of the President's aides. Did you have a good flight?' 'Yes thank you' Gary replied 'it must have been, he slept most of the way' added Emma. They followed Meads and the welcoming party to a large black 4x4 vehicle and got in for the short journey up to the Whitehouse itself. Around the back of the building they approached a security office where efficiently they had their photographs taken and identity cards issued to them both. Once inside they were led through a series of long corridors before coming to a set of elegant double doors. Once inside it was apparent this was a suite of rooms consisting of a sitting room, bedroom and bathroom. 'This is your room professor. Over there is a locked door adjoining Mr Barnes's room. Anything you need then just pick up the phone 24/7. It is late so we will let you get some sleep. Order breakfast when you like but please be ready to meet with the President at 9am. Lastly everything you need should be here, so please do not leave your room and wander the corridors at night as we have security devices that could be activated which will initiate an armed guard response, okay? They left Emma with a polite goodnight before going next door where there was an identical room for Gary. 'The same applies to you sir, anything you need just pick up the phone' said Meads 'Thanks, there is one thing. All the good clothes I have I am wearing and not really suitable for meeting with the President, anything you can do?' Meads nodded, 'of course, we have a selection of clothing for visitors for just such a contingency. I will leave a note for the early morning day staff to get you something suitable before the 9am meeting, okay?' 'Great' said Gary. Meads nodded politely and left Gary to survey his new home in the Whitehouse. The first thing he did was to quietly ensure the door adjoining Emma's room was locked before checking out the sumptuous bathroom and bedroom. 'Not bad Gary, not bad at all' he said to no one. Following Meads advice about not wandering the corridors, Gary opted for a beer from the fridge, some peanuts and more sleep. It was 7.30 am when there was discreet knock at Gary's door. A few seconds later there was another knock followed the slow opening of the door and small voice announcing 'your breakfast sir'. Gary sat up in bed and blinked before motioning the female staff member towards the coffee table. She set the tray down and poured some coffee into the cup before smiling and leaving. Gary yawned, did his morning check that both his balls were still where he had left them before stumbling over to the breakfast wearing just his boxer shorts. The breakfast looked and smelt good as he swigged at the hot coffee and shovelled down heaps of bacon and eggs, not all of which made it to his mouth but some ended up down the front of his shorts. He was halfway through breakfast and just starting to feel whatever normal was for Gary when there was a further knock at the door. Before he could answer the door briskly opened and a smartly dressed figure quickly entered the room. Speaking in clipped tones spoke 'Good morning sir, I am Marceau, the Whitehouse tailor. I understand you are in need of a wardrobe for today's press conference with the President. If I could quickly get some measurements I will have sorted in no time at all'. Before Gary could object he had been stood up and manhandled in a most efficient but camp way, so that all his vital statistics could be taken. There was only the slightest pause when Marceau came to measure his inside leg and found himself face to face with the egg yolk Gary had spilt down his crotch, but his professionalism shone through as he quickly said 'and I will ensure some fresh boxer shorts for you too sir'. In the space of thirty seconds Gary was measured up and still wondering what had happened when Marceau gave a slight bow and left him alone again. Head down, he continued the onslaught on the remaining breakfast, slurping eggs, pancakes and what the Americans call bacon into his greedy mouth. This time he was not surprised to hear yet another knock at the door, but this time he was ready and shouted 'Fuck off', spreading his food far and wide. Whatever the knocker thought he had said must have been similar to 'come in' because that is was Michael Meads did. However, he stopped as he caught sight of Gary and just presented his head. 'I can see you are not quite ready Mr Barnes, so I will be back at 8.45 to collect you, okay?' Gary said nothing and allowed his demeanour to convey the message. Meads nodded and left. Gary managed to finish the remainder of his breakfast in peace by taking a few seconds to lock the door to his room and then ignoring the two other anonymous knocks on the door. He then went for his morning constitutional and a hot shower, after which he was feeling more like greeting strangers and meeting Presidents. It was 8.30 when the knocking became more urgent, so Gary unlocked the door and allowed Marceau the tailor to quickly walk in to the room carrying various suits, shirts and bags. 'I see sir has showered but it leaves us little time to get him presentable before his first appointment' he said testily. Gary had never been spoken about in the third person before and was trying to reconcile it with his current position whilst Marceau set about removing his robe. Like a mother getting a late schoolboy ready for the bus, Marceau moved with consummate ease as he deftly dressed Gary from naked to sartorial elegance in about three minutes. Even Gary did not mind being manhandled when he turned to look in the mirror and saw himself dressed in a suit that he could never have afforded back in the real world. Marceau completed the ensemble by tying Gary's shoe laces then standing back to admire his handiwork. 'Given the time we had, is sir pleased with the overall result?' 'Very good work Marceau, I shall inform the President when I see him' said Gary flippantly. However, in the small micro world of the Whitehouse this was exactly the right compliment to pay to a staff member and Marceau was obviously pleased. 'Thank you sir. As I now have your sizes if you are staying longer I can arrange fresh clothes each day and something more casual for the evening.' He nodded his curt little nod and left Gary admiring Gary in the mirror. Emma has quite liked the idea of sneaking into Gary's room during the night but heeded the warning about security devices and guards, so thought better of it. She had enjoyed a long bath, a light breakfast and several hours to get ready, which meant she would only be a few minutes late. She was still fumbling with her shoes when Michael Meads knocked on the door to her room just before 8.45. Meads had deliberately gone to her room first, as he knew from experience if there was going to be time slippage it would be whilst waiting for the women to be ready. With one final smoothing of her clothes Emma accepted her time was up and followed Meads to Gary's room. She was amazed at the transformation the clothes had made to Gary and gave a little whistle of approval. 'Thank you' said Gary, growing into the part and adjusting his tie with a flourish. 'Please make sure your ID cards are on display at all times and obey all commands in the event of an incident. Also, the real people to worry about are the President's personal bodyguards, all of whom have a small white round lapel badge and a large concealed weapon'. Once he was sure that point had been made and understood, Meads led them around many magnificent corridors and stairs before coming to a security desk manned by two uniformed officers. Their ID was carefully checked and a phone call made before they were allowed to proceed along the corridor to an outer office. Inside were several secretarial staff, along with two round white lapel pin staff who eyed the strangers suspiciously. Meads introduced the group to the secretary who picked up a phone and announced their arrival. 'Yes sir' she replied before standing and opening a set of double doors. As they moved through the doors Gary recognised they were now in the famous Oval office and now understood why his egg stained boxer shorts would not have been appropriate. The President stood as they entered and warmly greeted Emma and Gary, saying how nice it was to see them again before introducing them to the two other men in the room, Secretary for defence Donald Weisman, and the other was the leader of the US Congress, Walter Crouch. Having got them seated and dismissed Meads, the President began the meeting. After outlining what they already knew, he made the point that they could no longer keep this thing secret so today he would be addressing the world. The meeting was to decide what he could actually tell the world without causing mass panic and chaos across the globe. 'Ladies and gentlemen that is why we are here now.' He paused for effect before continuing 'So, if we can start with the good news. Professor, as I understand it the recent dynamic weather situation has now abated and was in fact caused by the visitation and not a standalone natural disaster?' Emma lightly cleared her throat. 'That is correct Mr. President. What was looking to be a global catastrophic event was traced back to a point of origin in deep space. This eventually led us to the scientific conclusion that the cause was something headed this way at immense speed, casing the weather disruption we all saw, although we still do not know how it affected the Earth's weather. By tracking and studying the phenomenon we were able to predict a landing point, which as we all now know was near Lake Michigan. Once it had landed and stopped interfering with the weather things started to get back to normal pretty quick. There are a few residual rogue weather patterns still circulating the globe, but the most part that crisis has passed'. The President nodded 'Thank you Professor for that succinct and encouraging report. That brings us to the main topic, namely the visitation. Mr. Barnes if you could update us on what we have at ground zero?' Gary paused. Not just for effect but because he was somewhat overwhelmed to be sat in the Oval office with the President and his top men. 'The President tried again 'Mr Barnes, Gary?' It broke the spell and he began to speak slowly. 'Sir, sorry but it's the first time I have heard it called a visitation, it just threw me a bit. Taking over from where Professor Rowlinson left off, what I can tell you is this. There then followed a lengthy, sometimes vague, sometimes detailed description of Gary's involvement with JC. The only real lie Gary made was the how JC came to be known as JC. It was a non de plume that Gary had invented on the spur of the moment to give JC a non- threatening persona, but it was having far reaching consequences and that lie could not now be undone. It would have been equally shocking to other people if he had called him ET, but it would not have affirmed the religious connotations in some people's minds. Gary tried to explain the name by adding 'and when he was building his copy of me I was in a trance like state, but I clearly felt him transfer the name JC to me, hence why he is called that. But, as to whether or not he is an alien visitor or the second coming of the lord I simply do not know'. There was stunned silence from the group as they listened to an incredible story right from the horse's mouth. The President was the first to speak 'so, there we have it gentlemen. It was always going to happen in someone's presidency and JC has chosen mine. Do you have any questions before we get to discussing today's global broadcast?' The secretary for defence had already been privy to briefings from ground zero, but he was still shocked and opened mouthed hearing Gary's descriptions and conversations with JC. He managed to compose himself enough to ask the obvious question from a man with his job title 'Mr. Barnes, does JC either as god or alien pose any threat to the United States?' These was an uncomfortable few moments as the parochial question reverberated around the room, before picking up on the vibe he added 'in particular, or the planet and its inhabitants in general?' Gary sat upright in his chair 'well up until yesterday the only threatening thing I saw or rather heard, was JC shouting. This was as it turns out just a misunderstanding and he ceased to do it when asked not to. However, since he now has the internet connection and is gathering information and studying it, I found it more difficult to communicate with him, and there was a coldness to his communication. Also, when I told him I was coming to meet the President and that he should be careful not to be the cause of any aggressive action, his reply hinted at a vast amount of power and destruction that he reek on the planet if required.' This last comment caused a physical and audible reaction as each of them imagined images that Hollywood disaster movies had planted in their minds. The President spoke 'Well that is news even to me Gary'. 'Sorry Mr. President, but this only happened just before getting on the helicopter for the flight here' replied Gary before adding 'and this is the first time I have spoken with a god or alien, so I may just be misinterpreting something or missing a subtlety', which did little to lighten the mood. 'I think Mr. President that we should mobilise more forces and have more aircraft on standby in case of any aggressive moves' suggested the secretary for defence. 'I accept your assessment Mr Secretary but it must be done quietly so as to not to be seen to over react or upset the Russians.' The leader of Congress now slowly raised his hand. He was a third generation Jew, and not wishing for his people to be involved in the killing Jesus for a second time asked 'can we be quite sure Mr. President that he is not actually Jesus Christ and that we might just be preparing to attack him again?' 'No Walter we cannot, but as President of the United States I must prepare to defend my people until we know for sure. In god we trust, but only once we really know he is god' the President replied in a grave voice. 'Now, I think it is time we called in my director of press relations to discuss the upcoming broadcast.' There was no discussion as the President used his intercom to summon the press secretary, a smartly dressed woman called Eileen Cozak. The introductions made, the President took on the job of briefing the Ms Cozak with all that they definitely knew. As to the ambiguity surrounding the threat level, he explained what they currently position was, but also that it was not going to be part of his broadcast, which Ms Cozak agreed with. She had some comments to make about order of service for the President's speech and asked if he would take questions from the press on completion of his statement, to which the President replied that he would not, but would offer to give regular updates as things developed. Ms Cozak looked at her watch and then quickly left the room to prepare the written statement for approval and getting a copy onto the teleprompter. The President also checked his watch 'Ladies and gentlemen, we have one hour and ten minutes before we go live. Can I suggest you retire to the ante room for coffee whilst I carry on working?' Emma and Gary left the Oval office, leaving the three men waiting patiently for them to leave and the doors to close behind them. Meads was waiting for them and showed them to a large bright reception room overlooking the Whitehouse lawns. 'Coffee or perhaps would our English guests would prefer tea?' he asked politely, but was somewhat surprised when they both opted for coffee, strong, black and plenty of it. Whilst Meads organised the coffee, Emma and Gary stood alone looking out of the window. 'You did well in there prof.' said Gary, reverting back to his nickname for her. She now enjoyed the familiarity which she had once hated 'And you did a good job too. It was not an easy thing to brief the President' she replied 'but are you going to be okay in front of the whole world on TV?' she teased 'Oh that should be the easy bit 'Gary replied 'You have seen how the yanks do those disaster press conferences. We will be lined up behind him like a row of town mayors and police chiefs, whilst he does all the talking and claims the high ground. No worries'. They both laughed as Meads came back with the coffee 'Good to see you have still got a sense of humour, kinda gives me hope for the future' said Meads, partly in the hope of getting some snippet of information from their meeting with the President. Aware that Meads was fishing, Gary took the opportunity to nibble on his hook 'Yes well you have to laugh when you only have a few days left to live, don't you old chap?' Meads horrified face brought forth more laughter from the two of them before Emma let him back off the hook 'Relax, Gary is just having a little joke, aren't you Gary?' to which Gary pulled a non-committal face before dunking his biscuit into his coffee and stared out over the lawns in mock angst. Meads did not have a sense of humour and was not impressed. Putting his own coffee cup firmly down on the table he left them to tend to some paperwork in his office. Emma started the laughter again whilst Gary involuntarily spat coffee and biscuits over the large window pane. With five minutes to go Meads returned and escorted them through the building to a room where the press secretary was waiting. She gave them a final briefing about where to stand and what to do, but added one important change to the press briefing. The President had decided that as it had not been confirmed, there would be no mention of the word JC or god in the briefing. Gary and Emma both knew this was mainly to stop civil unrest or religious groups getting all 'I told you so' but in light of what they knew it made sense. They were joined by the President and a small entourage of officials and security men. He nodded at Gary and Emma 'You have been briefed about not using the JC title, and for the same reasons I have excused the secretary for defence from this press conference in case his presence should send the wrong message, okay?' They both nodded and Gary shifted uncomfortably as the coffee and nerves combined to make him want the toilet. 'You should have gone before we left' whispered Emma, recognising his symptoms. There was a door marked disabled toilet just behind them, so not taking any chances Gary made a bolt for it. His sudden movement caused some consternation amongst the security men and one of them reached into his lapel towards his weapon, but the head of security was quick to evaluate the threat and Gary's needs, and quickly calmed his man down. The press secretary emerged from behind a screen and announced everything was ready and for the supporting cast members to follow her, until she noticed Gary's absence 'where is Mister Barnes?' she started to ask before Emma whispered the reason in her ear. There followed an awkward minute as everyone waited for Gary's return, which was not helped by the way he came back drying his hands on the back of his trousers 'The blower is not working' he offered by way of excuse. 'Follow me please' said Ms Cozak. She led them through a door and then told them to wait whilst she walked in front of a screen The press secretary stood up to a microphone, which unlike in most movies did not feedback at all. 'Ladies and Gentlemen, The President of the United States' At that the President and entourage strode around the screen and up to the podium, to a chorus of camera shutters and flashing lights. Although they were expecting to see the press, neither of them were prepared for the hundreds of journalists, cameramen and TV cameras that stretch to the back of the long room. As briefed Gary and the rest of them closed ranks behind him. Reading from his autocue, the President spoke.

. '*My fellow Americans and peoples of the world. I am making this worldwide broadcast to try and stop any wild speculation and chaos that could come from such speculation. As many of you will know there have been some secretive events unfolding in a part of our great country and as 45th President of the United States of America, it is my duty to share them with you. For as long as man as walked on this planet he has wondered what lay in the heavens above and where he fits into the greater scheme of things. Some put their faith in god and religion, others in science and technology, some in both and others in neither. But, they all have in common the question of is other life out there somewhere'. I can now answer that question once and for all, and yes, other life does exist outside of planet Earth. '* There was a loud gasp and the cameras once again began their mindless chattering as photographers went through their learnt behaviour of pushing the button, despite themselves trying to take in the full impact of what was being said. Several of the reporters from Latin countries crossed themselves and began repeating religious mantras, whilst one fell to her knees. The President held up his hand and continued '*And furthermore, that life has recently visited planet earth and is currently in an area somewhere near*

Lake Michigan' Again there was an explosion of flashing cameras and comments from the throng as some of them spoke into microphones to pass the story as quickly as possible, the kneeling woman now fainted and fell forward, being tended to by Whitehouse staff. *'I can tell you we are in communication with it and it currently poses no threat to life on earth. Through circumstances I do not propose to go into right now, our world's ambassador here, Mr Gary Barnes has taken a lead and is communicating with the visitor on a daily basis, trying to find out who or what it is, and what is wants here on Earth. On a positive note, I am assured by experts that the recent weather phenomena we recently experienced was caused by the arrival of our friend, and now that he has landed the weather will eventually return to normal. Now, you will have many questions but at the moment I have very little information other than that which I have given to you today. Therefore, I will not be taking any furthers questions as I have to confer with other world leaders, but there will be a daily briefing here at 11 am or ad hoc if circumstances dramatically. Thank you for your time. God bless the world and god bless America.'* He gave a carefully rehearsed look around the room before leading the small team back through the double doors, which closed behind them. The President thanked everyone before turning to Emma and Gary 'Given that your friend does not currently need you down at ground zero, can you stay around here for a few days and help with detailed briefings of my people? You could also help with some of the technical aspects of the press briefings?' Although it was phrased as a question they both had doubted they could reply no to the President's request, so quickly acquiesced. 'Good' said the President, 'Meads will sort you out an office to work from and we will meet daily for updates, okay?' he said as he walked away, followed by his entourage. 'Do you not feel you should be back there?' asked Emma. 'Yes I do' replied Gary 'but he does seem to be in shutdown at the moment, so perhaps a few days away won't hurt, in fact it might be beneficial'. Emma chose to read more into that last statement than Gary intended but as she moved in for an intimate moment she was interrupted by Meads. 'So I hear you guys are staying with us for the foreseeable future and I have tasked with looking after your needs. You will need somewhere to work, so will sharing an office be okay for you?' 'They both nodded before Gary added 'It would be useful for me to keep an eye on things back at Lake Michigan, so can you arrange for a live CCTV feed for me to monitor?' 'Meads nodded, 'should not be a problem, the President is already getting that feed, so just tapping into the signal should not be a problem. I'll get the technical people on it'. He then led them to a lower level of the building that contained various offices and support services for the Whitehouse, stopping at each stairway to produce their identity cards. Meads reiterated the point about security and that they should always carrying their ID cards, but seeing the heavily armed security had already convinced Gary and Emma. Meads introduced them to the head of the support services, who within minutes had allocated them a spare office that he always kept for visiting dignitaries. 'By this afternoon I will have your CCTV feed patched to this room but for security that will mean you locking the door if you are not in here please' said Meads. 'So, what else can I get you?' asked Meads 'Lunch' replied Gary. Back at Lake Michigan the General was not a happy or completely sober man. Almost from the get go he had felt undermined by the micromanagement coming out of Washington. Then that damn limey journalist had got his nose into the action and had made himself keeper of JC or whatever it was. Now Morgan had broken the news that the brits had been whisked off to the Whitehouse to meet the President, leaving him here babysitting. He poured himself another drink as he talked to himself. He cursed everything and everyone who had put him in this situation. Gary got a double curse, but everyone from the President down to Morgan were included. His thoughts, influenced by his compulsive drinking and a perceived lack of respect conspired to make him focus him on the negative. 'I can deal with this' he said 'I can show them how the military can cut through all this bullshit and deal with the situation' he emptied his glass in one hit and growled 'I will show them' as he refilled his glass with whisky for the eighth time that day. Gary was impressed with the high class dining room his status afforded him. He ordered his third dessert from the uniformed waitress, who did not raise an eyebrow. Emma and Meads both teased him about the amount of food he had eaten. Emma had seen him eat before but had never seen him eat three desserts after a two course lunch. Gary made no apology. He loved his food, in truth probably more than he liked sex, but that was something he had not shared with Emma. Meads made his excuses and left Emma to wait for Gary to finish. They discussed recent events in general and somehow Gary managed to keep off the topic of their relationship. He was not adverse to how things were running but the inner single man shouted at him to keep running for as long as he could. He was just swallowing a mouthful of pancakes and cream and day dreaming about their last sexual encounter, when Emma's voice pierced his thoughts 'Hello Gary, are you listening to me?' she said impatiently. 'Yes, sorry, I was just wondering how JC is getting on' he lied unconvincingly. Seeing that she was not going to be discussing their relationship over lunch, Emma suggested they go and get their office arranged and decide how they could best use their time from whilst away from Lake Michigan. Due to the various security checkpoints it took them a full ten minutes to make their way back to the utility level where their office was located. Meads was there with some technician who had just finished installing another monitor above the desk. He stood back and pushed the remote control which after a few seconds showed a blue screen with password boxes. Meads thanked the technician, which also served as a dismissal so he left them to it. Meads produced a sealed envelope which he gave to Emma 'This is the password for the secure CCTV feed. Use it and then shred it please. Meads went to leave but Gary stopped him 'Stay and see if it works and you can also get a look at what we are working with'. Meads was unsure 'I am not sure I have the security clearance for that' 'Then I hereby give you the clearance 'said Gary, making a pretend anointing motion with his hand. Meads carefully considered the offer before making sure the door to the office was secure and replying 'Go on then, I am desperate to see this thing'. Emma opened the envelope and entered the long passwords into the two boxes. There was some flashing as the screen adjusted before the picture cleared and showed a screen spilt into four pictures. Each of the four views were from cameras positioned around where JC and the dome. Touching the screen to point out where JC sat made the screen change to a single full picture. 'Oh that is useful' said Gary. JC appeared to be exactly where he left him, in exactly the same pose. The only difference Gary could see was the addition of several microphone on stands which had been placed near JC, obviously to replace the mic that Gary had been wearing. Meads was transfixed at the overall image and stunned to see that JC did indeed resemble Gary, apart from the obvious shimmering effect. Gary gave Meads the virtual tour, along with the story so far. Ever the professional, Meads was both uncomfortable with having the information being shared with him, but also personally curious as to what had been happening at Lake Michigan. Emma started to weary at the new found boys club and logged onto one of the generic office computers to try and get some work done. Since the weather was no longer an issue, she had been working on the various readings coming from the area surrounding JC and comparing notes with the American scientists, so wanted to see how they were progressing. She was pleased that she had internet access and that her log in credentials to the main scientific server had not been revoked. One thing immediately jumped out at her in the scientific log. Readings from the dome and JC area showed some sort of power source, but one that could not be measured. She had to read the sentence three times over, becoming more curious at each reading. The author who was one of the team at Lake Michigan had managed to identify a power source but none of the instruments they had could quantify it. The analogy was offered that it was like trying to measure the contents of a lake using a thimble. She could probably come up with a more scientific description but for the layman it conveyed the immense power they were dealing with. Gary also logged onto a computer and when he opened the mail icon was surprised to find mail waiting for him on the Whitehouse intranet. There were three emails, one a generic system welcome, one from Meads and one from the President's secretary. The last one contained a short message telling Gary he could email the President at any time and she would ensure it reached his eyes immediately. The afternoon passed quickly, in a blur of study, report writing and in Gary's case an hour of solitaire whist watching JC on the monitor. They left and secured the office just after five and made their way back through the Whitehouse to their rooms. At the door Emma stopped and confirmed that they were meeting for dinner at 7.30. Deftly avoiding her implied offer of a kiss by ignoring her body movement, Gary quickly unlocked his room and left her outside with her head cocked and lips pursed. Somewhat cross, Emma would have spent the intervening period sticking pins into a Gary voodoo doll, but instead decided on a leisurely bath. Whilst the bath was running she thought she might emulate Gary in getting some nicer clothes and got through to the housekeeping department. The female staff member who was responsible for such things would be on duty till 10pm and would be delighted to bring a selection of evening wear to Emma's room at 6.30. Emma got into her bath with a smile on her face and a plan in her mind. In Gary's room the mood was somewhat different. Having flicked through every of the four hundred available TV channels and found little of interest, which is Gary's world meant no porn, he lay on the huge bed with his hands behind his head. He took stock of where he was and how he had got there, which basically amounted to him just being Gary. He thought about Emma and how he should handle that situation before his mind drifted back to JC. Just then he felt a presence and opened his eyes to find JC stood over him, his eyes open and that beaming smile that showed what Gary's face could do, if he only let go once in a while. 'What are you doing here?' Gary asked 'I have come to take you back Gary' JC shouted in his big voice 'Stop shouting' said Gary 'the guards will here you will batter the door down' 'No they will not Gary, only you can hear me'. Gary held two pillows over his ears to stop the noise 'what do you want JC?' JC's smile faded and he moved closer towards Gary 'It is you I want Gary' but as he spoke his whole head started to distort and rearrange itself, the features moving around and around in a blur before settling again into a familiar face, that being the face of Emma 'I want you Gary' the Emma/JC apparition shouted as it fell upon Gary. He screamed and still with the pillows in his hands he flailed wildly to fight the abomination off. That is when Gary suddenly woke up bathed in sweat and covered in an expensive duck down duvet. It took a few seconds for him to realise where he was and that he had been dreaming. Slowly gathering his thoughts and putting his fears back where they belonged, he suddenly jumped again at the loud banging on the adjoining door 'Gary, you okay in there?' he could hear Emma ask 'Yes, I am fine, just tripped over my shoes' he lied deliberately. Emma sat back down in the chair and smiled at Elspeth from the housekeeping staff. Elspeth, as promised had brought a range of evening wear for Emma to choose from but having seen what the professor had clumsily tried to do with make-up, she had offered to give her a complete makeover. It was all part of the service Elspeth like to offer and whilst Emma was essential a pretty woman, a lifetime of science had left her in need of help with girly type makeup. Elspeth scrapped, prodded, primed, cleansed, plucked and manicured Emma, before getting her to parade in each of the dresses before settling on one which she was happy with. Next door Gary was still getting over his nightmare and whilst sat on the toilet tried to fathom what the hell could that dream have meant. It was

7.35 when he opened the door to see if Emma was waiting outside for him but there was no one there. He tried again at 7.45, but again there was just the lone security guard sat at his desk at the end of the corridor. Waving his ID card on the chain around his neck, Gary walked to Emma's front door and knocked 'You still in there Prof?' The door was opened by a petite black girl 'Hi, I am Elspeth. Miss Rowlinson will be ready soon and will call for you, okay?' Before Gary could answer the door was closed and hushed voices could be heard laughing and whispering inside. Gary went back to his room pausing only to shrug his shoulders at the guard, who clearly understood this was a waiting for a woman scenario, and knowingly shrugged back. It was 8.05 pm and when there was a light knock on the door. Like the genie in the bottle, Gary was now a little pissed off at being kept waiting for so long. He impatiently swung the door open before doing at double take at the vision facing him. Whilst normally Emma dressed like an off duty professor and only applied makeup in little dabs to cover blemishes, Elspeth had accepted the challenge and had done a full makeover on Emma. Everything from head to toe and all points in between. Gary really was speechless for once. He tried to speak but no words would form, so he tried again before settling on the simple 'you look nice'. Trembling inside, that was all Emma needed to confirm that Elspeth had done a good job and with that her own confidence rose one hundred percent. 'Shall we go and dine then Mr Barnes' she asked formally, whilst holding out her arm. 'Gary took the bait 'yes Professor Rowlinson, let us go and dine'. 'Oh please 'she said in mock tones, 'just call me Emma'. 'Certainly Emma, and you must call me Gary' he replied. They set off down the corridor, with Gary taking a moment to return the wink offered up to him by the security guard. In the large VIP dining room there a dozen occupied tables. There were some military people who seemed to be hosting an event with several high ranking officials who they had seen around the Whitehouse since arriving. They were shown to a table where they ordered wine, still jokingly keeping the newly met personas that they had created for themselves. They made small talk about some of the people in the room before pausing to taste and then approve the white Pino Grigio wine they had ordered. With a glass in hand they chinked glasses, drank and made a silent toast, each unaware they were both wishing for entirely different things. 'Where did you get the clothes?' asked Gary 'the same place you got yours' she replied 'the Presidents casts offs' After the weak joke Gary tried again 'I am not very good at this, but you do look stunning tonight'. Emma blushed and nearly choked on her wine 'Well that sounded a pretty good start, and you don't look so bad yourself' she replied once she had recovered from her coughing fit. They ordered their food and with the help of the ambience and wine, settled into an easy and relaxed dinner. Between courses Emma excused herself to use the bathroom, which gave Gary the opportunity to order and glug yet more wine. Whether it was his surreptitious manner or conspiratorial tones that did is a moot point, but when Gary asked the waiter if there was any Champagne available his manner changed immediately and he whispered 'But of course. Is sir going to make a romantic gesture and pop a life changing question to madam? 'FUCKING HELL NO' Gary shouted, surprising himself, the waiter and drawing the attention and disapproving looks form other tables. Regaining some composure Gary spoke 'sorry no, just some general quaffing bubbles will do thank you'. Happy to accept it was obviously his fault, the waiter scurried away as quickly as possible. Emma reappeared and was more than a little surprised to see most of the tables looking in their direction 'Did I miss something?' she asked 'Oh no, It must just be the way you look tonight' he replied in his best lounge lizard accent. Emma was loving the compliments and attention too much to pursue the question and besides the answer had been the correct one. Timidly and still with an apologetic body language, the waiter appeared and presented the champagne and ice bucket. 'Oh champagne. Are we celebrating something?' said Emma. Gary scowled at the waiter 'see what you've done now', which despite the joke made the waiter even more uncomfortable. Once they had tried the bubbles Emma asked 'come on Gary, what did I miss? ' 'Oh, it's just our little joke' Gary replied but to change the subject added 'and talking of little jokes, I hope the General is being a good boy'. Back at Lake Michigan Morgan was having a problem containing the General's mood swings, religious fervour and obvious drinking bouts. Still waving his Presidential letter of complete authority over the operation, he had taken to walking around the compound issuing orders, which Morgan had then to unissue without the General knowing. He had found the best way of controlling the General was to keep him supplied with his favourite whisky, which whilst made him unpredictable, also made him sleep a lot. Morgan had raised his concerns with his superiors but due to inter service rivalries they could find no one to take their concerns to the President to try and have the General replaced. It was a problem Morgan knew he just had to live with, at least in the short term. Gary and Emma were on their second bottle of champagne and were really enjoying each other's company. Having told Emma about his earlier nightmare, they both joked about having a port and cheese course to finish the evening and set Gary up for another nightmare. He had of course left out Emma's part in his nightmare in case it should give her the idea she was in his subconscious. Mid laugh they were aware of an approaching male from another table. 'Excuse me' he said 'Are you the two British experts assisting the President with our visitation?' 'We are they' said Gary, 'and who might you be?' The American produced a business card, loudly announcing he was Dee M. Doyles 'chief reporter on The Washington Times, the most influential paper in Washington and probably the USA'. He told them he was being hosted by the high ranking military figures on the other table for helping them with certain stories they wanted in the press, hence him dining at the Whitehouse. They invited him to sit down, Emma out of politeness and Gary out of professional courtesy. They talked in general terms about the situation before the journalist leaned closer in 'So give me a break here. Just what kind of inside story could you guys let me have? Any little snippet or gossip that none of the other papers have got would be great for me!' Emma and Gary both laughed, to which the journalist joined in 'hey what's so funny?' 'Oh it's not you we are laughing at Mr Doyles. It is just that here I am, a world leading scientist and yet the one who has the real inside story on all this is Gary here' They laughed again before Doyles asked 'so why is that so funny' 'Because Mr Doyles' Emma tipsily carried on 'Gary here is one of you, a newspaper man, a reporter.' It was probably the alcohol that made Emma and Gary both think that A. This in itself was funny, and B. That Mister Dee M. Doyles would also see the funny side to it. They were wrong on both counts. Once it had sunk in that Gary really was a journalist and this was not some sick joke, Doyles went red and stated to shake 'you mean to tell me that the biggest story to hit the planet earth happens right here in the USA, and some, some British hack who I have never heard of is living in the President ass!' His voice had risen to a crescendo, causing the other tables to look across at them for the second time that evening. Luckily the Army General and his aide who been hosting Doyles were quick to react and came across to assist. With profuse apologies to Emma and Gary, they half talked, half pulled Doyles back to his seat at their table. His voice still raised as he tried to explain what he had just heard to his hosts. Recounting the story only made it worse, causing him to suddenly blow. Throwing his napkin onto the table he stormed out of the dining room, giving evil looks at Gary as he went. There was stunned silence in the room, which was broken by a loud pop as Gary opened yet another bottle of champagne.' Well I thought that went well' said Gary to the room, raising his glass in a toast. The remainder of the diners continued their evening, only occasionally sneaking glances across at the two Brits. Possibly it was the norm or maybe it was the change in atmosphere, but by 10.15 the room was empty apart from Gary and Emma, who were enjoying a brandy nightcap. The staff were professional and discreet, but even so Emma was aware they were waiting for them to finish 'Come on big boy, let's get out of here so these people can clear up'. Gary burped, nodded and burped again before getting to his feet. They thanked the staff and then made their way back through the Whitehouse to their adjoining rooms. They stopped at each and every security checkpoint, each guard getting the personal drunken account of their evening's entertainment. Once at Emma's door, Gary drunkenly assumed he would be going in with her for some jiggy jiggy, so was a little surprised when she kissed him gently on the cheek and bade him good night. He was confused, but before he could react she had gently closed the door behind her and locked it. He stood for a few seconds, confused, a little hurt but a lot horny, before he walked the few steps to his own door. He fumbled with his key in the lock but before he went in he looked hopefully back along the corridor in case she was teasing him, but there was no head or curled finger summoning him back. Crestfallen and confused he went into his room and then did a double take as stretched out on his bed was Emma. She had quickly come through the adjoining door and beat him to it. In her hand were two glasses of champagne that she had Elspeth arrange, along with the unlocking of the door whilst they were at dinner 'I thought it would better on the security cameras if we appeared to go to our own rooms' she said 'Good thinking Batman' was all Gary could think of to say. 'Get your clothes off Robin' was Emma's considered reply. Gary woke slowly, the light streaming in the windows adding eye pain to his hangover. He looked around at the bedclothes carnage, along with the men and women's clothing strewn around the floor but there was no sign of Emma. He groaned as he sat up and then groaned again as he remembered what had transpired the night before. It seems as if Emma had got her way again, but to be fair he had done some of the running and from what he remembered he had enjoyed the night wrestling. There was a knock at the door but before he could react it opened slowly and voice called 'housekeeping sir, your breakfast tray'. The small uniformed Latino lady deliberately avoided eye contact as she skirted the discarded clothing and made her way to the coffee table, where she carefully placed the tray. She retraced her steps and within seconds was gone from the room, grateful that she did not have to endure some of the groping she had in the past with other guests. Gary search his rooms but as there was no sign of Emma he correctly assumed she had gone back to her own room to freshen up. Looking at the time Gary realised he would have to hurry if he was going to make the 10 am briefing with the President, before the later scheduled 11 am press briefing. He ate, showered and had just put on fresh clothes when Emma appeared at the adjoining door. 'Good morning' she asked in that awkward morning after way. 'Morning' he replied, careful not to be either too keen or misunderstood. 'Looking at the mess on the floor she said 'Looks like someone had quite a party in here last night'. Emma's gaze spotted the dress she had been wearing, along with some of her underwear scattered on the floor. She quickly scooped up all the clothes and threw them on the bed before separating hers and taking them into her room. When she returned Gary was fully dressed and ready to go. 'Shall we?' he said, opening the door and allowing her to go before him. They made their way back to their new office, logged onto their computers and turned on the monitor. JC appeared to be still sat where had last seen him and nothing much seemed to have changed. The only problem arrived with an urgent email from the President's press secretary, which had been copied into the President himself. It seems that the self-important journalist from the Washington Times, Mr Dee M. Doyles, had made a big issue over Gary's involvement and had made a whole second page story out of it. There was a link in the email to the online version of the newspaper, which included the article. No matter how well it was written it was hard when reading the piece not feel as if it was based purely on professional jealousy. Of course there was the obvious angle abut Brits being involved within the USA but because it was written when Doyles had been drunk last night the little green man could clearly be seen hiding in the words. Gary printed a copy and showed Emma before they made their way to what they now knew was the press secretaries' outer office. They were seated and making small talk with Meads before the President and press secretary arrived. After some morning greetings the press secretary brought up the matter for discussion. Gary explained how they had been accosted in the dining room last night and yes, he had disclosed he was a journalist but did not have the chance to explain just how he was involved. The press secretary was horrified but the President was able to see past the issue and see where blame, if any lay. 'Mr Doyles gets more than his fair share of inside information from within the Whitehouse, much more than the rest of the press corps. I can see why his feathers are ruffled, but I will address that in today's briefing. 'Anything from Lake Michigan overnight?' 'No sir' answered Meads 'Special Agent Morgan's morning report states everything is as it was at close of play yesterday. However, there is a matter of internal admin which needs addressing by yourself. It is not for this group, so by early afternoon I will have a short report on your desk for consideration'. The

President nodded 'Okay, I got that. Anyone else have any input for today's press briefing?' there were no answers so the President stood up 'right lets have coffee and convene in the press anti room at 10.55' before he got up and left the room with an aide and security team member. Gary and Emma both liked his no nonsense way of dealing with matters and felt that they had his confidence. At the press briefing, Emma, Gary and the press secretary walked into the glare of publicity a few minutes before the President made his grand entrance. Gary was aware of a new focus on him as photographers took more shots of him and newspaper men scowled and pointed. The story was obviously the main point of conversation amongst the press corps and now here he was in front of them. Gary was pleased when the President arrived at last and took the heat off him. The President wasted no time in speaking:

'I would like to start by clearly stating that there has been no change in the overnight circumstances at Lake Michigan. Our visitor appears to be in a state of meditation or deep thought and has shown no sign of any aggressive act or further communication. Our scientific teams are still studying all aspect of its arrival and looking for possible threat from either an aggressive or passive act, but as

yet all fears appear to be unfounded. What I can you is that all the contact so far has been through our British colleague here Mr Gary Barnes'. The President paused here as he had set a trap and wanted someone from the press to spring it. He was not disappointed when a familiar face raised his hand. *'Mr Doyles, I was going to save question until the end but if you must'* Doyles stood up and announced his credentials 'Dee M. Doyles, Washington Times. Can the President comment on or explain why he has chosen a British journalist, above a US citizen to work with him on this unique event?' There was a large murmur of agreement amongst the American press throughout the room, all of whom felt it was an insulting imposition. The President waited for the murmur to calm down before speaking *'I can see why the indigenous press corps would see the inclusion of a non US reporter as an insult to their craft and integrity. However, Mr Barnes is involved not because he was chosen by me but because he was chosen by our visitor personally. Now, since this is a unique event where communication is the key to a successful outcome, if the visitor has chosen Mr Barnes to communicate with then it would be foolish and careless of me to try and replace him for the sake of internal politics or jealousies'* He allowed the logic and rebuff to sink in before carrying on *'therefore, Mr Barnes will remain a valued member of the team and will be world's ambassador to our visitor until circumstances demand a change'*. Gary grew an inch taller as he heard the President both defending him and announcing him as the 'world's ambassador'. With the President's approval still ringing out of the speakers, the cameramen and journalists shifted their focus back to Gary, but this time in a more positive way. The President once again wound up the press conference with the promise of updates at 11am each day, before exiting the room. In the back room the President was being congratulated by a posse of 'yes' men, which Gary thought a pity as this time he really deserved it. The President called Gary over 'That all okay with you Mister Ambassador?' 'Yes great' replied Gary 'just what does an ambassador earn?' but the joke was lost or at best politely ignored. The rest of the day went very much as the previous day, with the addition of finding things to say to Emma during the awkward silences. She had the good grace to not bring up the subject of their nocturnal wrestling, but he knew that would not last. He was grateful when Meads made several visits to their office during the day, either to catch up with what was happening at Lake Michigan or just to look at JC on the CCTV monitor. Gary had just poured a third cup of coffee for him in the hope that he would stay a bit longer. Meads was struggling to force it down whilst watching the live feed of JC in Lake Michigan. The picture was a little unstable this morning as something was causing interference and breaking up the picture and causing no sound to be heard. When he stared hard at the screen Meads could see there was something up. 'Is there something happening at ground zero today?' Meads asked. Gary looked up from his computer 'No there shouldn't be. JC should be studying and the site clear until I get back, why'. 'Well you had better come look at this' said Meads. Emma and Gary joined Meads to look at the screen. The picture was intermittent and without sound, but what could clearly be seen was an agitated figure moving around JC, gesticulating and from his body language obviously shouting. 'Oh shit' said Gary, as the four phones on their desks all started ringing at once. The General had awoke after a fitful few hours' sleep. The alcohol had conspired against his body, making him restless but also adding to his addiction and need. He stumbled to the coffee pot but while it started to hum into life he saw the half open bottle of whisky on the side.

Not even bothering to lie to himself with a rationalisation, he poured himself a drink and gulped it down. By the time the coffee was ready he had taken three shots of whisky and no longer wanted or needed the coffee. He got himself dressed and turned on the television to watch the press conference. It galled him to see that smug limey bastard stood behind the President, who had now just anointed him with the title of 'world ambassador'. It was the constant repeating of the title by the media after the press conference was over, complete with ticker tape strap lines along the bottom of the screen 'World Ambassador' the eventually drove the General over the edge. Finishing his drink and the bottle, he put on his braided hat and walked unsteadily down the steps of the motorhome. He berated some of the marines at the outer security for not saluting him quick enough, before making his way to the inner cordon. Alerted by radio, these marines saluted but did not challenge the General as he staggered passed them towards JC. The marines did call their colonel on the radio, who in turn called Morgan, but it was too late to stop the General.

The General continued his drunken gait getting ever closer to JC. The shimmering form of what appeared to be a sleeping Gary, only added to the anger the General felt. JC, Gary or whoever it was, was going to get a piece of his mind' 'You, you there wake up' he slurred but without response. He tried again but this time shouting 'Wake up you, I wanna talk to you and find out who the fuck you are!' But still JC did not respond. Drink fuelled, the General became more and more irate at being ignored. 'I'm a fucking General you know, you son of a bitch, you can't not not talk to me like that' There was a slight rise in the amount of static electricity crackling around but JC still did not open his eyes or react. The General finally cracked, he picked up a stone from the floor and threw it at JC, which did cause him a glancing blow. He threw several more rocks each with a varying amount of accuracy, but some did strike home. The General then upped the stakes by looking for and spotting a more effective weapon. He tore one of the microphones from its stand, then using the stand he raised it above his head and struck JC a half dozen times about the head. JC had been deep deep deep in thought and study. He had successfully managed to develop an understanding of what was useful and what was crap on the internet, and was now busy working his way through many topics. Anything that needed more detailed analysis was sent back to his main presence within the dome for filtering before being passed back to the replica of Gary's brain to be viewed in context. JC became aware of the approach of a being but was not concerned. The increase in noise levels also did not bother him or need a response. What did change was when a part of him felt a reoccurring physical sensation, which with the shouting indicated aggression. Bringing himself out of the study state he was in, JC slowly opened his eyes. The General was at first a little taken aback to see the eyes open, but once he had adjusted to that he figured he must have been getting through. Now was the time that he could save his beloved country in person from this being, god, devil, Jesus Christ, Allah or 'whatever the fuck you are' he shouted as he resumed his attack. He was on his fourth strike with the stand in his hand when JC open his mouth. Using his loudest loud voice he shouted 'GO AWAY' which he repeated over and over. The effect on the General was immediate and startling. He dropped the mic stand and covered his ears against the painful volume emanating from JC. Even then it still caused pain and his whole body could feel the blast from the sound wave. The General turned and half ran, half staggered back the way he had come, passing the marines who were also covering their ears and feeling the pain. Morgan had just been found and briefed about the General's incursion when the shouting started. Even though he and all the scientists and support staff were a hundred meters away from JC the noise was still deafening and painful. Whilst he tried to get a grip of what was going on, Morgan wished that JC would stop that infernal row, but he did not and would not for quite some time. Meads answered the phone while Gary and Emma continue to watch the screen and the events unfolding. Sound had been restored so they could both see and hear what JC was doing. Touching his shoulder Meads said 'Gary, it's the President for you'. Gary took the phone and confirmed with the President that he was seeing and hearing the same thing, and the cause was obviously the General's attack. The call ended with Gary saying 'yes Mr. President, I'll leave straight away' before he hung up. 'Well?' said Emma. 'We're flying back down there once the helicopter arrives, which will be in about fifteen minutes'. Both of them set off at a jog back to their rooms to pack what they could in the time allowed. Emma and Gary had acquired some new clothes and neither of them ever wanted to be caught out without clean underwear again. Emma with a small suitcase and Gary with a suit cover left the room and followed Meads outside. A black 4x4 SUV drove them back to the helipad at the rear of the lawn where the US Marine helicopter was just landing. Meads shouted 'good luck' as they were grabbed by the arms and led by the crewman under the spinning blades to the waiting helicopter. They were barely seated when the pilot pulled in the power, hovered, rotated the machine towards the northwest and then accelerated up and out of the Whitehouse. This helicopter was not the VIP transport that had taken them to Washington, but a load carrying workhorse. It was noisy and uncomfortable but using the intercom headsets they could talk to each other over the noise. Whilst enroute Morgan had been patched through to the helicopter to speak to Gary. Even over the radio JC's bellowing could be heard whenever it was Morgan was transmitting. He told them what he knew and promised them a full briefing when they landed in about two hours, although the cause and result were clear to see and hear. They sat mostly in silence for the flight, with Emma holding Gary's hand. The crewman finally held up his hand indicating they were five minutes from arriving, before getting everything set for landing. He briefed them that just like their departure, to save time the blades would keep spinning and they should follow him directly away from the chopper and not to turn right for fear of hitting the tail rotor. The machine made a swift and gut wrenching operational approach as the pilot perfectly judged the approach and set the chopper down on the helipad. The door was slid open and they ducked as they followed the crewman to where Morgan and his arrival party were waiting. Even over the sound of the helicopter JC's plaintiff wail could still be heard repeating the 'go away' mantra. Morgan was wearing ear defenders and carrying a set each for Gary and Emma, which he gave them. They were about to put them on when the helicopter engine was cut and started to wind down, allowing them to talk as they walked to the buggy. 'Still at it huh?' said Gary 'yes' said Morgan 'even out here it is loud but any closer than a hundred meters is painful. We have had to issue everyone these back at the site, but the scientists wanted to move their vans back, but I told them to wait until you arrived'. They mounted the buggy cart and started back towards the base area, the noise from JC getting louder with each yard they travelled. The put on their ear defenders as they reached the outer ring of the base and stopped by the CCTV cabin. Inside were the American scientific team, who all seemed genuinely pleased to see Emma and Gary again. 'Well I had better get down there and see if I can quieten the baby' said Gary with more bravado than he actually felt 'but before I do, where is the General? Morgan answered 'he is under military detention and will be flown out of here soon. He seems to have lost the plot completely' Gary nodded, adjusted his ear defenders and walked out the door like a film hero. Once outside the door he leant against the cabin and took a few deep breaths. He may well be the World's Ambassador but that didn't mean he could not be a little frightened, could it? Gary made the long lone walk through the base area, passing both sets of marines in the cordons. The all waved briefly before replacing their hands over their ear defenders to help keep put the noise. The repeated 'GO AWAY' was now deafening and Gary could feel it on his chest as he approached JC. He could see that the eyes were closed and the mouth opened in time with the chant. He got as close as he dare before calling 'JC' he shouted, but timed it wrong and was drowned out. He tried again, getting the timing right but sounding very puny in the two second gap between words. He tried for a third and fourth time, but without result, so he gathered himself for a huge shout. Taking a full breath he bellowed 'JC, it is Gary'. There was a deafening silence as JC slowly closed his mouth and opened his eyes. In a calm voice JC spoke 'Gary, you have comeback' 'yes, well I had to because of the noise you were making' replied Gary. 'Gary, I was being physically attacked and whilst it offered no real threat it did disturb my research, so I had to dissuade the lifeform from attacking me with noise or I could have ceased its life.' JC responded in a matter of fact way. 'You would have done that? Asked Gary 'only if it had been necessary Gary'. Gary thought it best to try and lighten the mood and certainly change the subject 'well since I am here now, how is your research progressing?' 'Gary I am making progress and have learnt many things. There are also things that are that I have not seen before and need to discuss with you Gary. So that you can prepare, I have chosen topics that need further clarification' 'I thought you needed six weeks to complete your studies?' asked Gary. 'That would have been the case Gary but I once I applied a filter to remove erroneous material then the information I needed was much easier to access. It seems Gary that nearly half of your internet is made up of images of your species mating, which you call pornography'. 'Only half?' replied Gary, 'wow who would have thought that'. Gary thought it best to avoid that so changed the subject 'But of course I am happy to discuss anything you want JC, if it helps you'. 'Thank you Gary.

Now I need to go and research more, but tomorrow I would like meet with you to answer my questions and discuss matters that are open to interpretation. Good bye Gary ' Gary went to speak but seeing JC's eyes close and knowing when he was not wanted, he just turned and walked away. Gary got a cheery wave and thumbs up from the marines as they removed their ear defenders. It was dark when Gary got back to the CCTV cabin where everyone was waiting for him. He accepted their congratulations but in truth was a little concerned about some of the things JC had said. Taking Morgan and Emma aside he told them of his conversation with JC and how he wanted things to progress, starting tomorrow. Morgan told him he was to call the President as soon as he returned, so led him to the communication van to place the call. The President was grateful to Gary for flying down at such short notice to deal with the situation and bringing it to a peaceful conclusion. Gary briefed the President on JC's request for further discussion and promised he would wear his microphone so that the conversation could be monitored in Washington. With little more to discuss, the President suggested Gary get some rest and wished him a goodnight. To everyone's surprise Gary refused going to eat and took himself back to the motorhome he had been using. He was sat quietly looking into space when after a quiet knock the door opened and Emma joined him. 'Something is up Gary, isn't it?' He waited 'I have seen a change in JC. There is an either an underlying threat or coldness that I just cannot get my head around' She stroked his head, she had never seen Gary like this before and she was worried. 'I am sure it will all work out' she said, but was talking more in hope than knowledge. The day's events had taken their emotional toll and before she finished her sentence Gary was asleep. Gary awoke on the sofa in the motorhome. He was covered in a duvet and had slept well, although he had some vague memories of dreams which he was glad he could not remember. He showered and got dressed before making his way to the catering cabin for breakfast. Emma was sat there with Morgan and a few of the technical staff. There were the usual pleasantries as Gary joined them with a large plate of cooked breakfast. 'Got your appetite back then Gary' said Morgan, drawing a few knowing looks from the others and causing Emma to blush. 'Yes, I just needed to get a few things straight in my mind and have a good night's sleep' replied Gary. 'What is your plan for today?' asked Morgan. Whilst chewing on a reluctant piece of bacon rind, Gary used his fork for emphasis 'Just to get down there and try and understand what he actually wants from us and more importantly whether to give it to him'. It was quite a thought provoking statement and not quite the flippant remark they had come to expect from Gary. Having raised a few eyebrows and knowing looks, the techies and Morgan made their excuses and left Gary with Emma. 'Thanks for tucking me in last night prof.' he said. 'That's okay. You obviously needed your rest, especially after the previous night's escapades'. He found the reference to their evening together warming and not as scary as he once would have done. 'Yes, you did rather take it out of me 'he answered, cementing their shared experience. Other people arrived for breakfast so they switched to talking about the general stuff that made up their day. After eating they caught up with Morgan and the American scientists for a briefing before Gary's one to one with JC. There was little advice they could offer him, other than to keep the microphone switched on and the earpiece in place so that they could help where possible. There were a couple of 'good luck' comments from the crew and a surprising kiss and hug from Emma, a public display of affection they had both avoided in the past. Gary set off for the now familiar walk but was feeling very alone.

CHAPTER TWENTY: THE EVIDENCE

Despite his inner self doubt, Gary was mentally refreshed and feeling sharp as he walked quickly through the base towards JC. He did have a feeling of impending doom that he could not quite place or rationalise. He was after all going to a meeting with an alien life form or god to answer questions, who wouldn't be apprehensive. His quick stride belied his thoughts as he waved to the marines at their checkpoints and they acknowledged him back. He started to whistle a mindless tune before his earpiece crackled into life and Morgan asked him if he could please refrain from whistling or at least form a tune they recognised. Gary smiled and was about to jokingly tell Morgan to 'fuck off' when he remembered that the President was also listening. As Gary approached JC he could see that he was sat quietly with his eyes closed. He stood in front of him, took a moment to gather his thoughts and then called his name 'JC, I am here'. The eyes slowly opened and the now familiar benign smile spread across JC's face. 'Thank you for coming Gary'. 'No problem' replied Gary 'it is my pleasure and it seems also my job as World Ambassador'. He included that last bit as he knew the President and others were listening in. 'So, where do you want to start?' asked Gary. 'My whole essence within the dome has examined the internet information and broken it down into categories. I have then ported these categories into your effigy here so that I can discuss them using your abilities to see if I have misconstrued anything' said JC as he continued to beam and shimmer in front of Gary. 'Well that seems perfectly reasonable' said Gary, feeling comfortable enough with his life experiences to answer some simple questions. 'That is good Gary. We have a lot to cover today so I will begin with making a statement and then you can explain why it is so. You might like to sit down' said JC. Not wishing to upset JC at the outset, Gary reluctantly sat on the bare earth. 'Go ahead' he said with as much confidence as he could muster. JC spoke 'Gary, my research has shown that your species is a very aggressive one. Your history shows that historically you always seem to have had war between different tribes, races and factions within your societies. It seems to be an inbuilt condition of the human species. Why is this so?' Gary sucked his teeth while he considered his answer but then was aware of a familiar voice in his earpiece. It was the President 'Gary, tell JC that yes, whilst there has been turmoil over the centuries, we for the most part are peace loving human beings'. Gary repeated verbatim what he had been fed whilst JC listened and processed the reply. 'Do you really believe that Gary? Let me show you some examples'. A tendril of light came out of JC and enveloped Gary's form. Before he could react Gary realised he was seeing vivid images in his mind that were not his own thoughts. The images were brighter and more real than his own imaginings ever were. He watched in 3d and full colour as JC projected graphic images and film footage of wars through history, everything from early Homo sapiens fighting to the latest technological warfare. There was plenty of blood, gore and human suffering that JC had found and now referenced to support his argument. Gary was unsure how long the presentation lasted but when it did eventually stop it took him a few seconds to recover back to the real world. 'Wow, that was very interesting' said Gary, 'but perhaps you could warn me next time you go inside my brain?' 'Yes Gary, I will. What comments or defence can you offer for what we have just seen?' Gary suddenly had the distinct feeling that he and the rest of the human race were somehow being judged. It must have occurred to others in the loop as the president's voice came through 'tell him we are not on trial here and not everyone on earth is engaged in war'. Gary was not entirely comfortable using the words fed to him but repeated them anyway. 'Given my reason for being here Gary, then yes you are on trial, or at the very least being held to account for your behaviour. It seems that all races of your species have been at war at some point in your history or another'. Gary remained silent 'To continue Gary, even outside of your wars, there is the matter to discuss of aggression and cruelty to other humans'. 'Tell him the good nature of people outshines the bad and as a society we are progressing' said the President in Gary's ear, which he told JC as prompted. 'If that were so Gary, then this would not be happening. Warning, I will send it to you Gary'. Before Gary could object he was once again subjected to the all-encompassing light and his mind used as a PowerPoint display whiteboard. These images and films that JC had dug from the dark recesses of the internet showed the depths that humans could plumb in their cruelty to each other. They included images of beatings, abuse, beheadings and a montage of thousands of depraved and disgusting acts, some of which were obviously recent. When it finished and Gary was allowed full use of faculty again, he leant forward and was physically sick at what had had been forced into his mind. 'Was that hard for you to experience Gary?' asked JC 'Yes of course, we're not all like that' Gary replied. He heard the President's saying something in his ear but by now the mental abuse and throwing up had taken Gary to a new place. He reached up and pulled the earpiece out and holding it up for the cameras to see let it dangle on its umbilical down his back. Others could still hear but not influence Gary's answers. 'I note you have removed the incoming communication device Gary, which may help you give honest answers which are your own' said JC. 'To continue. The matter of human cruelty also extends to others species that share the planet with you. It seems that your kind will kill and consume in one way or another, practically every other living species that inhabits this planet'. Gary was actually prepared for this question and jumped straight in 'JC, we have to eat, to consume other species to survive, it is what we have evolved to do'. JC spoke 'consuming to survive is one thing but consuming all without compassion is unforgiveable. Wait whilst I fetch the images' and quickly closed his eyes to have them ported from the dome. 'Warning Gary, projection is imminent' JC said. As before, the light shone and Gary was once more in the front row of his own HiMax movie theatre. There portrayed in his mind were some of the many thousands of cruel acts humans committed on animals. Animal make up testing, bear baiting, dog fighting, humans whipping, kicking and even cooking animals whilst still alive were seared into Gary's memory. The segment on battery farming was especially hard to watch but Gary did not have the luxury of being able to close his eyes and ignore it, as it was there in his mind for him to see. The episode finished with a dolphin bloodbath as they were corralled and into a cove and then clubbed or stabbed to death. 'Would you like to see more evidence Gary?' asked JC with a hint of something in his voice 'there is plenty more of it if you would like?' Gary's dry retching provided the answer but to eliminate any ambiguity he shouted 'No!' just to be sure. Gary rubbed his eyes as some tears had started to form at what he had just witnessed. As he looked up at JC he saw that he too had shimmering tears running down his cheeks. 'You are crying?' asked Gary. 'Yes, using your effigy also enables me to experience your emotions and those last images produced tears. It was a very interesting addition to my knowledge of you and your emotions Gary'. Now, my final question for today Gary is why your species seems so intent on destroying the place where you live on. It is a relatively small planet with limited resources, but all your commercial and industrial processes seem to involve the degradation of the habitat, can you not see this?' Gary had some idea how to answer this but thought it prudent to wait until he had seen the evidence first.' Probably best you show me first what you are referring to JC' and then prepared for the mind invasion. The images and films JC had gather showed not only the ravages of the human impact on the earth, but also a timeline of the Earth showing the past, present and future predictions' It had an impact on Gary, but this time he was not sick. 'JC' he started 'we have evolved on this planet and whilst we have not got everything right we are survivors and we survive by using what we have around us' Gary paused but JC spoke 'Gary, even your own human limited scientific knowledge shows you that your current behaviour is unsustainable. When you surely deplete this planet of all its resources what will you do and where will you live? Your technology will never evolve in time to be able to transport you to the next liveable planet, your species will die out long before that. Also, for the second time you used the word evolution, and used it as an excuse. Everywhere I have been in the cosmos Gary, evolution has been a good thing. It has been a force for good and improvement, but here on your planet you hold up evolution as an excuse for your own failings, which means here Gary, evolution has failed. In comparison to other planets and life forms your human species could be regarded as an infestation, one that has stifled other life and produced an evolutionary dead end for itself' JC paused 'how can you have let happen Gary, how?' Now knowing that humankind was on trial, Gary also felt out of his depth. He scrambled around his back and replaced the earpiece and the president's irate voice. 'Do not cut me off and try and deal with this yourself Gary, too much is at stake. I have a team gathered here of scientific and religious leaders who could have helped you! Now, we must have more time to consider our replies. Try and stall him so that we can come up with convincing arguments. Gary nodded to the cameras to show he understood and thought how he might phrase the answer and pose a question at the same time. 'JC. You will have seen from your research that we started off living in small groups and have slowly grown into bigger cities and nations. We hope to eventually grow into one nation, where war can be put behind us and we can then concentrate on just living productive lives without ruining the planet Earth where we live. Some people also believe that a god will save us before we get to a critical point in our evolution. From your studies you must know of our religious beliefs, don't you?' JC paused and his eyes remained closed for a full ten seconds whilst he considered the matter of religion. 'Gary, I think you are perhaps using this conversation to obtain information from me about your faiths, beliefs and god. I have decided that we will discuss this tomorrow. You must need to rest and I need to study more before we meet tomorrow. Goodbye Gary' JC closed his eyes which Gary gratefully accepted as it marked the end of the session. He groaned as he stood up and after brushing himself down he began a stiff slow walk back up to the base. Just outside the cordon Morgan was waiting for him in the buggy. 'Get in Gary, the President wants you in on a phone conference ASAP'. Gary looked up and saw the stars and was suddenly confused about the time 'How long was I down there?' he asked 'About nine hours' replied Morgan, causing Gary to try and put into context the discussion and time taken for the mind projections he had been subjected to. Once back at the CCTV unit Emma ran out and threw her arms around him. 'You look tired' she said 'absolutely knackered' he replied before being led into the cabin and given a coffee. The American scientists were a little cold towards him, anticipating the bollocking Gary would no doubt get from the President for going it alone. Morgan cleared out the technicians who did not have security clearance to be in on the phone call and invited everyone else to be seated. He hit the connect button on the triangular conference call machine in the centre of the table and established the secure link, and was then immediately transferred to the President's office. On the screen at the end of the room appeared the President and a group of advisors. A small inset screen showed Morgan and the others sat together also. 'Mr President, Special Agent Morgan convening this meeting at Lake Michigan. 'Thank you special agent Morgan' said the President. Mr

Barnes, Gary, you did a good job down there today but we feel it could have been better if you had stayed in communication with me and the team. Can I ask you to please refrain from removing your link to us in Washington?' 'I am sorry Mr President but the images that were being sent to my mind were both graphic and at times disturbing, to the point where I felt sick. Your voice at that point was not helping' said Gary. The President nodded and took the point before continuing 'It seems to us that as a species we are under some sort of scrutiny or judgement, if you will. It already will have lasting consequences for us but we must ensure we contain the situation. Given today's events we are looking at several options, ranging from complete capitulation and agreement with JC' through to a pre-emptive military strike. How do those options sit with you there? There was a murmur around the room but other than that no one seemed able to offer a constructive solution or even a comment on what had just been proposed. They looked at Gary 'Mr President, JC has already demonstrated powers way beyond our comprehension and a military strike would not only be futile it but would fit right in with his opinion of us as aggressive little fuckers. Capitulation is an option but in truth we are doing that already, so why don't we wait to see what tomorrow's meeting brings? He seemed to indicate we were nearing some sort of conclusion and since he holds all the cards why not wait for him to show his hand?' The President conferred around the table with his advisors for several minutes before replying to Gary. 'We have decided to go with your suggestion Gary but we must be in the loop when you are down there. We will make preparations for a military strike but will only implement it if the situation deteriorates and there is no other choice. Other than that, I suggest we all try and get some sleep and reconvene at 9 am tomorrow morning.' The picture went off and the line went dead. Emma rubbed Gary's arm and asked if he wanted food, but Gary was again emotionally tired and desperately needed sleep. Emma and Gary walked back to the motorhome together and went inside. She poured them both a large brandy from the cabinet and sat down on the sofa next to Gary. 'Anything you need to talk about?' she asked. 'Nope' he replied 'my head has seen things today I will never forget and my brain is fried. I need to sleep, will you stay with me?' Emma nearly choked on the brandy 'yes of course'. 'Nothing like that' he said, 'I just need you to hold me'. This was a vulnerable side to Gary she had not seen before but one that she could easily accommodate. Within seconds of spooning together on

the bed Gary was once more in a fitful asleep.

CHAPTER TWENTYONE: THE JUDGEMENT

Gary's nose woke him with the smell of coffee. As he opened his eyes he saw a smiling Emma sat next to him on the bed holding a cup of steaming coffee. 'Good morning' she said cheerily, as Gary sat himself up and took the mug from her. 'Thanks' he said, still trying to shake off the sleep.

'Did you sleep okay because you were shouting in your sleep?' said Emma with a concerned look on her face. ''Sleep seemed okay' replied Gary, happy not to be able to recall whatever he had been dreaming about. The images JC had projected into his mind yesterday had been graphic and very real to him, it was no wonder he had stored the horrors shown to him in his subconscious.

'I thought I had better wake you so you had plenty of time to get ready before the morning video conference with the President' she said. At hearing this Gary's eyes widened as he started to panic about the time 'what time is it?' he said. 'Don't worry, you have got an hour yet so relax and drink your coffee whilst I cook you breakfast. I have some bacon and eggs' she added with a smile, which soon changed when she saw Gary grimace. Some of the images Gary had been forced to endure yesterday included battery farmed chickens and pigs kept in squalid conditions, he could not face eating them right now. 'I am sorry Prof, but I am just not ready for a fat boy's breakfast, could I just have some toast?' Knowing that Gary turning down food was a most unusual occurrence but also that he had gone through quite an ordeal yesterday, Emma decided not to ask questions and just went and put bread in the toaster. When she returned and offered him the plate, she was surprised when he took her hand and kissed the back of it whilst looking at her. Whilst this was also unusual for Gary to initiate intimacy, she was not going to let that spoil the moment. She slid onto the bed beside him and kissed him gently on the cheek, to which he turned his mouth towards her and they began kissing. After yesterday's events Gary needed more than coffee and toast, he needed warmth, a distraction and loving contact. So, if the beautiful professor wanted to take advantage of his stiffening morning glory then so be it. The toast fell on the floor, butter side up. It was 8.50am when Morgan chose to panic and make sure Gary and Emma were ready for the video conference call. He was relieved to see they were both dressed when he entered the motorhome, and after the obligatory morning greetings he ushered them out of the door. The same scientists and

FBI people were seated around the table as Gary, Emma and Morgan entered. It made Gary smile that he had a reserved place with a name plaque in from of it. It read 'MR GARY BARNES, WORLD AMBASSADOR' 'I thought you would like that' said Morgan, who had organised the plaque as a joke, but in doing so had upset some if not all of the people sat around the table. At exactly 9am the machine beeped indicating an incoming call and Morgan answered. Once he was sure the security was scrambling the signals he pushed a button and the team in Washington flashed up on the screen. Seated centrally was the President, but this time there were more people sat around him, including several religious figures, some senior military officers and some serious looking men in suits. 'Good morning everyone' said the President 'you hearing me okay?' He then went on to make some introductions over the video link, ensuring everyone knew that Gary was the main actor in this play. In return the Washington people were also introduced. It surprised Gary that the new men in suits were the Russian and Chinese Ambassador's, and that there were also religious leaders of several different faiths. Gary counted twenty people sat at the big round table but they were lost as the camera zoomed in on the President.

'As a matter of good faith and openness, I have invited the Russian and Chinese delegations to this important meeting, so that they can report accurately back to their own leaders. Now, we have been meeting since 8am to decide how we should approach today and how we can assist Mr Barnes. Gary, we have decided we need more information before we can act, so we must insist that today you try and get some answers for us from the JC, okay?' Gary nodded 'It sounds like a good idea, but as you saw yesterday I am not entirely in control of things down there. However, just what questions do you have in mind?' 'We appreciate the difficult job you undertook yesterday Gary and under the most difficult circumstances, but we need to know the following'. The President picked up some A4 paper and began to read: One: What is the purpose of your visit here? Two: We, as the representatives of the people of Earth want to know if you intend any harm to its inhabitants or to the planet. And three: Are you god?' 'Wow' exclaimed Gary, 'the big three, all in one easy to manage sandwich'. 'Gary, I know it might seem daunting to ask you to go back down there today with an agenda, but after lengthy discussions with all parties it is essential that get answers to those questions'. Changing his facial expression slightly he continued

'Special Agent Morgan will provide you with a hard copy which I would like you to review now'. Morgan produced several sheets of paper which he passed to Gary. The top one contained a verbatim list of the questions but when Gary looked at the second sheet there was a message typed in capital letters.

'GARY, DO NOT READ THIS OUT LOUD. OTHER COUNTRIES ARE FEELING THREATENED BY JC AND ARE SUSPICIOUS OF THE USA'S HANDLING OF THE SITUATION. RUSSIA AND CHINA ARE CONSIDERING A UNILATERAL MILITARY STRIKE, HENCE THEIR INCLUSION IN THIS MEETING. PLEASE JUST AGREE TO TRY AND GET THESE QUESTIONS ANSWERED WHILST WE ARE STILL ON CONFERENCE CALL TO GIVE US MORE TIME WITH THEM ALSO.' This was a wow moment for Gary, firstly at being sent a private note by the President, but then the sheer weight of the content hit him. 'Okay Gary, you got that? Asked the President. 'Yes Mr President, I got *all* that' said Gary, trying not to let his body language give too much away. 'Thank you Gary' replied the President, with something of a relieved look on his face. 'Right, we had better let you get to it Gary. Keep your ear piece in please and good luck down there'. That was the President's final comment before the screen went off. Gary folded the paper and put it into his shirt pocket. He was about to leave when one of the scientists spoke 'and if you get a chance Mr Barnes, could you ask him about dark matter, it would be so useful to know? This opened the flood gates as several of the scientists also wanted him to answer questions about subjects close to their hearts and studies. Gary held up his hand 'Do like the President did and write them down and when I get the chance I will put them to JC'. The mere possibility of getting some scientific answers threw the scientists into a frenzy, as they all looked for pens, paper and considered how to phrase their questions. In the confusion Gary nodded to Emma and they slipped out of the room with Morgan. 'That should keep the children quiet for a while' said Morgan. 'Let's hope so, we have got bigger problems' said Gary, as he shared the second page with Emma and Morgan. They were both visibly shocked at the possibility of Russian and Chinese military involvement. 'Jeez' said Morgan, 'how will we deal with that?' 'Don't worry' said Gary flippantly, 'I have always liked Vodka and rice'. It was an obtuse enough comment to stop dead Morgan's train of thought. 'Hey Morgan here's one for you. If there was going to be an attack on JC, either by the Russians, Chinese or you Yanks, how would they do it?' Morgan pursed his lips as if to keep in a secret but then said 'What the hell, you deserve to know. The protocol in place is for a nuclear attack.' Emma gasped 'but that would kill everyone down here' she said. 'Yes' replied Morgan 'but it is a protocol that has not been actioned, so today is just another day'. Gary rubbed his chin 'Can I have moment alone with the prof?' asked Gary. 'Sure' said Morgan as he handed him his radio pack and microphone. 'I will be monitoring you from the CCTV room and will have a team on standby to pull you of there if it all gets too much for you. Good luck Gary'. As Morgan walked off Emma spoke 'There was already enough tension after yesterday but this Russian/Chinese thing really puts the pressure on you Gary'. Tell me about it' said Gary trying to laugh it off. The joke obviously fooling neither of them. Gary changed tack. 'Prof, I am here because every slippery and underhand move I have ever made has led me to this point. I have got no one to blame but myself, so I am just going to have to man up and do my best. But, at least I now have you in my life, so something good has come out of all this. Try not to worry'. Emma nodded 'I love you Gary' she said and waited for the time honoured response. Gary recognised the moment from a thousand films but somehow the single man in him managed to grasp him by the throat and limit his reply to a strangled 'me to'. It was a perplexing but not a negative answer, which Emma accepted in the short term as she hugged him. Gary smiled and was gone. Ready to accept his fate, using as upbeat a voice as he could muster Gary called 'Anyone home?' JC opened his eyes and beamed his familiar smile. Gary had quickly learnt that the smile was a learnt behaviour and not one that could be used as an indicator. 'Hello Gary. Are you well rested?' 'Yes thank you JC. Did you also rest well?' asked Gary using the polite convention. 'I have not rested Gary, it is not something I need. I have been busy researching, studying and coming to conclusions' JC replied. Instantly in Gary's earpiece was the President's voice. *What conclusion, conclusion about what?* Gary repeated the question out loud. 'My conclusions about the planet and the species that live here' JC simply replied, which gave nothing away. 'Could you be more specific?' asked Gary, knowing that his previous answer would not be sufficient for the President. '*Good Gary, very good*' said the voice in his ear. 'Not now Gary' said JC, 'my work will be completed today and then I will have reached my conclusions' his tone indicating the matter was at an end. 'Well what do you want to talk about today?' asked Gary. JC continued to smile in his faux benign way 'I felt that yesterday was a difficult one for you Gary, so today I thought we could discuss some of your questions. Is that good for you?' *'Yes yes yes'* hissed the voice in Gary's ear, which he thought was entirely unnecessary. 'Yes JC, that would good, thank you' he replied. Gary took out his piece of paper but once he had reviewed the questions decided they were too heavy to kick off with, so opted for a softer approach. 'Where are you from JC?' he asked, aware of the disparaging noises in his earpiece. 'Gary, I am from everywhere and nowhere, at least nowhere that you could comprehend'. Gary waited for further explanation but it soon became apparent that the answer was complete. Gary tried another starter question 'when will you leave this planet?' JC briefly considered his reply 'if my information is complete and my conclusions are arrived at, then Gary I will leave today'. Gary was again not entirely clear about the meaning of the answer 'So you are still gathering information as we speak, but once you have everything you will just leave?' 'Yes Gary that could be one interpretation' replied JC. *'The questions Gary!'* urged the

President's voice in his ear. 'I have here some questions from the president and other leading thinkers on our planet' said Gary, 'may I?' JC 'please ask your questions Gary, they may help me reach a conclusion'. Gary looked at the paper and quietly read 'yada yada yada, I think we have dealt with number one already'. Gary gave a little cough and went on 'Number two: We, the representatives of the people of Earth want to know if you intend any harm to its inhabitants or the planet Earth, is what it says here' said Gary, trying to take the pointy finger out of the question. JC closed his eyes and remained silent. When he opened his eyes they seemed somewhat wider than normal. 'Gary, I am experiencing a new emotion through your effigy, it is one of anger and the experience is enlightening. To answer your question Gary requires me to reflect back at you what you do you each other and what you are doing to the planet. Your question is based on fear as to what might happen, yet the consequences you fear are already happening, but are self-imposed. I came here to study you Gary, to judge you and then recommend what the future will hold, but nothing I propose will be equal to the misery and destruction you have imposed upon yourselves. Gary really did not like that answer, as it was both threatening and ambiguous at the same time. There was a raised voice in Gary's ear, which seemed to be some sort of plea to examine the religious question. In the hope that it might offer a more peaceable answer Gary went with it. 'JC, our religious leaders want to know if you are God?' JC did not seem to consider this question for more than a second before saying 'You are asking if I am God?' he then closed his eyes again for a further period of thought.' Gary, if by god you mean like the ones described in your religious books, then the answer is no, I am not that god. I have found the subject of your religions to be a very interesting but it is a phenomena that I have only seen on this planet. I examined all your various religions and digested all their books, but I could not find anything other than man made fiction, designed it seems to enslave other men or used as a reason to kill other men' In Gary's earpiece there was something of a commotion as the religious leaders sat with the President started shouting. JC continued 'However, if the simple measure of your god is to be all powerful, judgemental and at the beginning your creator, then yes, I am your god'. Gary felt a chill run down his back as JC's words sunk in. There was stunned silence in Gary's earpiece as the words hit everyone at the same time. 'You are our creator?' asked

Gary, the words forming slowly. There was no thinking time 'Yes Gary' said JC 'I have seeded this and many other planets over the millennia and throughout the universe. I have now returned to see what has spawned from my work'. Gary's brain was hurting trying to comprehend what he was hearing 'You started life on this planet, and from that we have grown and evolved?' he asked incredulously. 'Yes Gary that would be a simple way of putting it. Some of my work on other planets has exceeded my expectations, some of them still swim in the mire and will do so for ever, but here on Earth lies the biggest disappointment I have yet faced.' Gary went to speak but JC held up his hand 'Gary, nowhere in my journeys have I seen such a self-destructive, self-deluding, aggressive species as I have encountered here. Your meagre life cycle gives you an average of a thousand months on your planet, most of which is dedicated to death, destruction or wailing into the clouds at imaginary deities. Your language does not have the capacity to fully describe what my intellect thinks about your species. I came here with an open mind to meet you, to study and understand you before recommending to my species whether we should embrace you and gift you advanced technologies, but it is obvious that you would use any advancement for further destruction. What I have seen and learnt has shown me that you will either eventually destroy yourselves or worse still survive long enough to infest other nearby planets in your solar system, and we cannot be responsible for that. Despite the many voices in his earpiece, Gary groped alone for inspiration and a way out 'Who are the *we* that you refer to?' 'The *we* Gary, are my whole species. Individually we roam the cosmos, seeking other intelligence and seeding barren worlds to create life, or sometimes to extinguish it altogether if it poses a threat to others. Gary and the people listening in were not liking what they were hearing. In his earpiece Gary could not make out the President's words, as it was clear from the cacophony that various factions were trying to convince the President to take immediate action. From the few words Gary could make out it seemed the military advisors were actually being supported by some of the religious leaders, who saw JC as a threat and the ultimate heretic. One of the Generals had heard enough and was actually advocating a nuclear strike right now at ground zero. There was a second of clear air when Gary clearly heard the President's stressed voice say his name and a few short words 'Gary, play for time!' With literally the entire weight of responsibility for the world on his shoulders, Gary struggled to find a way out of the corner the human race had painted itself into. Always unconventional in his approach to everything he did, Gary opted for a bold strategy. Taking a strong stance he breathed in and shouted at JC 'Who the hell are you to come here and judge us. If, as you say you are our god, then where have you been during our evolution? You could have returned at an earlier point in our development and intervened, perhaps making us better, different or at least more to your liking. It is too late to turn up now like some absent father, expressing disappointment at how the child has grown up without your parentage. If you don't like what you have found then that is just too bad, we are human beings and proud of it!' Gary hoped his speech had carried some emotional weight to offset the practical things they were being measured against. JC was quiet, his eyes were closed as he considered every word of Gary's statement, considering every conceivable meaning in its content. When he at last opened his eyes they were different. His face contorted in anger and his body sat bolt upright. When he spoke his voice was loud and grew louder as he spoke 'You dare to challenge me by using angry words to defend your species Gary. Do you want to see what your human anger can do when combined with my limitless power?' As the volume of his voice increased JC's body also started to grow upwards and outwards until he was three times Gary's size. He looked down at Gary and continued his tirade 'Gary, I will show you how all my intelligence and compassion are negated when I use the same anger you humans thrive on. Using your anger I can suspend my own judgement and end your life, stripping you down to your component parts one atom at a time before I destroy this planet!' JC's hand moved and projected a single finger, the intent of which was obvious. Gary swallowed hard, closed his eyes and said quietly into his microphone 'I am sorry everyone, I did my best. I love you Emma'. As Gary prepared for his own death, some final thoughts did flash through his mind. They were not his first beer or sex encounter, family holidays or falling off his first big boy's bike, no, most of them included Emma. He could even hear her voice in his head calling to him, but was surprised when that thought became reality as her voice was really was coming from behind him 'STOP JC, STOP, PLEASE DON'T DO THIS' she shouted, as Emma ran up to Gary and stood in front of him to protect him. She had run all the way and was breathing heavily as she repeated 'Stop this please

JC'. She then turned and hugged Gary before taking his arm and holding him close. 'Who are you?' boomed JC's voice. 'I am Emma Rowlinson, a scientist and also someone who loves Gary very much'. Even at the height he was at they could see JC close his eyes to consider Emma's statement. 'I have examined your scientific achievements and whilst they are benign studies, ultimately even your work can be used for destructive or negative purposes. It is not your limited technology that condemns you, it is your limited intellect and compassion for other species and each other' he answered, his voice painful to their ears. Gary had listened to Emma's plea in hope and JC's reply in despair, but the combination caused something to stir, an idea that he hoped would give him a last throw of the dice. 'What about love JC, have you studied love?' Gary shouted. JC answered immediately 'the sordid internet images of your species mating is not relevant Gary and is not something I care to recall' boomed JC. 'No, not sex or pornography JC.I am talking above love, affection, tenderness, caring, it is the strongest emotions that we humans are capable of!' shouted Gary, unwittingly quoting from a Barbara Cartland novel. 'Not just procreation but the strongest emotion?' boomed JC in a questioning tone. He immediately closed his eyes as searched all meanings and sought understanding of the word love. There was silence as Gary and Emma looked at each other and hugged whilst they waited for a reply. There was nothing in Gary's earpiece as everyone watched and waited. It was a full three minutes and forty seconds before JC's eyes flashed open to see Emma and Gary exchanging what they thought might their last ever kiss. JC's countenance and demeanour changed, and his body and voice slowly shrank down to its original size. His face was now beaming and his normal shimmering had returned. 'Gary, using your effigy I have experienced and enjoyed most of your human emotions, except for the one called anger, which as you have just witnessed, the experience was not a good one. But now I have researched and experienced love as an emotion, and not just as an attachment to procreating. I can now see and feel it is the strongest force for good your species has. I am overwhelmed by the feeling I am currently sharing of your love for Emma, it has no equal in the universe that I am familiar with. This new enlightenment Gary has changed some of my views about your species. Gary, my intention is now to return to my collective and report to my family of intelligences all that I have found here, including love. They may still decide that the inhabitants of this planet still need eradicating so that a fresh start can be made, or they may decide that your unique love emotion is powerful enough and that you will still flourish before killing each other and destroying your home.' Gary spoke 'Thank you JC. Like me, I am glad you got to experience love first hand. But tell me, how long will it be before we know what decision your family come to about us? JC replied 'Depending on what route I take Gary, I should make the return journey in something between twenty and two thousand of your years.' 'Oh' said Gary ironically 'So I might just get to see you again?' 'That is a possibility Gary, but a distant one. Now I have everything I need I am leaving, so you should step back. However, I will leave you something as a reminder of my visit and that the future of your species is under review. Your species might use that to change their ways before it is too late. Good bye Gary' 'Goodbye JC' replied Gary. As they watched, JC's eyes closed in an altogether different way and shut for the last time. JC's form seemed to solidify as the shimmering stopped and whatever life force was within returned to the dome. Emma and Gary stepped back together as the static electricity sound increased and their skin prickled with the sensation. They watched as the dome began to pulse and then quicker than their eyes could follow the beam shot into the atmosphere forming a solid beam, quickly followed a second later by the end as it disappeared. Emma and Gary walked forward to where the lifeless effigy of Gary now sat. 'Some reminder' said Emma, as she touched the dull metallic surface. Gary looked up at the sky 'I wonder just how much time we have bought?' he said as he hugged Emma close. 'Well we do have at least twenty years together' Emma replied. 'Yes' said Gary 'let's go and eat'.

Made in the USA
Charleston, SC
16 December 2015